WOLF'S REIGN

WØLVES OF ODIN
BOOK TWO

MADELYN LAYNE

FREE BOOKS!

**Sign up for Madelyn Layne's
Newsletter and get access to
free books, bonus material, and
exclusive content.**

Madelyn's Newsletter:
www.madelynlayne.com

**Note to Reader: Originally, I published a different book as book 1 in Wølves Of Odin. That book was called First Kyss, and it was written in third person POV.

I have changed the covers, titles, POV, and book order in the series. Wolf's Kiss is now book 1, and Wolf's Reign (formerly First Kyss) is now book 2. Both books are written in first person POV.

For my mom, Marjorie.
Love you so much. Miss you every day.

PROLOGUE

Kristin

My father had always said I'd drive him to an early pyre. Now, I'd killed my mother too.

"Kitta, wake up."

I opened gritty eyes to see my mom, Gale, sitting upright on the bed we shared—but something wasn't right. She looked...odd.

Rubbing the sleep from my eyes, I rose to my elbow and squinted at her.

It didn't help. Her Valdyr side and wolf side were blinking in and out of existence on top of each other, making her blur together. Despite that, she looked healthy, which made no sense at all.

My mom hadn't been well for three years.

In that far, caged corner of my soul, my own wolf raised her head. The female sniffed the air and then lifted her muzzle and howled.

I reached for a handful of fur but caught only air. "Mom?" I questioned, my voice cracking.

Gale's chin wobbled, and the corners of her mouth pulled down. "You can't touch me, sweetheart. I'm in the helmingr."

Helmingr.

The familiar-sounding word sat heavily in my chest. I knew what it meant. I'd just…forgotten—one of the many things I'd forgotten since I'd been locked up in this house. There were no brothers to tease, no father to exasperate with my daredevil antics, no overblown teenage drama to lament.

My torment was all too real.

I inhaled sharply, and the familiar stench of sickness invaded my nose, the smell even stronger to my wolf inside. But now there was something else.

Something…something…

Dead, my wolf thought.

Shut up! I yelled, and my wolf lay back down with a whimper.

Jerking upright, I pushed tangled blond hair away from my face, my favorite headband lost somewhere in the covers. I hated it when the animal thought for me, when I could feel its emotions. I wanted it gone from inside of me and my life back to the way it was before my wolf had risen.

Before *he* had come.

A frightened shiver forced its way up my spine, and I dropped my gaze, trying to hide my fear from my mom.

But warm, tingly hands cupped my cheeks. "Look at me, svassa," Gale said gently.

Reluctantly, I raised my gaze to hers. She smiled at me, but I could see the pain in her eyes.

Her thumb brushed across my jaw. "Odin only knows why your wolf rose when you were so young. Or why your scent made the unmated males feral. But it wasn't your fault. You didn't do anything wrong, Kristin. You were just a pup."

"I was thirteen."

"Mine to protect. And your dad's to protect. He and your brothers would fight for you all over again."

"And they'd be just as dead." I clamped my jaw together, holding back a sob that had shoved up from my throat.

Something horrible was about to happen—was happening—and my brain refused to acknowledge it.

"Yes, Kitta. Dead. And now you're all that's left of us. Of our family. You have to fight. Let your wolf rise and escape. With my passing, there's nothing to—"

"No!" I pulled back from her caress and clamped my hands over my ears, refusing to listen anymore, but my thoughts kept coming.

The helmingr, I now remembered, was a perfect, magical merging of the Valdyr with their wolf. It happened the first time the wolf rose and the last time upon death. In between, a strong Valdyr could enter the helmingr at will—but my mom hadn't been strong enough to maintain it in years.

"You won't be alone for long, Kristin. I've seen someone. A girl. Different from you, but special in her own way. She'll be your family. And later, there's a male. A strong male. With Freyja's blessing, you'll join with him in the Kyssa."

"I don't want anyone else. I want you. Please stay, Mom. Don't leave me."

"I can't, Kitta. I've already passed over. I'm in Asgard, in a forest surrounding Valhalla. Your dad is here. And the boys. They see you through my eyes and can't believe how much you've grown. Your father's so proud of you for protecting me after I was injured, for taking care of me." She brushed her thumb over my cheek. "But now it's time for you to fly."

"I don't want to fly." I tried to grab my mom, but it was like sifting through energized air. "Stay with me, Mama. All I have is you."

"No. You have your wolf. Accept her, Kristin. She's a part of you to be embraced, not feared or hated. Let her rise when you perform the Hyrr. She'll help you escape."

Burn my mother's body. My fear and pain ratcheted up another level. "I don't know how."

"Your wolf will guide you."

I shook my head, a whimper pushing past my lips. Even if my wolf could, there's no way Hans would allow it. For once, I was glad to be a prisoner. Hans would never honor the Valdyr way, and my mom would have to stay.

"*He* won't let me."

"He will. He wants your wolf to rise so he can use her to bind you. But even he doesn't know how strong you are."

Behind me, the bedroom door opened. I spun around.

A monster, standing over seven feet tall, loomed in the doorway. His shining beauty made my eyes ache, and my stomach fill with acid. He wore a cream-colored silk shirt and perfectly pressed black pants. His hair and skin shone like moonlight, and his eyes were as black as the night sky. Yet, at other times, he shone like sunlight, and his eyes were blue.

I didn't know what he was. A Valdyr, maybe—I'd seen his wolf. A creature as big and cruel as he was. But he had magic, too, and had used it against me. Only female Valdyr were supposed to have magical gifts. Perhaps he was a witch or one of the Jotun— big, bad enemies of the gods. But the Jotun in the stories were ugly, and no matter how ugly Hans was inside, outwardly, he glowed like the sun and the moon.

He bared even white teeth at Gale in what I assumed was a smile. "Dead, already?"

I rose to protect my mom, my grubby, oversized T-shirt slipping off my shoulder, but Gale suddenly stood between us, her body a hazy blur. "My daughter's strong. Her wolf won't ever rise for you."

"Are you sure?" Hans leaned lazily against the doorjamb. "She'll need the wolf to enact the Hyrr." He shifted his gaze to mine. "Do you want your mother to be with the rest of your family? She can't go to Valhalla if she's not properly cremated."

Gale turned and squeezed my hands. For the first time, she felt truly solid to me. "Don't do it, Kitta. Odin will grant me favor. Whatever happens, *don't* let your wolf out."

But in my mind, she said loud and clear, *Let your wolf out. Then run like hel, baby.*

I closed my eyes. I didn't want my wolf to rise. Terrible things had happened the first time it tried to merge with me. The confusing mix of pain and pleasure, fear and exhilaration, the foreignness that somehow felt like homecoming, the shock as my brother's best friend, the sweet one I'd been crushing on for a while, turned on me.

He had been the first to die.

My mom said Hans needed the wolf to bind me, but what did that mean? How could I be more bound than I was now? I hadn't stepped a foot outside this house in three years.

Gentle pressure brushed my forehead—Gale's lips. "I love you, Kitta. Odin keep you safe."

Then she was gone.

The suddenness of it shocked me, and I spun to the bed. My mom lay under the quilts I had piled on top of her hours ago. She was pale, solid, and fully in her Valdyr form.

And she was dead.

The chill of the night air nipped my nose, but I didn't feel it—I didn't feel anything. Shock and sorrow had taken over. I barely noticed that I was free of my prison and back in the forest of the Appalachian Mountains. Even the presence of my old pack couldn't rouse me.

In that caged place deep in my soul, my wolf paced back and forth, agitated and grieving but also excited by the fertile scents of the wilderness surrounding us—the resin from the trees, the decay of foliage beneath the melting snow, the sweetness of new life beginning.

It was the first time my wolf had been outdoors...the first time the female had wanted to run.

I longed to bury my hands in the snow, and I almost dropped to my knees. The compulsion shocked me, and I grabbed onto a log for balance.

Roll! my wolf urged.

No! I shouted back.

My fingers squeezed around the rough bark, and it slowly dawned on me what I held. My gaze drifted upward until it rested on my mom's body lying on a wooden pyre. The breath exploded from my lungs as pain punched through my numbness. My wolf stopped pacing, dropped to her haunches, and howled.

Gale's body lay under a linen wrap, her head exposed. I drank in her pale skin, long dark hair, and peaceful expression. The knowledge that this was the last time I'd see her beloved face almost knocked me over, but I refused to let Hans see me weaken.

A wave of approval rose through my body from the wolf, which confused me. I'd never communed with my wolf like that before. Maybe I *should* let her out. It was what my mom wanted... what Hans wanted.

But how could anything he wanted be right?

Trust.

The wolf's thought echoed loudly in my head—warmer, somehow, like it resonated deeper within my body. I almost looked around. Had someone else spoken? But I knew none of the Valdyr surrounding me would speak without Hans's permission.

I heard a familiar wheezing cough and glanced over to see my old teacher, Mr. Stennersen, standing in the snow with his head lowered and shoulders drooped. The sweet smell of lilacs wafted beneath my nose, and I followed the scent, my eyes landing on the florist my mom had bought flowers from every Friday. The woman leaned weakly against a tree, her eyes downcast and chin trembling. To her right stood two of my former playmates, huddled together. They wouldn't—or couldn't—meet my gaze.

I recognized other packmates as well and knew they recognized me. I'd heard them whispering when Hans had led me out of the house behind two human males who carried my mom's body on a litter.

What did the pack think of humans serving Hans? Did they protest? Or had all the strong members been killed when my wolf first rose?

My stomach twisted as images of that day filled my mind—the crazed males, my father and brothers dropping one by one, my mother being ripped apart. Finally, I'd shoved my wolf back down, caged her, and the unmated males had come back to themselves, horrified at what they'd done.

But it was too late. Hans had come.

I pressed my knuckles to my forehead and squeezed my eyes shut. I would not think about that now.

Footsteps crunched in the snow, and then the monster laid a hand on my shoulder. Claws extended from his fingertips, and he dug the points through my clothing and into my skin. I gritted my teeth to hold back a pained cry.

"Here lies Gale Gullari," Hans intoned. "Beloved wife and mother. May she continue in death as in life. Blah, blah, blah." He turned to me, an excited glow brightening the whites of his eyes. "Do your thing, bikkja, and see if Odin listens to broken, worthless wolves. Call his fire, if you can, and seal your mother in Valhalla."

My wolf growled, and the sound tickled the back of my throat. Worse things had been said to me over the past three years, but still, my anger rose, bringing with it a grim determination to honor my mother in front of these piteous Valdyr that had once been my pack.

I would do as my mother had asked, and then I'd never have to look upon their faces or Hans's again—until it was time to kill him.

My wolf howled triumphantly, and the door inside my soul swung open.

Wrenching free of Hans, I strode to the other side of the five-foot-high pyre. Blood scented the air where his claws had ripped my skin, but it didn't matter. Nothing mattered but invoking the fire to seal my mom in Asgard with my dad and brothers and then honoring her last request.

To run.

My wolf leapt from her cage and slunk forward, focused on Hans. Three years ago, I had fought against the ulf-risa, but this time I welcomed my wolf.

Laying a trembling hand over Gale's heart, the words flowed over my tongue. "I am Kristin Marie Gullari. Daughter of Gale and Andrew Gullari. Sister of Adam, Joran, Garet, and Finn. I honor my mother by calling on Odin to welcome her home. She loved well, fought bravely, and will be met with great joy in the woods outside of Valhalla. As she burned brightly in life, may she burn even brighter in death."

I lifted my hand, drawing on the last spark of magic within my mom's body, and flames exploded from Gale's chest. They seared toward the stars, a myriad of colors blazing in the night. The Valdyr surrounding me gasped and stumbled back as heat rolled over them. Some cowered before the magical inferno. Others stared in awe.

I basked in it.

On the other side of the burning pyre, Hans gloated through the translucent flames. He reached out and played with the fire. "You're stronger than we thought."

My wolf waited just beneath the surface, wanting to lunge at the monster, but I held her back. Reaching for the flames as Hans had done, I somehow cupped the colored fire.

A stirring rose within my body, different from the wolf's presence. My magic, maybe? "Strong enough to kill you someday."

The glee fell from Hans's face. With a roar, he parted the flames and jumped toward me.

I threw the fire at him, my hands shaping it into a cage. Hans howled as it closed around him, but the cage held, giving me priceless seconds.

I darted my gaze around the pack, wondering how many unkyssed males were in the group. How many would turn feral and come after me once I—

A screech sounded behind me as Hans wrenched the cage bars open.

Too late.

I stopped thinking, leapt forward, and let go. Pressure built inside my body as my wolf filled my skin. Shivers raced up my spine. I heard a small pop and then felt myself dissolve. Wrenching pain tore through me as my wolf formed. Padded feet hit the snow, and I ran—a four-legged gallop. I wobbled at first over the uneven terrain, jumping logs and skidding through trees, and I lost precious time.

My wolf growled at me. *Release!*

This time, the wolf's thoughts were all around me rather than inside me. I was the wolf, or inside the wolf, or maybe the wolf was me.

A cacophony of sights and scents overwhelmed me, invading the dark hollow where I'd retreated, and I panicked, reaching for control.

Release! the wolf snarled again, and I yelped as something nipped my backside the way my mother had done when I was a pup. Was that her? Or my wolf?

In the distance, demented howls filled the air, making my heart race. The sound was chillingly familiar—as was the scent surrounding me. My scent. It poured off of me and carried on the wind to the unkyssed males, turning them feral as they fought everything in their paths to get to me.

My wolf knew what they wanted even if I didn't.

Mate.

Horror poured through me, and I shrank into the dark. Grunting in approval, my wolf found an easy, pounding rhythm, eating up the distance as she flew across the mountain through the snow. So fast. So strong.

We are strong.

In all the time I had been aware of my wolf, I'd never once thought in terms of "we." It had always been me against the wolf, an alien entity that had pushed its way into my body.

I tried to relax and was surprised to feel the pulse of muscle through a heavy horizontal form, the wind ruffling thick fur, the snow crunching beneath large clawed feet.

It was…exhilarating.

Can you…we…get away? I asked.

Ulf-mynd.

The ulf-mynd was the merging of the two souls. But wasn't I already merged? I was now the alien entity in the wolf's mind. What more could I do?

Heart.

The word confused me. In frustration, I crossed my arms over my chest, and my wolf stumbled. I uncrossed them immediately, but I couldn't stop my panic from rising.

My wolf slowed and barked at me frantically. *Heart!*

The deranged howls grew closer, and I sensed…him. His laugh cut through the frenetic yipping, and terror beat at me.

Faster! I yelled, but still, my wolf slowed. In desperation, I pictured my heart in my hands and shoved it into the wolf, who yelped and fell, rolling on the ground. I yanked my heart back, and the wolf dragged herself up. She took off again, whimpering in pain.

It hurt me too. I rubbed my chest gently with my opposite

palm, rocking back and forth, trying to be as small and inconspicuous as possible. Maybe if the wolf forgot I was there, we could still make it.

The pain eased, and the wolf's limping ceased.

We were connected.

Yes. Heart.

Connected through the heart. Through everything. I had to give of myself. That's what my wolf needed, what I needed. To become the wolf...become whole.

This time, I closed my eyes and imagined my heart expanding. It took over my body and the dark space where I hid until it encompassed my wolf. I seeped into bone, flesh, and fur. My eyesight changed, my sense of smell intensified, my hearing increased.

I didn't just feel the wolf. I was the wolf.

And the wolf was me—with all of her strength and power.

Yes!

A frenzied male appeared in front of us, eyes wild, and that strange stirring rose within me as my wolf jumped over him. The air whipped into a colorful wind beneath her, giving her height and speed. Another wolf leapt at us from the side, but she easily twirled in the whirlwind and kept going.

Stronger. Faster. We could outrun them all!

We broke through the trees, but ahead of us a vast valley fell away from a cliff's edge. My muscles bunched, and my claws dug in as I slid along the icy snow.

I reached for rocks, branches, anything to halt my forward momentum. Finally, I stopped just as my haunches cleared the edge. Sides heaving, I gingerly crawled away from the drop-off on my belly.

Hans's scent hit me, and I raised my eyes. A massive, snarling wolf stood fifteen feet in front of me before it morphed into Hans—naked, with one hand raised, angry amusement on his face. He was huge and scarily beautiful in the moonlight. Feral wolves flanked him, cutting off my escape.

"Shall I bind you first and then let them have you?" He lowered his hand and the wolves lunged, snapping at each other and straining to get to me. He raised his hand, and they quieted. "Or just work with what's left of you afterward? You don't have to be whole to be useful."

I couldn't get past Hans with the wolves there. Maybe I should shift back into my Valdyr form so my scent would—

Yes.

In a heartbeat, my wolf separated from me and retreated inside. Shock hit hard as I dissolved and then reformed with wrenching pain, lying naked in the snow.

The wolves surrounding me stopped snarling. Some of them shifted, looking shaken and confused. Others just looked weary.

I stood slowly and faced him, my mind racing. The fact that I was naked barely registered. It was the way of the Valdyr.

My hair whipped wildly in the wind. Blond strands the color of my father's hair obstructed my view, and I pushed them away from my face. The boys had all been dark like our mother. Maybe I would see them soon.

Closing my eyes, I said a brief, fervent prayer to Odin. *Save me from him. Please, Allfather!*

When I opened my eyes, Hans stood a foot away. I gasped and jumped back. Behind me, snow plummeted off the cliff.

"Odin won't help you, Kristin. The gods lost interest in you long ago. You have to save yourself now." He raised his hand, and heat warmed my skin—gently at first, then growing hotter until it burned. "Use your magic against me."

I nearly grabbed the raw energy and threw it back at him, but that's what he wanted.

My mom said he needed my wolf to bind me, but what if it was the magic gifted to all female Valdyr that he needed? I'd surprised myself earlier when I'd manipulated the fire. Could I do it again?

Could I win?

I raised my eyes, saw his eager anticipation, and had my answer.

No.

The snow at my feet had melted, and the rocky edge dug into my skin. Deep inside, my wolf raised her head. She stared me in the eye.

Fly.

Without hesitating, I shoved backward off the cliff. Hans roared in surprise and tried to grab me, but his claws barely scraped my belly. I started to free-fall down the rock face and smiled. Then I flipped him the bird—using both middle fingers.

The wind whistled past my ears, and the faces of my family flashed before my eyes. Peace filled my body, and I felt like I was changing…floating. *Not long now.*

My only thought—my only regret—was that my mother had promised I'd find a strong male to kyss.

I would have liked to meet him.

CHAPTER 1

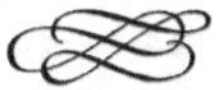

Missoula County, Montana
Twelve years later

<u>*Kristin*</u>

LEAVE IT TO GINA TO KILL ME BEFORE I EVEN GOT TO THE compound.

I stared into the grill of the black Range Rover as it barreled toward us, sure this was it. I tossed the gods a quick prayer, and for the second time in my life, I waited to die.

Gina swerved left, long red nails flashing on the wheel, and I slammed against the passenger door. Eyes closed, I braced myself for impact.

When the Mini came to an abrupt halt without the death blow I'd expected, I unclenched my teeth and took a deep breath. "I said pull over, not kill us now."

My foster sister cut the engine. "Technicalities."

Opening my eyes to a bright summer day and a gorgeous mountain view, I sighed with relief. Then I noticed the Mini convertible was parked sideways, a foot away from the drop-off —and there was no guard rail. "Not funny."

"Consider it behavioral therapy. I'm helping you face your fears."

"Uh-huh. Cause that's what you're all about. The helping."

Gina stepped out of the car and sauntered to the edge of the cliff. Her gauzy white skirt revealed shapely legs, and her crocheted pink halter top exposed way too much boob. She looked back, her dark hair blowing in the breeze, and smirked.

I gritted my teeth. I would not give my sister the satisfaction of seeing me climb out of the driver's seat. Instead, I opened the car door, planted my boots on the tiny ledge between the car and the drop-off, and forced myself to stand.

Do not look down. Do not look down.

Closing my eyes, I side-stepped toward the trunk of the car. My fear of cliffs was not real. It's not like I could fall, being supernatural and all. I was like Supergirl. Or, even better, Hawk-girl—my favorite comic book character when I was a kid.

When my right foot hit the back wheel, my lids opened just a smidge…and I stilled. Below, nestled in a wide, rocky valley, lay Wolf Ridge Industries. A thrill shot through me despite my fear, and if I hadn't been afraid of falling to my death, I would have started happy dancing.

This must be it.

I had no doubt the complex—hel, the entire valley—was guarded. Even if a pack didn't live in this range of mountains northwest of Missoula, Montana, the nature of the company dictated heavy security.

"Maybe you shouldn't go," Gina said. "It's a long way down. It could set your cliff-therapy thingy back years."

Her sarcasm grated, but I could hear the worry festering beneath the words, and I sighed. We'd been over this. I needed to get close enough to discover if Valdyr lived in the valley—close enough to scent them.

More importantly, to scent Hans. I'd been hunting him for years.

Still, every once in a while, it was nice to know my foster sister cared—which, right about now, as I stared into the jaws of death, was doubtful.

"They can't smell me, Gina, not unless I shift. And no way in hel is that happening with a bunch of unkyssed males around. When I met Dahlia in Denver, she didn't realize I was Valdyr, even though I scented her as soon as she entered the gallery. We don't even know if a pack lives here or not."

Closing my eyes again, I jumped over the back of the car instead of going around. I'd had about all that I could handle of my phobia right now.

When I landed on the other side, the jolt woke my wolf, who huffed before rolling over to go back to sleep. The pique that rose through me made me smile.

Lazy dog.

Inside, my wolf growled.

Where exactly "inside" was, only Odin knew. A Valdyr resided on two planes: the physical plane of Earth and a spiritual plane called Hjarta—or *heart*. Years ago, when my wolf tried to explain the supernatural realm to me, she relayed the image of a rock—a spherical geode—with thousands of crystals inside. I interpreted each crystal to be an individual cell or dimension within the spiritual plane.

Bonded wolves, whether kyssed pairs, family, or packmates, shared these special cells, and a wolf could exist in one or all of them, all at once. But since I had no mate, pack, or family, my wolf and I were alone.

Pinching the bridge of my nose, I made my way toward my sister. Thinking about things like higher dimensions made my head hurt. I was an artist, not a cosmologist or astrophysicist.

The only thing I knew for certain was that my wolf was

always with me and ready to shift at a moment's notice if I needed her. Or just to natter in my ear.

Another growl. *Natter?*

Sorry. I meant "give advice and express opinions...frequently."

When I reached Gina, I grabbed her hand and pulled her a safe distance away from the precipice.

"Maybe Dahlia did smell you, and this is a trap," Gina said. "You were locked up before. They might try it again."

"I was locked up by a psychopath who may or may not have been Valdyr. Hans had magic—only female Valdyr are magical. Anyway, if it is a pack, I'll look around and report back. If not, I'll sell a bunch of art for outrageous prices. Either way, I win."

"It is a pack—or something non-human."

I glanced at her sharply. "How do you know?"

"The entire valley is warded." Gina lifted her hands as if feeling the air. "The fortifications are strong...and old. I could break them for you, but..." She frowned, and I could see her fingers glowing. "It'll take me a few days."

"No. Keep your itchy-witchy fingers to yourself. We'll be gone before then."

A vehicle roared up behind us, and I spun around. Instinct had me stepping in front of my sister, who poked me in the back. "Hello. Daughter of Freyja here. I could easily turn the driver into mush."

It was an exaggeration—of sorts—and I didn't move. No way would I lose another family member. Gina might not be my real sister, but she was a sister of the heart, and I wouldn't be here if not for her.

A stinging electrical shock zapped me in the ass, and my wolf jumped awake with a yelp before snapping in my sister's direction. Gina didn't sense the wolf, of course—she was a witch, not a Valdyr—but I did.

I stepped to the side with a muttered curse, resisting the urge to rub my tingling butt. To hel with sisterly love.

"Language," Gina said smugly.

The big black Range Rover we'd almost hit earlier screeched to a halt, and my gut sank. Damn...the vehicle looked official. The last thing I wanted was to piss off people at Wolf Ridge before I even made it to my appointment.

Tinted windows hid whomever was inside, but when the driver's door opened, a familiar scent hit me, and I inhaled deeply. It reminded me of my brothers—strong, dominant, protective—and brought tears to my eyes. I quickly blinked them away.

My wolf raced forward, tail high.

Easy, I said, mentally clamping down on my scent even though I knew the Valdyr couldn't smell me as anything other than human. I'd mastered the ability to conceal my scent during the tragedy of my ulf-risa when the early rising of my wolf caused the unkyssed males to go feral. Too bad I hadn't mastered any other aspect of my magic.

Since my escape from Hans, I'd barely felt a spark in my belly.

But in other ways, I was stronger and faster. I'd trained with Gina for years, honing my skills against my sister's magic. I had no doubt I could take Hans—and kill him this time.

If I could find him.

The male who exited the driver's side was tall and broad-shouldered with buzzed black hair and dusky skin. He wore jeans and a tight gray T-shirt over a flat abdomen. All Valdyr carried a colorful aura I could see when I used my super-acute second sight—my avian sight, as my dad had called it—and this male, who leaned on the Range Rover's hood with his arms crossed over his chest, shone like a rainbow. Same as my sister.

It was the magic within them. Humans didn't carry nearly the same punch.

Dark sunglasses covered the Valdyr's eyes. He looked toward Gina—who'd cocked her hip and thrust out her chest.

Who'd have guessed? A man snookered by big boobs.

But then the man frowned. "What kind of idiot crosses two lanes of oncoming traffic without looking? You almost caused an accident."

Gina flicked her hair over her shoulder. "You're alive, aren't you?"

"I'm not the one who would've eaten the pavement, sweet cheeks. What's the matter? Too much silicone seeping into your brain?"

I groaned and quickly stepped in front of Gina, facing her just as my sister raised her hand to zap the man. I let my wolf shine through my eyes. "Just say you're sorry, Gina, and let's leave."

My sister's mouth set, and we glared at each other. Finally, she lowered her hand. With a sigh of relief, my wolf subsided. This could still end peacefully.

Then, a second scent hit my nose, and I almost dropped to my knees.

* * *

Erik

I sat frozen in the passenger seat of the Range Rover, watching the dark-haired woman argue with Gunn. The blond had turned toward the vehicle and was staring directly at me through the tinted glass.

Can she see me?

The darkness inside of me—the curse that had ravaged me since I'd sucked it out of the pack and trapped it inside the hjarta with my wolf—surged in response, almost breaking free of its prison. My wolf forced it back down, mentally fortifying the blocks of the well that contained it and stopping its poisonous spread of suspicion and distrust. When my wolf had finished, I turned my attention back to the women.

The dark-haired one was a knockout, but it was the blond

who held my attention—my wolf's too—which was unheard of for a human, or even a Valdyr.

The darkness was drawn to her too.

She was tall and slender with long legs encased in tight jeans that she'd tucked into high-heeled boots. A white T-shirt skimmed her curves, which were slight. Except for her ass. When she turned around to speak to her friend, it bowed out like an apple.

One I wanted to bite.

Compelled to see her eyes, I opened the passenger door and stepped out. Pushing my sunglasses onto my head, I stared. She met my gaze, wide-eyed, and tucked a strand of long, wavy hair behind her ear. My wolf gave an approving growl while the curse began to bubble.

Settle down, I told my wolf. *She's human, for Odin's sake.*

Mate, my wolf replied, bowing down on his front paws and tossing and tilting his head.

Damn. I'd been around wolves, natural and Valdyr, all my life. My wolf was flirting with her. No way should the big male be attracted to a human any more than I should be attracted to a natural wolf.

Gunn glanced at me, sensing my unease through the Alpha bond.

Advancing slowly, I scented the air. Had I missed something? Nothing unusual tainted her scent.

Gunn strode around the Range Rover to my side. "What's up?" he whispered.

"Maybe nothing. It's just...my wolf likes her."

"What's not to like? The woman's a living, breathing sex goddess. And a mouthy one too. Just my type."

I smiled, but it faded quickly. The arousal, whether mine or my wolf's, wasn't a laughing matter. "Not that one. The blond woman. Just be careful."

"Always." Gunn flashed me a leering grin. "But maybe your

wolf just wants to get laid. The pack won't fall apart if you take a night for yourself, you know." He swung his gaze toward the women, this time checking out the blond. "She's got pretty hair and great legs. And when she turned around, her a—"

My wolf snapped at Gunn through the bond, his lips pulled back in a snarl. Gunn—and his wolf—jumped back.

"I warned you." I knew Gunn hadn't meant any disrespect. My wolf shouldn't have been so possessive. The woman was human, after all.

The dark-haired "sex goddess" tossed a pebble at us. It hit Gunn on the shoulder. "Yo, rock star. You got a problem?"

Irritation, but also admiration, crossed Gunn's face. "Nothing to concern you, Miss Silicon Valley."

The blond briefly closed her eyes and shook her head. I understood why when her friend narrowed her gaze and sauntered toward Gunn, the sway of her hips matching the natural sway of her breasts.

"Freyja's tits," Gunn murmured.

I shifted my focus back to the blond, and when our eyes met, my wolf nipped at me to get moving. As I approached her, I tried to remember why I needed to be cautious. But that was hard to do when her eyes, a golden hazel streaked with amber, tugged at something deep inside.

"Hi," I said, my voice cracking at the end.

Her lips pulled back in a smile. "Hello."

And then I couldn't get my tongue to work. Silence hung between us. *Suave, dude*, Gunn said through the bond. I resisted the urge to give him the finger.

"I'm sorry my sister nearly hit you," the woman said. "She really is a terrible driver. If it's any consolation, I almost had a heart attack."

"Me too. Maybe you should drive from now on." I wanted to touch her and found myself raising my hand to her hair. I quickly shoved it in my pocket.

"I needed to navigate. Her driving is actually better than her sense of direction."

"Hard to believe. But it's better to be lost than dead. Where are you going?"

"Wolf Ridge Industries. I saw the logo on your car. Are you with the company?"

Gunn!

I heard.

"You need an appointment to get in." I tried to keep my voice relaxed, but it was tough with the tension that had invaded my muscles.

"I have one with Dahlia Kron. She came to my gallery in Denver last week and asked me to come and see her. She's decorating the offices."

Right. The artist. Dahlia wanted to buy some of her paintings—amazing depictions of wolves and other wildlife. I'd recently put Dahlia in charge of refurbishing the pack's den, trying to find a place for her, and she'd found this woman's work.

"You're the artist she mentioned. Kristin Andersen." I held out my hand. "I'm Erik Kron. Dahlia's my cousin."

She squeezed my hand briefly before pulling away. It was enough to make my wolf howl.

Settle down.

"I read about you when I researched the company. You're the CEO."

"Yes. And that's Gunnar Lang, Head of Security. We call him Gunn. You can understand why he's a little touchy about your sister's driving."

When Kristin looked over at the still-arguing Gunn and Gina, I stared at her. This time, I noticed all the little details—the long blond-tipped eyelashes, the faint white scar on the top of her left cheek, the stone Norse rune for strength fastened on a leather cord around her neck.

Hmm. That was suspicious too. I glanced at Gunn. *You getting anything?*

Just a bunch of sass. This woman has some mouth on her. Maybe if I got her to put it on me instead, she'd shut up.

I brought my attention back to Kristin. "Gina's your sister? You don't look alike."

Pink tinged her cheeks, and she pushed a self-conscious hand through her hair. "I know. I take after my dad. We really should get going. My appointment's in twenty minutes." She signaled Gina and then held out her hand to me—firmly this time, as if she'd prepared herself. "It was nice to meet you, Mr. Kron."

"Please, call me Erik." I took her hand, and a shiver of desire rolled through both me and my wolf. That other part of me, the joy-sucking darkness I detested, boiled up to the top of the walls that contained it. I released her and quickly stepped back. "Why don't you come with me to Wolf Ridge? It'll be easier to get past security."

"Oh, well…thank you, but that's not necessary. I'm sure it won't be a problem."

"I'm afraid I insist. We don't let strangers into the compound often. I agreed last week because Dahlia said you needed to see the space." I turned to Gina, who was striding toward us with a frown on her face. "You, unfortunately, won't be allowed in without clearance. And that can take weeks."

"Do you expect me to just sit here and wait?" Gina asked, planting her hands on her hips.

"Yes. But don't worry, you won't be alone. Gunn will keep you company."

Thanks, big dog.

You're welcome. In the meantime, why don't you use that mouth of yours in a nice, non-sexual way and see what you can find out.

How does that work again?

Repressing a smile, I took the keys from Gunn and turned to Kristin. "Do you have everything?"

She reached into the back seat of the car for a large portfolio bag, swung it over her shoulder, and then one-arm hugged her sister, who was gripping her other arm.

"I'll be fine," she said and then stepped away and strode ahead of me toward the Range Rover, her head held high and her rounded ass rocking my world.

I had the sudden feeling nothing would ever be the same.

Kristin

Erik's scent was thick within the Range Rover. I tried holding my breath, but eventually, I'd have to inhale and take Eau de Erik deep into my lungs. It was excruciating—in a take-me-now-but-don't-kill-me-afterward kind of way.

He could be my enemy.

My wolf, however, didn't care. She lay on her side, panting, having exhausted herself by running in circles. Once, she'd even stopped and raised her tail in Erik's direction as she watched him over her shoulder.

Hussy, I teased, only half joking.

Mate, she responded.

I'd been around other Valdyr males before Erik—in the Canadian Rockies and a few years later in Alaska. Much to Gina's disapproval, I'd searched them out, looking for Hans.

Never before had my wolf waved her fluffy ass at them like a feline in heat.

An insulted growl reverberated in my head, but its ferocity was dampened when my wolf rolled onto her back.

Nothing like a little subtlety.

One strong male in Alaska named Kell had piqued my interest, but he'd been grieving a human female who'd died. I'd liked him, but still, I'd been cautious. In the end, no matter how good it felt to be around other Valdyr, I hadn't revealed myself, afraid the unkyssed males would swarm if I shifted.

I hadn't scented Hans there or in Canada. Or anywhere else I'd looked. I'd even returned to my old pack in the Appalachian Mountains, but they'd disappeared.

Maybe this Montana pack would know something. And if not, maybe…maybe what? Maybe they'd be strong enough that I could let down my guard? Find a home and a mate? Did I even want those things?

I'd bet money Erik was the pack's Alpha. Gunn was strong, stronger even than my brothers, but his strength was more like a hammer. Erik's was a rapier—just as deadly but more precise. If Gunn was the bear, Erik was the panther waiting in the trees.

My wolf bared her teeth, not appreciating the second cat metaphor. I smiled.

"Something funny?" Erik asked as he followed the road down the rocky, semi-arid mountainside to the valley below. We'd been waved through security a few minutes before with little more than a nod.

"I was just…thinking of the expressions on Gina's and Gunn's faces when we drove away."

Erik snorted. The sound sent electrical currents that felt like fingertips down my spine. "They'll survive."

Gods, I had to get myself under control. I'd barely been able to form an intelligent thought since I'd scented him. Then he'd climbed out of the Range Rover, tall and muscled in a light-gray suit, his jaw chiseled, his eyes and hair a luscious chocolate brown that turned my knees weak. His nose looked like it had been broken at least once, which had to have happened before his ulf-rist. It was not so different from the scar I'd gotten on my cheekbone from jumping off a roof when I was little, thinking I could fly.

I'd dated good-looking males before, human and Valdyr, but

never one that smelled as good as Erik or made my wolf act so wanton.

Perhaps I was in heat? No, I was pretty sure females didn't go into heat until after they were mated. Maybe my mom had romanticized the details, thinking she could explain the process to me in greater detail when I was older.

My Valdyr knowledge was limited to what I remembered from childhood, but even that was suspect. If I found a strong enough pack, I'd gain more than just a sense of belonging—I'd recover my heritage.

But all that had to take a back seat to the reason I was here, the reason I'd trained so hard with Gina all those years.

To kill Hans.

"Now you're frowning," Erik said, pulling me back to the present.

"What? Oh, sorry, I was just…concentrating, I guess. I want to make a good impression on Dahlia."

I looked closely at the complex as we made our final approach. It was about a half mile long and a quarter mile wide, filled with buildings of all different shapes and sizes, including a couple about the size of a football field. Houses dotted the outskirts and rose up the mountainside.

I wondered if pack members lived there and if so, how they kept their existence a secret from the humans who worked for the company. Unless the whole complex was run by Valdyr? That would be incredible—there were over five hundred employees.

"I can't believe how big it is…and all the security. Wolf Ridge isn't a military facility, is it?"

"No, but we have several military contracts. Essentially, we build and maintain satellites, high-powered telescopes, and security systems and equipment for private, commercial, and governmental use."

"So you manufacture weapons?"

"Not exactly, but we're involved in projects with NASA and

the DOD that are strictly defense-related. I can't say anything more than that."

"Of course. Not that it matters. I'm only here to sell some paintings."

He glanced at me. "Dahlia says you're very good. She was especially impressed with your depiction of wolves. Have you spent time with them?"

Years ago, Gina and I had created false backgrounds and IDs, helped along by my artistry and Gina's magic. At the time, I never thought I'd need all the details my sister had included. I'd been wrong.

"There was a wolf sanctuary near my home in Ohio when I was a kid. I was fascinated by them. And I've observed them in the wild in Canada and Alaska. They're beautiful creatures."

"And deadly."

I knew it was a warning, and I barely repressed a shiver. "Yes, I've seen that too. Are there wolves around here? I'm assuming there must be because of the company name."

"There are now. They were extirpated from the western United States in the early to mid-twentieth century, but in the last forty years or so, there's been a concerted effort to repopulate."

"How sad. I'm glad they've made a comeback."

"Yes. Although they were never completely gone. People would still find traces of them—tracks or scat—or would swear they'd seen them. They probably came down from Canada."

Or they were Valdyr.

I gazed at distant, snow-covered mountains. The jagged peaks were so different from the Appalachian mountains where I'd been raised. "It's beautiful country. Did you grow up here?"

"The land has been in my...family...for generations. Originally, we were ranchers, and then, in the forties, my great-grandparents started Wolf Ridge Industries. It was a small company at first, but it kept growing."

"And now it's a billion-dollar success. I'll have to raise my prices."

"You can try. Dahlia's a mean negotiator."

I laughed. The docile Valdyr I'd met in Denver was too sweet to be mean.

We pulled up to a circular black-glass building built into the mountainside. It was four stories high with a domed glass roof.

"Is this the main building?" I asked.

"It's the, um, executive building. Dahlia will meet you inside."

I nodded and reached for the door handle, eagerly anticipating a breath of fresh air that didn't make me want to crawl into Erik's lap. He laid his hand on my arm. The contact stirred the heat in my belly, and I had to squeeze my thighs together to stop them from trembling. When I met his gaze, his eyes held a coolness that surprised me.

"Whatever you do, Kristin, don't wander around on your own. I'd hate for there to be a misunderstanding."

CHAPTER 2

"I'm so glad to see you!" Dahlia squeezed her arms around me in a tight embrace. The pixie-faced female, wearing a cute orange sundress, her brown hair cut in layers to her shoulders, was the same sweet Valdyr I remembered.

I grinned and returned the hug—despite my stomach twisting like a balloon animal after Erik's warning. Part of me was ready to shift and make a break for it, while another part was just pissed. *Stupid, overprotective Alpha.*

My wolf should have been pissed too—she was way too dominant to let something like that go—yet all she wanted to do was sidle up to Erik.

Floozy.

The scent of changeling wolves filled the air inside the foyer, bringing with it memories of my family and former pack—the good times in particular, like when everyone would gather together in the spring to celebrate the creation of the Valdyr, or when a recently risen wolf bonded with the pack.

My three oldest brothers had completed that ritualized

passage. My youngest brother, Finn, just five years older than me, had not. He'd died before his wolf had risen.

A sting of sadness pierced my heart, and I inhaled deeply. As if sensing my emotions, Dahlia squeezed my hand, her dove-gray eyes gentle. The sharp pain faded into melancholy, and I smiled again at the lovely Valdyr.

She really was a sweetheart.

Erik leaned in and kissed his cousin's cheek in greeting. My wolf strained toward him, pulling me out of my memories.

Oh, my gods. Did you hear how he threatened us? I asked.

My wolf huffed and lay back down.

"Gunn and I met Gina and Kristin on the way here," Erik said. "I offered to accompany her the rest of the way."

Now I was the one who huffed—silently. Accompanied? More like ordered. *Stupid, dominant Alpha.*

"Where's Gina?" Dahlia asked, sounding worried. "You didn't leave her with Gunn, did you?"

I raised my brow. "My sister's a tough cookie."

"I never thought I'd say it, but I think Gunn's the one you should be worried about," Erik added with a grin.

"You're sure?"

"Yes." We answered together, and the sound of our voices, echoing as one, left me breathless.

Now I was the one being stupid. My wolf thumped her tail in agreement.

We walked through the foyer, my boots clicking on the hardwood, toward a secure door that opened on its own. Stepping through, I stared in awe as we entered a large rotunda. Offices four stories high lined the rounded walls, which butted up against the rock face. The floor was copper slate and in the middle was a two-tiered sunken circle that continued into the mountain, forming an eight-foot-high cave at the end. At the point closest to me, facing the door, sat a large stone carving of a wolf.

The carving fascinated me, as did several Valdyr lounging on the steps. I shifted to my other sight, just to make sure, and their auras shone brightly—strong and vivid.

Erik had a strong pack. It thrilled me, but it also made me nervous. Could he control the unkyssed males if my scent escaped?

I eyed the sunken circle again. Did it become the pack's sacred circle when sanctified? It was so different from the crude hringr in the woods my pack had communed in.

Memories surged again, making my chest squeeze, and in an effort to hide the sudden wash of tears, I lifted my eyes to the domed ceiling…and noticed that the glass retracted, allowing the heavens to shine all the way down. "It's beautiful," I said, my voice tinged with awe.

"Thank you," Dahlia said. "You can see why I wanted you to see the space."

"Yes."

My gaze was drawn again to the stone wolf. An odd feeling tightened my belly and raised the fine hairs on my skin. The sculpture was majestic and intricately carved, but it also felt…wrong.

Was it the perspective or dimension of the work? The expression on the wolf's face?

All of that, and yet…none of that.

It was as if…as if—

"That's Rolf," Dahlia said.

I jumped at the words spoken softly in my ear. I didn't know how long I'd been staring at the sculpture, and my cheeks warmed. "I'm sorry. Did you say, Rolf?"

"Yes. That's what I call him. I have since I was a kid. It's like wolf, but…*Rolf*. You know, kind of regal."

I imagined a pint-sized Dahlia naming the wolf and smiled, then looked back at the carving. Maybe the bad feeling I'd had was just my imagina—

Something dark surged from the sculpture and prodded my shields. My wolf stiffened and growled low in her throat as my smile faded. Okay…so not my imagination.

I stared at Rolf, frozen by my uncertainty. Maybe the sculpture protected the pack by repelling strangers. It was positioned as if to guard the circle, and Erik and Dahlia didn't seem to be affected by it. Or maybe it sensed if someone had ulterior motives—like I did.

"It was a wedding gift for my parents," Erik said. "I met the sculptor years ago when my mom took me to visit him. He lived alone, high in the mountains. The sculpture is almost forty years old."

"It's…incredible. Who's the artist?" I desperately wanted to know, but at the same time, that feeling of dread intensified. Maybe the less I knew, the better.

"Bjarg Faegir. I think he's, um, Norse." Dahlia took my hand and tugged me toward the statue. "Come on. You can look at it up close."

We stopped a few feet away from the statue, and my wolf snarled viciously. The strange stirring in my body intensified, and I realized with shock that it was my magic. It had stirred before in the presence of danger. First, during my ulf-risa when my wolf rose so early and the unkyssed males attacked my brothers and father to get to me. Then, when Hans chased me the night my mother had died. I'd actually shaped the magical inferno that had cremated my mother's body.

But what exactly was threatening me this time, and how could I use my magic against it?

Erik leaned on the statue, unaffected. I linked my hands together to stop myself from pushing him away from it. It must have been some kind of talisman that only affected outsiders.

Stepping back, I glanced around the building again, pretending everything was all right. Many of the Valdyr watched me—males and females of various ages—all of them tall with sculpted muscles and a watchfulness that raised the hairs on the back of my neck. I considered myself strong and fast, but I'd need all of my skills to defeat these Valdyr—and then some.

They were almost as big as Hans. I shivered.

"Are you cold?" Erik asked. "The stone wall keeps it cool in here. I'm sure we can find you a sweater."

My eyes met his. As always, his gaze held a directness and intensity that made me want to nip him…before I rolled over in submission. "I'm okay. It's refreshing after the heat outside."

Dahlia looped her arm through mine. "I've got a jacket you can borrow if you need it. Let's go look at the space."

"Sure." I took a few steps with Dahlia before noticing that Erik wasn't following us. Disappointment pulsed deep within me. Was that my wolf or me? "Are you coming?" I asked.

"No, Dahlia can take it from here." He hesitated as if he wanted to say something else.

My wolf swiveled her ears forward, and I found myself holding my breath, wanting to catch every sound. For the life of me, I couldn't break the spell he'd cast over me.

Mate, my wolf thought.

Then he shook his head and dropped his gaze. He held out his hand. "Good to meet you, Kristin."

I took a breath, trying to pull myself back from whatever cliff he'd stranded me on.

"Good to meet you too." His big hand enveloped mine in a strong grip.

When he let go and walked away, I swore I wouldn't watch him leave, but at the last minute, I glanced back to see him ascending a spiral staircase near the door. At the top, he walked along an open landing and disappeared into one of the offices.

My wolf sat back and howled.

I turned to see Dahlia watching me closely, and the heat rushed up my face. Damn. Talk about making a fool of myself.

"If you're interested," I said hurriedly, "I have several stone and wood carvings I can show you. They'd be a nice compliment to Rolf."

"I didn't know you sculpted as well."

"I work in several different mediums." My eyes landed on the rock wall, and an idea began to form—a big idea.

The fact that it would allow me to see more of Erik never even crossed my mind.

My wolf grunted in disbelief.

Okay. How about the fact that we can look for Hans?

This time, she growled.

"Have you ever thought about carving the rock wall?" I asked Dahlia. "A stone mural in here would look amazing."

Erik

I leaned back against my office door and pressed my fingers into the wood to stop myself from returning to the landing to watch Kristin. What the hel kind of hold did she have over me?

I hesitated, then walked to a large black desk and switched on my computer. I clicked the video link to bring up live images of the compound and chose the one I wanted. Then I settled back to watch Dahlia and Kristin talking by the rock wall.

As the pack's Alpha, I could connect to Dahlia's mind and get a sense of their conversation, but I didn't want her to get the wrong idea. I wasn't interested in Kristin as a woman, only as a threat to the pack.

My wolf was drawn to her for a reason.

Yes. Mate, he said.

I squeezed my hand, and the pen I held snapped in half, leaking ink all over my palm. I sighed, tossed the pieces in the garbage, and shifted my hand into the helmingr—halfway to my wolf—so the ink no longer adhered to anything solid and splatted onto my desk.

She's human, I said as I wiped up the mess. *Haven't you smelled her?*

My wolf's confusion filled me, and I sighed. We were both in the dark here.

Closing the screen, I connected to a hidden camera at the overlook where I'd met Kristin. Spinning the lens, I found Gina lounging on the hood of her car, eyes closed, with her back against the windshield and the sun beating down on her. She'd hiked up her skirt to expose shapely thighs. Sexy sandals criss-crossed her calves.

Gunn paced in front of her, a scowl on his face and his arms tight across his chest.

You all right? I asked.

She's got me chasing my tail. When can I send her away?

Soon. Come see me when you're done.

After switching back to watch Kristin for a minute, I rechecked our security. Everything looked in order. I dug up the file my team had compiled on her. Nothing stood out.

So why was I certain something was wrong?

Because I'm a paranoid workaholic who's lived with the taint of the darkness for too long. I saw danger around every corner. But maybe Gunn was right—I just needed to get laid.

Still, I shouldn't be this attracted to a human.

And there *was* danger. Lots of it.

I wasn't just the Alpha of a Valdyr pack, I was the Fyrstr of the Varda—direct descendants of the original pack created by Odin to guard the mammoth wolf-changeling Fenrir and stop his sons, Hati and Skoll, from breaking him out of prison.

If the Varda and I failed, a monster didn't just go free. The world—all of the nine worlds—went up in flames.

The prophecy the gods had unveiled eons ago said that the oceans would heave, fire would rain down, and a great battle would take place between the gods and the Jotun, eradicating almost every living being.

Ragnarök would come to pass.

My eyes fell on a small stone pendant carved in the shape of a Viking longship. A leather cord looped through the sail and hung from the switch on my lamp. For a while now, I'd had a sense something was coming. My instinct, the warning system every Valdyr possessed, buzzed in anticipation.

Of what, I didn't know.

It was time for another trip to Asgard, the home of the Norse gods. Odin often spoke in riddles, but I needed guidance. However my maker chose to bestow it.

Snagging the pendant, I looped the cord around my neck. If I could send someone else, maybe Linnea, the pack's Alpha female, or Gunn, I would, but they were unable to sift between worlds. That skill had once been taught to every pup, but the pack had been under attack from the curse since before I was born. It was a type of magical poisoning that had slowly destroyed the bond between my Alpha parents and the pack, sowing distrust, deceit, and discord among the Varda. Much of our social structure, including the practice of teaching pups to sift, had collapsed.

It wasn't until the unthinkable happened that I had recognized the curse for what it was and contained it, all while fighting to become the new Fyrstr after my parents died.

Now, the darkness lived within me, growing every day until I could find the source and terminate it. Gods willing, that would happen before I died and the evil escaped back into the pack, amplifying their negative emotions until they destroyed each other.

Like my parents.

I'm on my way back.

Gunn's voice startled me from my dark thoughts, and I realized I'd been sitting at my desk for over an hour. Plenty of time for Dahlia and Kristin to finish their business, which meant—

My wolf sat up and howled. The plaintiveness of his cry struck an answering pain in my chest.

Kristin had left.

Hurry up, I said to Gunn gruffly.

I'll be there in five.

A second later, a knock sounded on my door before it pushed open. Linnea stood in the entrance dressed in form-fitting workout gear, scowling at me. The Alpha female was a gorgeous, shapely Valdyr who was over six feet tall, with dazzling violet eyes and long, wild red hair. And she could pin you to the floor in less than a second if you weren't paying attention—hel, even if you were paying attention.

But she was also a huge pain in the ass.

"Why was a human female in the den?" she asked. "She actually entered the domr. My wolf almost attacked her."

I pierced her with my gaze. "Linnea, you will leave, shut the door behind you, and knock again—this time waiting for my response."

"Did you hear me? She stepped—"

"Out!" I barely raised my voice, but my wolf snapped down the bond between us, his tail held stiffly behind him. In the hjarta, her wolf yelped, then lowered her body and tilted her chin up in submission to my wolf.

Linnea stared at me, jaw clenched, eyes mutinous. She turned, exited my office, and quietly closed the door. A second later, she knocked.

I held off for a moment before answering. "Come in."

She opened the door, closed it behind her, and waited.

"Start again," I said.

"The woman—a human woman—shouldn't be in our den. What if she saw or heard something? Or worse, what if she's working for Hati and Skoll?"

My wolf growled at her for suggesting such a thing.

"First, she's an artist, not a spy," I said. "Dahlia is buying some of her paintings, and they had to decide on the best places to hang them. I've seen her work, and it's outstanding. Second, she was cleared by Gunn before she crossed the boundary. Third, she did not enter the domr because the circle was not sanctified. Right now, it's nothing more than rock."

Linnea crossed her arms over her chest. "She rubbed my wolf the wrong way. I don't trust her."

"What do you mean?"

"She got all snarly and aggressive."

"Kristin?"

"No, my wolf." She shifted her weight and uncrossed her arms, holding them stiffly by her side. "More than usual."

"Okay. I'll take that into consideration."

"That's it?"

"What more do you want? She's left the compound, and as far as I'm aware, she won't be back." My wolf moaned pathetically. "Would you like to read Gunn's report?" I held it out to her. "Maybe you'll find something he missed."

Linnea hesitated before taking the file. "I'm not questioning you. I'm just…concerned."

"I don't mind you questioning me, Linnea, as long as you do it respectfully and you understand that the final decision is mine."

She nodded and turned to leave. At the door, she looked back at me. "I'm sorry I barged in. My previous Alpha didn't…he wasn't… Well, anyway, it's just different here. Better, but different."

I nodded, and she left, closing the door behind her.

With a frustrated sigh, I leaned back in my chair. Why was everything so difficult with her? The pack's previous Alpha female, who'd replaced my mother, had been an older, gentle Valdyr—the pack's doctor. She was what we had needed to heal after being decimated by the curse. Last year she'd died peacefully in her sleep, and I had decided the new female Alpha should have a power to match my own.

I'd chosen Linnea, who was certainly strong and fierce enough, but she rubbed people the wrong way.

When she'd arrived in Varda territory four years ago, bruised and bedraggled, asking to be one of my rekkrs, I'd said yes immediately, impressed by her ferocity. I'd believed she'd make a fine warrior. Odin had thought so, too, and had bonded her to the pack.

She'd turned out to be a fantastic rekkr, dedicated to the war against Hati and Skoll, but as Alpha, she wasn't a good fit. Instead of unifying the Varda, she ended up pissing everyone off. I knew her belligerence was a cover-up for insecurity, but I was losing patience.

In her defense, she hadn't wanted to be the new Alpha female and would never have entered the domr to fight for it on her own. Since there hadn't been any challengers, and the god had accepted her petition, she'd taken on the position—and she would keep it until she either died or was defeated, perhaps killed, by another challenger in the domr.

I'd thought I could teach her how to lead, but so far nothing had worked.

Maybe if we were kyssed in the way of most male and female Alphas, I could have helped her more, softened her edges. But I would never marry or have a family. I couldn't risk passing on the curse the way it had passed between my parents, twisting and fouling everything—their thoughts, their emotions—before spreading to the rest of the pack.

A knock sounded at the door. "Come in."

Gunn entered and frowned. "You look pensive."

"I was thinking about Linnea."

"What about her?"

"That she might have an easier time as Alpha female if we were kyssed."

A horrified look crossed Gunn's face, and laughter exploded from my lungs—and kept going. I leaned back in my chair, my stomach heaving. When I finally caught my breath, Gunn had crossed the hardwood floor and slumped in one of two gray leather chairs facing the desk.

"Hilarious," he said. "Don't scare me like that. I thought you were serious."

"You know I can't kyss a female and risk tainting her."

"You could if you let me and some of the other rekkrs share the curse. It's not fair you have to carry the burden all by yourself."

"We've talked about this before, and the answer's still no. I can't risk it."

"But maybe if—"

"No, Gunn. I *won't* risk it. Valdyr died before I caged the curse, including my parents, and the pack was almost ruined. What if the Varda had been destroyed? Do you think the other packs would have continued to fight against Hati and Skoll? Some packs don't even know the Jotun exist, and others don't care—as long as they're not affected."

"We've made progress with that. We have emissaries out to more and more packs all the time. And we'll find the lost Valdyr. Teach them our history and traditions. Their instinct guides them even if they've forgotten."

I nodded and rubbed my knuckles against my forehead. Sometimes, it seemed as if we'd barely made a dent in the mountain of tasks that had piled up during the years the curse had dripped like acid within the Varda. We'd suffered so many hits— the loss of our rekkrs, the inability of anyone but me to sift into Asgard, the destabilization of Wolf Ridge Industries. Not to mention all the diplomacy gaffes with other packs.

"We'll get there. And you won't have to sacrifice yourself by kyssing Linnea. Although I think you should look up that blond artist you like and screw her to Valhalla and back."

I shook my head, but part of me was tempted. What would it hurt? She was human; the curse wouldn't affect her.

"Speaking of Valhalla, it's time I took a trip across the bridge."

Gunn's gaze dropped to the stone pendant around my neck. "I wondered when you would go. It's been a while."

"I know. It's just hard, never knowing how long I'll be gone."

"I wish one of us could go in your place. Then the time difference wouldn't matter so much. You already have so many responsibilities."

I rolled my eyes. "Cry me a fucking river, rock star." I deliberately used the name Gina had called him, knowing it would distract my friend.

Gunn's scowl returned. "I can't believe you left me with that woman. How can someone so completely fuckable be so aggravating at the same time? Loki must have helped create that one."

I grinned. "Yeah, maybe."

I rose and made my way out onto the landing that overlooked the rotunda, Gunn at my heels.

"You think Loki's free?" Gunn asked. "I thought the myths said he was bound like Fenrir."

"You can't base everything on the myths. If he is free, I wouldn't be surprised. His relationship with the gods is complicated."

I found myself inhaling, searching for Kristin's scent. It was gone. Disappointment rocked through me, and I gritted my teeth.

She. Is. Human.

We descended, and when we reached the stone circle, Dahlia called my name. I paused at the entrance to the cave and turned to see my cousin hurrying across the circle toward us, a smile lighting up her face.

"I'll be in the Rover," Gunn said, and he pushed through a hidden door in the rock.

I smiled back at Dahlia. "What's up?"

"Kristin. That's what's up. Oh my gods, don't you love her?" She squeezed my arm. "I think I have a girl crush."

My smile slipped. "Dahlia, she's human."

"I know, but humans aren't bad—unless they've been recruited by Hati and Skoll. She's just so…cool, in that artsy kind of way. Plus, she doesn't make me feel like a freak."

My wolf growled low in his throat, and my gaze sharpened on Dahlia. "Who makes you feel that way?"

"No one. Not really. It's just…well, I'm not a normal Valdyr, am I? I'm like the runt of the pack. The size of a freaking human!"

I'd found a notation in one of the old texts about the pack's last foreseer centuries before and how petite she was. I hoped it was the same with Dahlia—that she was a foreseer—but it was rude to ask a female about her magic, and Dahlia hadn't told me.

"You have other gifts. And your magic, right?" I held my breath, hoping she'd confide in me this time.

She shrugged and then stepped toward the rock wall. "Anyway, you won't believe what Kristin's suggested. She's going to carve a mural in the rock. She has this incredible vision of an entire history of a wolf pack—pups playing, the pack hunting, fighting for dominance, even dying—mixed with other wildlife like eagles and bears in their natural settings. It's going to be amazing."

Eagerness and alarm shot through me at the same time. My wolf jumped up, tail high.

She returns!

"No," I croaked, tamping down my wolf's excitement.

"What?" Dahlia spun to me, her smile fading.

I rolled my shoulders to release the rising tension inside. "It will take her months to sculpt the wall—years, even. She'll be in our den, Dahlia, possibly learning our secrets. And the noise and dust…have you thought about that? People work here."

"She mentioned that, but she said she could work around our schedule and hang sheets to keep the dust contained. It won't always be noisy—just sometimes."

"And what if we're attacked? Dahlia, we're at war. Hati and Skoll won't stop just because Kristin's here."

"Then we'll deal with it. The same way we would if one of the other humans saw something strange." She reached out and grasped my hand. "I really want this, Erik. You asked me to contribute, and I'm doing it."

"I asked you to decorate the den. I didn't want you to put the pack—hel, the entire world—at risk. What if she's a spy? Are you willing to jeopardize everyone you know and love for a human?"

She looked me in the eye. "Yes."

Her conviction astounded me. "Why?"

"Because I trust her."

A tingle rushed up my spine. Maybe she'd had a foretelling. "Trust is earned, Dahlia, and you barely know her."

"I feel as if I do."

"Is that an opinion or something you *know*?" A divination?

Confusion clouded her eyes, and she dropped my hand. "I don't know. Maybe both. Kristin won't hurt us, and she's not a spy. She's an artist with a great idea. Please, Erik. It will be so beautiful."

I shoved my fingers through my hair. I hated seeing my cousin upset, but I wasn't the only one who'd had a strange reaction to Kristin. Linnea didn't trust her, and Gunn was way too riled by her sister.

Too many things didn't add up.

I pulled Dahlia forward and kissed her forehead. "I'm sorry, sunshine, but the answer is no."

CHAPTER 3

I SAT CROSS-LEGGED AT THE BASE OF A RED ROCK FORMATION IN A meadow high in the mountains. The afternoon sun shone down on me, but I couldn't feel its warmth while in the misty blur of the helmingr—equally present in mind, body, and spirit with my wolf, thinking and feeling as one.

And there was a hel of a lot to think and feel right now... Kristin, Dahlia, what to do about Linnea, and when and where the next conflict with Hati and Skoll would be.

Eyes closed, I tried to relax my mind, to soothe my thoughts and emotions, and let the colors that were just beyond my vision sift into me and take me to Asgard. A bright cerulean blue, tinged with fuchsia, drifted closer... And then I thought about Kristin, and the chaotic feelings that darted through me swept the color away. For the third time.

I sighed and solidified into my body. The sweats and T-shirt I'd put on before leaving the den now lay crumpled beneath me, having fallen off my body the moment I'd entered the helmingr.

The only object that stayed with me when I passed to Asgard was the stone pendant around my neck.

Nearby, Gunn leaned against the Rover, scowling into space.

"I love you, bro, but you're killing me," I said. "I have enough shit running through my brain without adding yours to the mix."

Gunn glanced up, startled, then crossed his arms over his chest. "I'm not a machine. I can't shut down my thoughts like you can."

"You could if you practiced. That's why the pups start young. It can take years to reach that state. Think of sifting worlds like painting a picture. Before you add the colors of another world, you need a blank canvas. Which is why we meditate."

I pointed to the ground beside me. With a sigh, Gunn pushed away from the Rover, stripped off his black T-shirt, and spread it on the hood of the vehicle. Then he did the same to his jeans. I raised my brow.

"What? I don't want them to wrinkle."

"And I don't have all day."

"Yeah, well, *you* don't have to do your own laundry." He made his way to my side, wearing black boxers covered in hot-pink lips, and sat cross-legged on the ground. "Two dudes meditating naked in the wilderness. Definitely not upping my fuckability factor."

"And who's going to see you?"

"You never know. A hot hiker might come by. Or two."

I shook my head. "Someday, you'll meet the right Valdyr, and your wolf will shut all that down."

Gunn grunted and closed his eyes. "Being kyssed is overrated. One female Valdyr can't do what unlimited human women can."

He shifted into the blur of the helmingr, and his socks, boots, and underwear dropped to the ground. A silence ensued, broken only by the wind stirring in the leaves and the birds twittering around them. "I read that some females, ages past, could use their magic to sift into Asgard from anywhere. They could see the colors all around them and didn't need to meditate at the bridge. They could actually bring the colors into our world, and other Valdyr could cross over. We need one of those."

I closed my eyes and shifted into the helmingr. "Tell me about it."

It took a while to calm my mind and let the colors sift into me, but I finally felt the warm, solid presence of Bifrost, sometimes called the Rainbow Bridge, under my butt. I opened my eyes. The colors, pure magic, flared up like fire through the white mist, giving the bridge its name.

I rose and walked forward, my body still in the helmingr. When I stepped off the end of the bridge, the mist dissipated.

Asgard, home of the Norse gods.

It looked like Earth, with a blue sky, green grass, and mountains in the distance, but everything was brighter, clearer, sharper. The colors were more vivid, the smells sweeter, every sound a pleasure. It was said if you ate while in Asgard, you would starve when you returned to Earth because everything would taste like ash in comparison.

I stood in a field surrounded by a tall stone wall. Simple buildings dotted the area, and when I turned, I saw the god Heimdall riding on his horse from the direction of his longhouse, Himinbjörg. Strapped to his body was a sword and his famous horn, Gjall, that he would blow to summon the gods to battle during Ragnarök—an event I prayed would never come to pass, especially on my watch.

"Vel finna, Erik Kron, Fyrstr of the Varda. I've been expecting you. Much time has passed. I had to return home for my midday meal."

I repressed a smile. The white god—so named, I assumed, for his long, white-blond hair, fair skin, and preference for white leather—was well known for his romantic dalliances. If the rumpled state of his hair and clothing was any indication, his "midday meal" meant something far more vigorous than food.

"Vel finna, Heimdall, guardian of the Rainbow Bridge. I had trouble crossing over."

"Yes, I heard. Your thoughts were loud enough to wake Brunhilde from her charmed sleep. Then your wolf-brother joined you, and it was like a fistful of Jotun were crashing through the river. Usually, the only sound I hear is the bubbling of your curse. It does not like being in Asgard—or maybe it likes it too much."

Well, that was interesting. I tucked that tidbit away for later. "Do you have any news before I see the Allfather?"

Heimdall swung easily from his horse, a beautiful white stallion with a golden-colored back. The god was shorter than Erik, with the appearance and size of a human male. A pensive expression crossed his face as he looped his horn over the horse's saddle.

"There is much news, Fyrstr, but none that I can tell."

"What about my parents?"

"No sight of them yet. Only Odin can see why, and he cannot share everything. And I still have no knowledge of your curse."

My jaw clenched in frustration. Odin created the Valdyr and made me Fyrstr of the Varda in order to protect the nine worlds against Hati and Skoll and stop Ragnarök. Yet the Allfather wouldn't tell me how the Varda could destroy the curse that had nearly ruined us. If the Varda fell, the gods wouldn't be far behind, let alone the rest of the worlds.

Odin was wise. He'd hung on Yggdrasil, the world tree, for nine nights and sacrificed one eye to Mimir for knowledge, but I couldn't for the life of me understand his secrecy about the curse.

But I couldn't do anything about it. The Norse gods—especially Odin, who ruled them all—did what they wished.

I forced a smile. "I'll let you get back to your *meal*. Enjoy your honey mead."

Heimdall laughed and slapped me on the shoulder. I had to brace myself to stay upright.

"You're welcome to some honey mead, too, Fyrstr. Lovely and

eager blonds—male and female—fill my hall every hour. They'll quench your thirst far better than this human artist you're pining for."

I stilled. It was bad enough Gunn knew of my attraction; the last thing I needed was the gods' interference. They'd been known to meddle.

"Thanks. Maybe next time. Vel finna, Heimdall."

"Vel finna, Fyrstr."

I turned toward the gate as it swung open and reached for my wolf. Familiar pain and pleasure ripped through me. Then big padded feet hit the ground at a gallop, the sweet-smelling wind ruffling my fur as I streaked toward the mountains.

It was a joy to run in Asgard—the scents and sounds so intense they almost overwhelmed me. My muscles bunched and stretched, my tongue lolled, and my claws dug into rich soil. Unfortunately, the curse also strengthened, and it reached out to corrupt my thoughts and twist my emotions.

I built the walls higher to contain the foulness within my body.

Odin

"He comes," Heimdall said, appearing by Odin's side. They sat on the top seats of a golden amphitheater along the shores of a small lake called the Well of Urd. Two ageless swans glided upon it.

On the opposite side of the lake, Yggdrasil, the great ash tree that united the universe, soared upward. Its sprawling branches and leaves loomed over the amassed congregation of gods and goddesses that filled the other seats, their colorful garments shifting and swaying as they argued back and forth.

"We shouldn't have agreed," someone shouted. "The stakes are too high."

"Can't Freyja work her magic and guarantee the sacrifice?" another asked.

"Freyja can't guarantee anything when it comes to love. One pairing, maybe even two, I would take those odds. But nine?"

"This surely has the taint of Loki."

The crowd roared at that, and Odin sighed, running his index finger along the top of the silk patch that covered his right eye socket. Not Loki, not this time. It was he who'd struck the deal with the three maiden Norns: Urd, Verdani, and Skold—Past, Present, and Future—the Fates who wove the great tapestry of life and lovingly cared for Yggdrasil. Odin had stood with them in their weaver's hut, pierced his palms with his spear, Gungnir, and, after wetting his fingers with his blood, marked two threads from the tapestry for each of the nine worlds.

Then the Norns, for the first time ever, laid down their wool, put aside their spinning wheel, and retreated into the hall that was their own, not to be seen since. Yggdrasil had suffered for it, as had every living creature in the nine worlds, even if they did not yet know it.

The threads, left unguided, haphazardly began to weave themselves.

For years, Odin had searched for answers and pondered ways to avert the prophecy of Ragnarök. He'd given an eye for greater wisdom and magic, outsmarted the Jotun again and again, and created the Valdyr from his own semen and the blood of a wolf-Jotuness to guard Fenrir.

But all he'd done was bought time for the nine worlds.

Finally, he'd had a glimmer of the one magic strong enough to change fate. Brilliant in its simplicity, yet so difficult to predict.

The power of love.

A magic even older than his own and stronger than anything in the nine worlds. But the magic needed more than just love. It also required sacrifice. For what was love without sacrifice?

Odin rose, standing tall and strong with Gungnir held

dangerously by his side. Around him, his great plum-colored robe billowed, and his red hair and beard shone in the sun.

Today, he played the role of monarch.

"The threads are in play, the lovers chosen." His booming voice quieted the other gods. "I have agreed, Fenris-Wolf has agreed, and the Fates have stepped aside. The hopes of the nine worlds lie upon Love's shoulders."

Erik

Two ravens circled in the sky above, and I knew I was close. One bird swooped low over my head, and I snapped at it playfully. Or rather, my wolf did. I thought about warning him—again—but it was a game my wolf and the ravens played every time. I prayed the wolf never won.

Best not to kill the Allfather's pets.

I followed the ravens into the soaring mountains, galloping over a field of wildflowers that poked through a shallow crust of snow. On the other side, a gurgling stream teemed with brightly colored salmon. My mouth watered as I leapt across.

Upon landing, two large natural wolves flanked me— although *natural* didn't quite fit when the wolves lived forever. They led me high up to a rocky pass where the air nipped the tips of my ears. It was cool but pleasant, and the view of the valley, the green so vivid it almost hurt my eyes, took my breath away. In the distance, Odin's eight-legged steed, Sleipnir, grazed in a field.

On the top peak, beneath a tree that bloomed lilacs, sat an old man with a long white beard and grizzled hair. He wore a tattered gray cloak, a black patch over his right eye, and a wide-brimmed hat. A wooden staff lay across his lap. The natural wolves flopped on the rocky ground to one side of him.

The man appeared to be sleeping, but I knew better. I shifted into the helmingr, then knelt and bowed my head.

A minute passed before Odin said, "Vel finna, Erik Kron, Fyrstr of the Varda."

"Vel finna, Allfather."

I stayed kneeling until Odin patted the spot next to him. "Sit. It has been a while."

I changed positions. "Are you well?" I asked. A silly question, perhaps, but Odin liked to pretend we were no different—when it suited him.

"I am old. My joints ache, and my eyesight fades."

A smile tipped the corners of my mouth. Not only was Odin ageless, he was also all-seeing. From his throne, he could observe everything in the nine worlds. A disturbing thought when you were seven and tempted to put a garden snake down the back of Brenda Sigurdson's blouse.

"You knew better, yet you did it anyway," Odin said, reading my thoughts.

"She got after me for eating too many raspberries. Gods save me from bossy know-it-alls."

"Ah, yes. The all-knowing ones are the worst."

The god was a fierce warrior who wielded deadly magic and could be cruel and merciless at times, but he also had a wry sense of humor that never ceased to amuse me.

"The absolute worst," I replied with a grin.

Closing his good eye, Odin stroked his finger over his brow and then tapped it. Deep in thought, he repeated this process several times.

Time moved differently in Asgard. It had been more than an Earth year since I had last visited, but that could be ten days, a decade, or one hundred years in Asgard. Coming here made running Wolf Ridge difficult because I never knew how long I'd be gone.

But I hadn't been able to delay the trip any longer. My instinct had screamed at me that Hati and Skoll were on the move, and my Alpha magic sensed that something deadly threatened the pack—besides my curse.

Taking a deep breath, I decided to quit worrying for a moment and enjoy the view, to allow the peace and beauty of Asgard to sink into my bones and soothe my soul. It was the first time in a long time I'd concentrated on anything other than the pack, the curse, or defeating the sons of Fenrir.

Duty was a heavy taskmaster.

"You have questions, none of which I can answer," Odin said, bringing me out of my reverie. "You are right to be concerned, Fyrstr. Dangerous times are upon us. Much will be sacrificed in the coming years." He raised his head and met my gaze. "But you may stay here if you like. Join the other Valdyr in the woods outside Valhalla. You have done well and liberated your pack from the curse—saved all the Valdyr and the nine worlds because of it."

I stared at him, stunned. "But I'm still alive. Only dead heroes live in that forest."

"I will make an exception."

Impossible. To live in paradise and never die? To pass on the weight of responsibility and worry with Odin's blessing?

"If I decide to stay, does the curse stay with me, or will it travel back to the Varda?" I asked.

"Your pack will be safe from harm. A new Fyrstr will be chosen to lead the fight against Hati and Skoll."

The air left my lungs in a loud whoosh as my thoughts raced ahead of me. The pack safe, the darkness no longer a threat. It was what I'd wished for all along.

But who would lead the Varda? My rekkrs were all strong and capable, Gunn and Robbie in particular. A few powerful lone wolves often helped the pack in the war against Hati and Skoll and might vie for leadership. And my brother, Aren, who'd been forced to leave after his ulf-rist when Odin hadn't accepted him into the pack.

Maybe this was why.

They were all strong contenders, which meant the deaths of good wolves as they fought within the domr to be Alpha male. But what if the wrong wolf ascended and the Varda was led by a Fyrstr who hurt the pack or couldn't unify them? Either way, Hati and Skoll won.

Looking back over the breathtaking view, I shook my head. I would not allow discord in my pack. I would not allow my wolves to die unnecessarily. I was their Fyrstr and would continue to lead them as long as I could. I just needed to tighten my hold on the curse and fortify the well that contained it.

Odin smiled and nodded. Then his eye rolled back in his head. His knuckles whitened as he gripped his staff, and his voice deepened:

> *Eagle eye. Earth to sky. Fly, wolf, fly.*
> *Lay her down. Wolf and crown. Cry, wolf, cry.*
> *One and one. It's begun... Love dies.*

With a flash of light, the words seared into my brain. I solidified into my body and grabbed my head to stop it from splitting in half. When the pain receded, I found myself curled into a ball, lying naked on the ground where I'd fallen. Alone.

I shivered, then shifted once again into the helmingr to protect myself from the cool mountain air. I didn't bother calling out. Odin had given me a choice, and I'd decided to stay with the Varda...and keep the curse.

I'd gotten all the help I could from the god—confirmation of the danger, which I didn't need, and a prophecy, which I obviously did.

But what did it mean?

The words ran over and over in my brain as I shifted back

into my wolf and streaked down the mountainside. The only phrase I felt certain about was "Wolf and crown." That had to be me. Crown not only stood for leader, but it was also the meaning of my last name: Kron.

And maybe "Earth to sky" was my visit to Asgard. Was I also the "Eagle eye"? My eyesight was good but no stronger than that of any of my rekkrs. No, it couldn't be that.

At the foot of the mountain, I paused and peered down a rocky trail leading away from Bifrost. The more time I spent here, the greater the likelihood that time was passing on Earth too.

Should I risk it and visit while I was here?

The word "visit" amused me, and I imagined myself showing up at the prison with a plate of cookies. The friendly jailer.

Turning toward the sheer canyon, I carefully maneuvered the trail to avoid razor-sharp stones, loose boulders, and sudden deep crevices, not to mention the snakes and scorpions that were poised to bite and sting me if I veered off the path.

I stopped in front of a rock face at the end, shifted once more, and pressed my hand flat against the granite. A sharp nip in my palm cut the skin, and my blood soaked the stone.

When I'd risen to Alpha after a series of bloody dominance battles seven years ago, Odin had brought me here and keyed my blood to the gateway. Only my essence, fresh from my body, could unlock the way to Fenrir's prison.

The rock disintegrated before my eyes, and a tunnel appeared. I moved forward, shifting once more into my wolf, and the canyon wall reformed behind me. Enough light existed from the minerals in the rocks for me to see.

The trail dipped downward, and I felt the change in my body as if I'd disintegrated and been put back together. Physically, the path didn't change, but I knew I'd been transported out of Asgard —to where was a tightly held secret.

Perhaps into Niflheim, the world of the dead, with Hel as its citadel.

Time had no meaning here, and I lost all sense of it as I continued downward for what could have been days, hours, or minutes.

Finally, the light brightened at the end of the tunnel. I rounded the corner and saw an enormous cavern filled with unnatural gray light emanating from a mist above a perfectly still, pitch-black lake. I shifted back to my body, and the stones dug into the soles of my bare feet.

I stopped at the water's edge, careful not to let any of the dark liquid touch my skin, and then slipped the leather cord and stone pendant from around my neck. After kissing the tiny carved ship for luck, I tossed it into the water.

When the pendant hit the surface, the liquid began to boil. A Viking longship with a huge square sail, oars, and a dragon head, erupted from the waves and sailed toward me. The ship beached itself, and I jumped aboard.

The boat reversed, turned, and set off toward an island in the distance.

It was eerily quiet, the mist absorbing all sound, and despite the ship's forward progression, no wind rushed past my face. But the strangest thing of all was the complete absence of smell. Even a bad scent would have been preferable to nothing at all.

Long and narrow, the island was covered with heather, and the boat slowed. I'd sailed around the land mass a few times out of curiosity, but it looked the same no matter where the ship anchored.

On the shore stood a monstrous wolf wearing a leash of ribbon that stretched to the middle of the island. The ribbon, called Gleipnir, had been made by the Dvergar eons ago, and it was the only fetter strong enough to bind Fenrir, son of Loki and the Jotuness Angerboda, who was both a wolf and a witch.

The wolf shifted, taking a human-like shape that was twice

the size and hairiness of the largest male Valdyr—and the ugliest creature imaginable. He was the opposite of his twin sons, Hati and Skoll, who rivaled the sun and the moon with their shining beauty.

Fenrir grinned at me, showing a mouthful of razor-sharp teeth—that should have been able to slice through anything, especially the pretty silk ribbon that encircled his neck.

"Don't you look sweet," I said from the prow of the boat. Fenrir's grin vanished, and his humongous muscles bunched. For a moment, I thought he might attack.

The fetter used Fenrir's strength against him—the harder he struggled, the weaker he became. If he tried to bite, a sword appeared in his mouth, the hilt anchored on his bottom jaw, the tip piercing the soft palate. Odin told me the sword took weeks to disappear.

"I don't need to be pretty to destroy the worlds," he said. "Do your best to keep me here, Fyrstr, but even the gods know I'll escape. And when I do, I'll hunt you down. And if not you, your descendants, and those of every Valdyr who kept me prisoner. I'll soon be coated in the blood of your pack. Your females will be torn in half as I fuck them, and your pups skewered on the very sword that so often pierced my flesh."

I kept my face expressionless. I'd heard worse from the monster. "There you go again, taking my compliment and twisting it. You should really see someone about that."

"I will. Sooner than you think. I hope you win this one, wolf and crown, because then, when the next pair fails, I'll come for you and your female first."

I stopped breathing. Trepidation crawled up my spine, and my instinct beat at me wildly. My wolf, who usually stayed quiet during my talks with Fenrir, rose to his feet, hackles raised, and rumbled in my throat.

It wasn't the promise of rape, murder, and torture that bothered me so much—Fenrir made those threats every time we met

—but the words he'd used. I didn't understand them. Win what? And he'd said "wolf and crown," the same phrase from Odin's prophecy.

I slowly released my breath. "Tell me what you hope I'll win, and I'll be happy to share. It's the least I can do for keeping you locked up."

Fenrir barked out a laugh. He walked to the shore, crouched down, and dabbled his fingers in the inky, silent lake. I watched him warily, prepared to shift into the helmingr if he splashed any water my way.

"That wouldn't be any fun at all," the beast said. "Besides, I wouldn't want to give you an advantage. Not that I'm worried. There's no way all nine will make the sacrifice."

I gripped the ship's rail to stop myself from leaping to the island and beating the answers out of the Jotun. And I just might succeed because Fenrir wouldn't be able to fight back.

The ship's oars dipped into the water, and the boat abruptly moved backward. Obviously, that wasn't part of Odin's plan.

"You, too, will die in Ragnarök," I said. "Have you considered that?"

Fenrir shrugged. "Maybe. Maybe not. Things change. Even fate. You would do well to remember that." Then he turned, shifted back to his wolf, and lifted his leg to piss in my direction.

I stepped off Bifrost and back onto Earth. As usual, I had a moment of acute disappointment as if my senses wept for the loss of Asgard.

I closed my eyes, breathed in the scent of pine, deer, and dirt, and took a moment to center myself. The summer sun warmed my back, and two squirrels chattered back and forth in the trees. In the sky above, a hawk screeched.

It was good to be home.

"Please tell me you finally hooked up with one of the females in Heimdall's great hall. I hear some of them are goddesses. Imagine how sweet they'd taste," a familiar voice said.

Very good to be home.

I glanced up and saw Gunn leaning against the Rover, his arms across his chest, his brow raised hopefully.

I shook my head. "It's one thing to drive to Missoula for a booty call, another to have to cross to Asgard."

"But that one sip. Can you imagine? It's sex in Asgard, for fuck's sake."

I rubbed my jaw, and images flashed in my head—they were filled with sex, all right, but I wasn't in Asgard, and it wasn't a serving girl or goddess riding me. It was here, underneath the trees and a moonlit sky. The woman was tall and slender with curling blond hair and bright hazel eyes.

Kristin.

My wolf rose in anticipation and sniffed the air. *Mate?*

Ah, hel. I scowled and stalked to the Rover. *No.*

He flopped over with a moan.

Gunn grabbed some sweats and a cotton shirt and threw them to me. I slipped them on.

"How long was I gone?" I asked as I crawled into the passenger seat and put on my shoes. Gunn started the Rover, and we headed down the dirt track.

"Just over three weeks."

Shit. The last time had only been four days. "Everyone's safe? No trouble?"

"Not if you don't count Linnea and the art—" Gunn's phone rang, and he checked the number. "It's my mom. I've gotta take this."

I suppressed a sigh as Gunn said into the receiver, "Yeah, Ma, I heard you the first three times. I said I'll be there, and I'll be there... No, I'm not bringing anyone...because I'm not... I'm just not, for Odin's sake. Leave it alone already."

He ended the call a few minutes later and shook his head. "Is there something wrong with me that I'm not attracted to Valdyr females? I mean, I like them and all, but it's way less work with a human."

"Your wolf's not involved with a human, so it's just sex, I guess. With Valdyr, the wolves interact—and not always how you want them to. You just need to meet the right one. Then it'll be different."

I believed that wholeheartedly. Gunn was the biggest hound dog around, yet when the time came, I knew he'd make the best mate and father. And I couldn't wait to see that happen—for a bunch of reasons. Number one, to razz him stupid, and number two, because my friend deserved to be happy.

It couldn't happen for me—not while I carried the curse—but it could, and would, happen for Gunn. If I asked anything of Freyja, it was that she bless the tough, protective, soft-centered Valdyr with a female and pups he adored.

If I asked anything for myself, it was that she never bless me with a mate—for both our sakes.

We pulled up to the den and headed to the large glass building. My wolf lifted his head, nose twitching. After pushing through the outer door, we crossed the foyer and waited for the inner door to unlock. With a happy yip, my wolf raised onto his haunches, thumped his tail, and stared straight ahead.

I frowned, but when the door opened, and the den's various scents hit my nose, one struck harder and faster than all the rest, causing my heart to race and my curse to boil upward.

Instant need shot through me, and I moved in a direct line toward the rock wall at the back of the den, which had been cordoned off with a long hanging tarp. Shoving the protective cover aside, my eyes traveled up the four-story scaffolding.

There. On the second level.

A woman crouched on the metal walkway, wearing safety glasses over her eyes and a mask over her nose and mouth. Thin gloves covered her hands, and ratty jeans, a dusty T-shirt, and work boots covered the rest of her. Her blond curls were pulled back in a ponytail as she chiseled away at the wall with a pick and hammer.

Kristin.

My wolf chuffed happily.

She spun toward me suddenly, and our eyes met. Then she rose, pushed back her glasses and mask, and moved to the edge of the walkway.

"Where the hel have you been?"

CHAPTER 4

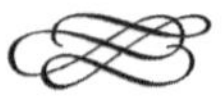

<u>Kristin</u>

I BIT DOWN ON MY LIP, REGRETTING MY WORDS THE INSTANT THEY left my mouth. Erik frowned up at me, nostrils flaring, dark hair ruffled, and eyes a little wild. He looked so different, wearing gray sweatpants, runners, and an oversized rugby shirt. Less corporate CEO and more testosterone-ridden workout guy.

Damn. I couldn't talk to him that way, no matter how vexed my wolf and I had been by his absence these last few weeks. And nobody would tell me where he was.

Not that I'd been able to ask...much. I'd chatted to Dahlia about it, but the petite Valdyr had claimed he was away on business. And that might have been true, except I could feel the tension rising through the pack the longer he was gone.

I tried a tentative smile. "I mean, hi, how are you? Long time no see."

He didn't return the smile. Instead, he reached a hand toward me. Those to-die-for lips pressed into a hard, straight line. "Come down from there. Now."

Did he want me to jump? I'd been careful not to use my

Valdyr strength and speed as I worked, clambering up and down the ladder at the edge of the scaffold every time I needed to change levels.

"Um…here?"

"Give me your hand."

The command turned my limbs to jelly at the same time as my spine straightened. My wolf bristled and bared her teeth, reflecting my feelings. Nobody bossed us around. But then the traitor rolled over and flashed him her belly—the ultimate in submission to a dominant wolf.

The hel of it was, I wanted to do the same, except I wanted Erik to climb on top.

Gods, he was sexy.

Arousal pulsed through my body as I leaned down and hesitantly placed my fingers in his. He grasped them firmly and then yanked me off the metal walkway.

I barely got out a shriek before his hands wrapped around my waist, and he caught me against his body, a solid block of muscle. His shoulders were broad, his torso was lean, and the biceps beneath my palms were rock hard.

The contact knocked the wind out of both of us, more emotional than physical on my part, and I exhaled noisily against his neck. His breath puffed through my hair.

I opened my mouth over his skin for just a second. Not tasting him, exactly—I didn't lick or nibble like I wanted to—but I craved the feel of him against my tongue and lips, his scent absorbed through the extra receptors located there.

My wolf panted happily, rolling around in everything Erik.

Drawing my head back, I met his gaze. His eyes were dark, lids at half-mast as he watched me. Slowly, he lowered me to the floor, rubbing our bodies together every inch of the way.

I closed my eyes for just an instant, reveling in the feel of him. For the love of Freyja, he was big and hard all over. More endowed in every way than any human male I'd been with. I hadn't been with many, mind you, but enough to know that once I'd gone Valdyr...

I couldn't help myself and rocked my hips against him. He dug his fingers in and held me tight, a subsonic moan only a wolf could hear rumbling in his throat.

Thank the gods, it wasn't just me. Then he stepped back.

The lack of contact left behind an empty ache. I resisted the urge to yank him closer and hold tight so he couldn't escape a second time. My wolf sat up and howled.

"Why are you here?" he asked. The coolness in his tone sliced through my sexual haze, and my stomach fell.

"What?"

"It's not a hard question, Kristin. You're obviously working here. Who authorized it?"

"Um...you did? After Dahlia gave me the go-ahead, I packed up my supplies and rented a place in Missoula. The carving's not as bad as it looks. I leave all the noisy work until night when everyone's gone, and the tarp keeps the mess to a minimum."

"Dahlia hired you?"

"I wouldn't be here otherwise. Do you think I just waltz through security every day? It's like getting into Fort frickin' Knox."

Erik stared at me. A strange kind of pressure bore into my head, and I mentally clamped my shields in place. When he dropped his gaze, I breathed a silent sigh of relief, but then he dragged me back toward him, making me yelp as our bodies slammed together.

"Did you coerce Dahlia into hiring you?"

My jaw dropped. "Like blackmail her?" Had he said no to the project, and Dahlia went ahead with it anyway? "Look, if you want me to quit, just say so, but I'm not returning the payment on the project. I won't be screwed around because you had some kind of miscommunication with your cousin."

He made a chuffing sound, then pushed his head into the

crook of my neck and inhaled, mouth open, tongue on my skin. I knew he was scenting me, and I stood stone still, heart racing and blood pounding in fear. But it was also the most arousing thing to ever happen to me, and my body flooded with heat, turning me soft, wet. My knees weakened and then threatened to give way. He tightened his hands on my hips and held me in place.

After trailing his mouth up my neck to the pulse beating frantically beneath my ear, he crossed my cheek to the corner of my mouth. All the places wolves expressed their scent.

Gods, would he smell me down there too? My wolf had all kinds of interesting scent glands above and below her tail.

Then he did something I'd only witnessed between mated Valdyr and natural wolves in the wild. He rubbed his cheek along mine all the way to my ear. As if he'd…marked me. No, that couldn't be right.

Could it?

"I'll be back," he said. Then he turned on his heel and marched away.

Erik

"Did you just mark that woman?" Linnea asked, shock and disapproval thick in her voice. She trailed me into my office and closed the door sharply behind her.

Hel, couldn't I have a minute alone to get my confused thoughts under control? Besides, the most important thing right now was to call Dahlia, not talk about me and Kristin.

Mentally, I reached out to my cousin. Her fear pulsed back at me through the Alpha bond. Usually, she was the first person to greet me when I returned. This time, she'd stayed away.

My office. Now. My words held the sting of command.

A brief knock sounded at the door—much too soon to be

Dahlia—and I closed my eyes. Fuck. Why didn't I just invite the whole pack in and get it over with?

Gunn entered, followed by Dane, a lone wolf who looked as dangerous and hard-core as ever with his shades, spiky blond hair, and black leather jacket. He was as tall as Gunn and an asset to the Varda in their fight against Hati and Skoll, despite his refusal to commit formally to the pack—or to anyone. He worked on his own, nursing a personal vendetta against the sons of Fenrir, and only shared information with the Varda when it suited him.

Which didn't suit me. But I couldn't afford to alienate the tough Valdyr. His sources were too good.

"Vel finna, ulf-einn," I said to him, reciting the ritual words for greeting a lone wolf. "Is the yla within your heart and upon your tongue? Do you ask Odin's blessing to join the pack?"

"Vel finna, Fyrstr," Dane replied just as formally. "The yla is not within. I choose to wander."

Big surprise there.

The Handsal ceremony bonded a wolf to the pack, be it a recently risen one or a lone wolf looking for a new home. The Valdyr in question sent out the howl, or yla, and the pack answered in a similar fashion. If Odin willed it, the magic of the Handsal tied the wolf to the pack. If not, the yla didn't reach its peak harmony and shattered.

I had howled for the pack immediately after my ulf-rist and been bonded by Odin to the Varda. My younger brother Aren had had his yla shattered. He still worked for the Varda, but in the same way Dane did, as a lone wolf battling Hati and Skoll and gathering information from other sources.

I dropped into my chair behind my desk, relieved to have some distance between my packmates, even if it was only a small barrier.

Maybe Dane had the right of it after all.

Closing my eyes, I tried to control the intensity of my

emotions. The desire to strip off Kristin's clothes and push inside her body was one thing. The need to mark her was something else entirely.

Which I'd done. Or my wolf had done.

Damn it—we'd both done. Her human scent now swirled inside of me. A part of me.

Linnea fisted her hands on her hips and frowned at Gunn and Dane. "We were having a private conversation. Wait outside."

"This is more important," Gunn said. "*You* can wait outside."

"More important than your Fyrstr marking a human female?"

Gunn gaped at me. "Holy shit. Kristin? No wonder you're all sexed up."

I pressed my knuckles to my forehead, wanting to growl. The wolves could smell my arousal. Nothing was private in the Varda.

"I was scenting her, looking for something more than human." At Gunn's disbelieving look, I threw my hands in the air. "I don't want to talk about it."

Linnea stepped forward. "Well, I do. I said it before. She shouldn't be here. Something is wrong with her—she sets my wolf off every time." My wolf snarled at the Alpha female. She flinched but stood her ground. "See? Your wolf is interested in a human. How unnatural is that?"

Which was why I had smelled Kristin so deeply, trying to pinpoint the danger.

"Maybe he just needs to get laid. Have you thought about that?" Gunn asked. He turned to me. "She's obviously willing. I say go for it."

"Getting laid isn't the problem," Linnea said in a scathing tone. "Go out and screw a thousand women, I don't care. But have you considered this desire for a human might be related to the curse? If it's becoming too much for you to handle, we need to know."

They all turned to me, silently assessing me. Damn. I wished

Dane wasn't here. I wished none of them were, but Linnea had a point.

Had my curse been more difficult to handle since meeting Kristin? The dark taint reacted to her in the same way it did when I crossed to Asgard, becoming more active, reaching toward her. But I hadn't had any trouble containing the foulness —in Asgard or with her.

No, as much as the curse was a pain in my ass and a viable threat to the pack, I didn't believe my desire for Kristin was driven by it.

"They're not related. The curse is still under control. But I am worried about Kristin being here. I assume you're watching her?" I looked at Gunn and Linnea, who nodded. "Good. Double her guard. I'm also worried about Dahlia." I considered keeping her part in this mess private but decided my senior rekkrs had the right to know. "I specifically told her not to hire Kristin before I left."

The Valdyr gasped as one, even Dane. Dahlia should have been the last wolf to disobey an order. She was unusual in the Varda for her extreme submissiveness. She always doubted herself and was afraid to make a mistake. When her wolf had first risen, and she'd howled the yla to join the pack, I hadn't thought she'd be accepted.

But she had been—and quickly—so obviously Odin had a plan for her. It was, perhaps, related to her magic, which I still thought might be the gift of foresight.

"She's on her way. I'll speak to her alone when she arrives," I said.

Linnea objected, but I silenced her with a pointed stare.

Glancing at the door, Dane said, "She's outside. And she's frightened. Do not make her cry."

My wolf snarled, offended not only by Dane's command but also by his assumption I would hurt my cousin. And why the hel was the uber-dominant lone wolf even aware of Dahlia? She wasn't exactly his type, was she?

Gods, I hoped not. Dane never talked about himself, but others did—especially the females who'd slept with him. Word was he dominated in bed, too, and put the *K* in *kink*. The idea of him strapping sweet little Dahlia to a headboard and having his way with her made me wince.

"She's a member of my pack," I said. "She has to answer for her actions—whether she cries or not."

"Which you know she will," Linnea said. We all frowned at her. "Well, she will."

Dane turned back to me, his mouth pressed into a hard line. "Then leave it to me. I'll find out what the human female has done to her."

A loud, vicious rumble erupted from my chest. Inside, my wolf battled to get free. "If you go anywhere near Kristin, I'll rip out your fucking throat. Do you hear me?"

The ferocity of my attack shocked everyone except Dane, who smirked. "Do you hear yourself?"

I knew I'd overreacted, but I was furious at Dane's threat. And if my wolf escaped, a fierce battle would erupt. One of us might end up dead. "You're not pack, Dane. Stay out of our business."

"Does that mean you don't want my information?"

"It means you choose to run alone, and I choose to run the Varda. Kristin—and Dahlia—are under my watch and protection. If you cross me, you cross the entire pack, and we'll take you down. No matter how good your intel."

We glared at each other, and then Dane sighed and sat in one of the chairs facing me. "Relax, Fyrstr. I just don't want to see Hati and Skoll get their claws into Dahlia. She's too trusting and… nice." He said it as if she had rabies. "It would be easy to use her. Not that I'm against that—I'll do whatever I have to in order to win this war—but in her case, it would be like kicking a puppy."

I held on to my anger for one more second, then matched Dane's sigh and let the rage drain away. "I know. I'll keep her safe. Tell me what you've got."

"The Jotun are preparing for something big. I think they're going to war, but I don't have any specifics about where or when. Or who they're warring against. Instinct tells me the information is good. My source wasn't exaggerating."

"Odin was full of doom and gloom too. He basically said the shit was about to hit the fan."

"Did he give any details?" Gunn asked.

"Nope. I got a prophecy instead. Cryptic as usual."

I recited the rhyme that had been seared into my brain:

> *Eagle eye. Earth to sky. Fly, wolf, fly.*
> *Lay her down. Wolf and crown. Cry, wolf, cry.*
> *One and one. It's begun... Love dies.*

"'Wolf and crown' has got to be you," Gunn said, "And maybe 'Earth to sky' means you're going back to Asgard."

"Yeah, that's what I thought too," I said.

Linnea had written down the prophecy and tapped her pen on the paper. "'Lay her down' could mean a female's going to die, which is why he'd cry afterward."

"Or he kills her, and it's a victory cry," Dane said.

Gunn rolled his eyes. "It's sex. The third line says 'love' and 'one and one.' It's all related."

"What if the cry is a wolf's cry—maybe the yla during the Handsal ceremony or the kalla during the Kyssa?" Linnea turned to me expectantly.

"I will not be calling for a mate," I said with a frown.

We tossed around a few more ideas before I stopped them. "We're going in circles. All we can do is wait for the prophecy to play out and hope we recognize it when it happens. We'll drive ourselves rabid otherwise."

I leaned back in my chair and squeezed my eyes shut, trying to block out the rhyme. It didn't work. Odin obviously didn't want me to forget. But for now, I needed to focus on other things.

"Did you dig up anything else on Kristin?" I asked Linnea.

"Not yet. So far, everything in her file is legit. Why not just kick her out? Get her the hel away from the den."

"I want to speak to Dahlia first. She may have a good reason for asking Kristin to stay."

"If Kristin *is* just an artist, why not let her finish the mural?" Gunn asked. "It's gonna be amazing."

Linnea rolled her eyes. "Who cares about the mural? You just want to screw her."

"No, I don't." He pointed at me. "He wants to screw her—and he should. I want to fuck her sister. Have you looked into *her* background? She's the one who's trouble."

"And you still want to have sex with her?"

"Hel, yeah. More than ever."

Linnea opened her mouth to protest, but I stopped her. "You're not going to change him, Linnea. Only one female can do that. And then we can both sit back and laugh as she runs rings around him."

"Not gonna happen," Gunn said. "If you can opt out of the mating game, so can I."

Dane rose from his chair. "Was there anything else?"

"No. I spoke to Fenrir, but he was worse than Odin. More gibberish. Something's going down, and I have the feeling we'll be picking up the pieces."

Dane scowled. "At times, I think it would be best if we were as ignorant as the humans. Let the gods and the Jotun sort out their own differences."

I grunted in agreement.

The lone wolf headed to the door. "I'll send Dahlia in." He

turned back. "On second thought, you should be hard on her. Scare her a little so she'll stay away from that woman."

My wolf growled at Dane again, not liking his tone. I didn't like it either.

Gunn made a point of sniffing the air, then smiled wickedly. "Dog, you've got it bad."

"Get out. All of you. I'll talk to Dahlia alone."

They left, and I drummed my fingers on the desk before Dahlia peered around the door, her pretty pixie face terrified. She was so small compared to other Valdyr females she still looked like a teenager, despite being in her mid-twenties.

Wearing jean short-overalls, a short-sleeved pink T-shirt, and tennis shoes, she stepped inside. Her teeth gnawed on her bottom lip—a habit I'd tried to break her of since she was a pup. I resisted the urge to soothe her and instead pinned her with a hard stare.

"I don't have all day. Shut the door and sit down."

She moved jerkily, and the door slammed shut. "Sorry," she squeaked, tripping over her feet in her haste to get to the chair. Finally, she seated herself.

"Out with it," I said.

The first glimmer of tears shone in her eyes. I ignored them. I was her Alpha, and she'd disobeyed a direct order.

"I know you told me to, um, not hire her, but I'd already said yes. And she was so excited, and I wanted her here so badly. I tried to say no, I really did, but…I couldn't get the words out. No matter how hard I tried, they wouldn't come."

"Then why didn't you tell Gunn or Linnea? They would have done it for you."

"I tried to, but I couldn't say it to them either." A different kind of shine entered her gaze, and she leaned forward, brushing the wetness from her cheeks. "Did you see the mural? I know she hasn't done much, but what is there is incredible. I swear it will be the most beautiful thing ever. Even the gods will envy it."

"Dahlia, I'm not interested in the mural. I want to know why you defied me."

She flinched and sat back. "I didn't."

"Yes, you did."

"Well, I didn't mean to. I told you it just…happened."

"Nothing just happens. Why, Dahlia?"

Her lips set in a stubborn line. "You were wrong. She needs to be here. She's supposed to be here."

"How do you know?"

"I just do."

Gods, it was like pulling teeth to get an admission from her. Was this Dahlia's gift showing her the future? If so, she'd be the pack's first foreseer in over a hundred years.

"What if I sent her away?" I asked, hoping to force her hand.

"You can't."

"Why not?"

"Because."

"Because why?" When she didn't answer, I marched around the desk toward the door.

"Where are you going?"

"Kristin doesn't belong here. I'm kicking her out of the den."

She bound to her feet. "No!"

I opened the door, but it ripped from my hands and slammed shut. *Magic.* Looking back at her, my excitement rose. "She's not Valdyr, Dahlia. She's a threat, and I don't want her at Wolf Ridge." I tried again, and this time, I found myself thrown against the door, my head banging back as she pinned me to the wood with her magic. The power that flowed from my cousin was off the charts.

Her mouth opened with shock, and a second later, she released me. My legs gave way, and I slid down the paneling to the floor.

She ran to kneel beside me, tears streaming down her cheeks.

"Oh, my gods. I'm sorry. I'm so sorry. Please, Erik, forgive me. I don't know what happened."

She crouched low, her head and shoulders tilted sideways, her chin raised. Avoiding eye contact, she nuzzled my jaw, her hands petting my throat and shoulders—like a subordinate pup.

I wrapped an arm around her, this time soothing her to my heart's content. "It's okay, Dahlia. It's okay. You're a seer. The pack's first one in over a hundred years. You couldn't let me prevent what you knew was meant to be. That's where your power came from." I grasped her head between my hands so I could see her face. When she met my gaze, I kissed the tip of her nose. "I'm so proud of you, sunshine."

"Really?"

"Yup."

Dahlia relaxed and leaned into my body with a loud sigh. "Does that mean Kristin can stay?"

My chest tightened. Damn. I didn't have a choice now, did I? And why did that make me so frigging happy?

"Yes, she can stay—for now."

CHAPTER 5

I SAT ON TOP OF THE SCAFFOLD, SHARPENING MY CARVING TOOLS—not that they needed it. The tarp around the mural was drawn, but enough of a gap existed for me to see Erik's office, and when I used my second sight, it was as clear as my hand in front of me.

Minutes ago, Dahlia had arrived and hovered on the landing, her fear scenting the air. A few times she'd scurried away only to return. It had broken my heart to see my friend so distressed—especially since my presence in the den had caused it.

Then Gunn, Linnea, and a dangerous-looking male I'd never seen before had walked out of the office. When Dahlia saw the second male, her scent had spiked—mortification as well as desire adding to the mix.

Well, that was a surprise. The badass male was sexy enough, but I hadn't thought he'd be Dahlia's type.

My wolf had crossed her paws over her muzzle in sympathy. Who wanted to be faced with their crush after being summoned to the principal's office?

The others had dispersed, saying little as Dahlia slunk inside Erik's office.

And now I waited—as I'd been doing for two weeks since I'd packed up in Denver and told a worried Gina goodbye. My plan to locate Hans and discover anything about the pack had been a bust so far.

The offices were either physically or magically sealed so no one could eavesdrop.

Good for the rest of the Valdyr. Bad for me.

And when the wolves were out in the open, they took care about what they said. I knew I was under guard, even though they weren't obvious about it.

Then there was that damn stone wolf. It still radiated dark energy, as if reaching toward me whenever I passed. Sometimes, I wanted to go over and smash it to pieces.

Like right now. I sharpened my chisel extra hard.

After a while, Dahlia exited Erik's office, eyes red and a little dazed. Hesitating for just a second, I hurried to the ladder, climbed down, and met my friend halfway across the rotunda.

"Hey," I said with a smile. "I'm getting a coffee. Want one?" I let my smile fade and pretended to notice Dahlia's tears. "What's wrong? Did this have anything to do with me? Erik seemed a little miffed I was here."

A delicate blush stole up Dahlia's cheeks, matching her red-rimmed eyes. "Oh no, don't worry about that. It's all settled. He's excited you're here."

Gods, she was sweet. And a terrible liar. The first part had been true, and I breathed a silent sigh of relief. The second part, however, was a big old-fashioned lie. I clutched Dahlia's hand and led her toward the break room. "Let's have a coffee, and you can tell me all about it. If it's not me that's upset you, it must be something else. Someone tall, blond, and dangerous, perhaps?"

Dahlia squeaked and then dragged me into the break room and closed the door. "Shhh!"

I repressed a smile. The sweet female's attraction to the tough-looking Valdyr was no secret. I'd seen and smelled it from across the rotunda. Surely, he had too.

Cocking an ear, I wondered if this room was also sealed. No. If I listened hard enough, I could hear the murmur of conversations outside—which meant others could hear them too. Well, maybe I could use that to Dahlia's and my advantage. Show that big, scary-looking male he wasn't the only wolf in the woods.

I placed my palms on the white counter and hiked myself up between the sink and the microwave. "Okay. Spill."

"I'm fine, really." But her lip wobbled.

I raised a brow and gestured with my hand for Dahlia to give up the goods. My friend flopped into the chair with a sigh. "I hired you without Erik's consent. He got mad at me. So mad I thought he would bite me or something."

"Bite you?"

"Oh…um…not a real bite. I just meant, like, metaphorically. I know he seems hard sometimes, but underneath that tough exterior, he's a darling. Did you know he's my cousin?"

"Yes, he told me the first day we met. Are you sure he's all right with me being here?"

"We sorted it out." She dropped her eyes. "But not before I started blubbering. I don't know if you noticed, but I'm not like the other females here…like Linnea."

"Sweetie, you don't want to be like Linnea. She's a crank." I raised my voice in case the bad-tempered redheaded wolf was listening. It was childish, but I couldn't confront the Alpha female directly, so this slap-down would have to do.

"She's not that bad, she's just…stressed. Her job is difficult, and she wasn't really prepared for it when she took the position. Plus, she had a pretty rough childhood, I think."

My heart softened a little. I knew about rough childhoods. "Linnea didn't grow up here?"

"No. She came to us a few years ago."

Interesting. A wolf could join the pack from somewhere else. It made sense. Wolves in the wild didn't always stay with the pack they were born into. And I remembered my mom saying something about wanting to join a new pack but being afraid it wouldn't accept all of my brothers.

"So what about Mr. Tall, Blond, and Dangerous?"

Dahlia hedged. "Which one?"

"Shades, shitkickers, and black leather?"

Another sigh escaped Dahlia, and this time, it was filled with longing. "Dane. He's not around much."

"What does he do?"

"He's kind of like a consultant. He helps Wolf Ridge with certain projects, passes on information, that kind of stuff—but he's not part of the company."

A lone wolf. "And why haven't you gotten down with him yet?"

Dahlia gaped at me and then dropped her head in her hands. "Yeah, right."

Reaching for the coffeepot, I hopped off the counter and poured two cups of the heavenly stuff. I sat next to my friend and passed one over. "What's that supposed to mean? You're a great catch."

"No, I'm not. I don't even know why I'm here. I'm a chicken. And I either talk too much, or I clam up and say nothing at all. It's pretty hard to carry on a conversation with someone who can't form a complete sentence. And I'm short—how weird is that? I still look like I'm freaking sixteen years old, for gods' sake. The males around here like strong women."

"Oh, come on. You're kind, sweet, funny. You have no problem talking to me, and you're not *that* short. My sister is as tall as you are, and guys fall all over her. Of course, she also wears tops cut down to her navel."

A smile tilted up Dahlia's lips. "Is she as pretty as you?"

"Prettier. She's like a goddess."

An idea formed in my mind, and I eyed Dahlia. The insecure wolf needed to see that just because she was different from the other females in her pack didn't mean she wasn't as good as them. Sure, she was submissive, and I could understand how that would bother her—especially growing up in a pack as strong as this one—but she had other wonderful qualities.

She needed to be shown how fun and sexy she could be. And I knew just the witch to do it.

"Gina's coming into town tomorrow and staying the weekend. Why don't you drive home with me Friday night, and we can hang out? We'll get something to eat, have some drinks, go dancing. There are lots of guys who'd love to spend time with you. Trust me. It'll be fun."

"I don't know. Won't you want to spend time with her alone?"

"No. She's a pain in the ass."

Dahlia laughed and then sighed. "Can you find me someone in black leather?"

"I can find you someone wearing a dog collar if that's what you like. Gina's a magician when it comes to makeovers. By the time she's done with you, you'll be beating the bad boys away."

Dahlia sat a little taller. "Maybe I don't want to beat them away."

The door swung open with a bang, making us jump. Dane stood there, frowning. He held his sunglasses in a clenched fist, and his stunning, ice-blue eyes bore into us. Dahlia gaped at him, the color rushing up her cheeks again.

"Come with me," he said to her.

A funny sound escaped her throat, but she didn't move. Probably frozen in place. I resisted thumping her on the back to get her breathing again.

The displeasure rolled off him in waves, but I also sensed something else. Protectiveness? Desire?

Definitely the need to dominate. Dahlia would be crushed by him.

He'd obviously heard us talking and objected to our girls' night out. But whether that was because he disapproved of me or of Dahlia getting it on with other guys, remained to be seen.

I rose from the table with my coffee, sauntered over to him, and held out my hand in greeting. My wolf puffed up and bared her teeth, sensing Dane's forceful nature. If he tried to boss her around, she would give him hel. It bolstered me but also exasperated me. Erik had been just as bossy earlier, and my hussy of a wolf had shown him her belly.

"Hi, I'm Kristin."

He ignored my hand and met my gaze. I expected frost to match his demeanor and his eyes, but a fire smoldered within. Wow. No wonder Dahlia was hooked.

I wondered if my wolf might change her mind about him, but instead, she snapped in his direction. Dane frowned and glanced around as if he felt the aggression but couldn't place where it had come from.

I mentally locked my shields in place. Bad doggy.

Dropping my hand, I turned to Dahlia, who still couldn't speak. "Do you want me to stay?"

"No," Dane said.

I ignored him and moved back to squeeze my friend's shoulder. "Dahlia?"

Dahlia cleared her throat and then shook her head. "I'm okay."

"All right. I'll talk to you later. We can make plans for tomorrow night."

Dane planted his hands on his hips and didn't step aside as I moved to the door. So I plowed right through him, elbow out, eyes cool, foot treading on his toes.

He didn't even wince. Jackass.

Entering the rotunda, I sipped my coffee and looked around. A few Valdyr stood in groups or sat on the steps leading down to the sacred circle. I was tempted to return to the break room and make sure Dahlia was all right, but I knew I had no place there.

The way of the Valdyr was different than humans, and to them, I was an outsider.

The thought bothered me, and I rubbed at an ache that bloomed in my chest. Maybe things could work out for me here. Maybe I could come clean and be more than just an outsider. I could belong to the pack, have pups and a mate.

My mom had said I would find a strong male to kyss. Maybe he was here.

My eyes drifted up to Erik's office.

Or maybe Hans was here, and I would finally kill him.

Not in the mood to work, I wandered around the edge of the ceremonial circle. When I'd first started at Wolf Ridge, I'd been reluctant to enter the sacred space, but I knew if I failed to do so when others walked freely across it, it would seem strange. Now I was used to it.

More Valdyr entered the rotunda, and the noise increased. Feeling claustrophobic, I headed for the outside door. But as I passed the stone wolf, I found myself slowing. Lethargy crept into my limbs, and I stopped.

The dark energy struck from the carving. My wolf jumped up, barking and growling. The darkness receded, and the snarls reduced to a low, threatening rumble.

I tried to clear my head and back away, but my legs were too heavy.

In my belly, a familiar stirring occurred. My magic. What was it about this statue that woke that other side of me? I'd tried numerous times to bring my magic out on my own, but nothing had worked. Maybe I should drop my shields and see what happened. Let my magic rise.

A whisper sounded in my ear. I tried to turn toward it, but I couldn't move. Was my wolf trying to tell me something?

Or someone else. Something else.

The stirring in my belly increased. *Let it rise. Let it go.*

My magic was my birthright. Why had I locked it away? I'd let my wolf free, why not my magic? It was as much a part of me as breathing. I needed to lift my shields and let the magic flow.

Let go.

"Hey! I'm talking to you."

The angry words ripped through me, and I gasped, stumbling backward, my coffee sloshing over the lip of my cup as my mental shields locked back into place. Strong arms caught me and shoved me upright. "What the hel? Are you drunk?"

Spinning around, I came face-to-face with a frowning Linnea. Well, not quite face-to-face. The gorgeous, muscled Alpha female topped me by several inches—in every direction.

Her aggressive energy was welcome after the mind-numbing attack of the stone wolf.

And that's what it had been—an attack.

If I had released my shields like I'd been urged to do, all hel would have broken loose, ending with my possible death as the unkyssed males swarmed, driven feral by my scent. Although maybe Erik could have stopped them.

But then, what would he have done? Locked me up like Hans had done?

"Hello. Anyone there?"

"I was thinking," I replied. "You should try it sometime." In reality, I wanted to hug Linnea for saving me. But I knew how the strong Valdyr would react—by face-planting me on the ground.

Not that I couldn't beat her in a fair fight. My wolf had sized up Linnea the moment we'd met, and while I respected the Alpha female's strength, I believed I could pin her, no matter our size difference.

Linnea leaned in close. "I know you're not who you say you are. You have everyone else here fooled, but I'm watching you. It's only a matter of time before you slip up. And when you do, I'll be there to take you down."

I couldn't help myself and matched Linnea's aggressive stance.

My wolf was too dominant to just roll over. "I'd like to see you try." I turned and flicked my hair, covered in rock dust, back into Linnea's face.

This time, I gave the stone wolf a wide berth as I marched toward the mural, my ears attuned to Linnea and the Valdyr around me, isolating their every move, waiting for them to pounce.

Had I given too much away?

When I reached the tarp, I closed it behind me—on edge and regretting what I'd done. Linnea would come after me even harder now. Why hadn't I just backed away, pretended to be afraid?

Because it went against every instinct I possessed.

I sighed and rubbed the nape of my neck. Working within such a strong pack was harder than I'd thought it would be. Maybe I should leave and never look back—cut my losses before something bad happened.

My gaze fell on the mural, and the stubbornness that had pushed me this far rose up again. Damn it. I didn't want to leave. I wanted to finish the mural, which would take months. I wanted to hang with Dahlia. I wanted Erik to scent me again like he had earlier. And I wanted to know if Hans was here—or if they knew where he was.

I had so much to do. Despite the danger, it was worth it.

Placing my cup on the scaffold, I noticed it was only half-full. Then I saw the coffee stains on my white T-shirt and jeans. Damn. I hadn't even felt the hot liquid splashing against my skin —that's how out of it I'd been. After wiping at the stains with a rag, I gave up and moved to my backpack that sat against the wall.

A wry smile tilted my lips as I pulled out a yellow tank top and jean cut-offs—they'd look funny with my work boots. Maybe I'd go home early today, sit in the afternoon sun for a while and regroup.

Looking back at the closed tarp, I decided I had enough privacy. The last thing I wanted was to cross the rotunda to the washroom and risk another confrontation—or an attack from Rolf.

I unlaced and slipped off my tan boots, followed by my wet jeans and T-shirt, which I used to dry my exposed skin. The bra and panty set I wore was a cream-colored silk that whispered softly against my skin.

Tossing the stained shirt on the scaffold, I'd just reached down for my cut-offs when the tarp swished open behind me, and a sharp intake of breath echoed in the enclosure.

CHAPTER 6

I STARED AT KRISTIN, WANTING TO CLOSE THE DISTANCE BETWEEN us, wrap those long, bare legs around my waist, and taste her. I wanted to touch every inch.

My wolf leapt in the air in agreement. *Mate!*

About to lose it completely, I spun around and reined in my need to run her down like a heat-seeking missile.

"Sorry," I muttered as I closed the tarp so no one else could see in.

The sound of fabric sliding over flesh, then a zipper and button slipping into place, reached my ears. With a snarl, my wolf tried to force me to look back at her.

Mate!

We struggled for dominance, something we hadn't done since my ulf-rist when we had to find a balance that suited us both. Now, the wolf pushed against my inner boundaries. Pressure built within. Even my teeth ached as I held my Valdyr form by will alone.

She's human.

She's ours.

No, she's not. Scent her.

I turned back slowly, barely containing my wolf. I kept my lids at half-mast, pretty sure my eyes had changed color, reflecting not only my inner battle but also my growing need for this woman.

Sniffing the air, my wolf whined anxiously and paced back and forth. I understood his confusion.

Human female.

Her arms and legs were long, lean, and tanned, and her hair was a mass of blond waves around her shoulders. A golden girl from head to toe.

I let my gaze drift over her. When I reached her ankles, I came to an abrupt halt.

What's...up...doc?

She wore pink-and-white striped socks with a picture of Bugs Bunny on the front. Amusement filtered through me. It was all I needed to wrestle my desire, and my wolf, under control.

"Nice socks," I said.

She glanced down, and her cheeks heated to match the pink stripes.

"Don't tell me you have a thing for the wascally wabbit. Is there a stuffed bunny propped up on your bed, with pink ears, a puffy tail, and a big, long—"

"Stop!" She raised her hand, palm out, and frowned, but I could hear the laughter in her voice. "I won't hear anything lewd said about Bugs."

"What? I was going to say a big, long carrot." Gods, I liked this woman. She brought out a side of me I'd thought lost, smothered beneath the curse, the mantle of leadership, and the ever-present sorrow of my parents' deaths.

Damn. I did not want to go there.

She turned to yank on her work boots. The sight of her ass in those cut-offs brought me back to the present with a resounding thud, erasing all thoughts of the curse. Which, for the first time, wasn't acting up around her.

She faced me again, tan boots now covering Bugs. All she needed was a tool belt to qualify for pinup status. I took a mental picture—I'd be saving that one for later.

"I spilled coffee down my shirt and pants. I had to change."

"Thank heavens for coffee."

Her lips twitched. "The heavens weren't involved. It was Linnea. She startled me."

"Thank the devil, then."

She laughed. "Okay, I'll give you that. She does come across as the spawn of Satan. Dahlia says I should cut her some slack."

"Dahlia's too nice. Stand up to Linnea, or she'll eat you alive."

Just like I wanted to—nibble and lick every inch.

Screw it. Instead of nursing the fantasy of her keeping me warm at night, why not have the real thing? She'd be at the den for a while, working on the mural. And the closer I got to her, the better I could watch her—just in case.

I inhaled deeply, my wolf doing the same. Her desire perfumed the air—along with her human scent.

Knowing she was sexually excited ratcheted up my own need. My wolf, however, slumped down and laid his head on his paws. I understood his dejection. For a moment, I felt the same. Then, anticipation took its place.

If she were Valdyr, we'd worry about tainting her with the curse. But a human woman can't be infected. And she smells like she's into us too.

No response.

Oh, come on. You've been pushing me to get down with her since we first met. Now I say yes, and I get nothing?

My wolf closed his eyes.

Fine. But remember—she's important. She may be human, but according to Dahlia, she's meant to be here. We have to find out why.

"Are you all right?" Her hazel eyes met mine with a quirked brow.

"I'm fine." I tried to think of something to say. Something flirty. "So, are you and Bugs exclusive?" To my relief, she smiled, which made my chest feel funny. I rubbed it with my hand.

"Nope. Just really good friends. My dad gave him to me when I was five. And yes, he's on my bed at home, holding a big carrot."

"I was more a Wile E. Coyote kind of guy." My wolf huffed disdainfully at my admission. "I hated that damned Roadrunner."

"Me too. I wanted him to roast the stupid thing for dinner. Or at least sue the Acme company. Their products were defective."

The laughter that punched up from my gut caught me—and probably everyone else in the den—off guard. It wasn't often I laughed out loud like that.

She laughed with me and even laid her hand on my arm—a good sign. I almost leaned down to kiss those smiling lips.

Raising my gaze over her head, I took a deep breath. There was no need to rush things. I had the weekend to wine and dine her. Although I'd heard her tell Dahlia her sister was coming to town. From the sounds of it, they were planning to hit the Missoula nightlife. And whatever men took their fancy.

My wolf growled territorially, unable to stay disinterested for long. The sound rumbled through me.

At her back, the scaffold rose, and I peered past it to the rock wall she'd started carving. I stepped closer. "Tell me about the mural."

Kristin turned and leaned on the metal walkway beside me, gazing at the wall. "Well, I thought since the company is called Wolf Ridge, and you already have other wolf sculptures and paintings, including mine, I would continue the theme. The life of a wolf pack, from birth to death."

She pointed to the cavern hollowed out in the middle of the rock where the sunken circle met the wall. "This is like a den. Life starts there with the pups being born. As the wall extends outward, we'll see the pups growing, each one on a different journey. They play, hunt, find a place in a pack, or wander alone.

If they're lucky, they court a mate or are courted, have pups, face danger, fight for dominance or for survival, get injured. Possibly die. You get the picture."

I nodded, focusing on one particular section of the rock where a wolf was carved in astonishing detail. Incredibly, it looked like the twin of my wolf. The shape of his head, the expression on his face, the position of the ears. Even the way the wolf carried himself.

The coincidence alarmed me, yet at the same time, I was bowled over by Kristin's talent. Awe rose at the magnitude and beauty of her vision.

Maybe that was why she was here—to create the mural.

"Why this wolf?" I asked. "Why carve it here?"

She furrowed her brow as she stared at that part of the rock. "It's hard to explain. I have a general idea for the carving as a whole, and I know what I want to express, but in many ways, I'm just the messenger. I let the rock guide me."

Reaching out, she traced her fingers over the stone wolf's face. I closed my eyes, imagining she brushed her fingers along my wolf's muzzle, brow, and ear.

When I opened my eyes, she was still gazing at the rock.

"It's as if the mural already exists beneath the surface of the rock. I get glimpses of it...like a puzzle. Eventually, I see all the pieces, and somehow they fit. I don't know where the inspiration comes from. It's just there, and I have to carve out the image."

She glanced at me and shrugged as if she thought she sounded ridiculous. Nothing could have been further from the truth.

"I get it. It's like that when I'm tackling a problem. Sometimes, the answer is just out of reach. I have to let it surface on its own."

"Yes. It's the same when I work on a smaller carving or a painting. Except the project is usually finished within a few weeks. This will take longer."

"How much longer?"

"I don't know. Months. Maybe a year."

Elation burst within me, followed immediately by unease. A human working in the den for over a year? Someone was sure to get careless.

But I couldn't kick her out. Dahlia had been adamant about that.

Ah, hel. If I sleep with her now, where will my judgment be?

In my pants.

I straightened my shoulders, determined to make better use of my time than just wallowing in her presence. I was the Fyrstr of the Varda, for gods' sakes, and it was my duty to protect my pack and the rest of the Valdyr.

"I look forward to seeing the mural finished. Why don't you show me your paintings and tell me more about yourself? I want to know all your secrets."

Kristin

I tingled from the top of my head to the tips of my striped, Bugs-Bunny-covered toes. I felt so…alive. My heart pounded, and my breath whooshed through my lungs as I moved through the den with Erik, hanging on his every word, watching for every emotion that crossed his face and all the ways his body moved. And the urge to laugh or, gods forgive me, giggle lurked just beyond the bend in my throat.

My wolf was no better, rolling and jumping around like an excited pup.

I'd picked up all kinds of I'm-interested vibes from Erik as I showed him the art I'd hung at Wolf Ridge—his gaze lingering, his arm brushing mine—but then he'd back off, fists shoved into his pockets.

Obviously, he was conflicted about me.

It made sense if he didn't date humans, although I'd known

lots of Valdyr who did, my brothers included. My mom used to tell the oldest boys to find a nice Valdyr female, settle down, and have some pups so she could be a grandmother. They'd roll their eyes, saying they had lots of time for that later.

If only that had been true.

And when I was in Alaska, the Alpha of the pack I'd infiltrated, Kell, grieved a human female who'd died. He'd loved her very much.

Not that I wanted Erik to love me. Right now, I just wanted him to push me against the wall and kiss me. Ever since he'd scented me earlier, running his tongue along my neck, I'd craved his mouth on mine.

"And what about this one?" he asked, peering intently at a painting of a wolf lying on the edge of a cliff. I glanced at him and noticed a muscle ticking in his jaw.

The painting hung in the foyer above the leather couch. I'd painted it a few years ago upon my return from Alaska. The wolf was a large male with blue eyes and a reddish-brown coat.

I'd been inspired by Kell and the deep sadness within him. This was how my wolf had envisioned the Alpha. It broke my heart every time I looked at the painting, but I knew it was one of my best.

"He lost his mate. He'll never recover."

Erik glanced at me and raised his brow. "In the wild, if a wolf's mate dies, they often take another."

"I know. But this one was just so sad. Can't you see it in his eyes?"

He nodded. "It almost feels like I've intruded on a private moment." Then he frowned. "Did you watch him? Was he one of the ones you studied?"

How could I answer that? I'd never seen this particular wolf, but I'd spent time with Kell in his Valdyr form. "Studied isn't the right word, but I guess you could say I met him."

Erik crossed his arms over his chest, his face inscrutable. What was he thinking?

"You're amazingly talented. The feel you have for the wolves is astonishing."

Pleasure mixed with guilt flashed through me. The fact that I pretended to be human—lied to him every moment we were together—made my stomach turn.

I had a feel for the wolves because I was a wolf.

But I couldn't tell him that until I knew if the pack was involved somehow with Hans.

"Thank you. It's a privilege to paint them."

He turned to the door. "Do you have time for a walk? There's a nice vantage point about ten minutes up the mountain." His eyes dropped to my work boots. "Those look sturdy enough to climb in."

"I'd love to go."

We stepped into the bright afternoon sun, the den and mountain at our backs and the complex spread out in front of us. Hearing a hawk cry in the distance, I looked skyward. The bird caught an updraft of air and glided effortlessly over the mountainside, searching for prey. A wave of envy surged through me. Freedom.

How I wished I could spread my wings and fly.

"They're beautiful creatures," Erik said before leading me around the side of the building to a trail that wound up the rocky, semi-arid terrain. My gaze lingered on his wide shoulders and drifted lower. I wanted to slip my hands into the back pockets of his jeans and squeeze.

Or the front pockets. That wouldn't suck, either.

Oh gods, I want to do that too.

"Um, I see you have a few eagles around here," I said, hoping he mistook my breathlessness for exertion. My boots crunched on the small rocks and twigs that littered the path as we entered the tree line. The smell of pine filled my nose, and my wolf panted happily.

"There's a nest about a mile west of here. We mounted a camera to watch the eggs hatch. Two of the three chicks survived."

"They look so funny when they're young. Hopefully, the older eaglet won't kill the smaller one before they leave the nest."

He glanced back, horrified. "Kill the smaller one?"

"It happens if food is scarce. Survival of the fittest, I guess."

"What about the parents? Don't they stop it?"

"No. And they give most of the food to the bigger chick. The smaller ones often starve to death."

"Ah, crap. Don't tell me any more. I'll never be able to look at the nest again."

The natural world could be harsh and the savagery heartbreaking, but Erik's concern for the eaglets warmed me. He cared for those weaker than himself and protected his pack. I couldn't see him being involved with someone as cruel as Hans.

Unless he had no choice.

I need answers.

"I was surprised to learn you transport many of your people in and out of Wolf Ridge. Is that for security reasons?" I'd been allowed to bring my own truck into the compound, but only because I had a lot to carry and wasn't working regular hours. Security checked the vehicle every time.

"Partially. It's also better for the environment. It saves space we would otherwise have to provide for parking, and it means our employees don't have to drive for an hour in and out of the city."

By employees, I knew he meant anyone who wasn't Valdyr. "I've seen houses higher up the mountainside. Some of the pa—people must live on site?" My stomach clenched at my near slip, but he didn't seem to notice.

"Yes. Some do."

When he didn't elaborate, I prodded again. "Are there places to rent? It would save me coming and going every day if I stayed here. I could work more often when my muse paid a visit." He looked back at me, and I placed my hand over my heart. "I promise not to pass any secrets to the Canadians."

His mouth quirked. "The Canadians are so last year. It's the Kiwis you have to worry about now."

"I promise not to pass secrets to them either. Or the Tahitians."

"Tahitians?"

"Mm-hmm. What do you think that dancing's all about? They lull you into a state of complacency, and before you know it, you've sold out your country."

He grinned. It thrilled me to see him smile.

We reached a bench that overlooked the compound. Erik pulled me up the last step. He didn't back up, so my body came flush against his.

Our fingers stayed curled together. His touch felt so familiar. So right.

"What about you?" he asked.

"What about me?"

"Are you trustworthy?"

I stared into the chocolate-brown depths of his eyes, heart racing, and wanted—no, needed—to speak truthfully. "I have secrets like anyone else. Bad things have happened to me and people I care about, but I would never hurt an innocent or betray a loved one."

"What kind of bad things?"

I dropped my gaze and focused on the pulse beating in his neck. How much could I say without compromising my cover?

"My dad was killed protecting me and my mom when I was young. A home invasion. Then, my mom died a few years later from injuries she sustained during the assault. Gina's my only family now."

A tremor shook me, and Erik folded me in his embrace. "Gods, Kristin. I'm so sorry."

Closing my eyes, I leaned into him, my face pressed against his neck. I let his warmth sink into me. Soothe me.

For the first time in a long time, I felt sheltered from the world. My wolf rumbled contentedly inside me.

"My parents were killed too," he said, the words muffled by my hair. "I found them together. My dad was holding my mom."

I raised my head to meet his pain-filled gaze and squeezed my arms around him. "Oh, Erik, that's awful. I'm sorry too."

He lifted a hand and caressed my face. "Were you close to them? You said your dad bought you your first Bugs Bunny."

"He did. He also taught me about eagles. He was fascinated by them. My grandfather too—kind of a family obsession, I guess. And my mom taught me how to bake. That's something I do when I'm in the middle of a project that's not going well." I swallowed past the lump that had risen in my throat. "I miss them both."

"I'm sure you do." His eyes dropped to the stone rune that hung from the leather cord around my neck. He picked it up. "Did they give you this?"

I glanced down. What looked like a drunken *n* was carved into the pendant. "No, Gina did. She went through a fortune-telling phase. That's the Old Norse sign for strength. She had me put my hand in a bag and pull out the rune that 'spoke' to me. This was it."

He ran his thumb over the lettering. "How did it speak to you?"

"Well, believe it or not, it was hot to the touch. The rest were cold."

The memory took me back to my seventeenth birthday, and I smiled. Gina and I had been living in a tiny apartment in upstate New York. My sister woke me in the middle of the night, holding the bag of runes.

I thought the rune I'd chosen was a sign from the gods—that I'd have the strength to kill Hans.

I still did.

"But, knowing Gina, she could have tricked me," I added with a laugh, wanting to change the direction of the conversation.

"Does she do that often?"

"She tries, but in case you didn't notice, she's not very subtle."

Amusement filled his eyes for a moment before fading. "Did they catch the man who killed your family?"

I lowered my lids as an image of Hans flashed through my mind. So big, strong, and stunning. Bigger even than Erik. But while Erik took care of those in need, Hans destroyed them.

A beautiful evil.

"No. He's still out there. Someday, I'll find him and—"

"And what?" Erik's hands cupped my face. "Go against him alone? Get yourself killed and leave Gina with no one?"

"I'm stronger than I look."

"I know."

I frowned at him, my frustration rising. "You don't understand what it's like knowing that someone so evil is out there and that at any moment he could show up and hurt you—or someone you love—all over again."

"Yes, Kristin. I do."

His gaze held mine until my anger faded. I let out a trembling sigh. "Right. Your parents. Did they catch the person who killed them?"

A muscle ticked in his jaw, and he tucked my head back beneath his chin. "Not yet."

"Do they know who did it?" Maybe it was Hans.

"No. It's...complicated."

More Valdyr secrets. It bothered me that he couldn't confide in me. Of course, there was an easy solution to that. All I had to do was let my wolf out.

And then what? What if I was wrong and somehow Hans was

involved with the pack? I'd lose my advantage and possibly my life. And then Gina would go after the monster herself.

"Do you live on the compound?" I asked, turning the conversation back to the pack's living arrangement. "I would think, as CEO you'd get the biggest house."

He huffed out a laugh. "It's not like that. We're more of a co-op than a corporation. I do live on-site, but the house has been in my family for generations. I told you my grandfather and others worked the land before they started Wolf Ridge."

"They must have been really tall because people here are huge. I fit right in. With the tall part, anyway. It's kind of nice."

He smiled, and I could just imagine what he was thinking—I didn't fit in at all. It made me sad all over again. I wanted to belong.

He kissed the tip of my nose. "You're kind of nice. So about those Tahitians. What type of dancing did they do?"

Obviously, he wanted to change the subject too. Well, why not? My fishing expedition hadn't led anywhere.

"You know, the hip-shaking kind." I swayed my hips from side to side against him, thrilled to feel his body's response.

His hands moved quickly to grasp my hips and hold me still. "Maybe that wasn't such a good idea."

I caught his gaze and held it. "Maybe it was."

He pulled me a little tighter, and I almost moaned at the size of him pressed against my pelvis. My boots added a few inches to my height, but his body still swamped mine.

"Are you trying to make me spill all my secrets?" he asked.

"You have secrets?"

"More than you know."

He trailed his palm up the side of my body, skimming the edge of my breast and collarbone to cup the nape of my neck. His fingers played with the tiny hairs there and rubbed over my necklace's cord at the back. I shivered in response.

He lowered his head, his lips inches from my mouth. "Question is, can I trust you with them?"

My tongue slid out, moistening my parched skin. "I guess it depends on whether I can trust you."

The moment hung between us. We shared the same breath, the same air, hearts beating together. He lowered his head another inch.

Then, a siren pierced the air.

Erik spun to face the valley at the same time as my wolf howled. I raised my hands to muffle the shrieking alarm before realizing it transmitted at a frequency only Valdyr could hear.

He turned back to me, jaw tight, eyes worried. Curving my fingers, I tucked my hair behind my ears, hoping he hadn't noticed my mistake.

"I have to go," he said. "It's an emergency—a silent alarm is ringing. My phone buzzed to let me know." He jumped back down the trail and looked up at me. I could see the wolf shining in his eyes, and when he spoke, I could hear the wolf's rough growl beneath his words.

"Don't move a muscle, Kristin. I'll come back for you. I don't want you to get hurt."

CHAPTER 7

I INCHED TOWARD THE EDGE OF THE CLIFF SO I COULD SCAN THE compound below. The blaring alarm and Erik's abrupt departure —as well as our near kiss—had set my heart racing. Now my fear of heights—cliffs in particular—added to the chaos.

It was ridiculous. I had nothing to be frightened of. No way in hel could I fall to my death.

It's not like I freaked out in airplanes or tall buildings. Or even driving a car over a bridge. It was just cliffs like this that turned my knees to jelly.

My very own kryptonite.

After a quick glance behind me, I went down on my hands and knees. *Gina would laugh her ass off if she were here.*

Pebbles bit into my flesh as I peered over the precipice. Down below, red lights flashed on the buildings, and figures darted to and fro. My eyes refocused so I could see clearly. Several Valdyr, including Gunn and Linnea, were running through the maze of buildings, weapons drawn.

Were they under attack? I had joked about being a spy, but

was that it? Had someone stolen plans to whatever the pack was working on?

Shift, my wolf urged.

No. Erik said to stay here.

Needs help.

I backed away from the cliff's edge and rose to my feet. Something inside battered at me to get moving—and it wasn't my wolf or my magic.

Instinct, my wolf said. *Must help.*

Yes, that was it. The inborn part of me that knew danger hovered nearby.

Turning, I raced back down the trail, unable to simply stand by and watch. I didn't shift, but I ran faster than any human could.

Around the bend, I caught sight of a black T-shirt, jeans, and boots lying haphazardly in the trees alongside the trail. Erik must have veered off the path to shift so his clothes would be harder to spot.

I wouldn't have seen them if I'd been human or even a regular Valdyr. A surge of pride at my family's special ability burst through me, and I wanted Erik to know about it, wanted to impress him.

Gods, I was pathetic.

He might not be impressed at all. He might be horrified. I didn't know any other Valdyr who had the ability to see like a predatory bird. They might lock me up if they knew.

Approaching the edge of the compound, I slowed, my breath rasping through my lungs. I heard movement and the occasional shout, but other than that, it was eerily quiet.

Which made sense. Erik's pack most likely communicated telepathically, like I had with my parents. If the Valdyr were under attack, they wouldn't want to give their positions away.

Reaching out, I tried the door to the first building I passed.

Locked. The compound was probably in lockdown to keep intruders out and the humans in.

If Gina were here, she would have a field day. She considered it her personal mission to crack any security device—physical or magical—that got in her way. Hel, she would have tried to break into the compound the first day if I hadn't stopped her.

Taking quick, quiet steps through the alleys between buildings, I came upon a small park with a large tree in the center. I moved forward cautiously, surreptitiously scenting the air. I reached the tree and pressed against it.

Instinct screamed at me that danger lurked nearby. My wolf was crouched low, close to the surface of my skin, and ready to attack at a moment's notice.

Grunts and a yelp sounded behind me. I spun just in time to see a large wolf being thrown off a huge man at the edge of the square. The wolf hit a concrete wall and crumpled to the ground. It tried to stand, then collapsed.

I knew the wolf was seriously injured. I wanted to help, but I couldn't breathe or move as I stared at the man standing with his back to me.

Sunlight-colored hair tumbled in waves past his shoulders. His blue silk shirt hung loosely over black leather pants that molded his muscular legs. Unhurriedly, he walked toward the broken, snarling wolf, his designer boots clipping across the concrete.

Shock and rage burst through me, along with soul-crushing horror. Memories of those terrible years when I was a prisoner with my mom came flooding back. I'd hated and often defied the vile creature who'd caged me, yet I'd been frightened too.

At times, petrified.

I tried to scream, to release the terror that now bound me, but my throat constricted. All that came out was a strangled croak.

He heard and spun toward me. Eyes the color of a summer sky widened in surprise. His beautiful face, etched like an angel, creased into an evil smile. Bright, white teeth shone against golden skin. Other times, his hair and skin resembled moonlight, and his eyes were as black as the night sky.

Either way, it was him—Hans.

"Well, well. Look what the wolf dragged in," he said in a deep, sexy voice. "What? No hug for Uncle Hans?"

My throat finally loosened, and I screamed—long and loud— at the top of my lungs, releasing the fear that paralyzed me. He stepped in my direction, but then a massive gray wolf leapt past my shoulder just as I was about to shift. Two more wolves jumped at him from the side, and a fourth—a female with reddish fur—raced toward him up the alley.

I barely held my wolf at bay. The urge to help the others kill Hans pounded through me, but I knew what would happen. I'd shift, and my scent would disorient the unkyssed males. By the time Erik regained control of the pack, Hans might have killed them.

For an instant, the monster stared at me, greed and frustration in his eyes, then he spun away and darted down the alley toward the red wolf. The female leapt at him with a ferocious snarl. He twisted, barely breaking his stride, and knocked her against the wall.

The red wolf hit it with a yelp, slowly getting up as the others raced by in pursuit, the big gray leading the way. She brought up the rear, shaking off her injuries.

I stayed in place, gripping the tree as Hans and the wolves disappeared around a corner. Tears streamed down my face.

I'd failed.

After all these years, I'd found what I'd been searching for. I'd had the opportunity to avenge my family, and instead, I'd stood there shaking in my boots. A child again, staring up at the monster who'd haunted my dreams.

Odin, forgive me. I'd let him get away!

Inside, my wolf howled, and I dropped to my knees, drawing

in great gulps of air. My stomach twisted as bile rose in my throat, and I vomited on the ground. When nothing else would come up, I wiped my mouth and scrubbed my fingers clean on the grass.

Useless coward.

Against the wall, the fallen wolf whimpered. I looked up and met his pain-filled gaze. It was an expression I'd seen too many times before when my wolf had first risen and my family had defended me against the crazed, unkyssed males in my pack.

Fear shot through me, this time for someone other than myself, and I scrambled toward him. Reaching his side, I cradled his head in my lap. He bared his teeth, but I stroked his muzzle anyway, my fingers trailing over his eyes and around soft ears.

"Don't worry. I won't hurt you."

Oh, dear gods. What if he was Erik?

No, my wolf said.

How do you know?

Smell.

I inhaled deeply and was glad I didn't recognize the wolf's scent beneath the stench of blood, sweat, and vomit.

"You're going to be okay. I won't let anything happen to you. Help is on the way." Someone would have called for medical assistance.

The wolf closed his eyes, every breath strained. I crooned to him, the seconds feeling like hours. "You were so brave, going after that monster by yourself. I'm sorry I couldn't help you. And I'm so sorry he hurt you."

My hands trailed gently over his back, and felt his broken spine and ribs, the thick brown coat matted and wet with blood. I noticed his aura coalescing around him and realized I was still using my second sight.

The beauty of the colors stole my breath but also stopped my heart.

The wolf's breath slowed, and a heaviness invaded his body as the iridescence thickened and drifted upward. In a small way, it reminded me of the magical inferno that had streamed to the heavens when I'd burned my mother's body during the Hyrr.

And then my chest constricted. "Oh gods, no! You hold on, do you hear me?"

I placed my hands over the flow, trying to stop it from leaving the wolf's body, but it passed right through my fingers, swirling higher. Panic squeezed my throat, and I grabbed at the colors, wishing for some way to hold on to the energy.

An odd feeling stirred in my belly—my elusive magic. The stream escaping the injured wolf slowed, and I gasped in surprise.

"Come on. Stay with me."

Once again, I took hold of the aura and pushed it down, remembering how I'd shaped the magical fire over my mother's burning body so many years ago and thrown it at Hans to cage him during my escape. Maybe I could shape this energy stream— or whatever the hel it was—and bind it to the dying wolf until help arrived.

In my mind, I sculpted the bright life force like clay, shaped it into a shield, and held it to his body. His chest rose as his aura seeped back into his fur. Then he opened his eyes and looked at me.

I wished I knew his name. "I've got you. I'm not letting go."

With a sigh, he closed his eyes, but this time, he was alive and staying that way.

Overcome with emotion, I dropped my head and sobbed. I may have failed to kill Hans, but I'd saved a Valdyr. Someone's son. Perhaps a husband and father.

And if he wasn't either of those things, now he had the chance to become one.

Still, the victory was bittersweet, even if it came with an incredible insight into my magic. I'd never dreamed I could do what I'd just done.

The sweet smell of Dahlia covered me like a warm, soothing blanket. I leaned my head back against the concrete building and looked at my friend, who knelt beside me.

"Are you all right?" Dahlia asked, her eyes scanning my tearstained face and the blood on my hands and clothes.

"No. I think the official term is *basket case*." I wiped my cheeks. How much had Dahlia seen?

I knew so little about being Valdyr. Could anyone else see the colors? Could they do what I'd just done?

Dahlia squeezed my shoulder and then lowered her hand and stroked the wolf. "Thank you. He's going to be fine. Help's coming."

As if she'd summoned the cavalry, a female wolf streaked across the park toward them. Dahlia moved aside, pulling my arms from around the fallen wolf. Something tugged inside of me and released. The injured wolf's aura surged toward the approaching female, melding their colors together before the white wolf snuggled close, licking and nipping the male's muzzle. He thumped his tail weakly in response.

The stirring in my belly settled, and I realized the injured wolf no longer needed me. I wanted to stay close to them—mates, probably—but Dahlia pulled me to my feet. When I swayed unsteadily, she hooked an arm around my waist.

"Lean on me," she said.

A van and a Range Rover roared into the park, and several Valdyr jumped out, carrying medical supplies and a gurney.

I glanced back as Dahlia led me away. "Are you sure he'll be all right?"

"Yes. The…vet will take good care of him."

I opened my mouth to tell Dahlia that I knew they were Valdyr…and that I was one too.

No. Mate first! my wolf said.

I hesitated. Yes, Erik should be the first to know. I'd snuck into the pack under false pretenses. It was only right I explain everything to him first—now that I knew Hans was his enemy too.

I closed my teeth around my bottom lip. Would Erik be angry with me?

Or would he finish what we'd started earlier?

I wanted him to scent me with his tongue on my neck again, to complete the almost-kiss we'd shared at the lookout. More than anything, I wanted to see his wolf, to run with him…and know that I finally belonged.

If he'd have me.

"There were wolves here, a lot of them. They chased a large man. What happened to him? Did the wolves catch him?"

Kill him?

Dahlia bit her lip. "Um…no. The wolves were just… They're like guard dogs. They've been trained to protect the compound. That's why Erik doesn't want you wandering around on your own. Not that they'd hurt you."

"And the man?" I asked. "He injured two of the wolves."

"Oh. He, uh, got away. He broke into Wolf Ridge and tried to steal something. We would have turned him over to the police if we'd caught him."

I nodded, my face a concerned mask, but underneath, a strange mix of disappointment and fierce exhilaration swirled through me. If Hans was still alive, it meant I'd have another chance to kill him. And this time, I wouldn't be too frightened to move.

"Were any other wolves hurt?"

"Nothing serious. Just the one you saved."

I halted in the middle of the road leading to the den and faced Dahlia. "What do you mean?"

The petite Valdyr smiled, her gray eyes shining. "I don't know exactly. All I know is you had to be in the park when that wolf was hurt. Otherwise, he'd have died." She reached up and hugged me. "I'm so glad you're here." After a strangling squeeze, she stepped back. "Erik says you're to take the rest of today and tomorrow off. And he wants you to see a doctor."

Relief flooded me as I realized Dahlia had spoken to him telepathically—and he was okay.

"That's nice of him, but I'm not hurt."

"I know. I told him that." Our eyes met, and Dahlia giggled self-consciously. "I mean, I *will* tell him."

My lips twitched, hoping we would laugh about this in a few days. I was pretty certain Dahlia would accept me into the pack with open arms. Gunn, too, maybe. Linnea, probably not.

But it all depended on their Alpha.

"Is Erik around? I thought I might speak to him before I go."

Resuming our trek, Dahlia paused before answering, most likely talking to him through their bond. "No. He'll be tied up for a while." We stopped in front of the steps leading to the den. "Do you need anything from inside?"

"Just my bag."

"Someone will bring it out. The building's been locked down."

As if in response to Dahlia's words, the door opened. A male Valdyr, whom I recognized but hadn't spoken to, came out with my backpack. The look on his face—open distrust—left me feeling cold. Hurt wormed its way into my heart. What had I done to deserve such hostility? Other than Dahlia, the Valdyr hadn't exactly been friendly, but they'd never shown aggression or outright suspicion before.

Except Linnea. Maybe she was behind it. No way would Erik think I was culpable. Would he?

I took my bag from the male with a barely audible "thanks." He retreated to the den, throwing a dark look over his shoulder before disappearing inside.

Disheartened by the turn my day had taken and sickened whenever I thought about my encounter with Hans, I headed with Dahlia toward my old black truck in the parking lot. The vehicle looked about as battered as I felt.

After throwing my bag onto the cracked bench seat, I pulled myself up. The air inside was stuffy, and I kept the door wide as I settled in.

Dahlia leaned on the metal frame. "Do you still want to go out tomorrow night? I can come by around five or so. I'd like to meet Gina."

I summoned a smile and nodded my head. "I'll email you my address. You can stay the night if you like. Gina will bunk with me, and you can have the couch."

A grin lit up Dahlia's face. "I would love that. I've never had a sleepover before."

"Well, whatever you do, don't fall asleep first. Gina's been known to wield a mean Magic Marker. You're likely to wake up with whiskers and a mustache."

Dahlia laughed as I turned the key in the ignition. After a sputtered start, the engine roared to life. I closed the door.

"Drive safe," Dahlia said.

"I will."

With a wave, I pulled out and maneuvered slowly through the sun-drenched complex, hoping I might see something—or someone. If not Erik, then Hans.

My mood soured again. Next time I'd be ready for him—and he wouldn't escape alive.

The security guards used extra care as they searched my truck before waving me through the gate. I drove quickly, feeling keyed up and on edge. The trip southeast through the Montana mountains to Missoula took just over an hour along the interstate. I checked the rearview mirror often and peered into every vehicle I passed.

Usually, the sight of the Garden City gave me a thrill. Not this time. I couldn't get the image of Hans, looking at me with such glee, out of my head.

The fucker should have been dead already.

Turning south, I drove through the ever-growing metropolis,

surrounded by steep hills covered in sandbar willows, cotton-woods, and ponderosa pines—not to mention the spreading suburbia.

As I entered downtown and headed toward my loft in an industrial area overlooking the Clark Fork River, I pulled out my phone to call Gina. Right now, I needed to hear my sister's voice.

Unfortunately, she didn't pick up, and I left a message. "Hi, it's me. I'm calling to confirm your flight info. I can't wait to see you tomorrow." My emotions pushed upward, clogging my throat, and I took a deep breath, not wanting to break down over the phone. Gina would only tell me to suck it up...and then she would dash to my side. "Maybe I can convince you to move your witchy ass up here. There are lots of brawny cowboys in town for you to scare. Love you. Bye."

After disconnecting, I swung into an underground parking garage. My apartment was a former concrete factory that had been turned into a series of artists' lofts. The space was suitable for my needs, and the rent was cheap. The neighborhood was a little rough, but I never worried about that. Humans were no match for me.

I parked and scanned the area warily—the first time I'd done that since moving to Missoula. Would Hans come after me? Probably. But I'd changed my last name from Gullari to Andersen since I'd been imprisoned, and I'd fabricated an entirely new background for myself. I wouldn't be easy to find—unless he'd followed me from Wolf Ridge.

After grabbing my backpack, I exited the car and walked toward the stairwell. My wolf paced back and forth just beneath my skin, scenting the air. The enclosed space was stuffy, and my echoing footsteps lent an air of impending doom to my three-flight climb.

An empty hallway appeared when I peeked through the steel door. I wanted a showdown with Hans, but on my terms and preferably with the element of surprise.

When I reached my door, which I'd painted purple, I placed my back against it so no one could sneak up behind me as I searched for my keys. Wasn't that how every woman died in a slasher film—unable to get the door unlocked in time? On the other hand, perhaps I'd make it through, and something would be waiting for me on the other side.

A smart Valdyr would have readied her keys before she left her vehicle.

"A fabulous end to a freaking fabulous day," I muttered.

And then my door suddenly opened. I shrieked as I fell backward into my apartment. My pack flew upward, scattering its contents everywhere.

Before I hit the floor, I shifted into my wolf, twisting in midair, and pounced. The intruder jumped back just as I snapped my jaws together. Then, I found myself immobilized on the floor by an icy blue light.

A pair of gorgeous violet eyes stared down at me. "Whoa. Who put the crack in your coffee? Seriously, sister, you have to chill out. Thor's balls, I could have hurt you."

CHAPTER 8

Kristin

THE GLASS OF RED WINE I CHUGGED AS I LOUNGED ON MY SOFA—hair pulled up into a messy bun and wearing comfy, Bugs-Bunny-covered pajama pants—hit the back of my throat with a satisfying gulp. Or five.

It had been a hard day, so I poured myself another.

Gina frowned at me from the opposite loveseat, and I took more time with the second glass, savoring the exceptional vintage.

Another bottle of wine, as expensive as the first, sat on the kitchen counter on the far side of the loft, along with the lock-picking tools Gina had used to break in. As a so-called private detective, she viewed security of any kind as a personal challenge —even if she'd been the one to install it.

"I thought you didn't steal," I said, resting my head against the sofa.

Gina took another sip before answering. "I don't. The guy who owned the wine was a scumbag whose ex-wife hired me to find his hidden assets. Consider the wine my finder's fee. The collection is worth about half a million dollars."

Which explained why it went down so easily.

That, and the crap day I'd had…although my time with Erik hadn't been so bad.

My wolf chuffed in agreement.

Boxes still cluttered the floor, but my home was slowly taking shape in a bohemian-chic kind of way. The only things I'd splurged on so far were the heavy, floor-to-ceiling gray drapes that covered the windows overlooking the river, the city, and the mountains in the distance.

My bedroom was tucked behind a folding Chinese screen, and my own brightly colored paintings covered the walls.

Gina was wearing a gauzy yellow shirt, a hot pink bra, big hoop earrings, and denim cut-offs. She sprawled on the restored blue-and-brown tie-dyed love seat that coordinated with the two chocolate-brown armchairs and the steel-blue sofa.

"Okay, spill," she said. "What happened today? You smelled like a frat-house bathroom at the end of the night—minus the booze."

I closed my eyes, tears of frustration and self-disgust welling behind my lids. I blinked them away. Gina had little sympathy for crying. "I was outside with Erik, and—"

"Wait…he's back? Where the hel was he? I called in a lot of favors to get the flight manifests for his private jets—he wasn't on any of them. And he didn't show up anywhere when I scried for him."

"I don't know. Does it matter?"

"Of course, it matters. Unexplained disappearances always matter." She waved her hand. "Carry on."

"Yes, Your Majesty."

"That's demigoddess to you."

I smiled, but my amusement soon faded, replaced by a growing anger. "An alarm sounded, and Erik ran off because of an intruder. I followed him into the compound, and I...I found Hans."

Gina sat up with a gasp. Her wine nearly sloshed over the rim of her glass and onto the loveseat. "Did he hurt you? Is that why you threw up?"

"No. He didn't do anything to me other than smile at me in that evil way of his. He was as surprised to see me as I was to see him."

"What did you do?"

I swallowed. I had to push the words past my clenched jaw. "I froze. And then I screamed—like I was being fricking murdered —which released me in some way."

"And he didn't come after you?"

"He started to, but the wolves attacked him, and he ran away."

Gina stared at me, her mouth falling open. After a second, she got up, circled the coffee table, and hugged me. "Okay. So now we know."

"Know what?"

"That you can't take down Hans."

I reared back. "Like hel, I can't. That was just a setback. Next time I see him, it won't be such a shock. I'm strong enough now. Ten years ago, you gave me this." I reached up to grasp the rune that hung around my neck—the rune for strength—but my hand closed around nothing but air.

I gasped and looked down. It was gone!

"Oh my gods, where is it?" I patted around my neck and down the front of my shirt, then stood up and checked the couch.

"What's wrong?"

"My necklace is gone. The rune you gave me." Panic beat at my chest. "I was wearing it this morning. I always wear it."

Gina rose and picked up a pillow, helping me search. "Where did you see it last?"

I stopped and tried to think. So many things had happened

today. "I went on a walk with Erik—before Hans showed up. Erik was asking me about it."

"Where did you walk?"

"Up the mountain to a lookout. Just before the alarm rang out."

"Did you shift? It would have fallen off then."

"No. I didn't dare. The unmated males would have come after me."

I headed toward the door. Maybe it had slipped off when I'd first come home. Gina had surprised me, and I'd turned wolfy.

But it wasn't there. I even opened the door and checked the hallway outside.

I came back empty-handed and sat down.

Gina sat beside me. "I'll scry for it later to pinpoint the exact location. I know how much it means to you."

"It means everything to me. It's my message from the gods… my mission—find Hans and kill him for what he did to my family."

Gina's lips tightened. "The rune wasn't from the gods. It was from me. And even if it was a message, it was canceled when you lost the necklace. No message, no mission. Got it? You can't take on Hans, Kristin. He's too strong."

"I can and I will, whether I lost the rune or not. It's the sign for strength. *My* strength." I grasped Gina's other hand. Squeezed. "The rune 'spoke to me.' Remember? Those were your words, Gina. It *spoke* to me. I am Kristin Gullari, daughter of Gale and Andrew Gullari, sister to Adam, Joran, Garet, and Finn. I'm going to kill the monster that murdered my family."

"You're also Kristin Andersen, my sister. And if you let Hans injure one hair on your fluffy blond head, I swear I will kill you."

My anger drained, and I sat back down on the couch. "Gods, Gina. I'm sorry, but I have to do this."

Gina sighed and sat beside me. "I know." She rubbed a hand over her forehead. "I don't suppose the wolves killed him?"

"No."

"Too bad."

I didn't agree. It gave me another chance to kill him.

"How the hel did Erik and friends cover up what happened?" Gina asked.

"Dahlia said the wolves were trained guard dogs, and Hans was a spy."

After a moment of disbelieving silence, Gina burst into laughter. "That's ridiculous. But I suppose it's easier for humans to believe in a trained wolf pack than werewolves walking among them."

I slapped my sister's arm at the same time as my wolf growled. "I am not a werewolf."

"Whatever." Gina stood and moved toward the window. Raising her arms, she started chanting.

Alarm skittered through me. "What are you doing?"

"What does it look like? I'm going to set some wards so no one can get in undetected. Hans may try to grab you now that he knows you're here."

I hurried forward. "Oh no, you don't. What if the Valdyr sense the wards and realize I'm not who I claim to be? I don't want Erik finding out that way. Besides, when I moved in, you installed enough physical alarms to keep out an entire army. No one could get through them."

"I did."

"Only because you're obsessed and have no sense of personal space. People put locks on things for a reason." I drew an imaginary box in the air. "Boundaries, remember?"

"Boundaries are for ball games."

I crossed my arms over my chest. "I forbid it. Hans doesn't know where I live. The only way he could find out is by following me home from Wolf Ridge."

"Or Erik could tell him."

I gasped, unable to believe my ears. "That's ridiculous!"

"No, it's not. You assumed that Hans was the intruder and the wolves chasing him were from Erik's pack. But what if the opposite is true? What if Hans is friends with the pack, and the wolves chasing him were some other Valdyr—like you—who tracked him down and tried to kill him."

"That's insane." I waved my hands in the air. "The pack helped the injured wolf. If what you say is true, why would they save the wolf who attacked him?"

"I don't know. Maybe they wanted to interrogate him. But until you know for sure, keep your mouth shut." Gina held up her little finger. "Pinky swear you won't say anything for at least a week."

"No way. I'm telling Erik the next chance I get."

"What does it hurt to hold off for a few days and see what happens? Hans won't risk losing you again by waiting too long. Then you'll know for sure if the pack is involved."

"The pack is not involved. Erik would never let such evil live. His nature is to protect people."

"You don't think he would throw you under the bus to save himself or his pack?"

"No!"

"Come on, Kristin. Quit thinking with your hoo-ha and use your head. His loyalty is to the pack, not to you." She raised her fist, finger out. "Pinky swear."

When I glared at her and stuck my hand behind my back, Gina leaned in close. "You owe me. I saved you twelve years ago, and I'm calling it in."

"You wouldn't."

"I just did."

I slowly wrapped my little finger around Gina's and squeezed. "I'll wait until after the weekend, but that's it."

"Fine. Now swear."

Through gritted teeth, I said, "I promise not to tell Erik I'm one of them until Monday."

We let go, and I flopped onto the couch. Then I reached for my wine and took a long swallow. "Some days, you make it really hard to love you."

"I do what I have to do to keep you safe."

That mollified me a bit. I filled Gina's wineglass and held it out. "What do we do now?"

"We stick together. Hans can't take us both at once." Gina took the wine and joined me on the sofa. "Your family is my family. I have as much right to avenge their deaths as you do."

The sentiment was sweet, but it still made me want to lock up Gina in a three-foot-thick concrete safe room.

Not that that would stop the queen—sorry—demigoddess of lock picking from getting out.

"No way in hel would my brothers consider you a sister."

"And why is that? I can be sisterly."

"Two words—tits and ass. Of which you have plenty."

"That's three words." Gina put the cork in the bottle. "We should probably stay sober, seeing as we might be fighting a monster at any moment."

"Good plan." I laid my head back, my emotions seesawing. I longed to tell Erik my secret, but if it made Gina feel better to wait four days, I owed her that. And if Hans attacked and something happened to my sister, I now knew how to fix her—at least until they found a doctor.

I sat up. "Oh my gods, I forgot to tell you something."

"There's more?"

"Yes. But it's good. Remember the injured wolf I told you about? I saved him."

"What do you mean?"

"Well, I was using my second sight, so the colors were bright around the Valdyr. Hans, too, now that I think about it."

"It makes sense. We know he's magical."

"Is that what you think the colors are? Magic?"

"I don't know. You only see them around non-humans, right?"

"No. Humans have an aura, but it's not nearly as vibrant. It's like one ping on a piano versus a whole orchestra. Anyway, I sat with the wolf, comforting him and waiting for help to arrive, when he died...or almost died. His colors sort of thickened around him before drifting upward—and I knew."

"Knew what?"

"That his life force, that magical essence that animated him, was leaving. So I stopped it."

"How?"

"I grabbed the aura and reshaped it into a shield, kind of like the barrier I imagine when I block my Valdyr scent. Then I forced the energy back into the wolf."

Gina's eyes widened. "That's amazing. What did it feel like? Were you weakened like I am when I do magic?"

"No. Not at all. Maybe because I wasn't creating something from my own magic. I just restyled what was already there. Funny, I never put those two things together before."

"What two things?"

"Being able to see the magic and giving form to it like I would a sculpture or a painting."

Gina put her wine down and grasped my hands. "Holy Thor. You're an artist, and the raw magic is your medium." She squeezed my fingers. "See if you can create something right now."

"Are you kidding? I can't create art out of nothing. I need raw materials to work with."

Gina pointed to herself. "Hello. How many times do I have to say it? Daughter of Freyja here. You told me my aura was fantastically brilliant. I am your raw material."

I scooted back, shaking my head. "First of all, I did not say 'fantastically brilliant.' Only you would take 'bright' and turn it into that. Second of all, no."

"Why not?"

"Um, let's see, because I'd be sucking away your life force?"

"You'd just take a little, same as I do when I do magic. Give me a few hours, and I'll be full up again."

"And what if I can't stop? Do you really want to be responsible for me killing you?"

"Oh, come on, Kristin. Don't you want to know? At least shift your sight so you can see my aura."

I crossed my arms over my chest, but a little voice inside said, *What can it hurt?* And it wasn't my wolf talking.

Hesitant, I brought Gina's aura into view. Hmm, it really was fantastically brilliant. Not that I'd tell my sister that.

The rainbow of colors not only glowed, they sparkled, dancing like sunlight on water. I reached out, almost hypnotized by the beauty of it, then snatched my hand back in horror. "I can't."

Capturing my hand, Gina placed it over her heart. It was like tossing a stone in a pond as colorful rings undulated outward. "Yes, you can. I trust you."

Breathing deeply, I tried to remember what I'd done before. It hadn't been enough just to touch the swirling energy. I'd had to wish for a way to stop it from leaving the wolf's body—give intention to the energy.

Okay, so what could I wish for? I'd created a cage to hold Hans the first time I'd shaped the colors, and I'd made a shield the second time. How about something totally different?

The magic stirred in my belly as an image came to mind. Touching my finger like a paintbrush to the reds, pinks, and purples, I drew a heart over Gina's heart and floated it between us.

"Can you see that?"

Gina's eyes widened for an instant, then rolled. "A heart? What are you, thirteen and doodling on your school binder? Anyone can make that. Do something else."

I clenched my teeth. "How do you feel?"

"A little tired, but not too much. Come on."

"All right." I pulled a lump of energy toward me—more than I probably should have because I was ticked—then shaped it with both hands like I would clay. Finally, I sat back, pleased and a little amazed at what I'd done. When I turned it to face Gina, my eyes lifted to my sister's face, and the excitement faded. Dark smudges circled Gina's eyes, and her mouth drooped with fatigue.

"Oh, gods. I took too much."

Even fatigued, an excited glimmer lit Gina's gaze. "Maybe a little, but it's worth it. So I feel fluish. You can redirect the magic back inside me afterward like you did with that wolf."

"Oh, right. I didn't think of that."

"That's what you have me for." Gina reached for the solid sculpture, fingers tracing over her own image, down her nose, and across her lips to her chin. "Now *that* I can get behind. Look at me. I'm a swirling mass of gorgeousness."

"Narcissist."

"Hel, I'm just owning what I got." Gina's brow creased in thought. "I wonder what would happen if you didn't put the magic back inside of me. Would it dissipate into the air? Or can you tie it off so it's a permanent fixture?"

I sat back, gnawing on my lip. "The shield that blocks my scent seems permanent, but I don't think it is. A part of my mind has learned to constantly reinforce it. Kind of like breathing. Since the sculpture's so new, it would probably disperse once I thought about something else."

"But when I create a ward, I can actually tie it off. And when I break someone else's ward, I essentially go in and untie it. Try with the heart. Imagine it being sealed in some way. Then stop thinking about it and see what happens."

"You just want a permanent magical sculpture of yourself," I said.

"No. I want *that* big lump of energy back. I can't afford to be weakened for a few days with Hans nearby. You can find some poor sucker later on and sculpt me using their raw magic. I'm sure they'd be happy to donate it once they knew their life force was going toward me."

I snorted, and then I turned my mind back to the heart, making sure to hold the sculpture of Gina in place at the same time. I imagined two strings coming off the point of the heart and then triple-knotted the ties into a big bow.

"Like that?" I asked.

"Sure. Now take your mind off the heart and see if it holds."

"Okay. I'll work with the sculpture. Tell me if anything hurts, and I'll stop."

It was hard to quit thinking about the heart altogether, but once I reshaped the image of Gina into a stream of water that trickled back into my sister, I had almost forgotten.

"How do you feel? Am I going too fast?"

"No. Kristin, this is amazing. My energy is increasing. Think of everything you can do with it. The lives you can save—or take. All you need is a magical source."

In a moment of clarity, my head snapped up, intent on what my sister had said. The heart lost form as it faded from my mind, and the magic drifted to the ceiling until it disappeared.

"I guess that answers that question," Gina said, looking upward. "Bye-bye, heart."

With a final push, I siphoned the remaining energy from the sculpture into my sister, who gasped.

"That felt weird."

But I wasn't listening. I stood and paced to the kitchen and back again, my mind centered on the idea of taking a life.

One life in particular.

Odin had given me strength and power to defeat the monster. I could weaken him with my magic the same way I had weakened Gina. And then I could cut off his head. Or I could just drain the life right out of him.

Either way, he was dead.

I stopped and stared at my sister, a tight smile stretching my lips. It felt more like a grimace.

"No wonder Hans murdered my family and imprisoned me. I'm a magical killing machine."

* * *

Erik

"We don't know that Kristin was involved," Dahlia protested, her eyes glued to the floor as four big rekkrs, plus Linnea and Dane, gathered together for a debriefing in my office. They were riled from the fight and the near death of one of their own.

I had asked my cousin to attend because she was the first to see Kristin after her encounter with Skoll. Maybe Kristin had said something to Dahlia.

"Are you saying it's a coincidence that Skoll attacked the compound while she was here?" Linnea asked, shifting in her chair to look at Dahlia. The Alpha female's right arm was in a sling, and her forehead was bandaged where Skoll had knocked her against the concrete. "How did he make it past the wards without help? They haven't been breached in decades."

The other rekkrs muttered in agreement.

Dane positioned himself behind Dahlia, hands clenched. He didn't touch her, but he scowled at anyone who raised their voice in her direction.

Right now, those daggers were aimed at Linnea.

I wondered if Dahlia knew Dane protected her—if she drew on his strength for the courage to speak. It pleased me she had finally found her voice, as tremulous as it was, but it did not please me that Dane was the one to watch over her when more suitable males in the den could do it. Males who wouldn't look twice in her direction if they thought they might tread on the dominant lone wolf's toes.

"She's human. What kind of h-help could she give?" Dahlia's gaze met the Alpha female's for a brief second before skittering away.

"Hati and Skoll have used human pets in the past. If that's all she is." Linnea turned back to me with an accusing glare.

I sat behind my desk, striving to appear calm, but inside, my wolf paced back and forth, huffing and growling. Skoll had broken through our security, almost made it to the den, injured one of my rekkrs, and come within forty feet of Kristin. He'd actually been stepping toward her when I'd jumped past her shoulder to chase him off.

The memory of her scream made me want to rip out someone's throat.

"What's the latest on Robbie?" I asked, forcing the words past gritted teeth.

"He's in surgery, but Kat said it looks good. Britta got to him just in time and held him to her through their kyss. Otherwise, he'd be running in the woods outside Valhalla right now."

Valhalla. The paradise for warriors killed in battle. A beautiful place, but it still meant leaving loved ones behind. I prayed every day that my parents would find their way to the sacred forest, no matter how they'd died.

"We have to assume Skoll didn't have inside help," I said. "That he found a way through our defenses on his own. Once the moon rises, Hati may also attack. I want every able wolf on four-hour shifts."

Gods, it was unbelievable. Skoll striking by day, Hati by night.

Linnea's lips pulled taut in a snarl. "How can you dismiss your human's part in this so easily? A Valdyr almost died!"

Rage burst through me like gunfire, and I shot from my chair to lunge forward over my desk. "Do you think I don't know that? I felt Robbie slipping away. I knew he might die before Britta got there, and I had to keep chasing Skoll. But I also heard Kristin scream. I smelled her fear. Whatever else is going on, she couldn't have faked that!"

All the Valdyr, including Dane, who'd grabbed Dahlia by the shoulders, stepped back.

Fuck.

Taking a deep breath, I reined in my wolf and my emotions. I righted my chair, which had toppled over behind me, and sat down. I had to keep everyone focused and calm, starting with myself.

Linnea squared her shoulders. "Maybe she was frightened for Skoll when Robbie attacked him."

"Rob was down by the time we arrived, and Skoll was going for Kristin. You saw what I saw." I noticed my hands were fisted on the desk, and I released them. "We'll continue to investigate her, but we must assume the worst—Hati and Skoll have found a way through the wards on their own."

A knock sounded at the door, and Gunn pushed inside. He carried a flash drive. "I have the video. You won't fucking believe it—we have Skoll on tape."

Shock rippled through the room.

Odin's bloody eye, what would happen next?

"That's what took me so long," Gunn continued. "Once I realized what I had, I tracked him backward using satellite images to find where and how he came through the wards."

I held out my hand. "Toss it here. I'll load it."

I caught the small device Gunn threw at me and inserted it into my laptop while Gunn crossed to a large monitor on the wall.

"Why is that unbelievable?" Dahlia asked, her brow crinkling in confusion.

"Human technology can't record magic, which helps keep our true nature hidden." I gave her a brief smile as I opened the file. "A camera, for instance, will record us in our Valdyr form and our wolf form, but it can't record us shifting from one to the other because of the magic involved. Hati and Skoll, because of their constant tie to the sun and the moon, have never been recorded. It's that magical bond we ward against, thinking they can never be parted from it."

"Until now," Gunn said as the satellite footage came up.

Silence fell as Skoll appeared out of thin air at the pack's western boundary, high in the mountains, his hands behind his head as if he'd just looped something over his neck. I zoomed in, bringing into focus a round, opalescent pendant that hung on Skoll's muscled chest. Something misty swirled inside.

"Any idea what that is?" I asked.

Everyone shook their head or said no.

I looked at Dahlia, who also shook her head. Damn. One of her visions would have been welcome right now.

I advanced the video, switching from satellite to the cameras mounted throughout the compound, tracking Skoll's progress.

"Here's where Kristin comes in," Gunn said.

A wide shot showed Kristin pressed against a tree in the middle of a park-like area. Skoll appeared behind her at the edge of the square, and then Robbie, in wolf form, attacked. The noise alerted her, and she spun around.

My heart pounded as Skoll threw Robbie down, stalked toward him, and then turned abruptly to Kristin. He smiled and said something to her.

"Can you turn it up?" I asked.

"It's as loud as it goes. The magic Skoll used to get through our wards must have made him visible but not audible. I'll get it to a lip reader and see what they say." Then, his eyes lit with excitement. "Having him on tape means we can update our security features for facial recognition. If he or Hati try to get in again, we'll be warned by conventional methods, if not magical. Fortunately, because they're twins, the different hair, eye, and skin color won't matter."

I knew what a breakthrough that was. Wolf Ridge was linked

to surveillance feeds around the world. If Hati and Skoll were using new magic to move around freely, the Varda would know.

"I tracked Kristin for the rest of it," Gunn said, turning back to the video. "We were hot on Skoll's tail until he grabbed a sunbeam and rode out."

"Get me the footage anyway," I said, shoving my hand through my hair. "Maybe he ditched that pendant before he grabbed the beam."

"They're searching the trail now. I'll let you know if they find anything."

"Did anyone else hear what was said?" I asked.

The rekkrs shook their heads.

No surprise. Everyone had been moving fast. With blood pounding in their ears, the slap of paws on the ground, and me shouting orders down the bond, I doubted anyone had been close enough to hear Skoll's words—other than Robbie, who should be able to tell us in a few days.

One part of me desperately wanted to know. The other part was afraid of what Robbie might say.

I'd heard Kristin scream. The terror-filled sound had flooded me with a gods-awful fear, driving me to dangerous speeds to get to her.

"Okay. You can play the rest."

When Kristin's recorded scream filled my ears for the second time, my wolf snarled viciously, pushing against me from the inside out to shift. I barely held him back.

She's all right. That's not really happening. It's just a memory.

Magic? my wolf asked.

Yes. Human magic.

My wolf stopped fighting me and paced anxiously. When I appeared in the video, leaping past Kristin and chasing Skoll, my wolf stopped to watch.

Then Kristin dropped to her knees and sobbed before leaning forward to puke on the grass.

Gunn made a face. "Sexy."

"Shut up, idiot," Linnea said at the same time as I hurled a pen at him, hitting the back of his head.

"Ow." He rubbed it with his hand, looking around for the culprit.

"See, she saved him," Dahlia said, pointing to the screen at the same time as Kristin hurried to Robbie and knelt beside him, placing his head on her lap and stroking his face, ears, and back.

I turned to her. "What do you mean?"

"She was the first one there. She comforted him when she could have run away."

"Why didn't she run?" Linnea asked. "She should have been afraid. Robbie's a huge, injured wolf. He growled when she approached."

"She has an affinity for wolves. It wouldn't occur to her to leave." It bothered me to see her so upset. It was as if she'd crumpled in on herself. Tears streaked down her face as she babbled soothingly to the wolf.

Then she did something odd. I leaned forward for a better look. "What's she doing?"

She seemed to grab the air above Robbie a few times before lowering her hands to his body and laying them flat on his side.

Gunn stopped the video and faced the room. "It looked like a witchy thing to me, but we're warded against witches by Freyja herself. Kristin's never set off the alarm."

We needed more answers. Soon.

"Dahlia, when are you seeing Kristin next?"

My cousin's eyes widened. Color raced up her cheeks as everyone turned to stare.

From behind her, Dane met my gaze and frowned. "No."

I didn't need the lone wolf's approval. I was well aware my plan might put her in danger. "Dahlia?"

"Tomorrow night. Her sister Gina is coming into town, and we're, uh, going out."

"Good. I want you to send an email saying you'll meet them at Savage." I named the nightclub the pack owned in Missoula. "We can keep an eye on you there."

Dahlia fidgeted. "I planned to go to her place first. Gina's, um, doing a makeover on us." She whispered the last few words.

Gunn's eyes bugged from his head. "Have you met Gina? You'll end up looking like the kind of women I date."

"Skanks?" Linnea asked.

"Free spirits," he replied.

I shook my head. "You won't be going to her home."

"She won't be going anywhere. It's too dangerous." Dane towered over her from behind.

"Actually, if she goes to Kristin's loft, we could place some bugs inside. Maybe a camera too." Gunn stepped forward excitedly. "Her place is impossible to get into. Locked up tighter than Fenrir's prison. And we could monitor Dahlia, so we know she's okay."

"I can't do that. Kristin's my friend!" Dahlia's eyes were bright against her red cheeks.

I rose and walked around my desk to crouch in front of her. A knot had formed in my stomach at the idea of using her, but we had no choice.

I grasped her clenched hands. "Please, sunshine. We need you. If Kristin's telling the truth, there's nothing for her to worry about. If she's not...if she's lying to us...we need to protect ourselves. There's more at stake here than just friendship. Kristin may be our enemy."

Dahlia dropped her gaze. After a moment, she nodded. "All right. I'll do it." I could see she was fighting back tears. "Can I go now?"

I gentled my voice. "Yes."

She left with her head still lowered. Dane frowned at me and then followed her out the door.

Damn.

"Anything else?" I asked the remaining warriors as I returned to my desk. When no one spoke up, I said, "Then let's get to work. I want hourly reports."

The rekkrs filed out of the room.

"Gunn," I called my friend back when he was almost out the door.

Gunn cocked a brow and returned to the desk. "What's up, big dog?"

I slipped my hand into my pocket and pulled out a leather cord with a stone pendant on it—the Norse rune for strength. "This belongs to Kristin. I want you to check it for anything unusual."

Gunn reached for it, and I found myself loath to give it up. My wolf agreed.

"Like what?" Gunn snagged the cord from my reluctant fingers. "Electronics?"

"Yes. But also magic."

"I'll get it to the lab." He looked up curiously. "Did Kristin give it to you?"

I shook my head, guilt twisting my guts. I'd stolen it. A low growl emanated from my wolf.

"No. I loosened the cord and pulled it off her when…we got close." During that almost-kiss up at the lookout.

Gunn eyed me, then shrugged, his eyes drifting back down to the rune. "You did what you had to do for the safety of the pack—and the world. Besides…" He looked up again. "She's not one of us. She never will be."

An image of my wolf running through a barren field on a cold, bleak winter day filled my head. Loneliness welled within both of us.

"I know."

CHAPTER 9

I STOOD IN FRONT OF MY CANVAS, BRUSH IN HAND, AND TRIED TO paint the stream of magic I'd seen rising from the injured wolf earlier—the magic I'd handled. But I couldn't do it justice. I couldn't get it to shimmer just right or the colors to shine brightly enough…luminous and effervescent, yet deep and dark at the same time.

I sighed, put down my brush, and looked toward the clock shining on the microwave—almost two a.m. Gina was dead to the world on my bed, snoring softly behind the painted screen. She'd lost a lot of energy when I'd drawn the magical life force from her aura. And not all of that energy had been returned.

Afterward, Gina had scried for my pendant, which she'd located at Wolf Ridge—somewhere near the den. Maybe it had loosened when I ran down the mountain, and someone had found it.

I would get it back. I had to. I'd speak to Erik about it on Monday—after I'd told him the truth about everything.

Surely, he'll be happy to know I'm Valdyr.

My wolf thumped her tail encouragingly.

A pinging sound caught my attention, and I peered at the window, the hairs on the back of my neck rising. Inside, my wolf rose onto her haunches and swiveled her ears forward.

I quickly turned off the light over my easel, switched to my second sight, and moved toward the drawn drapes. I was almost there when another ping sounded like a pebble hitting the glass. I ducked and peered out through a crack in the drapes.

My wolf whined happily—seconds before I spotted Erik standing beneath a streetlight below. He tossed a pebble in the air.

He's here!

I yanked back the curtain, and a happy smile crossed his face. I waved, and he waved back, dropping the pebble to the ground.

I held up my index finger, indicating for him to wait, then raced excitedly to the front door and disarmed the security system. Gina would kill me if she knew, but staying away from Erik hadn't been part of our pinky pact.

Returning to the window, I gasped when I saw him standing right there on the fire escape, so big, so Alpha, and so freaking gorgeous.

My wolf gave a happy yip.

So did I.

I quickly unlocked the window and pulled it up. "Hey!" I said as I crawled through to the other side.

He grasped my elbow to help me. "Hey, yourself."

When I straightened, our bodies brushed together—barely— and the heat from his skin washed over me. I shivered as our eyes met. It was the kind of shiver that started low in my belly and sizzled outward to all of my secret places, softening my body for him, welcoming him.

His eyes shone down at me in the darkness, and I inhaled deeply, taking him all the way into my lungs. I couldn't get enough of his Valdyr scent—musky, primal, yet as fresh as the mountain dew and pine-scented forests.

He released me and leaned back against the railing, a contented look on his face. "I saw the light. I hope I'm not disturbing you."

"You're not. I just finished painting." I quietly closed the window and then sat on the sill. "I would invite you in, but my sister's here. She's sleeping. She flew in from Denver today."

"Gunn will be happy to hear that."

"You think?" I let out an amused laugh. "They didn't seem too chummy the last time she was here. Although, if anyone could take on my sister, it would be him."

"It's not often Gunn meets a woman who can give back as good as she gets—and then some. I think he's a little obsessed with her."

"He *should* be obsessed with her. Gina's awesome."

He cocked his head, and I imagined his wolf doing the same thing, trying to figure me out.

"You're very different from her," he said.

"Yes."

"Yet you're so close."

"She's my family. I'd do anything for her. Does that bother you?"

"Not at all. I admire loyalty."

I let that sink in—reveled in it. "Me too."

His eyes continued to bore into me, and I felt his gaze all the way down to my wolf. The female preened at his attention.

Mate, she said.

Maybe, I replied.

Then he dropped his gaze to my lips…and I forgot to breathe. I wanted him to close the gap between us and brush his mouth against mine, to scent me like he'd done before.

Gods, I was desperate for that.

He cleared his throat and shoved his hand in the front pocket of his jeans. "I think this is yours."

Looking down, I saw him pull my rune from his pocket, the leather cord looped around his hand.

"My necklace!" I gasped, reaching for it. "Where did you find it?" The familiar weight of the stone rune warmed my palm, just like it had the night Gina gave it to me.

The sign for strength. My strength.

I glanced up when he didn't answer, and he smiled at me. But it didn't reach his eyes.

"One of my rekkrs had it," he said.

"Rekkrs?"

"My security team."

"Oh. Where did they find it?"

He shrugged. "I'm not sure. It went through a few different people before it came to me."

Right. People.

He was choosing his words carefully, and I wanted to growl at him—my wolf's growl—to let him know that I knew what he was…and what *I* was.

"Okay, well, thank them for me, please."

"I will."

I could only imagine that the pack was on high alert since Hans attacked that wolf. Maybe they'd found my rune and thought it was spelled or something.

And it could be. For all I knew, Gina had zapped the stone to heat it before she put it in that bag all those years ago. My sister always did what she thought was best—even if it meant a little subterfuge.

Erik straightened from the railing. The smile he gave me was real this time, and he grasped my hand. "Here. Let me." He pulled me from my seat and lifted the rune from my palm.

Suddenly, I couldn't breathe. Again.

"Turn around," he said, his voice deepening. I faced the

window, and when his fingers brushed aside the tendrils of hair at the nape of my neck, I shivered.

"Your hair is beautiful." He played with one of the curls that had fallen free of my elastic. "So bright and full of life."

I wanted to say something back, but I couldn't get my voice to work. He leaned even closer and looped the necklace around my neck. Then he connected the cord at the back.

His palms slid to my shoulders and stayed there, heavy and warm. Exciting. Knees weak, I leaned back against him. It was either that or lean forward and rest my hands on the window in front of me.

Desire shot through me as I imagined Erik taking me from behind and biting my neck in the way of the Valdyr as I supported myself on the window.

The sensitive muscles along my inner thighs quivered, and I had to squeeze my lips together to stop from groaning. Then his hands lifted, and disappointment flooded through me.

I straightened, only to feel a tug on my hair as he pulled out the elastic that held it up. My messy bun fell apart, and the strands tumbled down my back.

"Beautiful," he said again, digging his fingers into the mass of curls and sifting through them.

I tilted my head back and sighed. "That feels so good."

"I want you to feel good." His hands tightened in my hair, and the slight pull on my scalp—the inherent dominance—excited me. I could hear the growl beneath his words, could feel the predator in his body. Every part of him was hard and muscled. Ready to pounce.

My wolf rode me hard, too, and I arched my back, nudging my ass against his thighs. I couldn't speak. If I had, I was sure I would have panted and yipped in excitement just like my wolf was doing.

He dropped his head to my ear. "You are such a temptation," he whispered.

His lips brushed the skin below my lobe, and I stilled. Would he bite me?

Goddess only knew how much I wanted him to do that.

Instead, he pressed his lips against the side of my neck, and then the crook, then out to my shoulder, before he straightened behind me and exhaled loudly.

He stepped back, removing his hands, and I mourned the loss of his heat and hardness.

"I'm sorry. I shouldn't have done that."

Inside, my wolf howled at his rejection. I swayed forward and leaned against the window, just like I'd imagined. "Right. Just… give me a minute."

I was tempted to look at him with my wolf in my eyes and drag my hair over one shoulder in invitation—in temptation, just like he'd said.

It would drive his wolf wild. And I would get what I desired.

But then I focused on what lay in front of me through the window—my sister, sleeping, and the promise I had made to her.

I gripped the rune and asked Freyja for strength. My time with Erik would come. But it wasn't now.

Turning, I met his eyes. "Wow, you sure know how to show a girl a good time. A short time, but good."

He rubbed his hand over his face and then back through his hair. "I'm sorry. Again." He glanced down to the street. "I shouldn't be here. It was foolish of me to come so late, but I wanted to return your necklace. I know how much it means to you."

Heat blossomed in my chest, and I felt the prick of tears at his thoughtfulness. I quickly blinked them away. "Thank you. I *was* worried. It means a lot to me that you came all this way. And it's not like you woke me up."

"Good. And you're welcome. But I should have called first or something. I promise I'm not a stalker. Even though this is exactly what a stalker would do. Gods, I even sound like a stalker.

It's just...I was in town already, and I had the necklace in my pocket, so..."

He's rambling. How cute is that?

"So, you came over." I eyed him curiously. "How did you know where to find me?"

"Your address is on file."

"Oh, right. Of course. And I sent it to Dahlia, too, earlier."

He nodded. "She told me you were going out tomorrow night."

"Yes, with Gina. I think my sister will love her. Dahlia's so sweet."

Erik grinned. "She is sweet. She made me and my brother look not-so-sweet growing up. Are you sure Gina won't steamroll right over her?"

Kristin laughed. "I'm sure she *will* steamroll right over her. But Gina's a mother hen, so she'll tuck Dahlia in under her wing."

"Next to you."

"Yup. Except I don't need protection."

He looked like he might protest, and a little thrill shot through me. Valdyr mates were nothing if not protective—the males *and* the females. If he was mine, he would want to shield me from every danger.

Then he shoved another hand through his hair. "No, I'm sure you don't." He looked over my shoulder, and I wondered how much of my darkened loft he could see through the window.

"Do you often work late at night?"

"Sometimes. If I'm not too tired and the muse hits."

"So, you were inspired tonight?"

"Hmm. More obsessed than inspired."

"Obsessed with what?"

"Oh, just...colors. I was trying to get the tone and vibrancy of something just right." I shrugged. "And I was still wound up from earlier, so sleep was not my friend."

His gaze jumped to mine. He opened his mouth to say something but then closed it again. What could he say, really? It's not like they could have an open conversation about Hans.

"And now?" he asked. "Can you sleep now?"

"Maybe." I grasped my rune again. "And I have a better chance of it because I have this."

"Good. You need your sleep. And you probably won't get much of it tomorrow night."

Protective.

Inside, my wolf and I did a little happy dance.

"That's true. I seldom sleep in." I looked up at him through my lashes. "Unless I have a good reason."

A low rumble sounded in his chest, and every part of me melted. But Erik gripped the railing, his knuckles turning white. "I'll remember that." He took a step backward toward the stairs. "I should go."

Obviously, his wolf was getting harder to control around me. The knowledge left me feeling a little smug. I couldn't wait for him to let go completely with me.

Come on, Monday.

I stepped toward him, reveling in my role as temptress. His eyes glowed in the dark, and he took another step back, this time down the top stair, but I kept coming until we were nose to nose.

He held himself still, muscles bulging in his forearm as if he held on to the railing for dear life. Then I gently pressed my lips to his cheek, chaste and sweet.

"Thank you, Erik. I love that you came here tonight to return something precious to me. I love that you were thinking about me."

He gushed out a breath, and the air tickled my neck. He took another step back and down. Now, I topped him by half a head. When he spoke, the words were so low and ragged I could barely make them out. "Truth is, Kristin, I don't ever *stop* thinking about you. And that could be a problem."

CHAPTER 10

THEY'RE HERE, ONE OF THE YOUNG REKKRS SAID VIA THE BOND. HE'D been keeping watch for Kristin, Dahlia, and Gina in front of the nightclub. *Do you want me to bump them to the front of the line?*

Is it long? I asked.

No. Five minutes, tops.

Let them wait.

Gripping the balcony railing with both hands, I peered through Savage's dim light and over the mass of people gyrating on the dance floor below. Loud music pounded in my ears and vibrated every cell of my body. But it was nothing compared to the shiver of anticipation that ran through me, knowing Kristin would soon walk through the door.

Especially after what I'd said to her last night. What I'd confessed.

I don't ever stop *thinking about you.*

And then I'd turned and taken the fire escape down to the street in a few giant leaps, refusing to look back.

For fuck's sake. I'd totally lost control and even shown a little supernatural strength. I just hoped it had been dark enough to cover that up.

Well, tonight would be different. It had to be. I was the biggest, baddest Alpha of the biggest, baddest pack. I'd fought in the domr, under the watchful gaze of Odin, to lead the Varda. I'd fought the curse to save my pack. And every day, I fought Hati and Skoll to keep the world safe.

I could handle a human female.

I just…needed some distance between us.

It didn't help that I'd spent all afternoon connected to Dahlia as she hung out with Kristin and Gina.

The women had shopped for everything from boots to lingerie before going back to Kristin's loft, ordering Chinese food, and getting ready for their night out, laughing, teasing—and in Kristin's and Gina's case, arguing—about everything. And loving it.

It had taken hours, and some of the time spent in Dahlia's head had been torture—like when Kristin had tried on her new lingerie. I had kept my eyes averted and my thoughts on other things. At least I'd tried.

Dahlia had stayed safe. She was happy, excited, and a little bit nervous about the outfit Gina had picked out for her.

My day hadn't been as fun. Skoll had appeared on the perimeter of Wolf Ridge and in town as if he were looking for something—or someone. The rekkrs, alerted to his presence by instinct, had chased him down numerous times before he caught a sunbeam and rode out.

He could return to his original position by conventional methods but not by magic. The beam only drew him in the sun's direction.

His leash to the sun meant he couldn't stay once night approached. That was the domain of Hati, who was tied to the moon. When the sun dipped below the horizon, Skoll was automatically drawn around the world because of that magical bond —whether he wanted to go or not.

High noon posed an interesting conundrum for him. He was at his strongest and most dangerous, but to ride a sunbeam out at midday was impossible—he had nowhere to go but up. This meant when he released the beam, he landed in the same place he'd escaped from and had to face his attackers all over again.

When night had fallen, and Skoll had been inevitably tugged behind the sun to the other side of the world, my rekkrs and I received a short reprieve—but only until the moon rose and Hati made an appearance.

Yeah, it had been a day. Perhaps learning something from Dahlia about Kristin would make it better.

My curse suddenly surged to the top of the well that contained it, startling me. The dark whispers tried to take hold of my mind, insinuating themselves within my psyche, finding and escalating my doubt and fear. I mentally yanked myself free of the parasite while my wolf helped by charging the fetid tendrils.

Before they could latch on again, I built the walls higher and checked for any leaks.

To my surprise, there were several. Oozing from the bottom of the well was a putrid substance that looked and smelled like shit soup. Using all of my will, I forced the pollutant back inside and sealed the cracks.

In the beginning, I'd tried to cap the well, but that had only increased the pressure, and like water boiling on the stove, the curse rose even higher. Now, it was generally stable except at certain times—like when I went into Asgard. And, more recently, when I was around Kristin, although for some reason, it had been quiet the last few times I'd seen her.

The origin of the curse was still a mystery to me. It had been with the Varda since long before my parents had died, and I'd fought for the right to lead my packmates. The foul parasite had worked silently, treacherously, turning pack members and even kyssed pairs against each other.

With excruciating determination, I had used the Alpha bond to suck every last filament of the darkness from the hearts of my pack and into myself. Then, I'd battled to contain it.

And won.

But for how long? What would happen when I died or weakened and could no longer hold the evil inside? If the next Alpha wasn't strong enough, the Varda—the bastion of strength against the sons of Fenrir—would crumble.

We needed to find the source of the curse and terminate it.

I turned as Gunn joined me at the rail, dressed in his usual jeans, boots, and gray T-shirt. I had taken more care with my attire, pairing dark gray pants with a blue button-down shirt and fine Italian leather shoes.

"Any sign of Hati?" I asked.

"Not yet. But he doesn't usually crawl out of hiding until the moon is near its peak. Do you know why the twisted twosome has shown up?"

"No, but it must be related to Odin's warning." The prophecy flitted through my head, and I tried to fit the new events to the rhyme. "We never considered that 'Earth to sky/fly, wolf, fly' might refer to Hati and Skoll riding the sunbeams and moonbeams. They're not Valdyr, but they do shift into wolves."

Gun popped his jaw. "Thank you, Mommy Dearest."

Mommy Dearest was the Jotuness who'd birthed Hati and Skoll. She was part wolf, part witch—dangerous witch. Odin had killed her thousands of years ago.

"The two of you would get along perfectly," I said. "She'd approve of the way you hang your clothes and never use wire hangers."

Gunn flipped me the bird. "I don't think the prophecy refers to Hati and Skoll. The wolf in the second line is definitely you. So it makes sense the wolf in the first line is also a Valdyr."

"Yeah, but who?"

Gunn shrugged, focusing again on the door below.

Dane appeared on my other side, dressed in his usual shit-kickers and black leather. He still wore his shades even though the club was dimly lit. Come to think of it, I had seldom seen the lone wolf without his dark glasses. What was he hiding? Wolf eyes, probably. They were the sign of a Valdyr who never found balance with his wolf and fought constantly to stay in control. Or perhaps he'd stayed in wolf form too long and could never fully go back. The two often went hand in hand.

"Fuck me, Freyja."

Gunn's rasping curse had me whipping my head back to the door. My heart stopped. Beside him, Dane let out a disturbed growl.

Kristin, Gina, and Dahlia had entered the club.

A siren dressed in black leather, Gina's killer curves were on full display in a bustier, skin-tight black leather pants, and thigh-high boots. Her black hair tumbled to her waist, and her lips and nails were painted red. Not so shocking once you knew her.

Dahlia's sexy schoolgirl look, however—complete with a short plaid skirt, white knee socks, stilettos, a blouse buttoned low and knotted at her waist, and her hair caught back in two sassy pigtails—shocked the hel out of me.

But it was Kristin who held my attention.

She stood in the middle of the two women, looking like a cool, elegant, highly fuckable glass of chardonnay. Her blond hair was piled haphazardly on top of her head, revealing silver hoop earrings. Wispy curls floated down to frame her smoky eyes and glossy lips. A sleeveless silver dress fell loosely to the tops of her thighs, exposing a long expanse of shapely legs. Rhinestone-encrusted high-heeled sandals covered her feet.

My wolf huffed inside, panting and drooling.

I felt the same, my body aching, my cock swollen behind my zipper. Gods, what I wouldn't give to make love to her.

"Is that a dog collar?" Dane asked, leaning over the railing and lifting his glasses to get a better look. He sounded outraged—it was the most emotion I'd ever heard in the lone wolf's voice.

Hard-pressed to take my eyes off Kristin as she sauntered through the crowd, I followed Dane's gaze to Dahlia.

Yup. A thin leather dog collar with silver studs circled her neck.

Dane pushed backward, his teeth snapping together, and he dropped his glasses back in place. Shoving a hand through his spiky blond hair, he spun toward the stairs and headed to the dance floor.

"Maybe I'll go, too," Gunn said, still sounding a little hoarse. "We should stick close to Dahlia."

"Right. Dahlia. Try to keep your dick in your pants and not fuck things up with Gina."

"You're one to talk, horn dog. I bet you've already thought of a hundred different ways to wrap Kristin's legs around you."

My wolf snarled down the bond at Gunn, who backed toward the stairs, hands held up in surrender and a smug smile on his face. "Circling your waist, over an elbow, against your shoulder. Have you thought about what she might—or might not—be wearing under that dress?" He turned and shouted over his shoulder, "You won't find out from up here."

This time, I flipped him the finger. Gunn laughed and ran down the stairs.

Clenching my hands around the railing as if to anchor myself in place, I looked straight into Kristin's upraised eyes. The connection sizzled between us, and the air punched from my lungs.

What kind of hold did she have over me?

She lifted her hand in a small wave, her smile excited. I nodded in response, unwilling to release the railing and wave back. I was afraid if I did, I'd be down those stairs in an instant.

Right now, I needed a clear head. Hati could appear at any

moment. And, if we were wrong about Kristin, Dahlia might get hurt. This was not the time to lose myself over a female—human or otherwise.

Kristin's smile slipped, most likely at my less-than-enthusiastic response, and she spun back to her sister and Dahlia. The women stood around a high-top table with their drinks in front of them. Turning her back on me didn't help one bit. Kristin's long neck, exposed in such a vulnerable way, only roused me and my wolf further.

The nape and shoulders were highly erogenous zones in female Valdyr. To present one's neck was a sign of trust and submission. When kyssed pairs mated, in either form, the male, like a natural wolf, would often take the female from behind and bite her nape or shoulder to arouse and subdue her at the same time. Hel, they'd bite their mate in any position if they could.

All I could think about now was getting her on all fours, flipping up that short, shiny skirt, clamping my teeth around her nape, and fucking her from behind as she climaxed around me.

I wiped beads of sweat from my forehead. Gods, maybe I should just pick another interested woman so I could think straight.

I had a pack to protect. Until I was certain about Kristin, she was off-limits.

Wasn't she?

At least her necklace had turned out to be just stone. When Gunn had brought it back to me last night and declared that no magic had been detected, my relief was palpable.

And then I'd been driven to return it to her—to see her—at two in the morning.

Gods, I was losing it.

Erik. Dahlia called to me through the bond, bringing my attention back to the present...where it should have been.

Yeah? Even though I wasn't speaking aloud, the strain in my tone was evident.

Are you all right?

I'm fine. It's...been a tough few days.

She looked up at me. *I should have stayed to help.*

You are helping. We need to know all of Kristin's secrets.

Her resistance battered at me through our link, and she dropped her gaze. *I don't think there's anything to uncover.*

We don't know for sure. Until then, stay sharp.

All right.

She lifted her hand and fidgeted with the shiny dog collar. I watched her for a moment, then cast my gaze wider, looking for Dane. He stood a few feet from Dahlia, just behind her eye-line, arms crossed over his chest, stance wide, jaw tight.

What's with the outfit, by the way? I asked.

She dropped her hand from the collar as if it burned her fingers and tugged on her blouse and skirt to cover more skin. Gina, who stood with her back against the table, breasts thrust forward as she talked—or most likely argued—with Gunn, laid her hand on Dahlia's arm to stop her fussing.

I heard Dahlia sigh through the bond, and then she took a long swallow of her margarita. *It's just for fun,* she said. *Gina thought it might...draw some attention.*

Well, it's working.

She glanced up, startled. *Who?*

Behind you, two o'clock.

Dahlia whipped around to stare at Dane. Obviously, she'd never learned the fine art of checking out males without them noticing. If possible, Dane's jaw tightened even further. When she spun back, her eyes were wide, and panic spiraled up the bond.

He looks mad.

Hel, Dahlia. You don't know much about males, do you?

No, but you don't know much about females, either. Kristin's not what you think. Just talk to her.

She pulled out her phone and played with it as if she'd just received a text before leaning over the table to shout something into Kristin's ear.

Kristin looked over her shoulder at me and smiled. My pulse picked up until it pounded in my veins. I couldn't stop myself. I smiled back. She straightened as Dahlia pointed toward the stairs against the wall. Kristin grabbed her drink, looped her small silver purse over her shoulder, and made her way toward the staircase that led to the balcony.

To me.

I groaned. *Ah, hel, Dahlia. You don't know what you've done.*

Kristin

My heart raced as I ducked under the rope hanging across the stairwell at the edge of the room. With every step, my knees, wobbly with nerves and excitement, threatened to give way.

Which was ridiculous. Erik and I had really connected during our hike and then on my fire escape last night. He had to be attracted to me, or he wouldn't have come to see me so late. And he'd kissed my neck and shoulder—three times.

That had to mean something. Kissing and biting a Valdyr's neck was only for mates. Or that's what I remembered, anyway.

"Kristin."

I looked up from my halfway point on the stairwell. Erik stood at the top, so gorgeous he took my breath away. My wolf gave a happy yip. Gods, I loved a man who looked as good in slacks and a button-down as he did in a T-shirt and jeans.

His sexy, chocolate-brown eyes ran over me, and he shoved a hand back through his hair. "You're beautiful."

Heat blossomed in my chest. "Thank you. You too. Handsome, I mean. Not that you didn't look nice before—you did—it's just that I love that color on you. The deep blue is so nice with your hair and eyes."

I was babbling. By the quirk of his lips, he thought so too.

At the top of the stairs, I reached toward him. He was so broad and muscled through the arms and chest, and I wanted to dig my nails in. He quickly stepped back, leaving my hand hanging awkwardly in the air between us.

I pulled it back, embarrassed.

Earlier, when I'd waved at him, and he'd nodded so curtly, I'd been crushed…and confused. But then he'd asked Dahlia to send me up, and I'd thought maybe I'd misunderstood.

Now, I wasn't so sure.

But then he grasped my fingers, squeezed, and led me to a cushioned, U-shaped booth with a table wedged in the middle.

Okay. This is cozy. He must want me here after all.

My wolf agreed by thumping her tail. You didn't bring a female to a perfect make-out spot unless you were interested.

I scooted around on the seat. He followed me. "I know I said this before, but you look stunning. You always do."

"Even when I'm covered in rock dust and wearing steel-toed boots?"

"Especially then. That's when your passion shines through. It's sexy."

A wave of heat washed over me. "Thank you. I love your passion too. You're a great leader. Dahlia speaks highly of you."

"She has to, she's family."

"It's more than that. You take care of everyone. You're always thinking about the people around you."

Erik dropped his gaze to my mouth. He shook his head. "Trust me. I'm not thinking about anyone but myself right now."

"If it has anything to do with you, me, and this table, then I'm all for you thinking about yourself."

His eyes shifted back to mine. "Hel, Kristin. You're supposed to stop me, not put ideas in my head." For a moment, I thought he might lean down and kiss me, but then the air gushed from his lungs, and he moved carefully away. "This is not a good idea."

Disappointment crashed through me, but I knew it was the truth.

I didn't want lies between us when we first made love.

"I agree. Not yet, anyway." I scooted along the U-shaped seat until the table lay between us. It wasn't more than a few feet, but it felt like miles.

Leaning back against the cushions, he laced his hands behind his neck, and his shirt pulled taut against his biceps. I wedged my hands beneath my ass so I wouldn't be tempted to lunge across the table and squeeze them.

"I didn't ask how you were," he said.

"I'm good. And you?"

"Good."

The silence lengthened between us. He filled it again.

"And you slept well last night?"

"Uh-huh. And you?"

He shrugged.

The tension between us was palpable, thick with the need to screw formality and, well, screw. I blew a puff of air at my bangs in frustration.

He raised a brow. "That bad, huh?"

I nodded.

"All right, let's try again." He leaned forward, arms resting on the table. "I saw video footage of you yesterday at Wolf Ridge. You looked upset."

Color heated my cheeks. Oh gods, of course, he'd seen me. They had cameras everywhere. Not only had I screamed like a banshee, but I'd also puked my guts up and sobbed buckets, snot dripping from my nose.

"That has to be the understatement of the year. I was like the girl from *The Exorcist*."

"No. You were frightened, which made sense in the circumstances. Then you were incredibly brave."

"Brave?"

"You soothed an injured wolf. He could have turned on you."

Guilt hit hard, and I dropped my eyes to stare at a gouge in the table. "I wasn't brave. Far from it. The wolf wasn't a threat to me—he knew I wanted to help." I met his gaze again. "How is he, by the way?"

"The doctor says he'll make a full recovery."

"Oh, good. You mean vet, right?" It would be odd if I didn't question him.

"Right. Vet." He drummed his fingers on the table. "The man you saw—he scared you more than the wolves?"

I couldn't suppress a shudder. "Yes."

"That…surprises me. I've heard other people say they're attracted to him."

I half laughed, thinking perhaps he was joking. "Maybe if you're attracted to serial killers. Something was seriously wrong with him. I hope he doesn't work for you—or with you. He's not a friend of yours, is he?"

I tried to keep the question light, but his answer couldn't have been more important.

"No. He broke into Wolf Ridge. We've come across him before. He's dangerous."

Relief flooded through me, and tears pricked my eyes. I blinked them away before he noticed.

"What did he say to you, by the way? I saw his lips moving, but I couldn't hear him."

I cleared my throat. "Uh…it was weird. Something like, 'Look what the wolf dragged in.' It was creepy."

He nodded his head. "Anything else?"

Yes, but nothing I wanted to tell him. Still, it bothered me to spout another lie. "There was more, but I can't remember all of it. I was freaking out." Questions filled my head as I thought back to my run-in with Hans. "Has he broken in before? Who is he? What's he after?"

Erik shook his head. "Sorry. I can't answer your questions without compromising our security. But if you ever see him again, run. Then call me. I'll deal with him. He's a very bad guy."

"Okay." I wanted to demand answers, but if I did, I'd have to spill my guts and break my promise to Gina.

Thank the gods, Monday would be here soon.

I wanted to know everything about Erik—and not just sexually, although that was a big part of it. I wanted to lie in bed with him after we'd made love and talk until dawn. I wanted to putz around his kitchen baking brownies. I wanted him to watch me paint. I wanted to know everything he could tell me about being Valdyr—all the things I'd forgotten or hadn't learned yet.

I wanted him. Each sweet, tough, powerful inch of him.

"You're not going away again anytime soon, are you?" I asked.

"I'm not planning to. Why?"

"I just wondered if I would see you on Monday."

He gave me that intense look again, then his hands flattened on the table, and he leaned back.

My stomach fell.

"Look, Kristin, I really like you, but…"

"But what?"

"This thing between us, it can't go anywhere. My life is full. I don't do relationships."

"Ever?"

He shook his head.

I frowned. Surely he just meant because I wasn't Valdyr. "Well, what if I was…different?"

"I don't want you to be different. You're perfect the way you are."

"That's nice—I think—but I meant… Is it because I'm not a part of Wolf Ridge? I noticed you're all really tight."

He grimaced. "That would make it worse, trust me. Right

now, this is the closest I could get to being with someone. And…
there's something about you. You're hard to resist."

My breath stuttered. Before, he'd said I was a temptation.
"Like a bad habit or something?"

"No. I'm sorry, that came out wrong." He scrubbed a frustrated hand through his hair. "I just meant… Ah, hel, Dahlia
should never have sent you up here."

It took a second before his meaning sank in, and then a chill
ran up my spine. "You mean you didn't tell her—text her—that
you wanted me to come up?"

He looked at me regretfully. "No."

Oh, gods. He didn't want me here. His lack of a wave when he
first saw me had been his true reaction. He might have sex with
me if I kept throwing myself at him, but that was it.

Humiliation made my stomach heave. "Right. Sorry. I won't
bother you again." Avoiding his eyes, I grabbed my purse and
rushed to the exit.

"Kristin, wait."

I ran down the stairs, spurred on by the regret in his voice.
Great. Now he pitied me. I might as well have a big freaking *L* on
my forehead.

Weaving my way through the closely packed bodies on the
dance floor, I'd just caught sight of the door when someone
grabbed my hand and spun me around. I slammed into a hard
male body and exhaled the air from my lungs. On my inhale, I
was flooded with Erik's scent. So familiar. So tantalizing.

So heartbreaking.

I stared into his eyes, which blazed down at me wildly. He
pressed one hand to the small of my back and the other to the
nape of my neck, squeezing tight.

Heat engulfed me, and I melted against him, my breasts tight,
my core pulsing with need.

"I may not have sent for you, but that doesn't mean I didn't want to." Then he captured my mouth. I opened beneath his lips and allowed him to devour me.

He could take me right here, right now, and I wouldn't stop him.

At that moment, I was completely his.

CHAPTER 11

I COULDN'T GET ENOUGH.

The heat of her mouth scorched me as I swept inside. My tongue slid across hers, sparking frissons of need that shot straight to my groin with every stroke. I burrowed deeper, squeezed tighter, as her exquisite scent invaded my nose. Each tiny tug of her hands in my hair signaled her own desire.

Raising my head, I met her eyes. Her lids were half open, her mouth parted and wet.

Mine, I thought.

Ours, my wolf rumbled.

I kissed her again, trailing hungrily over her cheek and then down her throat, nipping and nibbling. Her breathy moans ratcheted up my own arousal, hardening my body to the point of pain.

Pushing the silver dress aside, I bit down on the petal-soft juncture at the crook of her neck—finally.

She whimpered, the grinding movements of her pelvis a steady pressure against my thigh. I tried to release my jaw, but my wolf was on me hard. Instead, I bit harder, licking and suckling the skin between my teeth.

She gasped, her sexual excitement perfuming the air as she pulled me closer. I slid my hand down, covering her ass. Her short, silky skirt had risen to the tops of her thighs, and my fingers curled into soft, bare skin. Growling in response, I lifted her a few inches higher so she rode me, one leg still twined around my thigh.

"Erik," she panted in my ear.

Gyrating bodies crushed around us, lost to the thrashing music and shadowy light, some in clinches as tight as mine and Kristin's.

A part of my mind yelled at me to stop, but I was too far gone to listen.

She was too far gone.

I would make her come, then take her back upstairs and lay her over the table. Keep her body pulsing—breasts aching, core wanting. I'd strip her down, sucking every inch. Finally, when I could stand it no longer, I'd push into her swollen center and find my own release, bringing her to climax around me again and again.

Erik!

The voice barely registered at first, even though I knew whoever it was had shouted at me.

Gods damn it, Fyrstr, he's here!

Reality seeped through my sensual fog like icy fingers. I came back to myself with a thud, my instinct raging. Breathing heavily, I released Kristin. She moaned as she slid down my body and landed on her feet.

Hati stood at the club's entrance, his hair and skin shining in the shadows like moonlight, staring at me over the top of Kristin's head. Four rekkrs, including Gunn and Dane, closed in.

A second later, the Jotun darted outside.

"Stay here," I roared as Kristin blinked at me dazedly.

I darted through the bodies on the dance floor, cursing myself that I was the last one through the door.

Dahlia! Find Kristin. Keep her with you.

Is she in danger?

I don't know. Maybe. I want someone with her. The need to keep her safe beat within me.

My shoes pounded on the concrete as I darted past people and vehicles in the street. Around me, I sensed the positions of the other rekkrs in the city, some in wolf form, others as Valdyr, as they closed in on Hati from different directions.

The young rekkr who watched the door had been knocked unconscious and now groaned through the bond as he rose to his feet, hurt but not broken. Hati had most likely ridden a moonbeam directly to Savage and caught the young rekkr unaware.

Go inside, I directed him. *Guard Dahlia and the others in case Hati gets through the net and doubles back. We don't know what he's after.*

Yes, Fyrstr. He attacked from out of nowhere. I'm sorry.

He landed behind you. It's my fault. I should have realized sooner that he was here.

Guilt over my failure, and shock that my instinct had been subsumed by desire, stole through me like poison. My curse reveled in the negative emotions and surged upward, seeking to infiltrate my mind and intensify the feelings. With gritted teeth, I shoved the parasite back down.

How could I have ignored my instinct? I'd put my pack and everyone else at risk. If the young rekkr had died, his blood would have been on my hands.

And for what? A human woman?

My wolf growled, upset by my cavalier dismissal of Kristin, and I growled back. For a moment, my anger threatened to overwhelm me. But I released it to focus on the chase. As always, the Varda sought to bring down Hati before he caught a moonbeam out.

But like Skoll, Hati was smart, fast, and strong, with powerful magic. The most the pack could ever hope to do was maim him.

The sons of Fenrir, on the other hand, attempted to kill us every time.

He jumped! Gunn said. *But I got my teeth into the bastard before he rode out. He tastes like shit.*

I relayed the information to the rest of the wolves as I spun back to the club, still worried about Kristin.

Squads one and two return to Savage. Patrol in pairs up to three blocks out. Squads three and four, resume your previous routes in the city. We don't know how far he jumped or if he'll come back. He's after something.

When I caught sight of the Gothic-looking nightclub with the blood-red sign, I slowed, catching my breath. My wolf nipped me to keep going, anxious to see Kristin.

I resisted, not because I didn't want to see her, but because I wanted it too much. I hungered to finish what we'd started on the dance floor. Hel, what we'd started the moment we'd met.

It wasn't just about sex.

I wanted to talk to her, tease her, be teased in return. I wanted to find out what scared her, what delighted her. If something made her happy, I wanted to provide it, whether it was cartoon socks, baking pans, or a hammer and chisel. I wanted to invade her home, her heart, to lounge on her bed and watch her paint. Then I wanted to show her all of my special places—the splendor of my mountains, the majesty of the wild animals and birds I loved, the fierce beauty of the wilderness.

Damn it. I wanted all of her. Every soft, sexy, talented inch.

What in Odin's name was I going to do?

Obviously, I couldn't put my pack at risk. She did something to me, made me lose control and ignore my instinct. Which, until now, I'd thought impossible.

But I couldn't just disregard my wolf, a separate yet whole entity. To override the animal within could cause a schism between us, which many Valdyr would consider worse than death.

Unless I could lessen my wolf's interest in Kristin, it was a no-win situation.

The roar of a motorcycle speeding along the empty street toward the club caught my attention. Alerted by the smell of blood, I shifted midleap, muscles stretching and joints popping as I transformed into my wolf and charged into the middle of the road to intercept the bike, warning my rekkrs at the same time.

The driver wore a helmet, but I knew it was Hati by the moonlit-colored hair that whipped around his shoulders. When he saw me rushing to cut him off, he smiled, going even faster.

The Jotun must have planned his earlier attack to draw the rekkrs away from the club so he could get in. I was only there because I'd been the last to leave.

My big padded feet hit the pavement hard. Ears flattened to my head, teeth exposed, my huge, lupine body a powerful bullet aimed for the motorcycle.

Hati leaned over the handlebars and gunned it, trying to outrace me. I adjusted my angle of approach to catch the Jotun. Fear that I wouldn't make it roared through me, giving me that extra push. The bike zoomed by. At the last moment, my heavy shoulder crashed into the back tire. The motorcycle swerved and fell, skidding across the pavement, and taking Hati with it. Then it bounced up, going end over end to land in a twisted, fiery heap farther down the street.

I also fell, hip smashing and back leg crunching as I rolled to a stop in the gutter. I dragged myself onto all fours and snarled at Hati, who pushed the bike's burning wreckage off him.

Gritting my teeth against the pain, I lurched toward the huge Jotun.

"Fyrstr!" the young rekkr I'd instructed to guard Dahlia and Kristin called out to me from the door of the club. He ran down the stairs.

Stay there! I yelled. *Don't let him past you!*

The rekkr stopped, the look on his face agonized.

I can handle him. Get back to the door.

The young wolf did as he was instructed. Hati scowled. He lifted his hand and hurled a ball of flaming, white light at me. The shot fizzled weakly, and I easily avoided it. It gave me hope. The Jotun was injured—worse than I was.

So why hadn't he beamed out?

Whatever he wanted had to be in the club.

I shape-shifted so I could speak but stayed partially in the helmingr, my wolf and Valdyr forms blinking in and out on top of each other.

"You're done, Hati. No way can you get inside before the rest of the pack arrives. You and Skoll failed."

"You think you can keep her from us? We'll come back every sun and moon until no one else is left. Your entire pack will be killed guarding a single female. Give her to me now, and we'll agree to a truce. Long enough for you to find the other packs and strengthen not just the Varda but your bond with the lost Valdyr as well. Just one of your females—in exchange for your entire pack and species."

Dahlia was the only female Valdyr in the club.

The shock that Hati and Skoll were after her hit hard, followed by fear that I'd miscalculated.

Protect Dahlia! I screamed at the young rekkr. *Tell me when you have her.*

I advanced on Hati, my stomach tied in knots. Sweet Frigg, I'd left my cousin alone with Kristin and Gina. What if this whole thing had been a setup from the start, and I'd been reeled in like a horny pup? Kristin may have lied and seduced me on Hati's orders.

My wolf growled at the suggestion. I ignored it.

I've got her, Fyrstr. She and the two women are secure.

Separate them quickly. Take Dahlia to the safe room.

Okay... They're not happy about it.

I don't care.

Furious at my dismissal of Kristin's safety, my wolf snapped at me, but then Hati hurled another white fireball, this one stronger and better aimed than the first. My wolf and I had to fight together or risk being burned to ash.

Just in time, the other rekkrs arrived, closing in fast. Hati caught their scents, and he was momentarily distracted. Shifting in an instant, I lunged at him. Another projectile singed the fur on my tail, but I used my strength to bowl Hati over, ripping my teeth through the Jotun's throat.

Hot blood squirted into my mouth an instant before Hati disappeared in a flash of moonlight. Landing hard on the empty pavement, my back leg crumpled beneath me. I gagged on the foul taste in my mouth.

It wasn't the first time I'd gotten a piece of Hati, and with Odin's blessing, it wouldn't be the last. Hopefully the Jotun would travel as far away in the beam as he could, holing up somewhere on the other side of the world to heal.

Like the Valdyr, the sons of Fenrir could repair grievous injury. Unlike the Valdyr, they never aged. That's not to say they couldn't die, just that it hadn't happened in the thousands of years since they were born.

"Erik!" Gunn knelt beside me, his body in the helmingr. Dane stood at his shoulder.

I shifted forms to lie naked in the street, too tired to care about modesty. "You're right, the fucker does taste like shit. Worth it, though. I got him in the jugular. He'll be out of commission for a while."

I glanced up, noticing the rekkrs—wolves and Valdyr—had positioned themselves around the club.

As always, I was amazed that no humans had seen the fight. Thanks to Odin.

Literally. The Allfather didn't intercede in the clashes between the Valdyr and the sons of Fenrir, but his magic kept the conflicts secret.

My senior rekkrs, including Dane, gathered around as Gunn helped me into a sitting position. Pain shot up my right side, and for a moment I thought I might throw up. "They're after Dahlia. He asked me to trade for her. He said he would call a truce for a while if I gave her up."

"What the fuck did you tell him?" Dane asked, his tone accusing.

If I hadn't hurt so much, I would have punched him. "I said, 'Here are the keys to the safe room. Go get her.'" I glared at Dane. "What the fuck do you think I told him?"

"She's in a secure place?"

"I just said that, didn't I?"

Linnea stepped between us, her long red hair wilder than usual around her hazy shoulders. "What in Odin's name would Hati want with Dahlia? What possible use is she?"

Both Dane and I growled at her.

Linnea continued, "I meant what use is she to him? She's not a fighter. She's not working on any of our scientific projects. She's an interior decorator, for Freyja's sake."

Everyone looked at me. No way could I tell them Dahlia foresaw the future.

Linnea stamped her foot in frustration. "How can we protect her if we don't know? I'm her Alpha female. Tell me." Understanding dawned in her eyes. "Unless this is about her magic. Is that what it is?"

I raised a brow. "If you want to talk about magic, Linnea, why don't you start by telling us about yours?"

Her mouth clamped shut.

No one asked a female about her magic. If she chose to share it with you, that was her choice—and your privilege. Of course, sometimes her talent was obvious if she used it in front of you. At other times, as in Dahlia's case, no one might ever guess.

So, how did Hati and Skoll know about it?

Dane turned without a word and marched toward the back door of the club. He was also in the helmingr, but I realized the Ulf-einn still wore his sunglasses. How the hel had he managed that? They should have fallen off with his clothes when he shifted.

Ah, hel. I had too much to think about without trying to riddle out that mystery.

I was still no closer to figuring out Odin's prophecy. I had to somehow convince Dahlia to stay safe in the den for the rest of her life, and I had no clue what to do about Kristin. Or if she was a threat to the pack.

I nodded to one of the other rekkrs. "Go with Dane. Show him where he can grab some clothes. Then send some of the junior rekkrs on pickup duty." Too many piles of underwear, pants, shirts, and shoes in the streets would make people suspicious.

After being helped to my feet, I tested my leg. It hurt, but I'd had worse injuries. It was nothing a few days wouldn't heal.

With a sigh, I looked at the club. What now? Fighting Hati had been the easy part. Walking away from Kristin would be nearly impossible.

But I had to try.

CHAPTER 12

"Are you okay?" I rushed toward Erik across the brightly lit storage room filled with boxes, barstools, and cleaning supplies. His hair was wet, he wore different clothes—jeans, a blue T-shirt, and boots—and he seemed to be favoring his right side, which worried me.

When I reached him, I laid my palm on his chest. He abruptly stepped back.

Hurt crashed through me, and I dropped my hand. He was back to pushing me away. It grated that I couldn't just ask what was wrong, that we still had secrets between us.

All because of my stupid promise to Gina.

I scowled at my sister, who lounged against a locked steel door between a young male Valdyr, whose "Security" shirt was soaked with nervous sweat, and Dane, who'd arrived fifteen minutes ago, dressed like Erik and smelling angry. He'd immediately pushed Gina away from the lock she'd been fiddling with, glared at the young Valdyr who'd failed to restrain her, and then stood in front of the keypad.

Because Dahlia was behind that steel door.

"What's happening?" I asked. "You run out of here like a bat on fire, and then Eddie"—I pointed at the nervous Valdyr—"arrives and shoves Dahlia into a safe room." I clenched a hand at my midriff. "Does this have anything to do with that psychopath at Wolf Ridge? Is he after her?"

I couldn't stop fear from cracking my voice. It was bad enough that Hans hunted me. I could protect myself and wanted him to attack. But if he got ahold of Dahlia, the sweet female would be easy pickings.

Erik lifted his hand as if to soothe me, then shoved it through his hair. "Don't worry about Dahlia. We'll protect her."

I lowered my gaze, not wanting him to see that he'd hurt me all over again. I wanted to help. I *needed* to help. Dahlia wouldn't be safe until the monster was dead.

I glanced again at Gina, who shook her head. As usual, my sister knew what I was thinking.

Frustration mounted. I would keep my promise if it killed me. *But it better not kill Dahlia too.*

It was a tough choice. I owed my sister my life, but Dahlia also felt like a sister.

Gina pushed away from the safe room and crossed to my side. "We should go. It's getting late."

"You promised me a dance," Gunn said, appearing in the doorway that led back to the club. Like Erik, his hair was wet, and his clothes were different.

Gina turned to him, jutting out her hip in a sexy yet confrontational way. "That's not how I remember it. You said, 'Promise me a dance,' and I said, 'Go suck on it.'"

"And I promised to suck on whatever you wanted—during our dance."

"Which I may have allowed, oh, say, an hour ago, but then you ran out of here...so I made do with Eddie." She turned and ran her fingertips over the young Valdyr, who flushed bright red. "Did you like sucking on me, puppy?"

"I, no…uh…that's not what—"

Gunn ignored him, not the least bit perturbed, and strolled toward Gina. When he reached her, he dug his hands into her hair, tilted her head up, and kissed her.

I gasped, expecting Gina to shove him away or zap him, blowing our cover. Which, when I thought about it, would be a good thing. Then I could tell Erik everything.

But to my shock, my sister did neither. Instead, she just kind of melted against him in the same way I had melted against Erik earlier on the dance floor.

Apparently, Gunn could kiss.

Unable to help myself, I glanced sideways to find Erik staring at me. Oh, gods. Was he thinking about our kiss, too? About how I'd totally lost my mind?

A moment later, Gina moaned softly. I looked back as Gunn raised his head, a look of satisfaction on his face. "You're not wearing lipstick. Your lips really are that red."

"Yes. Are you done?" Despite her words, Gina sounded breathless. Still leaning on him, she managed to look bored, but I knew my sister well enough to know she was faking it. She couldn't move without falling on her ass.

"For now," he said. "And Gina, you won't be able to stand when I kiss your other lips either." He released her, moved to the safe room, and punched in a silent, hidden code. The door swung open.

Dahlia rushed out. "What happened?"

Erik held out his hand to her, and when she moved to his side, he pulled her into a tight hug. "We'll talk about it later."

Gina got her sea legs back and trailed after Gunn toward the steel-and-concrete-reinforced room. "What kind of locking mechanism is that?"

"The secret kind," he said.

"Afraid I'll crack the code and get you into trouble?"

"Not a chance. Besides, you're the one who's going to get into trouble. Your fake PI license won't get you out of every jam."

Gina played with the front zipper on her bustier, threatening to reveal even more cleavage. "No, but this will."

Gunn stared at the bountiful sight, then dragged his eyes up and huffed out a breath. "It won't work on everyone."

Gina smiled and bit her lip. She stretched onto her tiptoes and leaned closer.

I knew what was coming and resisted shouting a warning. If I became part of this pack, the males had to learn that my sister played by her own rules.

"Then I'll do this." Gina's tongue darted out to taste him as she dragged her hand down his chest. Just before she reached the bulge in his pants, she shifted her weight and knocked his legs out from under him. He crashed to the ground with a curse.

Hands on her hips, she stood over him.

"That'll work," he said.

A snort sounded beside me, and I turned to catch Erik's amused gaze. My lips twitched with amusement.

"All right. Let's blow this Popsicle stand," Gina said, pulling my attention back to her. Hips swaying, she walked past Eddie, chucked him under the chin, and then grabbed Dahlia and me by the hands.

For all of Gina's brash, outrageous ways, she was a mother hen, and Dahlia had become one of her chicks.

"We're having a sleepover," she said. "Baby dolls, pillow fights, girl-on-girl action. You know, the usual."

"Gods, I think I love you," Gunn said, still lying on the floor.

"Hold on," I said. I looked at Erik. "My place is secure, but obviously, if Dahlia's safer with you at Wolf Ridge, she should stay there."

"I think she should come home, but it's her choice."

All eyes turned to Dahlia, who fidgeted uncomfortably. Her

eyes darted to Dane, who'd stepped forward, looking as if he'd been cut from granite behind those shades. "Um, well, it might be better for me to go home, but I left my stuff at your loft. Maybe you could bring it with you to work on Monday."

It was the answer Dane wanted, and he softened from granite to plain rock.

I resisted rolling my eyes. Gods save me from domineering men.

Gunn scrambled to his feet. "No need. We'll drop off Kristin and Gina to make sure they're safe and pick up your stuff while we're there."

He glanced at Erik, and another private conversation took place. This could get old fast. It was like talking to someone while they were texting.

"Okay, but you'll have to drive," I said. "We came in a cab."

Gunn shut the safe room door. "No problem. We've got a big-ass Range Rover."

Gina rolled her eyes. "You know what they say about men with big trucks."

"Yeah. They've got spectacularly big dicks. I'll take you for a ride anytime, baby."

Erik sighed and looked pointedly at Gunn and Gina. "You two should take your own car. I'll ride with Kristin and Dahlia." Then he tucked Dahlia under his arm, and they left.

"Me, too," Dane said, stepping after them.

Oh, great. Just like a double date. Except my date was playing hard to get. Trouble was, my wolf didn't take well to being ignored.

Neither did I.

Erik was inside my loft.

I glanced around, both nervous and excited, and tried to see my place through his eyes. It was a disaster. Makeup littered the kitchen table, empty wine glasses sat on the coffee table, dirty dishes filled the sink, and Chinese takeout cartons peeked up from the top of the garbage can.

And clothes were scattered everywhere.

Why hadn't I straightened up before we'd left?

Grimacing, I looked at Erik, who was peering in the opposite direction toward my bed. I'd pulled the screen back earlier, and the bed was covered in the clothes and shopping bags that Gina had discarded as she'd gone through our purchases and ransacked my closet in an attempt to find the perfect outfit for each of us to wear.

She'd succeeded.

Erik shoved his hands through his hair so the usually neat strands stood on end, then lifted his gaze past my bed to the paintings I'd stacked against the wall and on an easel by the window. It felt like a personal perusal. His eyes landed on the one I'd been working on when he'd stopped by the other night—the colors of magic—and I wondered if he recognized it. Could he see the magic too? When he looked back at me moments later, his eyes had darkened, his expression a little feral.

I blushed, cursing my fair skin that showed every emotion.

Why couldn't I shut him out as easily as he did me?

All six of us—Gina and Gunn included—had ended up piled into a giant Range Rover for the drive over.

Erik hadn't said one word to me, or given me a sideways glance. And I'd been closer to him than I was now.

"I won't be long," Dahlia said as she walked to the bed, most likely to find her clothes in the jumble.

Good luck.

I would have helped, but it meant stepping past Erik, and I wasn't ready to do that.

Dane had planted himself by the door as if he expected an attack, and he continually scanned the broad expanse of bare windows. Glad to have something to do, I crossed the open area and drew the drapes, shutting out the night. Then I picked up a paintbrush and fiddled with it, my eyes anywhere but on Erik.

Gunn passed me, examining and touching everything—my paintings, art supplies, lamps, pottery. Standing behind the kitchen island, Gina eyed him suspiciously, eating a leftover garlic prawn that she'd fished out from a carton in the fridge.

"Hey, hotshot," she said as she picked up a silver pen from the counter and tossed it at him. "You dropped this."

He caught it in one hand. "I didn't drop it. I *placed* it there so you would write down your number. It's a nice pen. You can keep it." He tossed it back.

Gina raised her eyebrow, then grabbed a pad by the phone and scribbled something on it. Ripping off the top sheet, she held it out to him with a sweet smile. He strode toward her, took the note, and read it.

"'Suck my ass.' Is this an invitation? Because we've been over this. I'm quite happy to indulge your oral fixation."

"It's a statement of derision. But thanks for the pen. I'll keep it." She walked to the sink, dropped the pen in, and turned on the garbage disposal. The sound of grinding metal ripped through the loft, making Gunn wince.

"Oops," she said.

I hurried into the kitchen. "For gods' sakes, Gina."

She switched off the disposal and then fished out the broken pieces of metal, which included a mangled recording device that she pointed to. Filling a bowl with water, she plunked the bug into it.

My chest tightened. Erik obviously didn't trust me, and he was right not to. I'd lied to him again and again. But had I done something to make him suspicious, or was this just a routine check on anyone who got close to the den?

"Okay, I have everything," Dahlia said.

The shy Valdyr moved to stand beside Erik. I lifted my gaze to his. He stared back. "I'll see you Monday. Have a good weekend." He shifted his gaze to Gina. "It was nice seeing you again. I'm sure it won't be the last time."

"If any harm comes to Kristin, you can bet your life it won't."

Flushing, I pinched my sister, who looked at me with wide eyes. "What? I'm just saying there's a lot of danger swirling around. The big boss and I understand each other." She faced Erik. "Don't we?"

Erik nodded, then grasped Dahlia's hand and turned toward the door.

"Wait." Running back to Gina and me, Dahlia wrapped us in a big, three-way hug. "I had so much fun today—and tonight. I think it's the most fun I've ever had. Thank you."

Gina tugged on one of her ponytails. "Next time, we'll get you hooked up with a bad boy. Then you'll really have a good time."

I held back a smile when I heard Dane's subsonic growl.

On their way out, Gunn patted Gina's ass. She lifted a hand to zap him, but I caught her fingers and squeezed. At the last moment, Erik glanced back. I bit my lip to keep from telling him everything.

When the door shut behind the Valdyr, Gina put a finger to her lips in a shushing motion. She retraced the route Gunn had taken in the loft, picking up everything he'd touched and examining it.

She found the first bug mixed in with all the makeup on the table. It was ingenious—an actual blusher in a pretty pink shade with a microphone under the back cover. I would never have looked at it twice. The second bug was placed on top of a lamp. The third was an actual camera on my bookshelf against the wall. Gina gave it the finger, then pocketed it.

Paranoid, I went through every book in the loft to make sure a new fake one hadn't been added. In the end, I decided there had to be a quicker way. Using my second sight and my wolf's hearing, I scanned the room, listening for electronic disturbances in the air.

Yup. Over there. Following the high-pitched buzz to my only plant, I found a tiny bug clipped on the stem and passed it to Gina.

One last irritating buzz remained, but I had a hard time pinpointing the source. Once I realized it moved when my sister did, I found a bug stuck to the back of Gina's belt, most likely placed there when Gunn had patted her ass.

Resourceful fucker.

Gina scowled at it. Grabbing the notepad and a pen, she wrote, *Any more?*

I shook my head. Then my sister added, *Follow my lead.*

She gave me a wicked smile as she placed all the listening devices on the coffee table, not including the mangled pen and the tiny camera she'd pocketed—a fortune's worth of electronic devices that Gina could use in her own line of work.

Sitting on the loveseat, she motioned me over to the opposite couch, leaned across the table, and moaned into the assembled microphones. "Kristin, you're so hot. I want to take your clothes off and plant my face in all your hotness. Let's get naked and rub hot oil on each other. That's hot."

My jaw dropped as Gina made faces to go along with her gods-awful dialogue—lips pouted, eyes closed, looking and sounding like a starlet in a bad porno.

Laughter bubbled up, and I shoved a pillow over my face. I hoped they were listening. It served Gunn right. Erik too. Although Dahlia was too sweet for such perversions.

"You are so bad," I finally said.

"Oh yeah. I'm a bad, bad, hot girl. Spank me with that hot paintbrush." Gina hit the loveseat with her hand. "Harder, sister. Spank me harder!"

Erik

Naked. Hot. Oil.

The words seeped into my brain and took root. Everyone else in the car faded away as I remembered Kristin riding me on the dance floor, her lips parted, cheeks flushed.

"I want to eat your love muffin—hot out of the oven. Lap you up like a hot little kitten," Gina's voice moaned again through the microphone. "Meow."

A snort sounded from the back seat of the Range Rover, and I glanced back. Dahlia had covered her face with her hand, and her shoulders shook with laughter. Gunn sat beside her, eyes wide and pupils dilated, wearing earphones connected to a sound system that lay in the middle of the seat. Dane was driving and eyed them through the rearview mirror.

"Do me now," Gina said over the airwaves. "Tongue me like a…like a…"

"A tiger?" Kristin suggested.

Another snort from Dahlia. Gunn's eyes glazed over. He was getting Gina's performance up close and personal through the earphones.

They're faking it. Of course, they are. Aren't they?

Gina had known the pen was a microphone. She wouldn't have dropped it in the garbage disposal otherwise. A thousand bucks down the drain. She'd probably gone through the loft as soon as we'd left, hunting down the rest of the recording devices. Which was why the camera Gunn had placed on the bookshelf wasn't working.

Guilt niggled at me for spying on Kristin, but we needed to know if she was involved with Hati and Skoll. It wasn't a matter of privacy. It was a matter of life and death. Trusting the wrong person could mean the end of the world—literally.

Gina moaned, bringing my attention back to her performance. She reached a breathy, panting crescendo before she screamed out a fake climax at the top of her lungs.

"Fuck!" Gunn yelled, tearing off his headphones and covering his ears. "Thor's balls, I think she ruptured my eardrums!"

My ears were ringing from the cry, so I could only imagine how loud it must have been for Gunn.

Then Gina sighed. I could hear Kristin laughing in the background, which made me smile.

"Sweet heavens, that was a good one. Was it good for you, too?" Gina asked.

Gunn scowled at the machine.

As if she could see him, she added. "No? Well, that's what you get for listening in. Pervert." Then the line crackled and went dead.

Gunn dropped his head. "I swear, she's a witch."

CHAPTER 13

<u>Kristin</u>

THREE DAYS LATER, I SAT BEHIND THE DRAWN TARP ON THE SECOND level of my scaffold at Wolf Ridge, listening to the murmur of voices in the building and the echoing steps as people walked across the rotunda. I wore my best jeans and T-shirt, and my freshly washed hair floated down my back.

I'd jumped out of bed this morning, eager to get to work, finally free to tell Erik everything. Except I'd been here for five hours and seen neither hide nor fur of him—or Dahlia, Gunn, or Dane.

What was going on?

And I'd been too keyed up to work, staring sightlessly at the mural until I'd given up. Another day wasted.

Despite the craziness of Friday night, the weekend had been fun. Gina and I had gone hiking in the mountains, seen a couple of movies, and had a Häagen-Dazs fest as we people-watched in the park. We'd also talked ourselves blue in the face, randomly blurting out bits and pieces of Gina's impromptu porno and laughing hysterically.

Earlier, I'd dropped my sister off at the airport to catch a flight back to Denver. She'd wanted to stay, but she was in the middle of a big case. I missed her already.

With a sigh, I lay back on the metal walkway and let my mind drift over the different scenarios of what Erik would say and do when I told him I was Valdyr. They all ended with him kissing me.

Then, the sweet smell and sound of Dahlia as she entered the den teased my senses, and I bolted up.

Hopping down from the scaffold, I peeked through the tarp. My friend crossed the rotunda dressed in khaki shorts, sandals, and a red tank top, looking stiff-legged and harassed. Linnea kept pace with her, talking nonstop, while another huge male walked closely behind her.

With a desperate glance toward my area, Dahlia tugged on one of her ponytails. She'd redone her hair in the same style from Friday night, almost as if she was reliving the memory.

Thrusting the tarp aside, I rushed toward her. "Dahlia!"

She turned, a relieved smile lighting up her pretty face. But then both Linnea, wearing Spandex workout gear over her strong, curvy figure, and the other large Valdyr stepped in front of her.

I stopped. Behind the wall of Valdyr protection, I heard Dahlia sigh. She sounded close to tears. I frowned, and my wolf snarled protectively.

What were they doing to her?

"Get out of my way," I said, planting my hands on my hips.

Linnea smiled, obviously jonesing for a fight. "Or what? You gonna take me down?"

Shockingly, I realized I could do just that. I could suck Linnea's colorful aura right out of her body until she dropped. And because I wouldn't have to shift to my wolf, none of the unkyssed males would turn feral.

Ah, hel, who was I kidding? I would never attack the Valdyr in such a way, no matter how big a pain in the ass Linnea was. Stealing someone's life force seemed like a super-villain thing to do. I'd save that particular trick for Hans.

Instead, I curled my fingers together and flicked the gorgeous redhead on the end of her nose—like I was scolding a misbehaving puppy. My wolf fell over onto her side in amusement.

Linnea's eyes darkened furiously, but before she could retaliate, Dahlia, who'd been all but forgotten, darted between us to protect me. "Stop!" she yelled.

Ignoring her, Linnea reached out to push Dahlia aside, but the petite Valdyr snapped at her like a wolf.

My jaw dropped. Sweet, shy Dahlia, challenging her Alpha female?

It obviously shocked Linnea and the other Valdyr, too, for they both came to a halt.

"If you touch her, Linnea, I swear I will scream. And I won't stop until everyone comes running. Do you really want that?"

Her voice cracked at the end, and I put a hand on her waist in support. She trembled like a leaf. My wolf growled again. Glaring at Linnea, I was tempted to let my wolf shine through my eyes.

Yeah, great idea. Tell everyone I'm Valdyr before I speak to Erik.

Throwing her palms in the air, Dahlia added, "What exactly do you think is going to happen? We're in the middle of the... Wolf Ridge. And it's not like I'm going to make a run for it. I can barely walk after the workouts you put me through the last three days."

I gasped. "You're working out? Good for you!"

"It's not good. I can barely get out of bed in the morning."

"That'll go away."

Linnea snapped her fingers, drawing our attention. "Would you focus? We're in the middle of a discussion here."

I huffed. "This isn't a discussion. This is you bossing Dahlia around. That...bad guy from Friday night isn't going to be able to get in here." Or past me. If Hans dared come near Dahlia, I would take him out, whether I'd spoken to Erik or not.

Glaring at me, Linnea tapped her foot. "Don't you have work to do?"

"I'm having a slow day. Let me talk to my friend, and my productivity may pick up."

"Fine. But don't leave the rotunda. I'm watching you." She directed the male Valdyr to the outer door and then stood on the opposite side of the sunken circle, pinning us with a heavy gaze.

Dahlia grabbed my hand and drew me in the other direction. By the time I noticed how closely we stood to the stone wolf that guarded the circle, it was too late. It made me uneasy, but with Dahlia there, I hoped the talisman wouldn't consider me a threat and attack me like it had before.

"Did you see that? I stood up to Linnea. You and Gina are wearing off on me," Dahlia whispered.

"Don't get yourself in trouble on my account. I can defend myself." I took a step into the sunken circle so we were on eye level. "Linnea won't be mad enough to hurt you, will she?"

"She'll probably make me lift heavier weights and run another mile, but that's all. Ever since Friday, she's been obsessed with teaching me how to defend myself. I swear she's trying to kill me. She makes that badass personal trainer on TV look like a fluffy kitten." Then she raised a brow. "Speaking of kittens... 'Lap you up like a hot little kitten'?"

My eyes widened, and then I burst out laughing.

Dahlia laughed, too, then moaned. "Oh, gods. Don't make me laugh. It hurts."

"You started it."

"I know." We took deep breaths to calm down, and then Dahlia said, "Harder, sister. Spank me harder!" and we broke into fits again.

I wiped away tears as I gasped for breath. "I swear when she started slapping the couch, I just about peed my pants."

"You should have seen Gunn. He totally believed it—or maybe he wanted to believe it—but when Gina screamed at the end, it just about ruptured his eardrums. He… he…" She tried to get the words out but couldn't stop laughing long enough to finish a sentence. "He was wearing headphones."

I bent over, hands on my knees. Killed by hilarity. What a way to go. "Thank Odin, the damage won't be permanent." When I realized what I'd said and how much it gave away, my laughter faded. I looked at Dahlia…who held my gaze and shrugged.

Straightening, I glanced back at Linnea, who stood with her arms across her chest and a scowl on her face. Had she heard that? Our laughter had been loud, possibly drowning out the words.

Facing my friend again, I whispered, "I'm going to speak to Erik today."

"Okay."

"Do you know what I'm talking about?"

"Not really, but I trust you. And I know you're supposed to be here no matter what anybody else thinks."

Tears flooded my eyes. Dahlia truly was a gift. Dane was a fool for not claiming her.

I pulled her into a tight hug. "Thank you. Gina's been my only family for a long time. Now I have you too."

Dahlia squeezed back. "I feel the same way. I never really fit in here before. I had my parents, obviously, plus Erik and Aren, my other cousin, but now Erik's the only one left. Oh, and Britta and Robbie. You'll love them. Although they're not actually family. And Rolf, of course. He's stuck with me, no matter what."

She reached out to pat the stone wolf on the head.

Instinct roared through me, and without thinking, I yanked Dahlia's hand away before she could touch the statue. But upon making contact with me, the sweet Valdyr gasped. Her body stiffened, and her eyelids closed and fluttered. Then she dropped to the slate floor. I caught her just in time, crying out in shock and fear.

"Dahlia!"

Staring down at my friend's pale face, I tapped her cheek. When she didn't respond, I turned toward Linnea for help, only to be hit by what felt like a Mack truck as the Alpha female pinned me to the cold stone tiles and yanked my arms behind my back.

"Get off me," I yelled. "Dahlia's hurt."

"Linnea, what happened?" Erik shouted from above.

Then, the ground beneath my cheek shuddered, and I heard feet pounding toward us. Had he jumped from the very top?

"Something's wrong with Dahlia," I screamed.

I tried to rear back, but my shoulder felt like it was being torn from its socket. My wolf barked furiously, but we both knew I couldn't shift. Gods, I couldn't do anything.

Shifting focus to my second sight for a wider view, I saw Erik drag Dahlia into his arms, but he was scowling at Linnea. "Ease up, Linnea. You're hurting her."

Linnea loosened her grip—barely. "She attacked Dahlia."

"I did not! She had a seizure or something and fell. What's wrong with her?"

"I'm not sure," he said. Other Valdyr gathered around as he patted her face. "Wake up, sunshine. Dahlia. Open. Your. Eyes."

As if unable to disobey a direct command, Dahlia moaned. Her eyelids fluttered, and she gazed at Erik. With a gasp, she sat up and pressed her hand to her head. "Oh, gods. What's going on?"

"You fell. Did...someone hurt you?" His hesitation as he asked the question pained me almost as much as Linnea twisting my arm.

"No, I just—" Dahlia looked around wildly. "Where's Kristin?"

Linnea grunted and yanked harder. "See. I told you."

I gritted my teeth, refusing to cry out. Then Dahlia flew toward Linnea. "Get off her!"

Linnea shifted just enough for me to twist around and push with my feet, throwing the Alpha female backward. I scrambled toward Dahlia. Behind me, Linnea growled.

"Everyone, stay calm," Erik commanded. A hush fell over the group. "Dahlia, tell me what happened."

"I just passed out. You know, from my thing." She whispered the last three words.

"What thing?" I whispered back, taking Dahlia's hands in my own. "Are you sick?"

She shook her head as Erik looked behind me. "Relax, Linnea. She passed out, that's all." He stood, lifting his cousin in his arms as if she weighed nothing, his biceps flexing against his tight black workout shirt. "Call for Kat and send her to my office when she gets here." Then he strode toward the stairs, wearing high-tech runners and black sweats.

I ran after him, clutching his elbow. "I need to talk to you. It's important."

He kept going, not even sparing me a sideways glance. "Later."

"I have to speak to you now!"

He reached the staircase and continued upward. I followed him. "Erik, you don't underst—"

A hand grabbed me from behind and pulled me back to the main level. Linnea blocked the stairwell, glaring at me. "You're not allowed up there."

Burning with frustration, I crossed my arms over my chest and watched Erik's retreating back. Dahlia peered down at me over his shoulder.

"Fine," I shouted at him. "But I'm not leaving until you talk to me."

I turned and marched toward the mural, closing the tarp behind me. Grabbing my biggest hammer and chisel, I climbed to the top of my scaffold and started hacking away at the rock wall.

Hopefully, I wouldn't butcher the whole thing in my fury.

———

Erik

I settled Dahlia in one of my office chairs and sat next to her. I tried to shut out the feel of Kristin's hand gripping my arm and the hurt in her voice when I'd refused to listen to her, but it was impossible.

Blowing out a frustrated breath, I made myself focus on my cousin. "Has this ever happened before?"

"Not really. So far, it's been different every time. Sometimes I sort of drift into a daydream, or I have this persistent feeling, kind of a knowing, that won't go away until I've acknowledged it. This time, it came on fast and strong. Suddenly, I was just there."

"What do you mean?"

"I was in some kind of a prison with tall, colorful walls. But I wasn't me. I was someone else, looking out through their eyes. And another being was in the prison with me. I couldn't see a face, just a tall and threatening presence. I kept thinking, 'Trapped again.'"

"You're sure it wasn't you?"

"Yes."

"Then who was it?"

Dahlia clenched her hands. "Kristin."

I stopped breathing. My wolf did too. "Are you sure?"

She nodded, looking like she might cry.

I pinched the bridge of my nose and tried to gain control of my emotions, but they careened all over the place—disbelief, anger, fear. My curse bubbled up, and tried to take hold of the negative feelings, but I shoved down the foul darkness. No way was I losing control to that parasite.

Not while Kristin was in danger.

I had to keep her safe—at least until I knew for sure if she worked for Hati and Skoll.

A knock sounded at the door. "Come in."

The door opened, and a willowy thin Valdyr female about Kristin's height stepped through, carrying a black bag and wearing gray pants with a white blouse. She had short dark hair, olive-toned skin, and bright blue eyes that somehow seemed sad even when she smiled.

She'd been with the Varda a few years now, but I still knew little about her private life—other than the fact that she was kyssed, yet she had no mate. I'd asked her about it when she first joined the pack, and Kat had simply said that her mate loved another.

I'd never brought it up again and forbid anyone else from asking about it. I could only imagine the pain she felt and didn't want her to relive it.

"Dahlia, how are you?" Kat asked as she crouched beside Dahlia's chair, a stethoscope around her neck, her hands and voice gentle.

"I'm fine now, Kat, really. I passed out because, well, it has to do with my magic. It's just something I have to learn to manage."

"Okay, but you don't mind if I check you out anyway, do you? It would make me feel better."

"Sure."

As Kat listened to Dahlia's heart, took her blood pressure, and looked into her eyes, I switched on my computer and accessed the camera that sat above Kristin's mural.

She appeared on screen, her glorious blond hair pulled back, a mask and goggles over her face, and a hammer and chisel in her hands. She was kneeling on the top level of her scaffold as she pounded on the rock. Angry energy radiated off her. It was all I could do to not go down and put all that passion to better use.

I sighed and clenched my fingers in my hair. I'd have to talk to her and see if I could figure out who would want to harm her.

No point in doing it now, though. She'd probably brain me with that hammer.

I'd wait until she was done.

The day passed agonizingly slowly. It was almost midnight now, and I paced my office, squeezing an orange stress ball in my hand. My wolf prowled and chuffed inside of me, feeling as edgy and aggressive as I did.

Hati and Skoll threatened my pack, Dahlia, and possibly Kristin too.

Even the den wasn't secure.

The clanging of Kristin's chisel was the only thing that kept me from losing it entirely. The sound let me know she was here. Safe. Not locked in a prison somewhere with a dangerous enemy.

My wolf barked, and I squeezed the ball so hard it popped, the gel inside squirting over my hand. With a muttered curse, I dropped the mangled mess into the garbage and then shifted my hand into the helmingr so the goo on my fingers dripped off.

The last three days had been hel. Luckily, Hati had been injured badly enough that we'd only had to deal with Skoll during daylight hours. But the Jotun had tried twice to get into the compound. He'd also appeared repeatedly in Missoula and the surrounding mountains, which confused me.

The bastard had to know we wouldn't leave Dahlia unprotected. Which meant we'd keep her in the den. So why look elsewhere?

Something niggled at me, but I couldn't nail it down. Too much other stuff whirled in my brain—and it always came back to Kristin. Gods, what was I going to do about her?

She wasn't mine. I couldn't keep her here and protect her indefinitely.

The clanging stopped, and I waited for it to start up again. After half a minute of silence, I leapt over my desk and ran out the door to lean over the railing, eyes intent on her workspace. She was still behind the tarp. I could sense her—her scent, her movement—almost as if I felt the displacement of air as she moved through it.

My body stirred, imagining that same air moving across me. Caressing me. Followed by her fingers and tongue. In the club, her body had felt like heaven against mine—the hard buds of her nipples and her soft breasts crushed to my chest. The heat at her core, hot and wet, only for me. I'd smelled her, had been inches away from sliding my fingers into that moist heat.

I could keep her here—keep her safe. I just had to ask her to stay.

It was what I wanted, what my wolf wanted. All weekend, I'd told myself to stay away, that she might be our enemy. And even if she wasn't, I had no right to a human woman I'd only end up hurting.

But things had changed. More was at stake than just losing myself in her. She was in danger.

Without thinking, I vaulted over the railing and dropped four stories to the ground below. Outside, my rekkrs patrolled and guarded the entrance to the den.

Moving decisively across the rotunda, my aggression barely contained, I dragged the tarp open. Kristin stood at the edge of the scaffold on the second level, staring down at me, eyes turbulent, body ready for me. I could smell her anger and desire, the intoxicating mixture as sweet to me as honey mead.

She'd discarded her mask and tools, but her hair was still messily restrained, her white T-shirt was dirty as if she'd used it to wipe the dust and sweat from her face, and her rune necklace was askew on its leather cord.

"What? You think it's finally time to talk?" she asked, cocking her hip belligerently.

It made me want to dominate her. To have her cock those hips, all right, but toward me and ready for my possession.

"Come here," I growled.

"Why, so you can escort me out? It's almost midnight—time to send the interloper home."

"You're not going anywhere. Get down here now, Kristin, or I'm coming up."

She continued to look at me, those golden hazel eyes bright with frustration. She balled her hands by her sides. "What do you want from me?" Her words trembled with emotion. "I have so much to tell you, and you won't even give me five minutes. Now you're here like a possessive Alpha wolf, telling me to stay. But for how long? What the hel do you want, Erik?"

My breath caught at her apt description of me. She saw so much. But I couldn't promise her anything—only pain in the end. Still, the word tore up from my gut.

"Everything."

Her throat moved as she swallowed, making me want to bite it. Not hard, but hard enough so she knew she was mine.

Reaching back, she tugged the tie from her hair, running her fingers through the wavy strands until they spread out like a cloak around her shoulders. I wanted to burrow my hands in it.

"I'm going to hold you to that," she said. Then she closed her eyes and jumped.

CHAPTER 14

Kristin

ERIK GROWLED JUST BEFORE HE CAUGHT ME IN HIS ARMS. MY FEET dangled above the floor, my hips were lined up with his, and my hands gripped his shoulders. I opened my eyes to find him frowning at me.

"I could have dropped you."

Despite his tone, I wanted to laugh, to nip him all over. Exhilaration bubbled up. It was all I could do to contain myself.

I wrapped my legs around his waist and rolled my hips against his. "I wasn't worried. I knew you'd catch me." I undulated against him again.

He inhaled sharply, planting one big hand on my ass and the other under my hair.

Oh, gods. Something about his strong fingers gripping the nape of my neck drove me wild. The dominant hold raised my temperature and melted my insides as if liquid chocolate were pouring through my veins. I couldn't press close enough, open wide enough.

Snaking my arms around his back, I licked his throat, the

earthy flavor of him delicious on my tongue. I could still taste the salt from his earlier workout, smell the tang of his sweat.

His breath gushed out, blowing into the sensitive whorls of my ear. With two long strides, he pressed my spine against the scaffold's cross brace. "Gods, Kristin, what you do to me."

Releasing my nape, he twisted his fingers in my hair and pulled back my head. I went willingly, lips open, hands tugging him even closer.

His dark eyes turned wild, and he kissed me.

I wanted him to fill my mouth, to thrust in boldly. Instead, he slowed down and teased me—lips shaping, teeth nibbling. He released his grasp and massaged the base of my skull, then rubbed down my neck.

I moaned into his mouth, needing more.

Impatient, I nipped his tongue, hoping my aggression would spark his dominant side and he'd give me what I wanted. He did. He clasped my nape again, harder this time, and my muscles liquified.

Total surrender.

Tilting my head sideways, I exposed the long, vulnerable line of my throat. He curled his thumb beneath my chin, captured my mouth, and drove his tongue deep inside.

Our hips rocked together, and the need continued to build. I crossed my legs behind him and pushed my calves against his backside, needing to get even closer.

It was an incredible feeling—this desire to be mastered.

My wolf huffed in agreement.

He kissed across my cheek, over my brow, and down to the tip of my nose, all while he continued his sensual assault with his hands, caressing the curve of my ass and along the seam of my jeans.

I lost my breath all over again as the flesh between my legs dampened in another rush of heat.

Lifting my head, I met his gaze. His eyes were bright and feral, his skin stained with a hectic flush.

The signs of his arousal enflamed me, and I nipped his Adam's apple, teeth on either side of the protrusion as I licked the hard ridge. The graze of his stubble against my lips had me riding him even harder.

I groaned, and I pushed my hands between our bodies to the tie at his waistband.

His fingers clasped mine. "Not here."

But then he grabbed the bottom of his T-shirt and yanked it over his head.

My eyes widened appreciatively as a muscular expanse of tanned skin over broad shoulders, sculpted biceps, and the hard planes of his chest appeared.

Goddess help me, he was built like a warrior.

A smattering of dark hair covered his pecs and trailed down at an angle over a set of washboard abs. I teased my fingers through the hair, and his muscles rippled in response. My palms flattened against his stomach, and I pushed upward, loving the contrast between soft skin and crisp, curly hair. When I found the hardened nubs of his nipples, I rubbed my fingertips over them.

A low growl erupted from his throat, and I looked up. The burning need in his gaze matched my own. I was just about to drag him down for another kiss when he wrapped his shirt around my eyes and engulfed me in darkness.

"I want to see you!" I protested.

When I tried to push back the soft material imbued with his scent, he caught my hand, kissed my knuckles, and placed my palm back on his chest. "I said not here. Trust me, Kristin."

He stepped away from the scaffold, taking my full weight in his arms. After a few steps, I felt him walk down two stairs—into the sacred circle—and continue before stopping again. The warmth and weight of his hand left my shoulder. After a second, a swish sounded, and he started walking again. The air was cooler now, and I had the sense of being enclosed.

Had he taken me into the mountain?

"Where are we going?"

"My place. I'm using a shortcut I can't show you." The hoarseness of his voice sent shivers down my spine. "I want you in my bed, not on the cold floor or against the scaffold."

I sighed. "Me too."

It sounded heavenly...cocooned naked with him beneath the covers, sleeping with my head on his chest, listening to his heart beating beneath my ear.

Then guilt tightened my chest. I dug my fingers into his shoulders. "We should talk first."

"Later. I can't think straight right now. I'll make you breakfast in the morning, and we can talk then."

I shivered at what that meant—all night, just the two of us, with nothing else to think about.

"Okay. Tomorrow."

I hugged my arms around his neck, excited but also filled with a growing insecurity about the step we were taking. He was a hugely powerful Valdyr, Alpha of his pack, surrounded by kick-ass females. I was a lone wolf who knew little of my heritage, had talents he might distrust, and couldn't even shift into my wolf around unkyssed males without causing an uproar. And death.

How could I possibly measure up?

A nervous breath escaped my lips. "I've never made love with someone like you."

"Like me?"

"You know...strong, dominant."

He grunted into my hair, a pleased sound, and I imagined his wolf all puffed up with pride.

His gait quickened. "I've never made love with someone like you, either."

"There's nothing special about me."

He squeezed me closer. "Yeah, right. Extraordinary about covers it."

Warmth spread from the tips of my toes to the top of my head, chasing away my doubts. I smiled and rubbed our cheeks together. "Well, I am a good artist. And by all accounts, I've got a great ass. Men swoon in the streets as I go by."

He snorted and swatted my stupor-inducing backside.

I giggled. "Hopefully, it will make up for the other, not-so-round parts."

"What are you talking about?"

Gods, why had I said that? The last thing I wanted was to draw attention to my smaller assets. "I'm just saying, when you caught me in my underwear that day, I was wearing a padded bra."

"Huh. Like some kind of bait and switch?"

I nipped his jaw. Then his hand on my back came up under my shirt until he cupped my breast. A gasp broke from my throat as he gently squeezed.

"Feels like enough to me." He strummed my pebbled nipple with his thumb, his voice deepening. "What kind of bra are you wearing now?"

For the life of me, I couldn't remember. Between his fingers on my breast, the hard length of him pressing between my legs, and his lips teasing my ear, my brain had stopped working.

He pinched the nub, and my breath gushed out. "A nice one. How close are we?"

He paused and removed his hand. I heard another swish. The temperature warmed again. Had we arrived?

"Almost there," he said.

Listening closely, I noted the difference in the sound of his footsteps, as if he now walked on hardwood. Were we inside? Maybe in one of the houses on the hillside? With a deep inhale, I scented his own unique scent—pure male, a hint of wolf— combined with the light smell of pine and fresh mountain air.

I could shift to my second sight and see more of my surroundings through the material of his black T-shirt, but that seemed like cheating. Which, considering I'd been hiding my true self all along, shouldn't have mattered, but it did. Before, necessity had trumped honesty.

Now, I no longer needed to lie. Tomorrow, I'd tell Erik everything.

He trotted up a flight of stairs, turning left then right, his footsteps softening as he crossed what sounded like carpet and then squeaking on a hard surface. A switch clicked beside me, and the light brightened.

He sat me on a hard, cold surface, then unwrapped the shirt from my head.

"Hi," I said, blinking up into that brown gaze, hands still clutching his shoulders.

He smiled and brushed his lips against mine. "I like how you say that. As if it's a new beginning with new possibilities."

"It is kind of new. And you make me feel like anything's possible."

He smiled and pressed our lips together. I absorbed his kiss for a second—the masculine scent and feel of him—barely believing I was here.

When he pulled back, I glanced around. We were in a large, luxurious bathroom with a walk-in shower, a soaker tub, and a gray granite countertop flecked with white and silver. Pewter fixtures perched above a white sink, and a large mirror covered the wall.

Hmm, we could have some fun with that.

I met his gaze again. "Are we in here for a reason?"

"I haven't showered since my workout, and you have rock dust in your hair. Besides, having you wet and lathered is one of my favorite fantasies."

An image stole through my mind of our slick bodies moving together under the water. My breath stuttered. "Oh, yes."

"I promise you won't regret it."

Lowering his gaze to the hem of my T-shirt, he slowly pulled it upward. I lifted my arms to help him. The material caught on the edge of my rune before he tugged the shirt over my head and dropped it on the white tile floor.

A slow exhale whistled through his teeth as he stared down at me. My breasts were small and well-shaped, and my nipples pushed red and stiff against the sheer white material that covered them.

The glazed look in Erik's eyes thrilled me, and the low rumble in his throat drove me wild with need. He leaned me back and closed his mouth, hot and wet, over an aching nub.

My breath escaped on a sigh that turned into a moan as he bathed my nipple with his tongue, soft yet rough, through the thin silk. He nibbled, then he opened wide over the tip and sucked hard.

I groaned and arched my back, tightening my legs around his hips to pull us even closer. I rocked against him, and he rocked back. Releasing my nipple, he kissed down and up the valley to my other breast, captured it in his mouth, and sucked on it too.

I tried to catch my breath as he played with me, back and forth, one then the other, sometimes hard, sometimes soft—teeth and tongue—before pulling back to blow on the wet material.

It was an impossible task, and I gave myself over to the rising tide of desire. I no longer thought, just felt, allowing the emotional and physical feelings to career through me—sexual want and the escalating need to be filled by him, but also an opening of my heart, leaving me tender, exposed...vulnerable.

Tears filled my eyes and trickled from my closed lids into my hairline. I didn't try to stop or hide them. I just let the emotion move through me, carrying me higher on that tumultuous wave of surrender.

He raised his head, kissing and nipping up my throat and along my jaw. When he reached my ear, he sucked the lobe into his mouth. A fresh surge of excitement crashed over me. What was it about him kissing around my neck that drove me so wild? It turned me into a complete puddle of need. I just wanted to be taken by him—impaled by him.

I kneaded his shoulders, digging my fingers in as he traced the whorls of my ear with the tip of his tongue. His muscles bunched beneath my hands as he tightened his arms around me, and I loved the restrained strength of him, his power to punish or caress, to kill or protect.

Dragging my palms down his chest, I scraped my nails through the crisp hair, and he shuddered. He kissed up to my temple and lapped up the trail of wet, salty tears, causing another trickle.

"Is it too much?" he asked.

"No. It's perfect."

He pulled back, sitting me upright again, and his nostrils flared as he scented me—just like a natural wolf.

It made me want him more, the ache in my core almost unbearable, the hot, heavy sensation full to bursting. I'd never desired a male this way—I doubted I ever would again.

His strong hands reached behind me and unhooked my bra. I dropped my arms so the silk slipped from my body.

"You're beautiful," he said, leaning forward with a reverent sigh to kiss the tip of each breast. The feel of him nuzzling my skin with nothing in between made me even needier.

With one quick tug, I loosened the drawstring of his sweats and pushed them down. He toed off his shoes and socks, then kicked the pants aside. Underneath he wore black cotton boxer briefs that molded his engorged cock and the heavy pouch beneath.

I couldn't believe his size and another flare of heat pulsed between my thighs, making me greedy. Desperate.

I gripped him through the material with both hands. His body shuddered as his breath gushed hot between my breasts.

"Gods, Kristin," he moaned. Then he pushed himself away from me. "Give me your foot."

I lifted one leg, leaning back on my hands. He grasped my heel and unlaced my boot. With a thunk, it hit the floor, followed by my white ankle sock.

"No bunnies today?" he asked as he massaged up my jean-clad calf.

I shook my head, lids at half-mast, then groaned when he trailed his fingers up my inner thigh. I wanted to be fucked. Hard.

My eyes dropped back down to his cock, and I reached out with my toes to massage the hard ridge. The vein at his neck pulsed heavily, and he leaned into my foot, rolling his hips against the sole.

Reluctantly, he lowered my leg and lifted the other one, moving faster this time as he took off my boot and sock.

Playtime was over.

Then he grasped my hips and tugged so I stood flush against him, my bare toes touching his, the tips of my breasts rubbing against his chest, my Norse rune pressed tightly between us, the pendant cold and smooth against my skin.

I wished to the gods my pants were off too.

Rising onto the balls of my feet, I kissed him, loving the way his crisp body hair tickled my nipples. My lips clung, and I wrapped my arms around his back, the power in his broad shoulders making the muscles along my inner thighs quiver.

"Turn around," he said hoarsely.

I was lost in a haze of desire and kept nuzzling the hollow at the base of his throat, loving the smell of him, the feel of him against my body and under my palms.

Without warning, he spun me around, pressing me back against his chest so I faced the mirror.

"Oh!" I gasped.

My eyes met his in the mirror, and I was struck by our reflection—the wantonness in every line of my body, the domination in his. I was tall and strong, but still, he dwarfed me. His eyes burned for me, and for a second, I swore that I saw his wolf.

His hands were splayed against my ribcage, rising and falling with my agitated breaths. Mesmerized, I watched his thumbs brush over the soft underside of my breasts.

My knees buckled when they reached my nipples, and he gave a wicked, wolfy grin in the mirror as he held me up. Then he dropped his head to bite my shoulder. Every nerve ending was saturated with pleasure, and I dropped my hands to the edge of the counter, arched the small of my back, and thrust my ass against him.

One hand clamped around my waist while the other slowly, inexorably popped the top button of my jeans, lowered the zipper, and pushed them down my legs, revealing high-cut, sheer white panties.

"Step out of your jeans and keep your legs spread," he commanded, his voice low, guttural.

It was like I'd lost control of my body. He could have asked me to do anything, and I would have, especially when his fingers slipped down the front of my panties and through my wet curls.

I kicked my jeans away, keeping my stance wide, holding my breath as his fingers dipped lower. When they rubbed against my slick center, the breath left me in a shuddering exhale. My arms reached back to circle his neck, needing something to hold on to, some way to anchor myself. My head dropped against his shoulder, and I watched in the mirror through heavy lids as he stroked me beneath my panties.

My hips moved with him in a steady rhythm, always wanting more as the pad of his finger circled my nub and down the slippery surface to my center before returning to my clitoris. Circle and stroke, circle and stroke.

I clenched my hand in his hair as I rocked my pelvis harder, wanting penetration.

"Gods, Erik. Please. Oh gods, I'm coming. Please."

Then, my panties were sliding down my legs. The hand at my core grasped my inner thigh and widened my stance. The other hand pushed on my shoulder from behind.

"Elbows down," he growled into my ear.

I did as he commanded and braced myself on the granite, my pendant clinking against the stone top as I mindlessly thrust back my hips. Then, he was there, pushing against me, and I cried out in relief. The blunt head of him penetrated my swollen folds, stretching me, filling me. One arm wrapped around my hips, holding me in place, while the other braced on the counter beside me. Our bodies pressed together, skin to skin, his head over my shoulder, his lids heavy and feral as he watched me in the mirror.

As he drove forward, I rocked toward him, enveloping the fullness of him within me. A feeling of completeness overwhelmed me, and I became aware that my wolf was wholly linked to me in the ulf-mynd, the merging of our two souls, making me wonder if Erik and his wolf were also joined at that level, allowing the wolves to mate at the same time.

I gasped as he pulled back and thrust forward again, my breasts swaying below my necklace, my channel tight and wet around him. His arm angled up to palm my breast, causing the tiny muscles low in my pelvis to ripple. I panted, so close to release I almost screamed.

This was lovemaking on every level—in the body and in the hjarta. Every cell filled with sensation until I was drowning in need.

He held me tight, rolling my nipple between his thumb and forefinger as he surged into me, his heavy sac swinging forward to nudge my swollen flesh. I arched my back, angling us closer. He grunted, then dragged my hair to one side and bit the soft skin between my neck and shoulder.

The pressure of his teeth on that sensitive spot burst the bubble, and I threw my head back, screaming as my orgasm hit. It surged through my body in hard waves as he continued to stroke inside me.

The pressure built again, just as fast, priming me for another release. Then his rhythm fractured. He dropped his hand from my breast to push the heel of his hand against my clitoris. I sobbed as I peaked again, crying out as I was swamped with pleasure.

He shot forward with a roar, pressing me flat to the countertop. His body shook behind me, and his cock pulsed within. He wrapped his arms around me, cushioning me against the hard granite. His body lay heavy on top of mine, his breath warm and uneven in my ear, matching my own jagged inhale and exhale.

Slowly, our breathing eased, and the shuddering stopped.

He pulled back, and I made an inarticulate sound at the loss of him. He soothed me with his mouth, nuzzling where he'd held me in place with his teeth.

"I'm sorry I bit you," he said.

I huffed out a laugh. "Don't be. I loved it. I want you to do it again. Soon."

He laughed with me, then gently lapped the area with his tongue, like wet velvet on my skin. Glancing in the mirror, I saw the oval-shaped indentation from his teeth. The skin wasn't pierced, but it would probably bruise.

I liked that he'd marked me—almost as if he'd branded me.

Sighing blissfully, I basked in the post-lovemaking glow. My wolf lay on her side, still panting. *Happy with mate*, she said.

Tears pricked my eyes. *Me too.*

Erik kissed the spot he'd been licking, then rose from the counter and scooped me into his arms. His chocolate-brown gaze met mine, making my heart trip over yet again.

"Don't even think of falling asleep. We're not done yet," he said.

CHAPTER 15

I HAD SLEPT WITH MY FAIR SHARE OF FEMALES—HUMAN AND Valdyr—when I was younger, inflating my ego to a decent size.

Hel, even bigger. Almost as big as Gunn's.

But since I'd become Alpha and taken on the curse, I'd been with only a few women. One-night stands—quick, forgettable. And a Valdyr female had been out of the question because of the possibility I might infect her.

Still, I thought I'd experienced all sex had to offer.

Until now.

Looking down at Kristin as she lay in my arms, her hazel eyes dreamy, her lips red and swollen from my kisses, I realized I'd been wrong. My previous trysts had been nothing more than preparation for the big game, and tonight, I'd won the Super Bowl, the World Series, and the Stanley Cup all rolled into one.

Before, I would have said it was impossible for me to join with my wolf in the ulf-mynd during sex—especially with a human. But to my shock, my wolf, who had never connected with me in any previous sexual encounter, even when I'd been with a Valdyr female, had merged with me, bringing the two halves of our souls together and enhancing every physical sensation, thought, and feeling.

It was similar, perhaps, to what happened between kyssed pairs. Something I'd never expected to experience—at least not while I housed the curse.

Mate, my wolf said, lying on his haunches and looking proud of himself.

Yes, I supposed she was, in a way. I couldn't be joined with Kristin in the Kyssa, talk to her mind to mind, or have pups with her like I would with a Valdyr female, but apparently, I could make love to her in the manner of mated pairs.

She was a gift from Odin—this human woman who could touch my wolf yet remain safe from our curse.

"What do you mean we're not done?" she asked.

Her husky tone made my cock twitch. Which, after the way I'd just spent myself, should have been impossible. "That was just a warm-up."

She laughed. "A warm-up? You've just altered my perception of reality. No way can you squeeze another orgasm out of me."

"Is that a challenge?"

I carried her into the large walk-in shower. The warm water came on automatically from the shower head and the jets on the walls. Rivulets turned her blond hair dark as they ran down her body. I couldn't look away, fascinated by the way her skin glistened beneath the drops. Bending my head, I lapped at the water that pooled at the base of her throat, nudged aside her rune pendant, and followed the stream as it trickled over her breasts.

Who knew I was so thirsty?

"Maybe," she gasped.

I continued to drink from her skin and around her reddened nipples, in the valley between her breasts, and down her torso to her belly button. Her jagged sigh added to the symphony of sounds around us—the water pounding from the jets and hitting our bodies, my blood thrumming in my ears, and my wolf's excited whine. Eventually I licked all the way back up her body and over her neck to her lips. She parted her mouth to let me in, snaked her arms around my shoulders, and held me close.

When I pulled back, her eyes were closed. Patiently, I waited for her to open them, wanting to see the golden hazel orbs heavy with desire.

Eagle eyes, I thought. Stunning, perceptive.

Her lids lifted slowly as if drugged. "Okay, I stand corrected. Maybe with a lot of hard work, like hours and hours, you could possibly make me come again."

I grinned at the breathy, teasing note in her voice, loving that she laughed so easily. Especially after the hardships she'd faced as a girl—she'd somehow found joy in life again after the terrible tragedy that had befallen her family.

"If I've got hours, one climax won't be nearly enough."

I lowered her feet to the shower floor, keeping an arm around her waist so our bodies touched. When she rubbed her wet belly from side to side against me, I groaned.

Leaning back against the tile wall, I stroked my palms down her back, over the curve of her ass to her thighs, and up again. "You feel so good."

Her fingers brushed through my chest hair before she took my nipple in her mouth and sucked, lapping the bud with her tongue and then kissing across to the other one. The sensation shot straight to my groin, and a growl rumbled low in my throat.

She laid her chin on the center of my chest and stared up at me. "You feel good too. And you taste even better."

Gods, I wanted her to gaze at me like that forever.

I pushed her hair behind her shoulders. "Tilt your head back."

She did, and the water ran from her forehead over her curls. I sifted my fingers through the length to soak it, then turned the spray away and reached for the shampoo. "Close your eyes."

Her lids drifted shut as I squirted the thick liquid into my palm. Smoothing it over her hair, I gently worked it into a lather and massaged her scalp. This time, she groaned, her body relaxing against mine.

"Are you trying to kill me with pleasure?"

"Always." I shifted the spray again and pushed her upright. "Rinse."

She moved under the water. The suds from her hair washed over her shoulders, around her pendant and breasts, and then along the small swell of her stomach before catching in the small patch of hair at the apex of her thighs.

Sweet Asgard, she was beautiful, long and lean with surprising strength in her body. The physical work of rock carving had toned her arms and shoulders, her back and torso. Her breasts were shaped like teardrops, and her nipples budded out high and tight. They filled my mouth and palm perfectly.

The shape of her stomach fascinated me—the slight dips and swells, her waist tucked in, her hips narrow. Sculpted, long legs led to adorable feet, nails painted pink, the second toe slightly longer than the big toe—more endearing for its imperfection.

I loved looking down and seeing them next to my huge ugly dogs, the water coursing around them on the tile.

"Turn around."

She did, confidence and desire alight in her face. The breath left me in a whoosh as her perfect, apple-shaped rear came into view. Like a kid reaching for candy, I squeezed the rounded globes, firm yet still soft under my fingers.

"Are you swooning yet?" she teased.

I looked up to find her staring at me over her shoulder, lips quirked, eyes laughing. My need rose to another level. "I've been swooning since the moment I met you."

"Me too." Then she turned and struck a pose. "Do you like what you see?"

I nodded, not trusting myself to speak. My wolf had merged

with me again and rode me hard. I'd be lucky if I could do more than growl.

She smiled slowly, wickedly. "I do too." Dropping her eyes, she focused on the stiff, hard length of me. "Is it me, or do they put something in the water here?"

"You." One word was all I could manage.

Her palms slid up my thighs and then cupped me, turning my legs to jelly. It was a good thing I leaned against the wall. One hand squeezed my sac gently as the other moved up and down my erection, her thumb circling the tip and along the sensitive spot below the head with each stroke.

The breath gushed from me, and I pulled her closer, salivating with the need to bite her. I resisted, nuzzling her shoulder instead.

"You're so big," she whispered. The excitement in her voice and the quickening pace of her hands had me thrusting into her palm. Gods, it felt good.

She felt good.

I slid one hand around her throat and then down to cup her breast, loving the weight and feel of it in my palm. The softness gave way to a pebbled areola and nipple, which I kneaded, making her roll her hips forward. I brushed the other hand over her ass and between her thighs, using gentle pressure to widen her stance, allowing me to wedge my thigh between hers. Off-balance, she leaned into me, pressing the heat of her core against my leg.

"Oh," she murmured in surprise, making me grin. I nibbled harder on the flesh I craved between her neck and shoulder as I strummed her nipple with my thumb. Her hips jerked in response, and her breath shuddered. The pressure on my cock faltered, but I didn't mind. I was pleased I'd made her mindless to everything but my touch.

When she rolled her hips again, I increased the friction against her core, creating a rocking rhythm with my hand on her ass. She dropped her head back, gripped my waist, and rode my leg.

I raised my hand to her neck and dug my fingers into her nape. She gasped. Taking advantage, I stroked my tongue into her mouth, lingering for a few minutes before kissing down her chest and pulling her nipple into my mouth. The bud dragged along my tongue as I suckled on it, stimulating me as much as her.

I squeezed her backside and gently stroked between her legs from behind. She stilled for just an instant, then arched her hips back to give me greater access. When she rubbed forward again, her center was slick and hot on my leg.

"Erik. Oh gods, don't stop. Please don't stop," she panted. "It feels so good. Don't stop. I'm coming. Erik, I'm coming!"

I gripped her nape hard, holding her in place as I opened my mouth wide over her breast, stroking it with the flat of my tongue. Lifting my leg, I increased the pressure, holding her core tight against me.

She came on my thigh, shuddering and rocking, her hot flesh pulsing out her orgasm.

Before it receded, I dropped to my knees, my hands holding her up as I pulled her leg over my shoulder. She braced herself on the shower wall behind me.

"Erik, what are you…ohhhh gods."

I tasted her, licking and nuzzling every warm crevice. I wanted every drop. The scent of her drove me wild, and the swollen heat of her made my wolf howl. She came once more against my mouth, quivering on my lips and tongue.

I let her relax against me, kissing up her stomach and chest as I stood. Shutting off the water, I scooped her limp body into my arms and carried her from the shower. It hurt to walk, I was so engorged, but I wanted Kristin in my bed—my weight pinning her down, her arms and legs wrapped around me as I pushed inside.

I planned to take it slow this time. To savor her.

Last time, we'd both been too excited, and the unleashed passion had pushed us to an eager, almost rough, joining. Now, I was in control. I could draw out our lovemaking. Allow myself to be cocooned by her.

Supporting her against the counter, I grabbed a fluffy white towel from the warming rack and rubbed it over her hair and body before quickly drying myself and scooping her up again.

"I could get used to this," she said.

"Good."

Leaving the bathroom light on, I crossed the threshold into my bedroom, my feet sinking into a plush, cream-colored carpet. Her head lifted from my shoulder as she looked around my dimly lit bedroom, making me see it through her eyes—dark wooden furniture, sand-colored walls, the bedspread a mix of slate green, gray, and a rusty red.

I lowered her feet to the ground near the bed and then pulled back the covers. When I straightened, I hesitated, feeling uncertain all of a sudden.

She smiled, kissed me, and crawled into the middle of the bed on her hands and knees. The perfect curve of her ass waved to me like a red flag to a bull. My wolf lowered his head and stalked forward with nostrils flared.

I did the same, quickly crawling after her and insulating us beneath the quilt. Turning on her side, she faced me, looping her top leg over my hips as I pressed our bodies together. I couldn't wait and rolled her onto her back, moving between her legs. She twined one calf around the outside of my thigh and bent the other leg at the knee, foot flat on the mattress beside my hip.

"Mmm. You feel good against me," she whispered in my ear.

"It gets better."

Hooking my elbow beneath her knee, I tilted her hips upward. The blunt, sensitive head of my erection nudged her opening, and I slid inside, loving the silken feel of her cushioning me.

She sighed, matching my satisfied groan.

We rocked together slowly at first, kissing and stroking, nibbling and caressing. Her hands explored along my shoulders, arms, and chest, then scraped down my abdomen to urge me on. I licked, sucked, and nuzzled—inhaling her, tasting her, wanting her to peak again even though she'd already come so many times.

When her nails curved into my ass and her breath caught on a jagged moan, I increased the tempo. A tingling rose up from my toes, spread heavily through my groin, and tightened my sac. The need to dominate overtook me. I bit her neck, making her whimper. She pulled her knees wider, and I sank deeper.

My weight pushed her down, and my arms crushed her against me, one hand tight in her hair, the other holding her shoulder. Our bodies surged together, hard chest grazing soft breasts, the edge of my pelvis rubbing her clit.

Her hips rocked frantically, and I dropped my hand to hold her still. All the while, my wolf urged me to bite harder. I did, and she climaxed around me in waves, head tilting back as she cried out, heels digging into the small of my back. I followed immediately, growling into her flesh as I came, the velvet walls of her sheath clamping around me, milking me until I collapsed on top of her.

I somehow had the presence of mind to unclench my teeth from the crook of her neck and roll onto my back, taking her with me. She lay boneless, head pillowed above my racing heart, arm limp across my chest.

Finally, she heaved out a long sigh before falling asleep.

I stared at the top of her head and along her arm to her hand lying peacefully over the dark hair on my chest. I wanted to stay awake as long as possible to savor the reality of Kristin in my bed.

A single thought flitted through my head before I lost the battle and fell into a deep, contented sleep.

Mine.

Erik. Wake up!

My eyes popped open, my arm tightening protectively around Kristin, who still slept, draped across my body.

Gunn?

Yeah. Come to the containment room on the lower level. There's something you have to see.

The cells located on that level were seldom used, especially the ones with extra security—both physical and magical. Whoever or whatever Gunn had imprisoned there had to be a threat.

What is it? I asked, easing out from under Kristin. She moaned softly and curled into my pillow, her blond curls strewn every which way in a sexy tangle. Gods, what I wouldn't give to stay and make love to her all over again.

Come see for yourself. Is Kristin with you?

I didn't respond right away, compelled to keep my budding relationship with her private even though it was an exercise in futility. There were no secrets in the Varda.

I crawled from the bed and strode to the bathroom, finally saying, *She's sleeping.*

Good.

Had there been something in Gunn's voice, or was it my imagination? *What does that mean?*

You don't want to have to explain yourself. This is Varda business. Come as fast as you can.

Then he was gone. I could have reached out to him, and was tempted to demand more information, but I knew I had to get my head right first.

After splashing my face with water, I dragged on the clothes that lay scattered across the floor. Stopping for just an instant, I pressed my shirt to my face and inhaled, loving that it smelled like Kristin.

Catching sight of myself in the mirror, I had a flash of us together—her arms wrapped around my neck, her eyes closed and mouth open, her hips rocking into my hand as I touched her beneath her panties. Then I'd pushed her over the counter and spread her legs as I thrust into her from behind, rounded breasts swaying every time I plunged forward.

The image made me groan. Thor's balls, I had to get myself under control. I should have been out the door by now. Obviously, the situation was urgent, or Gunn wouldn't have disturbed me.

I yanked the shirt over my head, shoved my feet into my runners, and picked up Kristin's clothes. On the way out, I dropped her stuff on the end of the bed.

"Erik?"

Her sleepy voice stopped me, and I turned back. She was propped up on her elbow, the quilt dipping low to reveal the tip of one breast while her hair tumbled around her shoulders. "Where are you going?"

I changed direction and sat on the edge of the bed, tempted to forget everything and crawl back under the covers. I could just imagine how soft and warm she was. Instead, I stroked blond curls from her face and kissed her forehead. "Gunn called. Something's happened that I have to deal with. I won't be long."

She sat up and pulled the quilt under her arms. "Do you want me to leave?"

"No. I want you to stay right here." I pushed her down onto the pillow, kissed each eyelid, the tip of her nose, mouth, and chin, then pulled the quilt away and kissed each rosy nipple before tucking her in. "It's still early. Go back to sleep. I like knowing you're here. I'll make you breakfast when I get back, and we can talk."

She smiled groggily, already drifting off. "Okay. French toast. With strawberries and whipped cream."

The idea of cooking for her made me happy. "Your wish…my command."

Feeling reenergized and focused on the emergency, I strode quickly through the door and down the hallway. Instead of taking the stairs, I leapt over the railing to the great room below, trotting past the gleaming kitchen and into my study.

My home was built into the mountainside, and while the front of the house was wall-to-wall windows, the rooms at the back, like my study, were completely enclosed. Both me and my wolf liked it.

Dahlia had chosen overstuffed leather chairs, cherrywood for the floor, and lighting in every corner, keeping it warm and cozy.

Stepping behind my desk, I placed my hand on a stone carving of Odin in his wanderer guise—that of an old man with an eye patch, a long beard, and a staff. The statue sensed me, and a portion of the wall slid away. A well-lit passageway appeared that burrowed into the mountain. I stepped through, and the wall sealed behind me.

The tunnel could easily fit three Valdyr side by side. The walls were smooth rock, and the floor was made of hard-packed earth.

When I'd carried Kristin through here earlier, I'd worried about meeting up with my packmates. I shouldn't have used the secret route, but desire had won out.

I couldn't let it happen again. It was one thing to have a relationship with a female of a different race, another to put her above my pack and duty.

The path sloped downward, with tunnels veering off in different directions. I turned down a short passageway that led to a secure door. It opened at my touch.

A lit stairwell descended sharply in front of me. I met several rekkrs on my way down who greeted me with a tilted head—a sign of respect and submission. At the bottom, I crossed a vast room, the hub of Varda security, where row upon row of computer terminals and video screens relayed information from Wolf Ridge and the rest of the world—and the heavens too.

Off the main area, dorm rooms housed many of the young, unkyssed rekkrs. Next to the dorm was a large communal kitchen, a recreation room, and a well-equipped gym.

Laughter and cheers came from the rec room where the rekkrs relaxed, watched movies, and played the latest video games, many of which were modified for their faster reflexes.

But it wasn't all high-tech. A game of ping pong was constantly in play, using special balls, paddles, and a table that wouldn't burst after one powerful hit. Gunn and I still held the record for the longest volley, set when we'd both been too young to think about anything beyond our latest assignment or night on the prowl.

Things had changed.

Finally, I reached the door to the lower cells, guarded by the young rekkr who'd been at Savage last week and had hustled Kristin, Dahlia, and Gina to the safe room when Hati had attacked.

It pleased me that Kristin and my cousin were friends.

"Fyrstr," Eddie greeted me.

"Eddie," I responded before putting my hand to the sensor.

"I couldn't believe it when they carried her down," the young rekkr whispered. "She's not dead, is she?"

I stopped as the door slid open. Ice filled my guts. I stared at Eddie for a moment, unable to think past the horrific vision that flashed through my head. Then I raced down the second set of stairs, my heart pounding, my wolf howling frantically.

A long, barren hallway preceded me with doors on either side. Behind those doors were reinforced concrete cells with a magical seal. Gunn stood in front of one of them about halfway down, staring through a window in the door. Dane leaned back against the opposite wall, arms over his chest.

They looked at me, their expressions grim, as I ran toward them.

"Dahlia?" I yelled.

Gunn shook his head and stepped aside so I could peer through the glass. My blood thundered through my veins.

The inside of the cell was barren except for a metal slab attached to the wall for a bed. These prisons were for the worst offenders and were not intended to be cozy.

But this particular cell had a mattress added to the bed, on which a female lay facing the wall. A doubled-over blanket covered her body, and a fluffy pillow supported her head. Her dark hair was twisted into a low, tight bun. Beneath the covering, she wore a black turtleneck.

Shock ricocheted through me.

"Is that Gina?"

CHAPTER 16

<u>Kristin</u>

"Get up!"

My eyes popped open, my heart racing as the quilts were ripped away, leaving me naked on the bed except for the rune that hung around my neck. Inside, my wolf lunged forward, snapping and snarling.

Sitting up, I dragged the pillow around to cover myself, my shocked gaze landing on Linnea as she towered over me. At the bedroom door stood two tough-looking Valdyr I hadn't seen before—one male, one female.

What the hel was going on?

"Where's Erik?" I asked, all traces of sleep deserting me.

"Not here. You're dealing with me now. Waving your tits in my face will get you nowhere."

Oh. Shit.

Had Linnea gone rogue and come for me on her own, or had Erik sent her? No. He would confront me directly if he thought I was a threat to the pack.

So, it comes down to me and Linnea.

The gorgeous Alpha female topped me by several inches, and pure muscle filled out her hourglass figure beneath the stretchy black workout gear she favored. But even with all that strength, I was sure I could beat the Valdyr in a fair fight.

Not just because of my magic—Linnea had her own magic to fight with. No, my wolf just knew I was faster and more dominant than Linnea, impossible as that might seem.

"Grumpy much in the morning?" I asked, my mind racing as I glanced around. Should I go along with the Valdyr and see what happened? Or fight my way out of here? They'd never be able to stop me once I was out in the open.

Linnea stalked to the closet, grabbed one of Erik's white dress shirts, and tossed it onto the bed. "I said get up—or we'll drag you out of here naked. You and I are going to have a little chat."

I picked up the shirt, resisting the urge to press it to my nose and inhale Erik's scent. Just having the material close and knowing it had been wrapped around his body comforted me. After putting it on, I spotted my underwear at the end of the bed and pulled it on too.

I knew the Valdyr weren't as conscious of nudity as humans—they couldn't be when they lost their clothes every time they shifted—but the shirt, which hit midthigh, made me feel less vulnerable.

"I don't understand what's going on. Do you think I'm a corporate spy or something?"

"Cut the crap, bitch." Linnea grabbed my arm and yanked me toward the door.

Okay. They knew I was bluffing, hiding something. But did they know what? And did this have anything to do with Hans? Maybe Linnea was working for him on the side.

But that didn't jibe with her personality. She saw the world in black and white, pack versus non-pack. Most likely, she'd discovered something incriminating about me and had taken it upon herself to interrogate me since from Linnea's perspective, Erik's judgment had been compromised.

"Look, I don't know what you think you know, but—"

"Save it for later. You're in deep shit, Kristin—if that's even your real name. We don't tolerate liars."

Linnea marched me from the bedroom with one guard in front, the other behind. They entered an open hallway that overlooked a great room. My gaze flitted down, calculating distances and working out escape routes.

Floor-to-ceiling windows afforded a view of the valley below, allowing the first streaks of dawn to light the room. Dark leather couches and chairs surrounded a huge slate fireplace that took up one wall in the living room. Beautiful paintings of wilderness and wildlife, including one of mine, covered the walls.

The dining room was on the other side of the great room with a large, well-appointed kitchen behind it, making me wonder if Erik liked to cook—and if he'd ever make me French toast and strawberries. As promised.

Pain squeezed my heart as I imagined him wanting nothing more to do with me, but I pushed it away. I hadn't done anything wrong—not really. It could only be a good thing I was Valdyr. Once I explained my situation, everything would be all right. My lips tilted with forced optimism.

"Keep smiling. You won't be doing it for long," Linnea said.

"Don't count on it, bitch." I deliberately repeated Linnea's slur from earlier.

The Alpha female swung the back of her hand at me, but I ducked out of the way. Linnea's knuckles hit the wall, cracking the drywall. She glowered at me.

I smirked. *Two points for me.*

"Temper, temper, Linnea. I'm sure Erik won't be pleased to know you've lost control and damaged something that belongs to him." The Valdyr were possessive, and Erik's scent from our lovemaking was all over me.

I belonged to him.

"You'd be surprised what pleases Erik, especially when it comes to traitors."

The seriousness of my situation sank in. I was in the custody of three strong, hostile Valdyr, being led toward some kind of interrogation.

"I'm not a traitor," I said quietly.

It was possible Erik might never forgive me. I'd worked in the den and slept with him under false pretenses. But I'd had good reasons for keeping my true self hidden.

Plus, I'd tried to talk to him beforehand. He'd remember that when the time came. *Wouldn't he?*

They led me across the gleaming wood floor toward a burgundy door at the front of the house. I sighed inwardly with relief. If I needed to make a quick escape, it would be easier in the open rather than the mountain tunnels I was sure Erik had carried me through last night.

The guard in front opened the door. The chilly air hit my bare skin as I passed through, making me shiver. Two black Range Rovers idled in the driveway, with two additional Valdyr beside each one. My panic mounted, and I contemplated the forest around me and the open sky above. An eagle circled high overhead, and I almost shifted, wanting the bird's freedom for myself.

But I wanted Erik by my side when I revealed my true nature.

I either had to stand on my own now and gain the pack's respect and a possible future with him, or I ran and avoided the fallout if things went wrong—possibly never seeing him, Dahlia, or the pack again.

And I wouldn't get to finish the mural. I knew the rock carving was insignificant in the big picture, but the artist in me hated to leave it.

What do you want to do? I asked my wolf.

Fight.

Fight to get away now? Or go with them and fight for our place in the pack?

Go. Fight. Pack.

My breath escaped in a silent sigh. That's what I wanted, too, despite the possible consequences.

Gina would kill me for taking such a risk, but the idea of my sister's anger also made me smile. If things went bad and I was imprisoned, the Valdyr wouldn't know what hit them. Gina was a force to be reckoned with when she was pissed.

How long would it take her to figure out something was wrong and come back from Denver for me?

Three days at the most.

Which was nothing. Hans had imprisoned me for three years.

I lifted my chin and pulled my shoulders back, then marched to the lead Range Rover. Climbing into the back seat, I slid across the gray leather. Linnea followed behind me. We sat in silence as I absentmindedly rolled up the sleeves on Erik's shirt, watching as the driver followed the gravel road through the woods toward Wolf Ridge.

After pulling in front of the main building, we exited the car just as the sun breached the horizon. Morning rays hit the black glass, reflecting toward me, and I squinted. Inside, my wolf paced back and forth, focused, alert, and almost eager for what was to come.

Do you know what's going to happen? I asked.

My wolf stopped and cocked her head as if listening. To what, I had no idea. Maybe it was instinct. After a moment, my wolf said, *Challenge.*

Okay. A challenge I could deal with. I even looked forward to it. I was sick and tired of pretending to be someone I wasn't.

It was time to prove I was worthy of the pack and of Erik. I wrapped my hand around my stone rune necklace and squeezed.

Strength.

Linnea grabbed my arm, trying to drag me up the stairs and

toward the den, but I shook her off and walked inside on my own. The hardwood felt cool against my bare feet. The door to the inner sanctum was open, and a loud, uneasy murmur came from inside, interspersed by a raised voice or growl.

On the threshold, I paused, one guard in front, Linnea tight on my heels. My eyes widened. I'd been working here for weeks, and I'd never seen it so full of Valdyr. And they kept coming, young and old, streaming out of hidden entrances in the mountain and pushing past me in the doorway. The area around the circle was filling up, as were the upper landings and my scaffold. A few even perched on the wolf carving, making me shiver.

For a moment, I worried the scaffold wouldn't hold their combined weight. Then I shrugged. If the structure collapsed, it was their own fault.

Just as long as they didn't mess up my mural.

Silence fell as the pack turned suspicious, wary eyes in my direction.

Obviously, they were here to witness something to do with me. From the looks of it, that something would take place in the still-empty sunken circle. Once sanctified, the circle would become either a hringr for low celebrations or rituals, or a domr for high rituals in which the gods or the pack's Alpha male or female brought judgment upon a Valdyr or other creature.

I had a sinking feeling it was the latter.

I lifted my eyes to the domed glass ceiling, wondering with nervous excitement if the gods would actually descend upon us. That's when I noticed the glass was retracted, allowing the morning sun to shine down. Surely if Odin were to pass judgment upon me, he would know I'd meant no harm.

And if it were Linnea or Erik who judged me, I'd be able to explain my actions. Hopefully.

Glancing over the crowd, I saw a few familiar faces, all of them tight and guarded, but no one I was close to. Not Erik or Dahlia. Not even Gunn or Dane.

If events worsened, I'd use the open roof to escape. No way would I allow them to lock me up. I could use my strength and magic to jump to the top and then continue up the mountain.

"Move it," Linnea growled behind me.

I glared at her and then stepped forward. The Valdyr in front of her divided, opening a path all the way to the circle—right past the stone wolf. I proceeded cautiously. Not because of the agitated crowd, although that was a valid concern, but because I was wary of another attack by the sculpture.

A heavy hand stopped me from stepping into the sanctified ring. "Wait."

Linnea moved past me down the stairs, and the two guards behind me seized my arms. It was all I could do to stop myself from ripping free, taking out their throats in the process. My wolf growled in agreement.

Patience.

Turning my attention back toward Linnea, I watched with curiosity and rising excitement as the female strode toward a raised altar at the far end of the circle, where a small knife, candle, bowl, and pitcher of water sat. Linnea lit the candle with a match, held her palms over the flame as she muttered something in Old Norse, pricked her thumbs with the knife, then poured water into the bowl and washed her hands.

The ritual brought tears to my eyes. I'd seen my mother perform it many times in our home. The scorching of Linnea's palms represented sacrifice for the pack. The bloodied thumbs represented sworn duty—to what, I couldn't remember—and the washing represented a cleansed soul to greet the gods.

The last caused me to shiver, and I looked through the open ceiling to the heavens again. Would Odin actually appear?

"Linnea, stop!"

I whipped my head around. Erik stood at the back of the crowd. His face, looking like it was carved in stone, topped the masses of Valdyr between us. Gunn and Dane stood behind him on either side. He did not meet my eyes. Instead, he pinned Linnea with his gaze.

"I'll deal with her," he said.

I was suddenly shoved forward, and I yelped as I fell down the steps. Tucking into a roll at the bottom, I came out of it in a guarded crouch.

A growl ripped through the room, torn from Erik's wolf, and everyone stilled. Then he leapt forward with blinding speed.

Linnea lifted her hands and cried out, "In Odin's name, I anoint myself Domari. I call judgment upon this creature, Kristin Andersen, and by rights cast the sacred domr. None shall enter or exit until the Varda is protected and Odin's will done."

A snap in the air sounded just as Erik's big body hit an invisible barrier that trapped me and Linnea inside.

Panic threatened at the thought that I was once again imprisoned, but it was tempered by growing awe as I sensed the force of the magic around me. I shifted into my second sight and gasped with pleasure as a fluid, colorful wall became visible, streaming toward the sky. It was vivid yet translucent, allowing me to see Erik and the other Valdyr on the opposite side.

Beautiful.

I gazed upward in wonder, knowing this was the energy of Asgard, of the gods. It was life itself. Pure creativity. The same as when my mother had been cremated and when I'd saved that wolf the other day.

Slowly, I turned, marveling at the brightness and clarity of the colors around me, colors I hadn't even known existed.

"I'm talking to you."

I was so enthralled the angry words barely registered. The hard slap across my face brought me screeching back to reality. I was knocked against the floor, and I skidded to the perimeter, right in front of Erik.

"If you touch her again, Linnea, I swear you'll regret it!" He roared the words, his wolf's incensed snarls underlying every syllable.

I shivered at the dominance and power that emanated from him. Gods, he was magnificent, eyes blazing as he stared at Linnea, hands fisted against the domr wall, his lips pulled back from sharpened canines.

"Unsanctify the circle. Now!"

Linnea's sides heaved as she struggled against Erik's command. She wouldn't meet his gaze. Instead, she kept her eyes, a wolf-enhanced, shining, pale green, on me. "As Alpha female, it's my job to protect the pack. To protect my Alpha when he needs it. This…woman…whatever she is…has lied to you, tricked you. She's tricked us all." Taking a labored breath, she lifted her gaze to Erik. "You've been compromised."

Then she leapt forward.

I yelped and tried to roll out of the way, but Linnea twisted her hand into my hair and yanked my head back, using her greater height and weight to throw me off-balance and pin me face down on the cold slate, my arm jammed painfully behind my back.

"Holy hel. Get off me, you sadistic bitch!"

"I want answers," Linnea said, "and I'll beat you bloody until I get them." She yanked me up and dragged me toward the altar.

"We'll get those answers, Linnea. Together." There was an edge of desperation to Erik's voice. "I know she lied. I know she's not who she says she is, but she's also human. Weak and fragile. You can't treat her like one of us. You've already revealed too much."

My wolf huffed in indignation at being called weak. I turned to glare at Erik, but Linnea hauled me around and slammed my face down against the altar.

"Ow!" So much for Linnea taking it easy on the "fragile" human.

"You don't know she's human. She could be a witch like the other one. Or something worse."

Like the other one? They must have figured out Gina was a witch. Maybe they'd followed her back to Denver. But I would bet they had no idea just how strong a witch she was.

"Kristin's human," Erik said again. "She would never have made it through the wards otherwise. And yes, she's probably working for Hati and Skoll, and maybe she was responsible for the breach the other night, but you should never have involved her in a Valdyr ritual."

"Then why did Odin allow it? If I didn't have his blessing, the circle wouldn't have been sanctified. You know what that means. Either she tells me what I want to know, and I release the barrier, or she takes it from me. It's what the Allfather wishes." As if to emphasize her point, Linnea picked up my head and smashed it against the stone.

Stars flashed behind my eyes. "Fricking Xena Warrior Princess, that hurt!" I yelled.

"It's going to hurt a hel of a lot more if you don't start talking. Why are you here?"

I closed my eyes. Inside, my wolf was poised, eager for the fight, eager to test herself against the other female, to claim her place in the pack and earn her right to be with Erik.

When I opened them, I saw Dahlia pressed against the barrier. Everyone else had moved a step back, leaving a path for their raging Alpha. His wolf was on him hard as he paced around the enclosure, pounding it in frustration.

"Let. Her. Out. You'll kill her!"

I'd wanted to tell him who I was over breakfast, preferably in bed. I'd imagined him overjoyed at the news, wanting to make love again, wanting to see my wolf and going for a run in the forest, as giddy as pups.

But as Linnea had said, it was as Odin wished.

Tears trickled down Dahlia's face. I met her gaze and mouthed, *I'm sorry*. Dahlia nodded and mouthed back, *Fight*.

"I'm here," I said to Linnea, my voice deadly calm, "to kick your Amazonian ass." Then I shifted my weight forward onto the altar, lifted my feet, and shoved them backward into Linnea's stomach, throwing her hard against the wall. Linnea hit with a loud "oof" as the air was knocked out of her lungs.

Silence fell in the rotunda. Shock, probably, as I showed my strength. I straightened and turned, rubbing my hand against my head where Linnea's fist had held me tight.

Erik stopped pacing and stared at me. His sides heaved, and his body winked in and out of the helmingr, signaling he was about to lose complete control.

Behind him, I heard Gunn mutter, "Fuck."

Linnea stood and shook off the hit. "Bad call," she said to me. "Now everyone knows."

"Knows what?" I asked.

"That you're our enemy." Then Linnea leapt back across the circle.

CHAPTER 17

Kristin

HOLY THOR! LINNEA WAS FASTER THAN SHE LOOKED.

I spun just in time to evade the Alpha female's full-body tackle, scraping my knees on the copper-colored tiles. The crowd reacted with shouts and indrawn breaths.

My head stung where a few hairs had ripped free, probably trapped in the other female's fist. I quickly tucked the unruly blond mass under the collar of Erik's shirt and scrambled up.

"With speed like that, you're obviously not human," Linnea said, her eyes narrowed and watchful from across the circle. "Did you know what we were when you came here?"

"I suspected. But I never intended to harm anyone. Not unless he was here."

"Who?"

I hesitated, still uncertain if I should name Hans. I was already in deep shit. "A male. I've been looking for him. He's not Valdyr, he's…something else."

Behind me, Erik growled, making me realize I'd almost backed up against the colorful, translucent wall. I turned and stretched out my hand to him, wanting to soothe the frown from his brow and kiss along his jaw until it softened.

I brushed my fingers where one of his fists rested on the barrier, causing an energetic buzz to fill me. For a moment, I was drawn back into my enthrallment, the kaleidoscope-like patterns hypnotic to my senses. Then he stepped away, his rejection like a bucket of freezing water in my face.

"What are you?" he snarled. "A witch like your sister? A Jotun?"

"No, I—"

Linnea leapt, and the crowd's murmurs surged again. I dived low, spinning and kicking with my feet. I caught the powerful Alpha in the thigh and pelvis, but Linnea also hit hard, her wolf's claws digging into my calf.

Pain seared my leg as blood poured from the wound. I cursed and limped behind the altar. Some of the crowd cheered.

Hand pressed low on her side, Linnea rose from the floor. I could still see her claws. Obviously, the Alpha female was able to partially manifest into her wolf. By magic? Or was it a skill any Valdyr could master?

Well, I had my own magic and skills. I could end this fight in a second by either drawing on Linnea's aura and weakening her or using my magic to create a cage, trapping the other female within.

My wolf barked a negative response. She wanted to win this fight in the lupine way, not with magic. She wanted to impress the pack and Erik with her strength. Her dominance. She would bring Linnea to heel like a pup to master.

"Fine," I muttered to my wolf, even though I doubted Erik could be won over so easily. I'd known he'd be mad at my deception, but now I worried he might never forgive me.

"What's fine?" Linnea asked.

I glared at her. "I wasn't talking to you…cheater."

Linnea's jaw dropped. "You're being judged, Kristin. By me, by the pack, by the Allfather. You're the cheat…and the liar. You've admitted that."

"I never cheated, and I had good reasons to lie. Besides, you're the one who used your claws. Afraid you can't take me down without magic?"

Color flushed Linnea's face, clashing with her wild red hair and making those gorgeous green eyes pop. "I'm the Alpha female of the Varda, chosen by Odin in this very circle to lead my pack. You haven't a chance in hel of defeating me. With or without my magic."

I stepped out from behind the altar, the pain in my leg receding. "Then prove it."

We attacked at the same time, coming together with a thud, feet kicking, heads butting, claw-free hands punching. The noise of the crowd egged us on like two gladiators. Linnea dragged me beneath her, but I managed to get one leg between us and shove the larger female into the air. As she came down, I grabbed her leg and twisted. A loud pop sounded from Linnea's knee.

She landed awkwardly and crumpled to the floor. I jumped on her and then swung my fist into her jaw. "That's for using your claws on me." I punched again, hitting her cheek. "That's for being such a grump the whole time I've been here. And that"—I karate-chopped Linnea's windpipe—"is for being mean to Dahlia. How can you yell at someone so sweet?"

I'd pulled my punches. The display had been more about dominance than crippling my opponent. My wolf growled at Linnea, and to my surprise, the Alpha's eyes widened. We weren't connected in the way of packmates, so we weren't communicating through the bond, but somehow our wolves were together in the hjarta, fighting it out as hard as we were.

Did it have something to do with being in the domr, surrounded by Asgard's magic?

"What are you?" Linnea asked.

"The last one standing, that's what."

"We'll see about that."

Sensing the other female was about to flip me, I jumped off, loose and limber. Looking frustrated and a little uncertain, Linnea rose and limped warily along the edge of the barrier. My torn leg had already healed—faster than normal. Had the energy from the wall sped things up when I'd touched it?

"If you answer my questions, we won't have to do this." Linnea's voice was hoarse, her face bruised.

"Yes, we will. Neither one of us will give up. I'm afraid it's gonna get bloody."

"You would bleed for them?"

"For who?"

"Hati and Skoll. I know you work for them."

"Who?"

"Hati and Skoll." The big Alpha drew the names out like she was talking to a child. "Come on, Kristin. You can do better than that."

"Nope. Don't know them. I just don't like to lose. It's a flaw, really."

"Liar."

Linnea attacked again. I spun and smashed my elbow backward into the Alpha's face. Then I swept Linnea's legs out from under her. Linnea landed hard but managed to kick upward and drill the toe of her shoe into the small of my back, then grab my arm and flip me onto the slate floor. The back of my head smashed into the stone, and black wavered around the edges of my vision. Linnea took full advantage, jumping on top and holding me down.

Ah, crap. It was the worst position I could be in. My advantage was speed and agility, not strength. I tried to swing my legs around, but Linnea sat on my thighs rather than my waist this time. Blood dripped down her chin and landed on my chest.

"You either tell me what Hati and Skoll want you to do, or I'll tear you to pieces and let you bleed to death. No one will stop me."

Back to Hati and Skoll. What the hel could I say? The names rang a bell. I may have heard about them as a child or read about them in mythology, but I couldn't place them.

Gazing past the Alpha's scowling face, I saw Erik pressed once more against the barrier. He looked savage, eyes burning and face drawn as he winked in and out of his solid Valdyr form into the blur of the helmingr, just a breath away from becoming his wolf.

"We'll do this another way, Linnea," he said, his wolf's deep growl distorting the words. "Ask Odin to judge."

"Odin is judging. Through me. Whatever happens within the domr is his will. You know that."

Erik smashed his fists against the barrier and howled. I couldn't stand to see him so ravaged. What if he and his wolf fought each other over me? That could do irreparable damage. I had to end this quickly.

"I told you before, I don't know Hati and Skoll." I heard the panic in my voice over Erik and quelled it. "The names mean nothing to me. And I had no clue a pack lived here until Dahlia came to see me in Denver."

"Why should I believe you?" Linnea asked.

"Because it's the truth."

"That's reassuring, coming from a liar."

"Okay, how about the fact that I won't kill you…but I'm sure as hel going to make you my bikkja."

Linnea lunged forward, incensed by the Old Norse slur, which was just what I wanted. I drove upward at the same time and smashed my forehead into her nose. The Alpha cried out as more blood gushed down. Her hold loosened enough for me to twist my body and throw Linnea off. Then I clambered onto the Alpha's back and tied her into a pain-wracked pretzel against the floor.

"Give up, Linnea. You know you want to. Your wolf wants to."

"Fuck you," she grunted, straining to get free.

I yanked harder on Linnea's arm, aware the tendons and muscles were stretched to the tearing point. "It's in your nature to submit to the strongest female. Your wolf knows it, and you know it. How can you ignore her wishes?"

"You don't know anything about my wolf."

"I know that if you continue to force her to fight, you'll lose her. The two of you will schism, and you'll never get her back. Is that what you want, Linnea? To kill your wolf? Yourself?"

Linnea tried to rear up, but I held her tight. In the hjarta, my wolf bit down on the other wolf's throat. The faint taste of copper filled my mouth. With a gurgling sound, Linnea slumped back to the floor.

"I won't hurt you or your pack, I promise. I came here to avenge my family, nothing more. I won't stay if I'm not wanted."

Silence stretched between us, filled only with our jagged breaths. Finally, Linnea said, "Swear it on Odin's one eye." Her voice was tinged with desperation.

"I swear it." I put as much truth into the words as I could. "Let go, Linnea, before you hurt your wolf for good."

A tear trickled down the Alpha's cheek. Then, with a sob, she went limp in my hold. She was no longer dominant—in spirit or body. A hush fell over the crowd.

At the same time, I was hit with a force that knocked me backward off the Alpha female and squeezed tight around my body before releasing me. I gasped for air.

She's no longer Alpha, my wolf said, satisfied. *We won.*

It was a good feeling, although I hadn't intended for Odin to take away Linnea's Alphaship. Who else would he pick? The pack needed someone.

Oh, well. That wasn't my problem.

I lay on the floor, dazed, staring upward, barely aware of the shocked, whispering Valdyr on the other side of the colorful barrier. My head throbbed, and my body ached, but it was a good kind of ache.

It felt like victory.

Still, I felt…strange. Strong yet shattered at the same time. No, not shattered—scattered, as if I'd been thrown to the wind and put back together again. Closing my eyes, I tried to figure out what was happening. I sensed Linnea, as clear as day, slumped on the floor a few feet away—in pain, humiliated, and demoralized. The former Alpha felt not only defeated but worthless to her pack.

Which irritated me. I'd gone through much more—for three years, at the hands of a monster—than just being beaten in a fair fight. Granted, this defeat was in front of Linnea's entire pack, but her family wasn't dead or her pack subjugated by a sadistic freak.

I pushed onto my elbow. "Suck it up. If all it takes is one fight to defeat you, you never deserved to be Alpha in the first place. You still have a job to do."

Linnea didn't move, so my wolf, still connected to Linnea's in the hjarta, snapped at her like she would a sulky pup. Linnea scrambled backward on hands and feet until she sat with her spine against the stone altar, her eyes cast down.

Huh. My wolf had bitten Linnea's before, but she hadn't reacted so strongly.

Unless things were different now.

Yes. Pack, my wolf said.

What do you mean?

We are pack.

My throat tightened on a sharp inhale. Tears pricked my eyes. I was part of Erik's pack? I just had to beat someone, and I was in?

But I hadn't beaten just anyone. I'd beaten the pack's Alpha female.

Blinking to clear my eyes, I glanced at the colorful walls. No, it had taken more than that. I was in the presence of the gods. Odin had found me worthy.

That was why I could feel Linnea's emotions so clearly, why I felt scattered to the wind. A part of me was connected to every wolf in the room, although I suspected the other Valdyr were muted to me, and me to them, by the domr wall.

Did they realize what Odin had done?

I looked through the translucent colors to my new packmates, taking in their stunned faces. Would they ever accept me? I'd meant what I'd said to Linnea. I wouldn't stay if the pack was hostile toward me.

The former Alpha huddled against the stone altar, broken and bloodied, unable to meet my gaze. Ah, hel. I'd done what I had to in order to win, but perhaps the price was too high. Maybe Linnea really was hurt.

Closing the distance between us, I crouched by her side. The other female opened and closed her mouth several times as if to say something, but all that came out was a squeak.

"I think I can heal you," I said. "I've never really tried before, but there's something about being in this circle. We're surrounded by…life force. Pure creativity." I placed my hands on Linnea's bare, swollen knee. "Tell me if this hurts."

Closing my eyes, I imagined the colors around me soaking into my skin and seeping out through my hands. Linnea flinched, then sighed.

Opening my eyes, I saw the knee looked normal again. Satisfaction bubbled up. I'd been right. The energy around us was pure creation, and I had been the conduit. I reached for Linnea's battered face next.

"No," she whispered. "Those I will keep as a reminder of Odin's will."

"At least let me straighten your nose. You don't want it to heal crookedly."

"Why not? I'm a warrior."

"You're also female. Hold still."

Linnea did as she was told, even though she didn't want to. I was quick and poured a little energy into the injury to take the sting out as I aligned the bone and cartilage. "There. You can thank me later."

Rising to my feet, I glanced around the circle and spotted Dahlia standing with her hand on Erik's arm. He looked like he'd been to hel and back. But he'd stopped flashing in and out of the helmingr, so he must have stabilized.

Regret rose swift and hot within me. If I'd been more insistent earlier rather than carried away by sexual need, I could have warned him, and this never would have happened.

He was also naked, his clothes on the floor around him. A side effect of the helmingr. When he saw me watching him, he snagged his jeans from the floor and pulled them on.

Pity.

Slowly, I crossed the circle toward them, aware my hair was a wild, blood-matted mess and my shirt was ripped. Dahlia met my eyes, smiled, and then stepped backward to merge with the whispering crowd.

At least one member of the pack was happy to have me.

I stopped in front of Erik. His fist shimmered on the barrier. Okay. Maybe he wasn't as stable as I thought.

I shifted back to my regular sight so I no longer saw the colors in the wall between us and could see him more clearly.

"Is anything you said over the past month true?" His voice and eyes were filled with anger.

"Most of it. Except Gina's my foster sister, not my biological sister, we didn't grow up together in Ohio, and I'm not human."

"That much is obvious. Which leaves the question…what are you? You smell human, but you have the speed and strength of one of us—or a Jotun. And you have magic, like a witch or most of the other races. Are you a hybrid?"

"No." I placed my palms flat against the invisible barrier

between us, frustrated I couldn't feel him skin to skin. "Erik, I didn't mean any harm in coming here. I admit I was curious, and I probably shouldn't have stayed to finish the mural, but it was hard for me to leave. Being around your pack was… comforting…exhilarating." I glanced back at Linnea. "Most of the time."

"So why lie? Why insinuate yourself amongst us and hide who you are? We deal with the other races. If you weren't a threat, we still would have bought your work."

"It wasn't that simple. And I tried to tell you."

"Not hard enough."

"I know. I'm sorry. I should have said something as soon as I felt I could trust you, but…I had to know you were strong enough."

"Strong enough for what?"

"To protect me." My heart thumped, and I took a breath to calm it. "And to control the others."

A low rumble sounded from deep within his chest. "What do you mean? Does someone want to hurt you?"

I scrunched my brow, knowing I wasn't explaining things well. "Not yet. But they will…when I…"

My words trailed off, seeming inadequate. Or was I just afraid to tell him? Afraid that admitting I was Valdyr wouldn't be enough? That he'd still walk away?

Even worse, perhaps he'd be unable or unwilling to control the unkyssed males, and then I could never be with him. I glanced around the rotunda, sensing the vast number of strong, unmated males. Could I get away in my wolf form before they turned feral and attacked me?

I raised my eyes toward the open ceiling and the sky above. My magic, especially since being in the circle, would help me jump all the way to the top. That would give me a head start. And then, if things didn't go well after that, I could always shift again. They'd never be able to catch me in that form.

"Talk to me, Kristin. Who wants to harm you? Is it Hati and Skoll?"

"No. I really don't know anyone named Hati or Skoll. It's…" I hesitated again, and my wolf huffed in annoyance, metaphorically rolling her eyes. She wanted to shift and show Erik and her new pack who she really was, wanted to preen and parade in front of them, to greet everyone as the strongest female in the pack.

Fine. Better you than me, seeing as I've made such a mess of things. But don't forget they're going to come after us. You have to be careful.

I glanced back at Linnea. "How do I get out of here? Can you drop the shield?"

Linnea's eyes widened, and she mutely shook her head.

"Then how…?"

"You control it, Kristin," Erik yelled, his frustration finally shattering his restraint. "You beat her and took control. The circle is yours." He began pacing back and forth, his knuckles white from the pressure of his fists.

Gods, he was so angry with me. "So I can just…disintegrate it?"

"No. You ask Odin to release the circle. If you were Valdyr, it would be easy, a simple request. But seeing as I don't know what the fuck you are, you and Linnea could be trapped in there forever!"

"That's not going to happen."

"How do you know?"

"Because…because…" I threw my hands in the air, unable to say the words. "Oh, crap. Please, just…do your best to hold them back." Then I said a quick prayer to the Allfather and reached for my wolf.

Erik

I stared, stunned, as Kristin dissolved into the helmingr just a few feet away, her clothes and stone necklace falling to the tile. My wolf howled triumphantly at the sight. The other wolves in the pack picked up the cry until a crescendo built inside my head, singing through the pack's metaphysical bond.

But my curse surged at the same time. It spilled like black, polluted oil over the walls and reached for her, hitting the still-sanctified circle's invisible barrier.

"No!"

Kristin looked at me, startled. "I'm afraid so," she said, mistaking my meaning.

I ignored her as my wolf and I forced the curse back, determined not to let it have her. We built the walls higher and thicker, plugging any crack that looked like it might burst.

The thought of that happening made me shudder. If the walls ever came down, the pack, me, and now Kristin would be swamped with the foul, negative entity intent on sucking us all into soul-destroying distrust, jealousy, and murder.

I couldn't let that happen again. The pack couldn't stand another direct hit.

Then suddenly, Kristin morphed from the blur of the helmingr into her wolf, her pelt a sleek honey color, her eyes golden amber.

I forgot to breathe. Gods, she was beautiful.

The she-wolf gave an excited jump and a series of yips, then trotted around the circle, showing off. Part of me wanted to laugh and jump around with her, wanted to lick and nuzzle her.

The other part was horrified, and my blood ran cold.

At any time, I could have infected her with the curse, especially when we were making love. I forced myself back from the domr wall.

Kristin, despite her human scent, was Valdyr. That was why my wolf wanted her so badly, why she'd been able to take the circle from Linnea, why she'd passed through the wards around Wolf Ridge without setting off any alarms.

"You're one of the lost Valdyr," I said in a whisper.

She came to a stop and turned to me, cocking her head. Something trickled into my consciousness, and I realized she was trying to communicate with me, mind to mind, but couldn't get through the barrier.

Which meant one thing. Kristin was pack.

Suddenly, she streaked like a golden ball of lightning toward the altar and used it as a springboard to leap toward the ceiling, just as the domr unsanctified and the barrier around the circle came down.

I watched for an instant, amazed by her height as she soared toward the open roof. She barely made it. Fear lodged in my throat as her back legs dangled over the edge of the retracted glass ceiling. I darted forward until I stood directly below her, arms raised. But she pulled herself up and disappeared.

Then, a scent swamped me. Her mouthwatering, sexy scent, with hints of her wolf, the mountains, and the open sky all rolled into one. I recognized it from the taste of her skin when we'd made love. But this scent—the scent she'd released when she became her wolf—was magnified a thousand times over. It swirled up my nose, in my head, and then seeped through the rest of my body, pooling in my groin, stroking the sensitive nerves.

My mind fogged, but my body hardened. I couldn't help thrusting my hips upward, palming and squeezing my rigid cock through my jeans. I wanted her, needed her. I had to have her.

Mine! my wolf cried, howling to get free, as driven as I was to get to her.

Rational thought ceased as the higher functions of my brain shut down. I was intent on just one female. My female. Her scent was so powerful, so enticing, I could do nothing but chase her down. Mount her.

Help me!

The words drifted through the feral haze in my mind—Kristin's voice, tinged with her wolf. Anxious, worried. Pleading and commanding at the same time.

Was that doubt I sensed? Doubt that I could...that I could what?

Control them!

Her fear broke through, and I snapped back to myself, panting and aching.

Kristin was afraid.

The she-wolf I'd unknowingly buried myself deep within just hours ago now ran for her life through the forest, two large males who'd been on sentry duty in the woods hot on her heels.

If they caught her, she would die. I recognized what they were driven to do—I'd felt it myself only moments ago—and I knew she would never submit. Females accepted their males. It was their choice, always. She would never give in, and the two in pursuit, as mindless as I had been, would kill her in the process.

Hold on! I commanded. *They're too strong. Do not engage them.*

Relief poured down the Alpha bond at my response. Our communion, mind to mind, was like biting into a succulent peach, the flavor of Kristin bursting addictively through my brain.

My wolf howled in anger that the other males dared poach his female, dared to harm her. Part of me objected to my wolf's possessive claim, but I let it go, and my wolf leapt down the metaphysical bond toward the male closest to Kristin, attacking viciously until the other male submitted and gave up the chase. Then, my wolf subdued the second male.

Both wolves slowly returned to themselves. Their shock, horror, and confusion filled the bond. My wolf huffed at them aggressively.

Kristin slowed as happiness and hope burst through her.

Come back! I commanded.

No. Others.

I frowned and released my connection to her. In doing so, I realized that chaos reigned around me. Scanning the rotunda, I saw Valdyr in both their forms, many of them acting rabid. Some jumped upward as they tried to trace Kristin's path—either leaping toward the roof as she did or going from floor to floor. Many wolves fell from the top and hit the stone tiles only to get up, even when injured, and try again. Others streamed for the doors. Still others fought with their packmates, who held them back.

With a sinking feeling, I saw that the males in pursuit were all unkyssed. This was what Kristin needed protection against. The feral males. They were the ones she feared.

"Stop!" I yelled. The chaos subsided for a moment, then picked up again. Fury erupted within me. I would not allow any of them to harm a single golden strand on Kristin's head. Or fur on her wolf's body.

I gathered up as much power as I could, dragged it down the Alpha bond from the pack, and siphoned it into myself.

"You. Will. Stop." My voice vibrated with the strength of command, with the Alpha magic only the Alpha female and I possessed. Not magic, really, more a life force that I could draw on. At the same time, my wolf howled at all the other wolves in the vicinity, claiming Kristin as his own, swearing vengeance and swift justice to any who crossed him.

Slowly the chaos subsided, and the unkyssed males in the rotunda returned to themselves, dazed, bruised, and in shock.

I slowly let out my breath. Many of the Valdyr crawled on their bellies toward me—in both forms—accepting my dominance and leadership and reestablishing their place in the pack. I reached out and touched a few on their muzzles.

Then, I strode toward the door, the pack following me. There were other wolves out there. Strong and fast. Kristin would draw them to her from miles around.

I connected to her as I stepped outside and shifted into my

wolf. She seemed almost giddy, safe in the knowledge that I came for her.

Then I sensed another male, bigger than the other two, jump at her from an upwind position. She never saw him coming and tumbled beneath the large lupine body.

He did not belong to the pack.

CHAPTER 18

Kristin

DIRT FILLED MY MOUTH AS THE CRAZED MALE SHOVED ME ONTO the forest floor. I twisted my head and snapped at his muzzle. He didn't retreat like a normal wolf when pushed back by a female. Instead, he chomped on my ear, ripping through tender flesh.

With a yelp, I struggled to get out from under him. I threw him off with a blast of energy and sprang away, but he was right behind me, biting at my tail.

Erik! Please help!

I raced over the rough mountain terrain, twigs snapping beneath my paws, claws scraping on rocks, other animals running for cover.

He's not pack. Run!

A chill shot up my spine, but I didn't panic. I'd escaped Hans when I was barely more than a pup. I could get away now, although the wolves that had chased me all those years ago weren't the warrior wolves in Erik's pack—or lone wolves who had Varda potential.

Spotting a twenty-foot-high rock face ahead of me, I swerved toward it. When I reached the base, I leapt, channeling the magic within me to create an updraft that carried me up and over the edge. I kept running, swiveling my ears back to listen for the feral wolf. Demented barks and howls came from below, along with thumps and scraping sounds, as the male attempted to follow me up the cliff.

Lost him, I informed Erik. I tried to sound cool, but my wolf practically crowed at my victory.

It was strange talking to him when I was merged with my wolf—and he with his wolf. I thought in complete, complex sentences, but the message my wolf relayed over the bond was just a few words, the ideas transmitted and received mostly as smells, tastes, and images.

I had a spatial sense of where Erik was on the mountain, where every packmate was, and I knew he raced in my direction. Because I was focused on him, I heard him clearly, but if I focused on someone else, that other Valdyr's thoughts became clear.

It had been the same in my family, and I'd missed that intimate communion. A spurt of pleasure warmed my chest. After all these years, *I belonged.*

A part of me couldn't believe it.

Some distance away, the pack spread out as Erik directed them into a net-like pattern. Were they herding me, the other feral wolves, or both? My wolf yipped excitedly at the challenge, still wanting to prove herself, to win.

Enough already, I groused. *Can't we just go find Erik? It will be safer.*

No. Beat him too.

Oh, come on. Showing off is not attractive. Erik's wolf won't like it.

He will.

Obviously, I didn't understand Valdyr courtship. *Okay. You're driving this boat. Just don't piss him off more than I already have.*

My wolf leapt onto a log and trotted along, tail high, ears

perked. Her excitement was infectious, and I couldn't help smiling. Erik had come to my rescue and had corralled many of the unkyssed wolves in the pack. Surely he would accept me, want to be with me.

I was Valdyr. Nothing stood in our way.

A snarl sounded to my left. I whipped around to see a young pack male barreling toward me. I thought my wolf would run, but instead, she charged back at him, angry that he dared challenge her.

Holy crap, what are you doing?

Disrespect. Teach lesson.

I closed my eyes, then popped them open when my wolf growled fiercely at the male on both the physical and metaphysical planes. He hesitated, and she snapped in his face, causing him to tuck into a submissive position with his tail curled over his rump and his body crouched low to the ground. The crazed look left his eyes, and he actually rolled onto his back, exposing his belly and neck.

Standing stiff-legged over him, she huffed for a minute, then leaned down to lick his muzzle.

I couldn't believe it. My wolf had dominated the feral male and actually pulled him back to himself. It had to be because he was a packmate. No way would that lone wolf have submitted.

I sensed Erik and the rest of the pack closing in. My wolf darted in the opposite direction, making me roll my eyes.

You know, if you don't let him catch you, you'll never get to be his female.

Must prove himself.

The fact that he's Alpha of the biggest, strongest pack we've ever come across and that he single-handedly controlled all those feral males isn't good enough for you? Or how about the multiple orgasms he provided? Personally, I thought they were kind of cool. I'd like to have more of them if you don't mind.

She sniffed in disdain at my ignorance. *He'll catch us.*

She galloped through streams, water splashing everywhere, and leapt over downed trees and rocky boulders. Her stride lengthened, and her body twisted and turned, sensitive to every nuance in the landscape.

The chase invigorated her—us. Several times, I thought we were caught as the pack moved in, but we always managed to escape. A few times, I suspected it wasn't so much an escape as we were let go.

But why?

She was attacked again by another feral wolf, but Erik brought that male under control. In fact, he brought several males under control before they even reached her. And she faced another one down by herself.

When we were forced high into the mountains, where snow still covered the ground, and the trees were few and far between, I realized he'd been herding us. My wolf's padded feet sent snow flying as she raced full out, the wind ruffling her fur, her tongue lolling out the side of her mouth.

As she crested a hill, I saw the windswept land come to an end at a cliff that looked out over a river gorge. In an arc behind us, the pack closed in, Erik at the center. My wolf slowed, and the other wolves followed suit.

It was déjà vu, in a way. Just like the last time we'd been chased by a pack—led by Hans. Except then, we'd been running for our lives and hadn't wanted to get caught. We'd almost slid over the cliff's edge. That wouldn't happen now—Erik would never herd us toward a dangerous spot.

My wolf walked closer toward the precipice, and my fear rose. *What are you doing? Stop!*

No fear, she huffed.

Easy for you to say! You're not the one with cremnophobia. I squeezed my eyes shut and tried to calm myself.

She stopped. *Look.* She sounded pleased, and I pried my eyes open.

Wolves weren't only behind me but on the cliffs below and on the opposite side of the gorge. Maybe a few hundred of them, including the twenty or so behind me. All were looking up at me.

And you're pleased about this because...?

Smart, strong male. My male. Then she howled, long and loud, her nose pointed to the sky.

A wolf picked up the call behind me, and I knew it was Erik by the dominance that flooded our bond. The rest of the wolves joined in until a beautiful chorus filled the air, the sounds harmonizing. We reached a musical peak, and the song swirled around us before colors burst across the sky. The same colors that had surrounded me in the circle.

As one, the wolves stopped singing, and the colors slowly dissipated.

I gasped for breath, tears coursing down my face. I remembered this ceremony—the Handsal. I'd experienced it when two of my brothers had howled to join our pack, but I'd been young, and the ceremony had never been as wondrous as what I'd just witnessed.

I thought I was already part of the pack. I could speak to Erik mind-to-mind.

Yes.

But this was necessary too?

Acceptance.

So, Odin had accepted me in the circle, but the pack had accepted me here. My eyes welled up again. I hadn't realized until today how much I wanted to belong to this pack.

And Erik had been the first to answer my call.

Facing him, my wolf sat on her haunches, relaxed and happy. I recognized his wolf immediately. He stood out front, larger than most of the others, almost double the size of a natural wolf. His eyes shone a deep, golden brown, surrounded by white fur that continued down the sides of his muzzle.

The rest of his coat was dark and glossy, all the way from the points of his soft-looking ears to the tip of his fluffy, raised tail.

A gorgeous creature, just like his other Valdyr form.

My wolf barked in greeting.

His wolf stalked forward until we were separated from the rest of the pack in our own little world. Connected to him like this, I could sense his conflicted emotions. And something else, something...dark. It flared toward me and then withdrew, causing my wolf to stand and growl.

What was that? It felt...evil. It wasn't a part of Erik but was attached to him in some way.

I shifted back to my Valdyr form, keeping my body in the blur of the helmingr—

for modesty's sake, but also because it was too cold at this altitude to stand naked in the wind.

"Are you all right?" I raised my hand and stepped toward him.

He shifted, not bothering to obscure his nudity. I couldn't help but stare at his muscular chest and arms, remembering how he'd touched me, held me, as we'd made love. My eyes continued downward over his washboard stomach to see he was aroused, his cock engorged and heavy. The sight sent an answering wave of heat through me, tightening and softening my body at the same time.

Emboldened, I took another step forward.

"Stay there," he said with a growl, shifting into the helmingr.

I dropped my hand. "You're still mad."

He didn't answer for a minute. The flaring of his nostrils was the only sign of his unrest. I suspected he was trying to control himself. "If you had just come to me and explained the situation, all this could have been avoided. Instead, your lies put everyone in danger. I lead this pack, Kristin. I don't know how it was in your old pack or if you even had one, but here, what I say goes. And if you ever lie to me again, I swear you'll find my jaws squeezed tight around your throat. Got it?"

"Yes." Tears pricked my eyes. "You have to understand. The first time I shifted around my pack, the results were disastrous. I was young, and I didn't know how to control it. I had to know if you were strong enough, if I could trust you to keep me safe. Keep the others safe."

"So you thought you would win me over by sleeping with me first?"

Alarm ripped through me. "No. That had nothing to do with it. I planned to tell you before last night, but…things got out of hand. You said we would talk in the morning. Then you left, and everything went to hel."

"You can say that again." He lifted his hand to rub the back of his neck. A muscle ticked in his jaw.

I took another step forward, wanting to soothe him, but he glared at me, and I stopped. "Erik, everything's okay now. We got through it without any serious injuries." I remembered the tear in my ear and lifted my hand to touch it. The skin was tender, but the cut had healed.

"You're not hurt?" he asked.

"I'm fine, and everyone else seems to be okay. Believe me, that's a huge step up from the first time I shifted."

"When was that?" he asked.

"During my ulf-risa. A lot of wolves died that day. I haven't lived openly with a pack since then."

He frowned. "You took a risk coming here. The Varda have a high number of unkyssed males. Odin chooses them for their strength and speed. We're warriors."

"I know. Believe me, it scared the hel out of me. But I had faith in you. I knew you were powerful enough. And I controlled some of the males too. My wolf subdued two of them." I couldn't help the pride that filled my voice.

Erik nodded. "She's strong."

"Tell me about it. I wanted to come to you as soon as you were in control, but she wanted..." I trailed off, fearing I'd make my wolf look foolish.

"To make me work for it. I know. My wolf relished the chase."

Relief poured through me, and I smiled. "They're quite the pair. I think... I think they were joined when we were together last night. They mated as we made love." Desire flared in his chocolate-brown depths, and my heart flooded with warmth. "I had an amazing time."

He exhaled heavily and dropped his gaze. Regret carved itself into every inch of his face. "Kristin, I can't—"

I raised my hand again, afraid to let him speak. "No, just listen. I know we got off to a bad start, and I realize you have all the reasons in the world to distrust me, but I'll tell you everything. I'll answer any questions you have—where I'm from, why I lied. I'll even tell you about my magic." I breathed deeply to quell the tremor in my voice. "We're good together, Erik. You can't just throw me—us—away."

"I'm not throwing you away. I want you to stay with the pack..." He paused, and I had the impression he was fighting with his wolf—with himself. "Just not as my mate."

The words didn't penetrate at first, and then they crashed over me. My wolf paced in agitated circles. "But...I'm Valdyr, just like you. There's nothing to stop us being together."

"I'm stopping us. You're a strong addition to the pack, but your place will never be by my side. It can't be."

"Why not?"

"Because..."

I could feel his wolf protesting. They must have come to an agreement as a mournful yowl siphoned down the Alpha bond. "Look, there's more going on here than you realize. It's a long story, and I don't want to get into it right now. We'll talk about it later." He raised his chin, and that muscle in his cheek jumped. "Just know that the pack needs you, but I don't. Not in that way. I won't ever take a mate."

I stared at him, stunned. My wolf whined, hurt and confused. This wasn't right. My wolf knew it. His wolf knew it. We were supposed to be together. He was the strong male my mother had told me about, the one I would kyss, create a life with, belong to—and he would belong to me.

That he would dump me now was unthinkable.

After everything I'd just been through, and after the way he'd fought for me, saved me, how could he walk away?

Gods, I was a fool.

I'd slept with the Valdyr once. A few wonderful hours in which we'd used each other's bodies. We hadn't even been on a date. Of course, he didn't want to mate with me. Why would he? I'd lied and put his pack in danger. Hurt and shamed his Alpha female. Took away Linnea's place in the pack. For all I knew, Erik may have been involved with her—that's how it was with natural wolves.

Needing to put space between us, I took a step back. Then another. I couldn't even run away because the pack had trapped me here. Everyone a witness to my humiliation.

"Kristin, I—"

I heard the regret in his voice. Or was it pity?

"I'm sorry," he continued. "It's my fault. I never should have gotten involved with you in the first—"

"Shut up." The words burst from my mouth in a desperate attempt to get him to stop talking. I pressed my fist to my forehead and blinked back tears. The last thing I wanted was for him to see me cry. "For Odin's sake, you've said enough. Just take your pack and go. I won't bother you again."

"You are my pack. Bonded by Odin to serve the Varda. I don't think you understand—"

"Quit telling me what I do and don't understand! So we fucked last night—who cares? Obviously, not you. Well, not me either. And you know what? I don't want to be part of your stupid pack. I have Gina. She's all the family I need. You and everyone else can go to hel."

I stomped toward the edge of the cliff, my cremnophobia consumed by my anger, pain, and bewilderment. At the edge, I turned back to him. He'd followed me out, a concerned look on his face.

"And good luck finding an artist as good as me to finish your damn wall. I hope you choke on rock dust for the next millennium."

He closed the distance between us. "Kristin, you're—"

"I said, shut up." Then I turned back to the edge, flipped him the bird over my shoulder, and leapt into the abyss. Behind me, he roared in shock and horror. Fingers brushed my heel as I tumbled down, but he was too late to stop my descent. I careened off the cliff, my terror forgotten in the sting of his rejection.

Jagged rocks and the odd tree growing out of the sheer mountainside flew past me. Wind froze the tears on my cheeks and drowned out my sobs. Gods, I'd been such a fool! We'd had one night together, and I'd assumed that meant a lifetime commitment?

Mate, my wolf said.

He's not our mate. He's nothing to us.

The ground rushed up toward me so fast it made me dizzy. A strange lethargy had come over me, mixing with my despair. It stole over my limbs and into my brain. I knew I needed to act, but still, I let myself fall.

Shift, my wolf urged. I barely heard her.

Shift!

Teeth snapped in my face, and I came back to myself with a jolt. Adrenaline raced through me as the bottom of the gorge loomed dangerously close. Reaching my arms out to the side, I let go of myself, dissolved, and reformed. My sight sharpened, the prick of feathers burst through my skin, and my toes formed into razor-like claws.

Wind buffeted a golden wingspan that stretched well over six feet. I slowed, but it wasn't enough. Using my magic, I thickened the air, which slowed the rate of my fall. Still, it would be close. I managed to catch a draft at the last second and glide over the river that wound around rocks at the bottom of the gorge. My claws skimmed the ice-cold water as I fought to stabilize my avian body.

Finally, I gained control and flapped my wings to avoid the rapids and boulders. I hadn't flown for a while—and certainly not off the edge of a cliff. The closest I'd come since the first time I'd shifted into my eagle was from the top of a tree.

Even though my heart felt like it had been ripped in two, my eagle—the last part of my threefold nature—was pleased to spread her wings, and a bittersweet joy filled me.

I gained height, seeing the pack with my eagle eyes. Magical colors burst with vibrancy around every wolf. Through the bond, I could feel their shock and awe, their amazement as they witnessed my flight—soaring, looping, spiraling slowly upward.

Surprisingly, I didn't sense any horror or disgust in them like I'd feared.

Not that it mattered anymore. I didn't need or want any of them. Especially their Alpha.

Then, a special aura caught my eye on the opposite side of the gorge, the colors delicate. Dahlia, in wolf form. She was so small and brown next to a huge blond wolf with black around his eyes, in his ears, and at the tip of his tail. He looked terrifying and gorgeous all at the same time.

Dane, I thought, even though I couldn't connect to him.

I swooped low over my friend and sent out a sharp cry as if to say I was sorry. The feeling that came back through the bond was excitement, love, and acceptance.

Okay, so I'd miss the petite Valdyr a lot. But just because I left the pack didn't mean I couldn't see her anymore.

I came around for another pass. This time, Dane jumped

upward and snapped at me. Dahlia barked at him. He was such an ass. As if I would ever hurt my friend. Stupid, dominant, overprotective wolf.

Rising quickly on an updraft, I soon crested the top of the cliff. Erik, still naked, lay half over the precipice edge with a huge black wolf, Gunn most likely, pinning his legs to the top.

I flew over him, screeching my pain and anger. He scrambled back onto land and pushed Gunn away.

"Kristin!"

The sound of my name on his lips only infuriated me more. He'd said it many times last night when we'd made love. Whispered it, groaned it, shouted it.

How could he just throw away what we had?

I swooped over him again, coming in low and fast, my claws extended. At the last moment, he ducked. I barely grazed the skin on his back. Then, I circled a final time over the gathered Valdyr before heading south across the mountain range to Denver and Gina—my hopes and dreams dashed.

For the first time since I'd escaped Hans, I'd revealed my true nature to a pack, become one of them, and made love with a male of my own kind. And yes, I'd been hoping he'd want me as a mate, but even just dating for a while would have been nice.

Wham, bam, thank you, ma'am.

Well, screw him. I was done.

And if I ever saw Erik again, he'd better pray I didn't claw his balls off.

CHAPTER 19

"YOU'VE GOT TO GET HER BACK!"

I closed my eyes and tried to block out what little I could hear of Gunn's voice above the mournful howling of my wolf—and my own mourning too. It was sharp like a knife with regret, disbelief, and anger stabbing deep.

Added to the cacophony were Odin's words, which had repeated in my head ever since Kristin had flown away:

> *Eagle eye. Earth to sky. Fly, wolf, fly.*
> *Lay her down. Wolf and crown. Cry, wolf, cry.*
> *One and one. It's begun... Love dies.*

"She's the wolf from the prophecy," Gunn roared, hot on my heels, as I pushed on the hidden door that led from the tunnels into the rotunda at the back of the cave. "We need her!"

I rounded on him, eyes burning, teeth grinding, wanting to rip him apart—rip everyone apart. "You think I don't know that? You think I don't know better than anyone else what's at stake?"

The noise in the rotunda swelled as the rest of the pack swarmed into the den from every direction, all of them looking to me for answers. They'd seen what I'd seen. They knew the prophecy.

Secrets didn't last long among the Varda.

I turned sharply and started across the open area—then stopped short when I saw my shirt in the middle of the circle, along with Kristin's silky underwear and her necklace. The clothes and the Norse rune had fallen from her body when she'd shifted into the helmingr.

I quickly scooped them up.

Kristin. A wolf and an eagle. A Valdyr prophesized by Odin. A female who was supposed to be my mate.

I knew it. My wolf knew it. She knew it.

And I'd pushed her away.

I had to. I couldn't risk infecting her or the rest of the Varda with the curse.

Still, the look on her face, the pain and anger and bewilderment in her eyes, had just about killed me, especially as she'd been so happy just moments before.

"Fyrstr!"

The summons drew my gaze up toward the fourth floor, and I saw Elli, a Valdyr in her late teens who hadn't gone through the ulf-risa yet, peering down at me from the landing, a sheaf of parchment in her hand. She lowered her head in submission when our eyes met.

My whole pack, besides Gunn, had been doing that since I'd asserted such dominance over them to control the unkyssed males.

It had to stop.

Grinding my teeth together, I took several quick steps and leapt to the fourth floor. I grasped the handrail and swung my body over the edge. Elli gasped and stepped back, her gaze fixed on the wooden planks at her feet.

I placed my fingers under her chin and gently lifted it. "What is it, ulf-ungr?"

"She's a Gullari," Elli said, her cheeks flushed and eyes shining.

"A what?"

"A Gullari. I've been helping out in the library, cataloging and transferring the texts into digital files, and I came across a number of old stories—myths, really. But not myths because she's real."

"Who's real?"

"Kristin. The stories are about a powerful female Valdyr who is both wolf and eagle. She has special powers and is only born in times of great danger. In the tales, she and the hero always defeat Hati and Skoll before Freyja joins them in the Kyssa. It's so romantic."

I smoothed the frown from my brow. I didn't want to frighten or intimidate the young Valdyr, but the last thing I wanted to discuss was romance or the Kyssa—especially in connection with Kristin.

I grasped the parchment. The paper crackled in my fingers, and I had to squint to read the faded words written centuries before.

"I already transferred them," she continued, pulling a flash drive from her pocket. "The manuscripts were low priority, but I did it on my own time because I love the stories."

All week, we'd had our best Valdyr searching the library for clues to the meaning of the prophecy and come up with nothing. Not enough of the old texts had been transcribed, and during the years the curse had poisoned the pack, the library and manuscripts had fallen into disrepair. Some of the more ancient works were crumbling with age.

No one had thought to look through mythical stories.

I placed a hand on her shoulder and squeezed. "Good job, Elli. We'll read them."

She beamed up at me. "I'll keep looking. Maybe other stories will help." She spun and ran back along the landing to the hidden door in the stone wall.

I reluctantly returned my gaze to the anxious throng of Valdyr standing on the rotunda floor and gazing up at me. They needed to be reassured, but I had little to tell them.

I had to try. It was my responsibility—they were my responsibility. I breathed deeply and tried to calm my mind and savaged heart. Tried to find my center.

Placing my hands on the railing, I selected my words carefully. "Every one of us was chosen by Odin to be a part of the Varda. We fight to keep Fenrir imprisoned, defeat Hati and Skoll, and ensure the world's safety. War is constantly upon us, and every Valdyr has suffered because of it. No one said it would be easy." I lifted the parchment. "If the stories are true, a Gullari has been sent to us. Hidden by the Allfather until the time was right. Chosen like you to fight in these dangerous times. We'll get her back, and Kristin will help vanquish this threat. Trust in the Allfather who created her, trust in your wolf, and most importantly, trust in each other. We will prevail."

The crowd calmed, and I strode toward my office. Gunn appeared from the opposite direction and followed me inside.

"What's the latest on Gina?" I asked as I sat behind my desk.

"She's still unconscious." Worry filled Gunn's voice. "She doesn't appear to be hurt, and she's breathing, but if she doesn't wake soon, we'll have to move her to the infirmary."

"Is it safe?"

"Would you rather have Kristin's sister die on us? We need Kat to take a look at her and see if she has any internal injuries. We don't know what Freyja's magic did to her when she tried to break through the wards."

"Send rekkrs to Kristin's apartment in Missoula. I want to know if she returned there. Gather anything that might tell us where she's gone. And patch her phone through to us just in case."

"We know where she's gone. Back to Denver. Unless you think she's done a runner?"

"No. She's angry and hurt but not scared. She'll return for Gina. Then we just have to convince her to stay."

"*You* have to convince her to stay." Gunn shook his head. "All it would take is one little kiss. Surely, you can sacrifice that for the pack."

My anger exploded out of me, searing through every cell and nerve ending, pounding in my head. I almost jumped across the desk. Hands fisted, I lunged at Gunn, my chair crashing to the floor behind me. "Don't fucking talk to me about sacrifice! You think I don't want Kristin here? You think it didn't kill me and my wolf to push her away?"

Gunn's fingers clenched on the back of the chair he stood behind as if to hold himself in place. "Then why did you?"

"To keep her safe from the curse. To keep us all safe, including the gods-damned world. What do you think will happen if the Varda falls?"

"Hati and Skoll will free Fenrir."

"And then?"

"Ragnarök."

"Yeah, the bloody end of the world in a storm of flood and fire. The Jotun fighting the gods. Odin killed by Fenrir. All because I couldn't keep it in my pants."

Gunn's brow furrowed as he tried to understand. "How is one thing related to the other?"

"If the curse slips from me to Kristin, it could infect the entire pack. It almost destroyed us last time."

"And you think you're the only one powerful enough to contain it? For fuck's sake, Erik. Let us help you. Odin chose us all for our strength. Not just you."

"You are strong. Every one of you. But he chose me for this."

"Are you certain?"

I sighed, the anger suddenly draining away from me. I

straightened my chair and slumped in it. "I know it as surely as you know your name. Instinct whispers it to me. This is my cross to bear."

Gunn's face fell. He looked as depressed as I felt.

The only chance I had of being with Kristin was to destroy the curse at its source. Wherever the hel that was. We'd been searching for it for years and come up empty. I'd almost given up.

But I wouldn't give up on Kristin. She belonged here with the Varda, if not with me. That was my cross to bear too.

"Did Gina have a cell phone on her? We'll find out where Kristin is and call her from it. She'll pick up, and she'll have to listen. We have her sister as ransom."

Kristin

My eagle spread her wings to slow her flight and landed none too gently on a darkened high-rise balcony, knocking over a wooden lounge chair.

I was spent. Emotionally and physically. I'd barely slept the night before, fought a tough battle with Linnea, run from an entire pack of warrior wolves, jumped from a cliff, and flown all the way from Missoula to Denver—no small feat, even for my large and powerful eagle.

Oh, and I'd been dumped by the male I thought would love me forever.

It had been a long, sucky day.

All I wanted to do was curl up on the couch with a bottle of wine and cry on Gina's shoulder.

I shifted back to my Valdyr form, not bothering with the helmingr. Gina had seen me naked before. Besides, the apartment was dark. My sister was probably out.

Hopefully, she wasn't undercover or on a stakeout.

After locating the key in a secret compartment behind the planter, I unlocked the sliding door and stepped inside.

Home sweet home. Except it wasn't.

Home was a mountain cavern buried deep in the rock, miles of forest to run through, the crisp scent of snow, fresh air, pine needles, and the comforting connection to my pack.

And Erik. More than anything, he felt like home.

My wolf howled again, something she'd done for half the trip here, and I lost it.

Quit yowling! He doesn't want us, and there's nothing we can do about it.

I flipped on the light by the door and was met by disaster. If I didn't know better, I'd have thought someone had tossed Gina's apartment. Clothes, books, and even a towel, which I was sure had been wet, covered the brown faux-suede couch. Empty mugs sat on the end tables, and surveillance gadgets covered the coffee table. A camera had been taken apart and the pieces scattered everywhere.

I was afraid to go into the kitchen or, heaven forbid, the bathroom.

On the counter between the kitchen and dining room, a phone sat on a base with a blinking red light. As I reached for it, the phone rang. The display read *Gina's cell.*

Misery welled up, and my throat thickened. I had to swallow several times before I picked up. "Where are you? I just got in, and I was hoping you'd be here. You won't believe what's happened."

Silence.

"Gina?" I said.

"It's not Gina, it's Erik. Don't hang up."

I went hot, then cold, and inside, my wolf barked joyously. "What do you want? And why are you calling from Gina's cell?"

"Because she's here, Kristin. I don't think she ever left Missoula."

"Yes, she did. I dropped her off at the airport yesterday morning. She had a 9:00 a.m. flight back to Denver."

"Well, she didn't get on the plane. Last night, she tried to break through the wards around Wolf Ridge. That's how we knew she was a witch and you weren't who you said you were." He paused as if searching for the right words. "The wards are strong, Kristin. Freyja set them herself. Gina was knocked unconscious."

The blood drained from my head, and I gripped the counter to stay upright. "Is she okay?"

"I don't know. We moved her to the infirmary, but she still hasn't woken up. Our doctor has looked at her but can't find anything wrong. It's like she's just sleeping."

"Then she'll wake up. She has to. Freyja would never let her die."

"I'm sorry to say this, but you can't count on the gods for anything."

I chose my words carefully. "Gina's a daughter of Freyja. Surely, she has some sway with the goddess."

"I don't know that Freyja pays much attention to her witch 'daughters.' But maybe if Gina's coven—is that what it's called?—prayed to her or asked for a boon, Freyja would respond. I'll do the same. I'll cross to Asgard if I have to. I promise."

His words sank in slowly. Cross to Asgard? As in the home of the gods? "I'm sorry. What did you say about…Asgard?"

"If Gina doesn't wake up, I'll petition Freyja myself."

My mouth dropped open. "You can do that?"

"Yes. It used to be that every Valdyr could. Now I'm the only one. But we're teaching the pups."

"I had no idea. There's so much I've forgotten."

"Forgotten?"

"Pack history. I've been on my own for a long time."

"It's likely your pack didn't know. Our kind splintered and went their separate ways thousands of years ago. We call packs like your old one the 'lost Valdyr.'" Another gust of breath sounded at the end of the line. "We have so much to talk about, and you'll want to see Gina, of course. I have a helicopter standing by. Can you make it to the Wolf Ridge building downtown? We have a landing pad on the roof."

"You want me to come back?"

"I never wanted you to leave. Your home is here."

"Just not with you." I clamped my lips together to hold back the grief that flooded me again.

He sighed. "We'll talk about that too. There are reasons I can't be with a Valdyr female. How soon can you get to the landing pad?"

I looked at the clock on the wall, cursing myself for having said anything about our botched relationship. It made me sound desperate and weak. "Twenty minutes. I just have to put some clothes on."

"You're naked?" His words came out strangled.

Glancing down, I saw that not only was I naked, I was aroused too. Nipples hard, skin flushed. All it took was hearing his voice.

"Shut up, Erik," I said, then hung up.

The rhythmic *whump, whump, whump* of the rotor blades above my head drowned out all sound as the helicopter landed gently in the empty parking lot in front of the den at Wolf Ridge. It was pitch black, but I sensed Erik immediately through our bond and knew he waited close by.

After unbuckling my belt, I opened the door and jumped down, hunching over to avoid the blades. Two steps later, Erik grasped my hand and led me toward the main entrance. The warmth from his palm traveled up my arm and into my heart before I could protect myself.

Once we'd cleared the blades, I tried to tug my hand free, but he tightened his grip. My wolf pranced around with happiness.

I scowled. *Oh, come on. He dumped us!*

No. Confused.

Not confused. And definitely not our mate!

I tugged on my hand again, exasperated and annoyed with both my wolf and Erik. "Let go of me," I said above the sound of the helicopter.

He stopped on the stairs and faced me, finally releasing his grip when the helicopter lifted into the air. The wind blew back my hair, and I glared up at him for good measure. A whispered expletive reached down the Alpha bond toward me—*Fuck.*

"Not bloody likely," I said.

His eyes widened. "Sorry. I didn't mean... I just..." He clenched his jaw together. "This is going great."

"What were you expecting?"

"I don't know." He glanced up as the helicopter turned and veered away from us over the mountain. When he looked back, he held out his other hand. "Here."

Nestled in his big palm was my necklace.

"I found it in the rotunda," he continued. "It fell off when you shifted into the helmingr. Do you want me to do it up for you?"

"No." Trying not to brush my fingertips against his skin, I gathered up the rune and the black leather cord and brought the ends together at my nape. But I kept missing the clasp, even though I'd fastened it a thousand times before.

Frustration rose, and I glared at him in anticipation of his offer to help.

His eyes widened. He shoved both hands in the back pockets of his jeans and waited. After a moment, he said, "You should know that I stole it from you."

"What?"

"Your necklace. You didn't lose it. I stole it when we were up at the lookout the other day."

The clasp finally clicked into place. "Why on earth would you do that?"

"Because nothing about you added up, starting with the fact that my wolf was going wild for a human woman. The same woman that my sweet, submissive cousin hired after being told not to. She defied me for you. A human. And on top of all that, you were wearing a Norse rune." He rolled his head on his neck as if working out a kink. "I had it tested."

"And?"

"And nothing. It's just a stone."

"Surprise, surprise." Although, if it had been magical, that wouldn't have surprised me either.

He continued up the stairs, and I followed. We entered the den and headed toward the cave that was carved into the rock wall. "The infirmary's this way."

Old, soft-looking jeans hugged his thighs and butt as he led the way. Work boots covered his feet, and a black T-shirt stretched across his shoulders.

Gods, he made my mouth water. My wolf yipped in agreement.

At the back of the cave, he pushed through a hidden door. "You won't have any trouble getting past the wards. You're keyed in now. You can go anywhere except private homes and offices."

"You're not afraid I'll spill your secrets and betray the pack?"

He stopped to face me in the excavated tunnel. "To betray us would be to betray yourself. We're guided by instinct, Kristin, which was instilled in us by Odin thousands of years ago. You couldn't be disloyal even if you wanted to—which you don't."

"You don't know that."

"Yeah, I do." He turned and continued down the tunnel.

I tore my eyes away and looked around, comforted by the enclosed space. The tunnel was well-worn, and it intersected with other passageways as we continued deeper into the mountain.

My eagle didn't like it, but my wolf did.

"Do you know many others like me? You know, wolf and eagle? I was the only one in my pack."

"No. You're unique. Odin created you that way for a reason." He glanced over his shoulder. "It's an amazing, remarkable gift."

Pride and pleasure flooded through me at the same time as disappointment did. It would have been nice to talk to someone who'd gone through what I had.

"So, you've never heard of any others?"

He didn't answer. Instead, he pushed through another door. "We're here. Gina's in the room at the back."

It was like entering a modern hospital with every kind of high-tech equipment I could imagine. Valdyr, young and old, all looked at me as I walked by. When I met their gaze, they dropped their eyes and nodded.

Respect, my wolf said, puffing up and trotting in a regal manner.

I don't care what it is. It creeps me out.

At the end of the hallway stood two large Valdyr on either side of the door to Gina's room. "Is she a prisoner?" I asked, my voice tightening.

"No, but we'll want to question her when she wakes up. She did try to break in."

"That was to protect me. She was afraid you'd hurt me or lock me up."

"If you trust her, Kristin, that's all we need to know. We won't hold her."

"I'm not sure you could. Gina's a powerful witch. And besides, I said *I* trusted her. I didn't say you should. She'll ferret out your secrets and break through your security. Not that she'll need to. I'll tell her everything." I said the last defiantly, glaring at him as I planted my hands on my hips.

His lips quirked. "You'll do whatever instinct tells you to. And that's whatever's best for the pack. It may be that Gina has some role to play. You never know who the gods have recruited for their purposes."

"And that doesn't bother you?"

He paused before answering. "Sometimes."

He opened the door to Gina's room, and I hurried inside, focusing my second sight—my avian sight—so I could see my sister's aura as she lay on the bed. Her black hair was spread out on a pillow, and her body was covered with a light-pink blanket. A white hospital gown peeked from beneath the covers, and several machines flashed and beeped as they monitored her vitals.

But it was her aura that made me gasp. The bright colors were denser and more vibrant than ever, fluctuating wildly like a solar flare.

"Help me roll her over," I said urgently.

Erik pulled gently as I pushed until Gina lay on her side. Her hospital gown threatened to open at the back, and I held it together.

"What are you doing?" Gunn yelled at us from the doorway.

I looked up to see him striding protectively toward us. Behind him, a dark-haired, slender female in a white coat met my eyes. The doctor, I assumed. But, like the rest of the Valdyr except Erik and Gunn, she couldn't hold my gaze.

"I'm looking for any leaks." I turned back to my sister.

"You mean energy," the female said, her eyes wide, voice excited.

"Yes."

"You can see that?" Erik asked.

"Not with my normal sight. But when I examine her through my eagle's eyes, I can."

"What does it look like?" the doctor asked.

"Vivid, colorful. The more powerful or magical the being, the brighter the aura. It looks similar to the fire that burns a Valdyr on the funeral pyre. You've seen that, haven't you?" I had been able to see the magical fire that cremated my mother before I even knew about my eagle. I assumed the other Valdyr could see it too.

"Yes."

Erik put a hand on the female's shoulder and ushered her forward. "Kristin, this is our doctor. Kat, this is Kristin, Gina's sister."

"Foster sister, technically—just in case that makes a difference. She's a witch, not a Valdyr."

Kat bowed her head in a show of submission and respect. "It's an honor to meet you, Fyrsta."

I clenched my jaw. I didn't know what Kat had just called me, but I assumed it was meant in a nice way. All this obsequious behavior, however, was getting on my nerves.

"It's nice to meet you too. Thank you for looking after my sister."

"I haven't been able to do much other than monitor her. According to my tests, there's nothing wrong with her. She's just...sleeping." Again, she didn't meet my gaze.

"Kat."

"Yes?"

"Look at me when you talk, please."

She lifted dismayed eyes to me. "I'm sorry, Fyrsta."

"That's okay. I know I'm different, being part eagle and all, but other than that, there's nothing really special about me. Females all have their talents, right?" I was pretty certain only the female Valdyr had additional magic, but I could have mixed up that memory too.

"Right," Kat replied with a slow smile.

Gunn made an impatient sound. "What about Gina? Is she leaking or what?"

I gently rolled my sister back into place and pulled the blankets up. "Not that I can see. Her aura is strong, really strong, and it's bound tightly in place, which is good. I've seen life-threatening injuries before, and the aura streamed up and away from the body toward the sky until it disappeared. Passing over to the woods outside Valhalla, I hope."

"Like with my ulf-verr."

Once again, the voice came from the door, and I glanced over. A pregnant female, slender with a dancer's sculpted body, stood in the entryway with tears in her eyes. Her long brown hair hung around her pale face, and dark shadows surrounded her eyes. *Ulf-verr* meant *husband*, and my heart broke for her. "I'm so sorry. I'm sure your mate died a warrior, and you'll see him again someday. My mother was reunited with my father and brothers upon her death. She appeared to me in the helmingr one last time and told me."

"My mate didn't go to the heavens. He was dying—I felt him leaving me—and then something...someone...forced his life force back into him. It was you, Fyrsta. You held Robbie here long enough for me to arrive and intertwine my energy with his. He's alive because of you."

Realization hit. This must be the mate of the wolf I had saved after he was attacked by Hans—when I first understood I could manipulate someone's life force to either revive or kill them.

The female came forward, tears now flowing down her face. She knelt on the floor before me, and my vision blurred as my eyes filled with tears as well.

"I'm Britta, Fyrsta. I pledge my life to you—and that of my mate and pups. It is a blessing by Odin to have you among us. I'll gladly call you Alpha."

I knelt beside the woman and wrapped my arms around her. "You don't owe me anything, Britta. Consider it one packmate helping another. And you'll call me Kristin. Let's leave the Alpha bit to Erik and whoever else Odin chooses."

A shocked gasp escaped Kat's lips, making me peer up at her. Deafening silence filled the room, broken only by the beeping and whirring of machines.

I glanced around. Everyone, including the guards at the door, stared at me. Some, like Kat, had surprise written all over their faces. Gunn frowned at me while Erik looked pained. He lifted a hand and pinched the bridge of his nose.

I slowly rose to my feet, facing him. "What's wrong?"

"Kristin, you fought with Linnea in the domr and won. You took the circle from her."

"She forced me into it. I didn't want to fight her."

"That doesn't matter. You beat her, and Odin accepted it. Accepted you."

"Yeah, to belong to the pack."

"No. To lead the pack."

Alarm sizzled up my spine, causing my heart to pound and my mouth to dry. It was so dry, in fact, I had trouble getting the words out. "I have no idea what you're talking about. For gods' sakes, Erik, speak clearly."

"You are the Fyrsta of the Varda. The first female. Chosen by Odin to lead by my side." He stepped around the bed and grasped my shaking hands. "Kristin, you're the new Alpha female of our pack."

CHAPTER 20

Kristin

I BOLTED AS FAST AS I COULD THROUGH THE TUNNELS WITHOUT breaking into a run. The tunnels no longer comforted me. Instead, they boxed me in. Trapped me.

Occasionally, I'd pass someone who'd gawk at me and then drop their head in submission, irritating me and upping my panic.

Alpha female of the pack? No friggin' way. These Valdyr were cracked. As if anyone would listen to me. I knew little to nothing of our history and had no idea how to run a pack. Up until yesterday, everyone other than Dahlia had wanted me gone.

Now, all that had changed?

Like hel.

I'd long since lost my way, and finally, I stopped dead in the middle of an intersection that looked like every other intersection I'd crossed. Through our bond, I sensed Erik close by, probably just around the bend. He'd been trailing me since I'd run from the infirmary.

Giving me space. Letting me calm down.

Yeah, right.

"How the fuck do I get out of here?" I yelled.

He came around the corner, eyebrow raised. "Language, Fyrsta. There are pups about. You don't want to set a bad example."

I scowled at him, and his mouth twitched. Then he turned to the left down one of the tunnels and indicated for me to follow.

Along the way, we passed other packmates who greeted Erik with a nod. Then they saw me and got all weird again. Erik was Alpha too. More senior than me. How come he didn't get the royal treatment?

"What gives with all the bowing and scraping? They don't do that to you."

"They did when I first became Alpha—and many of them had known me since I was a pup. They're greeting you formally."

"Yeah, well, it gets on my nerves."

"I can see that, Fyrsta."

"Quit calling me that."

Erik turned down another tunnel, reached a dead end, and pushed on what looked like solid rock. A door swung open. Fresh air wafted through the opening, and I greedily inhaled. Outside, a star-filled night sky beckoned.

I squeezed past him, a little too close for comfort, causing my heart to pound and my inner wolf to pant in excitement.

Hussy.

Stepping out onto the mountainside, I spread my arms wide and took a few more pine-scented breaths. Maybe I should just fly away.

No, something held me here, and it was more than just Gina. My wolf, perhaps? Or maybe instinct? I hadn't realized how much that inner drive controlled my life until Erik had explained the mechanics of it. Deep down, I knew he spoke the truth.

He stood silently behind me. I had a sixth sense for his whereabouts at all times now.

"We have to talk," he said.

"I seem to recall saying that to you a few days ago. You ignored me."

"I didn't—"

"Yeah, you did."

He sighed. "Please, Kristin. A lot has changed since then."

I didn't answer immediately. Every inch of me wanted to give in yet resist at the same time. How could he have just pushed me away?

Well, this was my chance to find out. And, depending on how long Gina was unconscious, I might be here for a while. Maybe I could convince Erik to reverse the Alpha female bond, if that was possible.

I nodded curtly. He gripped my hand before I could stop him and led me up a mountain trail lit by the full moon. It was the same path we'd taken the day he almost kissed me for the first time. The day Hans had appeared in the compound, and Erik and his warrior wolves had fought him off.

A shudder passed through me at the memory. What if Erik had been killed? Or if he hadn't been there to save me and I'd been taken? Now, I would relish the chance to kill Hans, but at the time, I didn't know the extent of my magic.

I was a virtual killing machine.

Maybe I should tell Erik. Then he'd never want me to lead the pack. He'd probably boot me out as fast as he could.

At the top of the trail, he kept walking toward the edge of the cliff. The familiar panic rose, and I dug in my heels. The sharp scent of fear burst from my body.

He spun around, concerned, checking the woods for danger. "What's the matter?"

I tugged my hand free and retreated to sit on the bench, taking a deep breath—in through my nose, out through my mouth—like my therapist had taught me. "Nothing."

His eyes widened. "Kristin, I could smell your terror. One

second, you were fine; the next you were petrified. It's still there but not as strong."

I scowled and waved my hand toward the cliff. "It's just a little phobia, that's all."

He frowned and looked in the direction I'd indicated. "What phobia?"

"Cliffs, okay? They freak me out. They have since I was a teenager. You were dragging me toward the edge."

He turned back, that incredulous look in his eyes again. "It's not like I was going to throw you off. Besides…you can fly. Yesterday, you jumped off one much higher than this."

"I didn't say it made sense. That's why it's a phobia. Cremnophobia," I added as if to give my terror more weight. Who could argue with such an official-sounding word? "And yesterday was an exception. I was upset. Otherwise, there's no way I would have gone near the edge. I prefer to take off from the ground or a tree." Like a normal person. Who the hel would want to run off a cliff?

He stepped toward me and sat down. I gripped the bench tighter to stop myself from scooting either toward or away from him—I wasn't sure which.

"When did this fear start?" he asked.

"Not fear. Phobia. I was sixteen."

"So you hadn't gone through your ulf-risa yet."

Of course, he would think that. A female's wolf didn't rise until her late teens or early twenties. Males generally were a little earlier than that. I was the exception to the rule.

"Uh…no. My wolf rose early. Maybe because I was an eagle too. I don't know."

"How early?"

I hesitated. "Thirteen."

"Thirteen?" His shock turned to dismay. "Did they attack you? Could your Alpha control them?"

I understood his horror. It had been a terrible time. "No. He wasn't very strong, but neither was the pack. I wasn't hurt—at least not physically. My father and brothers fought them off. My mom too."

"Ah, hel, Kristin. Is that how your family died?" He grasped my hands again, this time gently, and I had to fight the lump that rose in my throat. "When we came up here the first time, you said your dad was killed and your mom hurt when an intruder broke into your house."

"Yes," I whispered, blinking away sudden tears.

"And your brothers?"

"They were killed too. Attacked by our own pack—by wolves we'd grown up with and called friends. My brothers and dad were strong, but in the end, there were too many of them."

"How many siblings? It's unusual to have more than two pups per mated pair."

"Four. Adam, Joran, Garet, and Finn. Finn was only eighteen. His wolf hadn't even risen yet."

A bittersweet image flashed in my mind of Finn standing in front of the mirror, giving his hair that perfectly messy look the females loved. I would make faces at him behind his back, mimic him, and then run away screeching when he gave chase.

A grim light filled Erik's eyes. "Odin provided many protectors for the Gullari."

I pulled back, startled. "How did you know that?"

"Know what?"

"My real name. Kristin Gullari. When I met Gina, I changed it so Hans couldn't find me."

"I didn't know." His brow creased as if trying to figure out how to explain things to me. "We have stories—old stories—of a powerful female Valdyr who is both wolf and eagle. She's called a Gullari and is only born during times of great danger. I had no idea it was your last name. In old Norse, Gullari roughly translates to golden eagle."

My stomach clenched. As much as I wanted to believe it was a coincidence that my last name matched Erik's stories, I knew better. "When was the last one born?"

"This particular manuscript was written over three hundred years ago, but that doesn't mean there haven't been other Gullaris since then. Our library fell into disarray, and many of the old texts were lost or destroyed." He frowned. "And who is Hans?"

"You know…big, blond, beautiful, and as evil as they come." I rolled my eyes at his continued confusion. "You guys chased him away from here last week. If I hadn't been so shocked to see him, I would have chased him too. And he wouldn't have escaped."

Erik stilled, his eyes shifting into the brilliance of his wolf. Inside, my wolf lifted her head, sensing the change in him. "Tell me you're not talking about Skoll." His voice was low, deadly.

"No. His name is Hans. I don't know if he's a Valdyr or a Jotun or what, but he imprisoned me and my mom for three years after my dad and brothers were killed. He wanted my magic. I escaped after my mom died."

"The creature we chased that day was Skoll Hrodvitnir, son of the monster Fenrir and twin brother of Hati, who tried to get into Savage the next night." Then realization hit. "Odin's bloody eye. I thought he was after Dahlia, but it was you!" He sprang from the bench and peered into the darkened woods. "We need to get back to the den."

"No." I rose, too, arms crossing my chest. I knew I was being stubborn, but I didn't care. "I'm not ready to go in. Besides, there's still a lot to talk about."

"You don't understand. I can't fight off Hati by myself. If he gets through the wards, he could kill or take you."

I tossed my hair. "I'd like to see him try. I've been searching for the bastard—bastards—for years." The fact that there were two of them actually made sense. I'd always noticed a certain duality in Hans and slight differences in his appearance. Not that it changed anything. "I'm going to kill them both for what they did to my family."

"You can't. If you get close, they'll use a moonbeam or sunbeam to transport out. Skoll's magic is tied to the sun, and Hati's to the moon. The most you can hope to do is maim them."

Not if I weakened them first. I was about to tell Erik that when he looked back down the trail.

"Hold on," he said to me as Gunn and Linnea appeared. "Set a perimeter," he told them. "Turns out Hati and Skoll are after Kristin, not Dahlia."

"Okay," Gunn said.

Linnea planted her fists on her hips and glared at me. "Is she going to stay?"

No bowing and scraping here, which pleased me. In fact, maybe the tough warrior would like to go another few rounds. Like my own personal stress ball.

Erik's jaw hardened. "Linnea—"

"No. She's our Alpha. Odin chose her. She has a responsibility to the pack, to the war we've all sacrificed so much for, and to the world." Linnea huffed out a breath. "The prophecy clearly names her. We need her to stay."

Apprehension bloomed in my chest, and I looked at Erik, my desire for a fight fading. Just when I thought things couldn't get more complicated…

"What prophecy?"

His nostrils flared, the only sign of his annoyance with Linnea. "Go," he said to her. Gunn grabbed Linnea's arm, and they moved out of sight.

Erik turned back to me. "That's part of what we have to talk about. But first, finish telling me about your family."

My stomach twisted like it always did when I thought about that time, and I lifted a hand to rub it. "Well, after my wolf rose and the unmated males attacked, I finally figured out how to hide my scent. It's part of my magic." I felt a rising need to apologize for my weeks of deception, but I quickly squelched it. Screw that.

"But it was too late by then. My dad and brothers were killed, and my mom was injured. She never recovered."

"When did Skoll appear? Hati?"

"Right after that. I don't know if they happened upon the fight by chance or if they were responsible for it, but they took over the pack. They were so powerful—and cruel—and everyone else was so…battered. They locked my mom and me in our house for three years. I didn't escape until after she died."

Erik groaned and pulled me into his arms. I couldn't help but melt into him. It felt good to let go, even though the rational part of my brain knew I shouldn't.

"You were sixteen by then. What happened with the cliff?" His breath was warm in my hair. It somehow made telling the story easier.

"I cremated my mom. Hans—I mean Hati—wanted me to use my magic so he could bind me in some way, but I surprised him. I let my wolf rise, and we ran for it. The unmated males came after me, of course, but this time, I was strong and fast. I knew I could escape. Except I trapped myself on a cliff."

Erik cursed softly. "Where was this?"

"The Appalachian Mountains. I went back a few years later. The pack was demolished. There was nothing left of them."

"I'm sure Hati and Skoll destroyed them." His hand slipped beneath my hair to rub my neck. "Is that when you fell off the cliff and discovered you could fly?"

I hesitated. "I didn't fall. I jumped." His arms tightened around me. I took another deep breath to settle my voice. "I couldn't go back. No way could I let him lock me up again. Plus, I didn't want him to get my magic. He was already so powerful. I prayed that Odin would forgive me and I'd reunite with my family in the woods outside Valhalla."

"You fought until the end."

"If you call throwing yourself off a cliff fighting. I truly thought I'd die, but then…you know."

"Your eagle rose."

I nodded. "Along with a permanent case of cremnophobia. And I don't care how stupid it is—the fear's real to me."

Erik pulled back and looked me in the face. "How soon after that did you meet Gina?"

"I'm not sure, exactly. Months. I lost myself to my wolf for a while. Then, in upstate New York, I came across her doing some kind of witchy ritual in the woods. My wolf was half-crazed by then and attacked her. She zapped me with her magic. My wolf retreated back into me, and I was left lying in the snow. She's taken care of me ever since."

"You take care of each other."

"Yeah, we do. I know she's a pain in the ass sometimes, but I wouldn't have it any other way. I'd sacrifice everything for her."

I pulled out of Erik's arms and was left feeling cold despite the warm summer night. Talking about Gina was a good reminder. She, not Erik, was my family. He couldn't be relied upon, no matter how good it felt to tuck my head beneath his chin and rest against his chest.

I walked behind the bench to put some distance between us, trailing my fingers along the top of the wood. "Gina trained me to fight. Not in the way of wolves—my wolf already knew that—but by attacking me with her magic whenever I least expected it. Believe me, I learned how to move fast and anticipate an opponent's next move. Since I was determined to hunt down and kill Hati and Skoll, she was determined I'd survive." I shook my head. "Gods, I can't believe there're two of them. What are they?"

"Jotuns—enemies of the gods and us. We've been fighting them since our very creation. We've tried to trap them, but as soon as the sun or moon drops from the sky, they're pulled along behind."

My eyes snapped to his. "Trap them? Why in hel would you do that? Cut off their heads, tear out their hearts, whatever it takes. Just kill them!"

"No. We don't know what that would do. You can never kill—"

Suddenly, shouts, curses, and fighting erupted down the Alpha bond. They came from the infirmary, and I groaned. An instant later, the clanging alarm ripped through the compound.

"Gina," we said at the same time.

I took off at a run down the trail, Erik hot on my heels. I pushed at the boulder through which we'd exited the den. To my surprise, it opened automatically.

"This way," Erik said, taking the lead.

We took a different way back, and within minutes, we'd reached the infirmary. He held the door for me, and I came upon a scene of utter chaos. Beds and equipment were overturned, sparks filled the air where Gina had wielded her magic, and warriors—including Gunn, who must have arrived just before us —were scattered about, some injured, some fighting Gina.

"Don't hurt her!" Gunn roared.

Gina turned to him, incensed, her fingers raised and glowing, her hair floating around her. She looked like a gorgeous demigoddess—in a shapeless white hospital gown. "Where is my sister, you knuckle-dragging, big-headed moron?"

"I'd tell you if you weren't acting like a deranged loon."

Gina's eyes narrowed, and she flicked her wrist, sending energy particles in his direction. Gunn swerved and raced toward her, but she kept shooting. He'd almost reached her when one of her missiles caught him right in the package.

"Thor's balls," he cried, toppling to his knees and grabbing his crotch.

She cackled gleefully. "What did you say? Sore balls? Somebody, give me a medal for saving all of womankind."

"Gina!" I yelled from the doorway, a strong reprimand in my voice.

My sister whipped her head around, and relief crossed her face. Then her gaze dropped down to my footwear. She cocked her hip and frowned. "Are those my boots? And my clothes? What did you do—wait for me to almost die and then raid my closet?"

I glanced down, taking in the heeled, knee-high red boots, the leggings, and the fitted black T-shirt. "You weren't dying. You were unconscious. And I had to wear something because I was naked. And where were you? Oh, let me guess—here. Breaking through the wards."

Gina smirked. "I told you I could do it."

"Yeah, and it almost got you killed!"

"You just said I wasn't dying. I was unconscious."

I marched toward her. The boots had a high, thick heel, and I felt invincible in them. I flexed my hands by my side, knowing what was coming.

"Oooh, feeling all Rambo, are we?" Gina asked.

"Bring it on, witch."

I jumped an instant before Gina struck—right where I had stood. I'd been hit many times in the past and empathized with Gunn, who still groaned in pain where he'd fallen. Those damn energy particles hurt like a son of a bitch.

Gina struck again, but I noted that my sister shifted to the left and aimed high. I dived low and rolled. When I came up, I had a blanket in my hand. I tossed it over Gina to restrict her movements and then pounced, trapping her arms and legs against the floor.

"You couldn't have woken up nice and slow and just asked to see me? They would have called me immediately. How do you think it makes me look to have my sister trashing my pack's hospital with her ass hanging out of the back of her gown?"

"I have a fabulous ass, so I'm sure I made you look fantastic." Gina cranked her head toward Gunn, who rested on his elbow, watching us. "Right, wolfy?" she asked.

"I wasn't here for that," he grunted. "Why don't you turn over, and I'll let you know?"

"Gina, I'm the Alpha female now. You have to behave." Much to my dismay, the title felt right on my lips and the acknowledgment settled my anxiety. I groaned inwardly. This was where I was meant to be.

My sister's eyes widened. "You're the what?"

"The Alpha female. Thanks to your little stunt, I had to fight Linnea in a sacred circle sanctified by Odin. I won, and he made me Alpha."

"Odin was here? In person?"

"No. Through magic. He bonded me to the pack, and every time you zap one of us, I feel it. A lot." I exaggerated—it was barely more than a tingle—but I'd try anything to keep my sister in line.

Gina burst out laughing. I sat back and glared at her. "It's not a laughing matter. I had to shift, and the unkyssed males came after me. Erik controlled them."

"So I guess they're not working for Hans."

"No. And Hans isn't Hans. He's Hati *and* Skoll. Big, bad, magical enemies of the gods. I'm part of some fricking prophecy about a Gullari. And they're not talking about my last name."

Gina stopped laughing and sat up. Her eyes sought Erik, who'd moved into the room and stood just a few feet away, his gaze impenetrable.

"You received the prophecy?" she asked.

"Yes. From Odin himself."

"In person?"

Erik nodded. Gina paled and pushed me away. When she rose to her feet, her gown gaped at the back. I hurriedly tied it in place.

"That's where you were when you went off-grid a few weeks ago," she said. "In Asgard. I scried all over for you, but you'd disappeared." Gina pressed the palm of her hand to her forehead. "What did the prophecy say?"

Erik looked at me, and I nodded. The other Valdyr stepped

closer, and Gunn pulled himself to his feet. Erik recited the prophecy:

Eagle eye. Earth to sky. Fly, wolf, fly.
Lay me down. Wolf and crown. Cry, wolf, cry.
One and one. It's begun... Love dies.

I frowned. "What does it mean?"

"Obviously, you're the flying wolf," Gina said, "and Erik's the 'wolf and crown.' Did you guys hook up yet?" She looked from me to Erik.

My cheeks heated. I whacked my sister on the arm.

Gina flinched and rubbed the spot. "I'll take that as a yes. So that's what 'lay me down' means." She scowled at Erik. "And you obviously made her cry, or she wouldn't have flown back to Denver. She's an artist. They're sensitive, you know."

My cheeks went from hot to scorching. "Would you shut up?"

Gina ignored me. "That's two-thirds of the way through. Great. All that's left now is someone dying." With a loud curse, she spun in a circle and marched toward her room. "Where are my clothes? We're leaving."

I gaped at my sister's retreating back, then ran and caught up with her. I grabbed Gina's arm. "We can't just go. I'm the Alpha female. I have a responsibility to the pack. We need to see how this plays out."

"No, we don't. We need to get out of here before it all goes to hel. You can't trust the gods, Kristin. They're selfish, petty, and don't care about anything but themselves. If we stay, you'll end up dead. And I won't let that happen." She clenched a hand around mine and stared into my eyes. "What have I always said?"

I hesitated. "You and me first, everyone else second."

"Yeah, well, I'm putting us first. Right now. We're out of here."

CHAPTER 21

Kristin

I SAT CURLED UP IN A BURGUNDY VELVET ARMCHAIR IN DAHLIA'S cottage. Gina snoozed on the couch beside me while Dahlia puttered in the tiny yellow kitchen, making another pot of tea.

Instead of leaving like Gina had wanted, we'd ended up at Dahlia's for the night. Possibly longer. Despite my uncertain relationship with Erik, I hadn't been able to leave.

Exhausted, I glanced at the clock on the mantel—2:00 a.m. I ought to be sleeping, but a strange restlessness consumed me. So much had happened in the last few days.

"Here you go." Dahlia handed me a steaming mug.

After wrapping my hands around it, I sniffed appreciatively— mmm, strawberry—and took a sip. Dahlia dropped into an antique rocking chair next to me. It squeaked comfortingly when she set it in motion with her toe.

"This is a nice place. Did you grow up here?" I asked.

"No, my parents had a bigger house further up the mountain. I no longer needed the space when they died, and another family took it over. The pack owns everything in the valley collectively."

"What about going to school? I didn't see one on the compound."

"It's tucked away. Valdyr only."

"A normal school?"

Dahlia laughed. "As far as I know. It was the same as any other school, except we had more to learn. I had classes, homework, teachers I hated, crushes that left me heartbroken, and parents who didn't understand me. Just like a regular kid."

"I missed all that—those teenage years. I would have loved to tell my mom she was ruining my life instead of it being the other way around."

Dahlia put her tea on the table and squeezed my knee. "It wasn't your fault, Kristin. Hati and Skoll murdered your family. You couldn't have stopped them."

I closed my eyes and sighed. "My mom said the same thing, but I always felt responsible—still do—like maybe I did something wrong when my wolf first rose."

"You didn't. The sons of Fenrir did. And now you're here, fighting them. I'm sure it's the last place they'd want you to be."

That made me feel better. I smiled at my friend. "I have so many questions about being Valdyr. There's a lot I don't know, or maybe my pack didn't know."

Dahlia set the rocker in motion again. "Ask away."

"Okay. Um…start with the Norse gods."

"Well, they exist, but not necessarily how they're portrayed in the human myths. Odin, Freyja, Thor, Loki, and lots of others. Have you heard about them?"

"Yes. I remember my parents reading me stories about the gods and Asgard when I was little."

"So you know about Ragnarök? And the Jotuns?"

"Kind of." I sat forward, excited to finally get some answers. "Do they live on Earth, too?"

"No. They have their own world called Jotunheim. It's one of the nine worlds, including Earth and the underworld Hel. The gods have Asgard, and the Dvergar live on Nidavellir. Our stone wolf in the rotunda was carved by a famous Dverg who lives in the mountains around here. Erik's mom was fond of him. He gave it to her as a mating present when she kyssed Erik's dad. Maybe someday you can meet him. I'm sure you'll have lots to talk about."

"Maybe." But I knew I'd never want to meet the creator of that particular statue. There was something seriously wrong with it. Although, now that I was Alpha, perhaps the malevolent energy directed at me would change. "What about the Valdyr? Do they have their own world?"

"No. We were created by Odin for a specific purpose—to guard the wolf-monster Fenrir that the gods locked up."

"I've heard about him. The big bad. He's the father of Hati and Skoll, right?"

"Yup. And the son of the trickster god Loki."

Surprise flashed through me. "I thought Hati and Skoll were Jotun."

"They are. Believe me, it's all very incestuous and complicated. Anyway, Fenrir is imprisoned by the gods in a secret location because of the prophecy of Ragnarök."

"The end of the world," I said, staring into my tea.

"The end of *all* the worlds. Ragnarök will begin when Hati and Skoll swallow the sun and the moon. We don't really know what that means, but something bad will happen, maybe to do with their magic. Then they'll release Fenrir, who'll fight and kill Odin. A battle will erupt between the Jotuns and the gods, and the usual apocalyptic stuff will happen."

"Fun times."

"Yeah."

I took a small sip. "How long has the fight between the Valdyr and Hati and Skoll been going on?"

"Eons. The stories say that Odin created the Valdyr after killing Hati and Skoll's Jotun mother, who was a witch and a wolf. He then mixed her blood with his semen and fed it to his favorite wolf pack. The first Valdyr burst fully grown from the wolves' stomachs in the spring, killing the wolves."

"That's terrible."

"I know, right?" She picked up her tea, tested it, and sat back in the rocking chair. "Originally, we were all one pack and lived in Northern Europe close to where Bifrost, the Rainbow Bridge, connected Earth to Asgard. Any Valdyr could cross over. But a polar shift occurred thousands of years ago, and the bridge moved."

"To where?"

"No one knew. The pack left their home in search of it. We wandered the earth for another thousand years like the Roma. Eventually, some of the Valdyr lost faith, and the pack began to splinter. Hence the 'Lost Valdyr.'"

"Like my pack." I tapped the outside of my mug with my fingers. "Did they ever find the bridge?"

"Yup. In the Montana mountains, which is why we settled here. The pack became known as the Varda, which means *guard against* in Old Norse. We are the last ones to fight Hati and Skoll and keep Fenrir imprisoned."

"Wow. That's quite the legacy."

"What about the bridge?" Gina asked, surprising us that she was awake. "Can anyone cross to Asgard? Have you been?"

Dahlia shook her head. "That talent was lost. It used to be every Valdyr could come and go. Then, it was just the Varda. Now only Erik can pass over—but the pups are learning."

"So, you don't know what it looks like?" Gina asked.

"Asgard? It's supposed to be beautiful. Amazingly so."

"No, I meant the bridge. You mentioned rainbows. Could someone cross over on their own by mistake? Like a child?"

"No. It's hard to access from this side, and the god Heimdall guards it on the other end."

I forgot about my own troubles for a moment as I looked at

my sister. We both had our secrets and for a long time, we'd been each other's sole confidant. But now, most of my secrets had been revealed.

It felt good.

Gina, however, still carried hers deep inside.

Stretching my leg, I rubbed my foot against my sister's arm. The gesture was meant to be supportive, but she shrugged it off. Suppressing a sigh, I was about to ask another question when a knock at the door made us jump.

"Who in the hell is that?" Gina asked, sitting up.

I listened through the Alpha bond, but the wolf on the other side of the door didn't belong to the pack.

"Let's find out." Dahlia took one step toward the front entrance, but Gina and I both jumped in front of her. "What?" the petite Valdyr asked, alarmed.

"It could be anyone," I said.

"Who's there?" Gina yelled, hurting my ears. Dahlia's, too, by the way she winced.

"It's Dane."

Dahlia gasped, and her cheeks flushed.

"What do you want?" Gina asked.

"To speak to Dahlia."

"It's almost three in the fricking morning."

"The lights were on."

"Please let him in," Dahlia said.

I took pity on her and walked around a scowling Gina to the door. I opened it and had to tilt my head back to look at Dane. Damn, he was big—and bad. So not the kind of wolf Dahlia should be going after.

Not that Dahlia would ever make the first move.

He glanced past me, jaw hard, eyes unreadable. "Out of my way, Fyrsta."

The way he said it made my hackles rise, but I could sense Dahlia's anxiety through the bond, so I backed off.

He strode directly to the sweet female, taking in her messy ponytail, fluffy pink bathrobe, and bunny slippers, of which I wholeheartedly approved. "You shouldn't be here with them," he said. "It's dangerous."

Dahlia's jaw dropped. "Kristin's my Alpha. I couldn't be safer."

"You don't know that. Her sister is a witch."

Gina's hands lifted, fingers sparking. "Hey, asshole. You want dangerous, I can give you dangerous."

I stepped between them. My wolf bristled furiously. "I'll let that pass, once, because you don't know what it means to belong to a pack. Or maybe you've forgotten. But if you ever say anything like that again, you'll regret it."

Dahlia's fear pounded down the bond at me. I wasn't sure who the petite Valdyr was afraid for.

"Dane, you don't understand," my friend said, her fingers small against his bared, muscled bicep. "Kristin and I are bound together. Just like everyone else in the pack, but more so. I'm as safe with her as I am with Erik. She'd kill anyone who tried to harm me."

"Including the witch?"

My sight shifted into that of my wolf. It was all I could do to stop the lupine from rising. "I'd never have to make that choice, Ulf-einn, because Gina would never hurt her."

He faced me, his eyes also shining with his wolf, and was just as deadly. "If you do, and you make the wrong choice, you'll be the one regretting it."

After stalking to the door, he paused in the entryway without looking back. "You trust too easily, Dahlia. It's a liability." Then he stepped into the darkened night.

* * *

Erik

I sat on the top step of the circle in the rotunda, my elbows resting on my knees. I still couldn't believe what had happened in the last twenty-four hours—from making love to Kristin to discovering she was not only a wolf but an eagle too.

The eagle from Odin's prophecy.

It had been agony watching her fight Linnea in the domr. I was so afraid she'd die…until I realized my Alpha female was the one in danger. Then, a mixture of emotions flooded me—fury at Kristin's deception, anger at myself for having been fooled, worry for Linnea's safety, and awe at Kristin's fighting skills.

Not to mention that she was a gorgeous, honey-colored wolf with gleaming amber eyes *and* a sleek golden eagle.

My wolf had been ecstatic when she'd shifted. I had been devastated. It had taken my curse overflowing repeatedly to reach her before my wolf had fully accepted the danger of us being together. It was only a matter of time before I could no longer contain the foul poison.

Her scent reached me just before I saw her, causing both me and my wolf to sit up in anticipation. She stepped from the passageway in the back of the rock wall—the same entrance I'd used when I'd taken her to my home.

Had it been only last night?

She stopped, and her gaze swiveled to meet mine. Wariness and hurt seeped toward me down our bond.

When my curse bubbled up yet again to reach her, I shut my eyes and reinforced every barrier I'd sealed in place.

"Do you think if you can't see me, I'll just go away?" she asked, disdain in every word.

I held up my index finger, asking her to wait. She sniffed, and I heard her march toward the mural—still in Gina's red boots by the sound of it. Their staccato beat was louder and more forceful than any other footwear she'd worn.

It spiked my temperature.

No surprise there. I'd been hot for her since the moment I'd seen her step out of the helicopter, hips swaying in tight black leggings that molded her ass to perfection and those damn red boots.

Suppressing a sigh, I opened my eyes and found her at the scaffold, rummaging through her backpack. She pulled out an elastic band and tied back her hair, then bent over to unzip Gina's boots.

Damn, I did not need to see that.

"Are you planning to work?" I asked.

"Yes."

"At this time of night? Shouldn't you be sleeping?"

"Shouldn't you?"

"Kristin, you've been up for almost twenty-four hours without much sleep the night we…the night before. You had a hel of a fight with Linnea, you raced through the mountains, and then you flew all the way back to Denver. You must be exhausted."

She didn't answer right away, taking the time to put on her work boots. "I'm not, and now that I'm living here, I can carve the mural whenever I want. Day or night."

"Does that mean you're staying? Despite what Gina said?"

She shrugged, and my frustration grew. The curse responded to the negative emotion, amplifying it. With a snap, my wolf forced the foul darkness back down.

I let out a sigh. "I'm not a hundr, Kristin."

She didn't look up, but her lips twitched.

"Do you know what that means?" I asked.

"My brothers used to call each other that. A hound dog?"

"Right. Keeping Fenrir imprisoned and maintaining the safety of the pack are my priorities. Not getting laid. No matter what might have happened between us."

She picked up her tools and faced the mural. "Whatever."

I stood in one quick movement, wanting to stride over there and make her pay attention to me. Instead, I stayed glued in place, fists clenched by my sides. "There's no 'whatever' about it. It's the truth. I slept with you because I was attracted to you, and I thought you were safe."

"Safe?"

"When you pretended to be human."

"Now that I'm Valdyr, I'm dangerous?"

"No. *I'm* dangerous. To you. And, through you, to the rest of the pack."

She laid her tools aside, her brow creased in confusion, and moved toward me. My curse surged again, almost gleefully, and I retreated, battening down my mental hatches. "Stay there… please. I'm not stable right now. It's been a stressful day. Hel, it's been a stressful week."

At the other side of the circle, she stopped, her confusion turning to worry. "Tell me what's wrong."

"I'm cursed, Kristin. Or rather, the pack is cursed. For many years we didn't know it. The destruction was slow and insidious, but when I became Alpha, I could feel it. I drew the dark energy into myself and contained the foulness as best I could. The Varda was almost destroyed."

"What happened?"

I scraped my fingers through my hair. "The curse feeds on negative emotion. Greed, anger, jealousy, suspicion. It amplifies those feelings in each Valdyr. The bond between packmates and kyssed pairs, even parents and pups, was nearly destroyed. If that had happened, the Varda would have ceased to exist."

"And there'd be no one to guard Fenrir or stop Hati and Skoll."

"Right."

She sat on the top step across from me, hugging her knees. "When you and the pack cornered me on the cliff, I felt something malevolent attached to you. It surged toward me, then withdrew. Was that it?"

"Yes." I rubbed my hand over my face. "I'm sorry. I usually have better control."

"So, it was attacking me?"

"Trying to get a hold of you in some way. It's become more concentrated within me over the years. And hungry. I don't know if it could seize you completely. Or if it did, what would happen."

She tapped her fingers on her legs. "Who cursed you? Was it Hati and Skoll?"

"Probably, but we're not even sure when it started. The years since I became Alpha have been about rebuilding—our defenses, our relationships with the other packs, our forces. When my father was Alpha, no pups but me were trained to cross to Asgard. We restarted that program too."

"Why did he stop training them?"

"Who knows? The curse twisted something inside of him, as it did to every one of us. Looking back, it was obvious something was wrong, but we were too immersed in it to see clearly."

She met my gaze, and I noticed her eyes had changed, becoming the brilliant gold of her wolf. Or perhaps her eagle. She lifted a hand in my direction.

"What are you doing?" I asked, alarmed.

She hesitated. "I told you I can see auras with my eagle's eyes, but I can also work with them. I sensed the darkness in you once. Maybe I can draw it from you."

Panic surged. "No. I have it contained. If you pull it out, it could go everywhere. The only way to destroy it is to find the source, and believe me, we've searched high and low."

"Maybe I could cage it outside of you."

"You can do that?"

"Theoretically. I use my magic to block my scent. That's like containment. I should be able to do it with the curse too."

I blew out a breath. "I'm sorry. But it's not a risk I'm willing to take."

Regret rose over what might have been. And it was amplified, of course, by the curse.

Suddenly, the weight of it seemed unbearable. I needed time alone. Away from here, from Kristin. Time with just my wolf to come to terms with my choices.

Duty. Sacrifice.

She rose to her feet and met my eyes. Need burned within her, reflecting my own desire. I turned away and strode to the door, willing myself not to look back.

When the night air greeted me, I couldn't let go fast enough. I broke into a run and shifted midstride to my wolf. Long legs stretched, lungs pumped, and I raced full out, trying to sweep her scent from my nose and her image from my mind.

Until the next time I saw her, fought with her, wanted to make love to her.

I should have stayed in Asgard when I had the chance, because my life had become hel on Earth.

***

Kristin

I stood at the door, squinting after Erik as he raced away. I was certain that if I stared hard enough at his bright, flickering aura in the predawn light, I'd see something.

Moments ago, when he'd walked by the stone wolf, a sudden blackness had engulfed him, making me gasp. Then he'd passed the sculpture, and a line had stretched out between them before disappearing when he exited the building.

The shadow felt alive...a living, breathing malevolence attached to him yet not a part of him. The same energy I'd felt on the cliff.

And it came from the stone wolf. The wolf everyone loved. The wolf I'd hated from the very beginning.

After Erik disappeared into the tree line, I carefully moved back toward the sculpture, my wolf and eagle on full alert.

Erik claimed they'd looked everywhere for the source, but what if it had been right under their noses the entire time? Carved by the Dverg, who lived in the mountains, as a mating gift for Erik's mom.

Or a Trojan wolf.

Lifting my hands, I summoned my magic, amazed at how easily it came to me now that I knew what I was doing. The familiar stirring in my stomach rose until my hands warmed and my fingers tingled. Reaching toward the carving, I focused my eagle's eyes as sharply as possible on Rolf.

Studying every inch down to the individual particles, the darkness stayed hidden until I reached the eyes, where it glowed like two deadly black orbs.

"Gotcha."

Erik said the curse couldn't just be released. It had to be caged like he'd done within himself. But he hadn't contained it so much as siphoned it down the Alpha bond from the sculpture into himself, leaving the curse with nowhere to go until it broke free.

We needed to destroy it. But how could we do that without allowing it to spread evil wherever it wanted? At least now it was bound to the sculpture.

Perhaps a magical vessel of some kind, like Pandora's box or Aladdin's lamp, could seal it inside. Either forever or until we could figure out how to destroy it.

With a sigh, I straightened.

It was tempting to try to draw the curse out of the sculpture—and out of Erik—right now, but I wanted to speak to him first. Gina too. She might have some ideas.

A whisper of excitement stole through me at the thought of what I'd done. Alpha female for only one day, and I'd already pinpointed the source of the evil—something the rest of the pack hadn't been able to do.

I smiled a little smugly, thinking I was a thousand times the Alpha female Linnea had been, and even though—

It hit me hard. A black force almost knocked me over. My teeth snapped together over my tongue, and I tasted blood.

That was what saved me.

Roused by the blood, my predator wolf and eagle lunged at the entity that had grabbed me. It backed off just far enough that I could throw up a shield. But not before I was dragged forward. My hand made contact with the stone wolf and sank up to my wrist into the rock.

Seething rage poured into me, filling me with a burning, blinding heat. Every negative emotion I'd ever experienced shoved upward as darkness surrounded me. Consumed me.

It felt good to hate, to want to punish.

And I could do it, too. Lash out at everyone with my magic through the Alpha bond. That's what I wanted to do, what I was born to do. I was a killing machine.

All I had to do was let go.

CHAPTER 22

Sudden pain seared through me as I raced up the mountain in wolf form. I stumbled and crashed to the ground, skidding hard on plants, rocks, and sticks. I slid past the edge of a ravine and toppled ears over tail to the bottom.

The bone-crushing impact tore the air out of my lungs, but it was nothing compared to the burning hatred aimed at me that scorched every nerve, muscle, and vein. The cells in my body screamed in agony, and I curled into a ball deep within my wolf, clutching my abdomen. I couldn't think, couldn't move, couldn't send a message down the Alpha bond to see if the rest of the Varda was under attack.

Slowly, the loathing and pain withdrew. I gulped in air, my sides heaving, nostrils flaring, before I dragged myself up and braced for another attack. It didn't come.

Dread rose like a black cloud, and I turned inward to focus on my curse, but instead of an impenetrable fortress of stone, I found a crumbled pile of rubble, the foul sludge undetectable.

There was no sign of it on the rocks I'd used to build the entity's prison or the concrete I'd used to patch any leaks.

Or anywhere else within my mind, body, or soul.

The curse was gone. I had failed. The Varda was destroyed.

I turned back to the den, the metallic taste of fear in my mouth, my stomach tied into a sickening knot. Running faster than ever before—my reflexes quicker, senses sharper, body stronger—I reached out to my pack and to Kristin.

No one responded.

Kristin

Kill. Maim. Hurt. Punish.

Kill. Maim. Hurt. Punish.

The words reverberated through my mind and body, coming from deep inside. I knew I was responsible for them, that I chanted them softly, yet at the same time, they didn't stem from me but from some dark shroud that had overtaken every cell of my being.

I'd retreated to a far, caged corner of my soul. Except instead of locking my wolf inside as I'd done after my ulf-risa all those years ago, this time I'd locked myself in. Outside, my wolf and eagle fought a vicious battle with the malevolent entity that had a hold of me—or most of me.

A nugget of independence remained, and it refused to let go as the curse wanted. I sat stranded in a safety zone while not only my wolf and eagle were on the brink of destruction but the rest of the pack and Erik, too, for whom the curse had a particular hatred. It soured the back of my throat like the most putrid vomit.

I tried to think, but the chaos of the battle raging inside me battered my senses. How could I help without losing the last piece of myself?

I couldn't fight physically, but I had my magic. If I sucked enough energy through the Alpha bond—or from any other source—I could create a cage for the entity.

Maybe.

But what if I opened myself up to the bond, and the curse poured into me the rest of the way? If that happened, the only thing that would save the Varda, save Erik and Dahlia, would be my death.

I didn't mind dying. Once, I'd even welcomed it. But now I had more to live for—friends, a lover, and a pack of my own I wanted to lead. I could help in this fight with Hati and Skoll. I had a purpose.

If I could just access the magic in time to force the curse back.

<hr>

Erik

I bounded up the stairs to the den, shifting from my wolf form midleap to land on my bare feet. Wrenching the door open, I raced inside to find the inner door also open, and my pack jammed shoulder to shoulder in the rotunda.

The scene resembled Kristin's challenge, except I could see over their heads that the circle was not sanctified. Instead, it was filled with more Valdyr—all facing the top of the circle where the stone wolf sat. Anxious whispers filled the air, and the acrid smell of fear wafted up my nose.

"Erik!"

Gunn's voice broke the hushed atmosphere like the crack of a bullet, and the gathered Valdyr turned to their Alpha, crying out for answers and reassurances I couldn't give. I had no idea what had happened other than that I no longer contained the curse.

Had it leaked to them? Were they also unable to communicate mentally with their packmates?

And where was Kristin?

I pushed past them toward Gunn, squeezing every hand and shoulder I came into contact with. "I can't reach you through the bond," I said as I drew closer. "I can't reach anyone."

"No one can."

Then I saw both Dahlia and Gina crouched on the ground beside the sculpture—as if they held something up.

Or someone.

Blond curls floated past Gina's shoulder, and horror struck like a snake in my gut. "No!"

I darted forward the rest of the way, my wolf howling.

Dahlia rose to face me while Gina turned frightened, furious eyes on me, holding her sister close. "This is your fault," she yelled. "If we had left like I wanted to, she would be okay. Now look what you've done."

Kristin lay slumped half on the floor, half in Gina's protective embrace. Her eyes were closed, her breath shallow, her skin devoid of color. With shock and dismay, I saw her hand was buried up to her wrist in the cold, hard stone of the statue. "What in Odin's name happened?"

"You happened. And all the rest of your fucking pack. If my sister dies, I swear I'll obliterate every single one of you!"

Dahlia knelt behind Gina and wrapped her in her arms. A single tear trickled down Gina's cheek, and she dashed it away— but she never shrugged out of Dahlia's embrace.

I took hold of Kristin's free hand, trying to think over the pounding of my heart and my wolf's ferocious barking. I had to restrain myself from tearing Kristin away from Gina. My need to hold her was a palpable force within me.

"She was fine when I left. Did anyone see what happened?" I glanced around the rotunda. No one came forward.

"I did," Dahlia said, tapping her temple. "Up here."

"Tell me."

"She stood a few feet back, peering at the statue, and then its eyes went black." Dahlia lifted her gaze to the stone wolf's face. Its eyes, like the rest of it, were now the same gray as the rock from which it had been carved. "I swear, Erik, it was like Rolf was alive…swirling with evil."

Of course. Why the hel hadn't I seen it before?

"The curse must be in the statue. Did she try to extract it?"

"No. She was pleased, though, that she'd found it. I think she intended to wait for you so you could decide together what to do."

"Then how did this happen?" I gestured toward Kristin's trapped hand.

"It attacked her. She was dragged forward and into the wolf. I don't know for sure, but I think it wanted to draw her all the way in. She somehow fought back—she's still fighting."

I looked at Gina, who was as white as Kristin, her mouth a grim line. "Gina, please. I need to hold her. We're connected, but something's interfering with our bond, and I can't reach her. Touch may help. My wolf can go after her in metaphysical ways that you can't."

Another tear rolled down Gina's cheek before she reluctantly handed Kristin over. "Bring her back to me. She's all I have."

***

Kristin

I put my hand on the cage door and pushed. The ugliness from outside immediately swamped me, and the livid, seething presence of the curse tried to squeeze through the opening. I slammed the door shut, filled with horror that my wolf and eagle were out there, fighting that.

I had to help them, but if I was overcome by the entity, we

were all as good as dead. Maybe I could take my shield with me. I sustained it through my magic, drawing on my own energy. Maybe I could change it to suit what I needed now.

Closing my eyes, I pictured my body as a canvas and then painted on my shield. Metaphysical armor. As the cage shrank to fit me, the entity raged closer until it battered me like a hurricane, seeking even the tiniest entrance.

Bracing my feet, I wound up and punched with my magic. The curse reeled back.

Get behind me!

But my wolf and eagle ignored me, both too dominant to give up the fight. I raced after them as they continued their attack, my wolf snarling and snapping at the black mass, my eagle tearing at it with her beak and claws. I tried to cage the evil, but it was too massive. All I did was further drain my magic, thinning my protection.

I needed help.

Erik!

But my voice bounced back to me. What had happened to our bond? I listened for him as hard as I could, but all I heard was static. The entity had to be interfering with our connection.

A faint barking sounded in the distance. I twirled around, trying to pinpoint it. Was that him?

Erik! I screamed again, using a sliver of my magic to project my voice. For an instant, the barks increased in volume and then faded away, but at least I knew what direction they came from. If I could reach him, I could tap his aura and, through him, the rest of the pack's. With luck, we could generate enough force to cage the curse.

I'd only have one chance to get to him. My wolf and eagle had better follow.

Be a good doggie and birdie and heel this time. Got it?

Disgruntlement flowed back to me, but also their agreement. Their strength was waning as well.

Imagining a concrete tunnel, I plowed it through the curse in Erik's direction and sprinted inside, my wolf and eagle hot on my heels. I prayed to the gods that Erik waited at the other end.

Behind us, I collapsed the tunnel, but the black mass found holes in the rubble and eagerly swept through. My eagle scouted ahead while my wolf nipped at my feet, urging me to run faster.

I'm going as quickly as I can. In case you haven't noticed, I only have two legs.

My wolf drew abreast of me and nudged my arm. I grasped her fur and jumped on board, then held on for dear life as she streaked forward, her paws eating up the distance.

But as fast as my wolf ran, I didn't know if we would make it. Cracks formed in the walls and ceiling, and the magical life force I needed to plug the holes was spent.

My eagle screeched, flying back toward us.

He's here, my wolf said, finding an extra burst of speed from somewhere.

Erik? I can't sense him.

Listen.

Closing my eyes, I tried desperately to hear his voice. Nothing.

I don't think—

Then, a familiar large wolf appeared behind my eagle, barreling toward us. The bird flew overhead to attack the black mass in pursuit.

Faster, I screamed as the ceiling began to crumble. My wolf leapt over the rubble that crashed in our path.

I need the bond! I have to draw energy from you and the pack, I yelled at Erik.

He jumped toward me, changing his form at the last second, so his strong arms wrapped around me as we tumbled to the ground. The bond snapped into place between us, and I reached into it, drawing the energy I needed from him and the rest of the pack.

Above us, the tunnel collapsed, and the curse surged in. Erik covered me with his body, but I barely noticed as I used his aura to dig a mammoth hole that acted like a vacuum and sucked the entity inside. Faster and faster, it sank into its new subterranean prison until nothing was left of it.

I slammed an iron door shut, then sealed it.

But the job wasn't done yet.

When I opened my eyes, I was in Erik's naked embrace, half lying on the rotunda floor in the den. Dahlia and Gina crouched beside us, and Gunn towered over top. The rest of the pack gathered around.

"Put some clothes on. It's distracting," I croaked to Erik. "And have someone bring me my carving tools. We're not out of the woods yet."

He held me even tighter. "Sweet Freyja, you scared the hel out of me. Is the curse locked away for good?"

I shook my head, but before I could explain, Gina wrapped her arms around my neck and squeezed.

"I swear, if you do that again, I'll fricking kill you," my sister said.

"Hug me any harder, and you might."

Dahlia gasped. "Kristin, your hand is free. And look at Rolf."

Everyone glanced at the stone wolf. Malevolent, swirling black orbs stared back at us where lifeless stone eyes should have been.

Gina huffed out a breath. "Crap. I guess this means we can't leave yet."

"I'm not planning on leaving, Gina. Ever. And this isn't over."

"What do you need?" Erik asked. Someone had tossed him sweats, and he'd pulled them on.

Gunn handed me tools, and I wobbled as I stood. Erik kept his hands on my waist to steady me.

"I'm going to re-carve this pain-in-the-ass wolf. I don't know how the sculptor enchanted it, but I suspect he's mixed magic into the stone."

"I was cursed once," Gina said. "An attack by a coven in New Orleans when you were in Alaska. They used Norse runes embedded into an amulet to sustain it. I had to break into their headquarters and smash the amulet—and other stuff while I was there."

I shook my head. "Well, I can't just smash the statue. The evil within it is too great." I glanced over my shoulder at Erik. "Don't let go of me. I have to draw from everyone's aura to do this. It may take a while."

"I won't. We're here for you."

The pack drew closer, and before long, a chain developed, everyone touching everyone else right down to Erik, who had his arms around my waist. "Obliterate the motherfucker," he said.

Such sweet nothings.

I glanced at Gina. My sister was the only one unconnected. Then Gunn put his hand on her shoulder. After a second, Gina shrugged it off. I caught her eye, reading the resistance there. An island unto herself.

Yeah, right.

Turning to the sculpture, hammer in one hand and chisel in the other, I took a deep breath. My eyesight shifted so I could see every molecule. A trance-like state, that often overcame me when I carved, descended upon me.

Odin guide my hand.

With the first swing of my hammer, I knew it would be a battle. The stone barely chipped despite the strength of my blow and the sharpness of my tool, so I used my magic to heat and soften the rock as much as I could and finally made some headway.

The curse fought back, using my raw emotions and doubts against me.

He'll never love you. He's in love with Linnea. They are the true mates. You're not pretty enough, strong enough, smart enough.

You're not normal. He can smell the stench of your eagle a mile away.

But the taunts just angered me, and I chiseled harder, shouting in triumph, when I found a golden rune, the rune of Ansuz, hidden in the wolf's forehead. Like all runes, Ansuz had a dark and light side. This particular rune related to the transmission of omens or messages.

A necessary component for the curse to infect the Varda.

I knocked out the gold, and it smoked when it hit the ground, turning black.

"Gina," I said, knowing instinctively my sister knew what to do. Gina shielded it so it couldn't infect anything else, then destroyed it with a loud bang.

The unexpected noise startled me, and the entity struck again, besieging me with horrific memories of my ulf-risa. Once again, I experienced the unkyssed males of my pack attacking me, my father and brothers dying one by one in an attempt to save me, my mother being injured and taken prisoner by Hati and Skoll, the three years of hel locked in our house as my mom wasted away—all because of me.

You did this. They died to save you. You're a freak and an abomination. They should have let you die.

I had no idea how long I was lost in the memories, but I came back to myself with tears streaming down my face.

Erik held me tight. "Keep fighting, Kristin," he whispered in my ear. "Don't let it win. Whatever it says to you, remember you are loved. By your family, by Gina, by your pack. We need you."

I scowled into the black eyes of the wolf and kept carving. In all, I found thirty runes hidden within the rock, each one relaying a message of dark destruction, fear, and hatred. One by one, I knocked the runes out until my arms shook, and I was covered in sweat. It took hours.

Still, the attacks came. *You're not wanted. You're not good enough. You bring pain and devastation wherever you go.*

Certainty filled me when I uprooted the last rune. The statue was a mess, covered in jagged edges, disfigured features, and the leftover imprints of the runes. Working on instinct, I remodeled the sculpture into a new wolf and either obliterated or reshaped the runes' indents into a positive message—one of hope, joy, triumph, and peace to match the energy of the new, smaller wolf I'd created.

Little by little, the malevolence in the wolf's eyes disappeared until they were stone once more. Now, they projected a sense of love and laughter that came through as I refined the face.

Hammering my chisel for the last time, I leaned back against Erik, glad for the strength of his arms as he held me up. He dropped his forehead onto my hair and released a long, pent-up breath. Dahlia took my tools with a teary smile while Gina walked around the statue, checking for any missed runes.

A warm energy buzzed through the pack despite their fatigue and depleted aural reserves. I had tried to siphon the raw magic from each Valdyr equally. I was the only one running on empty. It would take me days to recover.

I rolled my head back to look at Erik. "Take me home."

Then I closed my eyes and slid into oblivion.

Kristin

I SLOWLY OPENED MY EYES AND ROLLED FROM MY BACK ONTO MY side beneath the fluffy duvet. Dawn light seeped through the uncovered windows, and I recognized Erik's bedroom—as well as the brawny triceps, shoulder, and back in front of me.

Yum.

He slept beside me on his stomach, his head turned away, his hand stretched back to curl loosely around my forearm. I wrapped my own hand around his and snuggled closer, my heart filling my chest.

The last few days—or weeks, for all I knew—were a blur. I remembered Erik, Dahlia, and Gina waking me up to eat and drink, Dahlia coaxing sweetly while Gina yelled at me to "get up!" Erik had the most success, using his wolf to rouse mine.

I also remembered being in the shower with him, falling asleep upright against his chest as he washed my hair and body, helped me brush my teeth, and carried me back to bed.

The way he'd cared for me, the way they'd all cared for me,

even the doctor Kat, made tears well in my eyes. Gina would always be my beloved sister, but I had a bigger family now too.

And a mate…I hoped.

My wolf thumped her tail in agreement.

Unable to resist, I pressed light kisses along Erik's muscular triceps. When I reached his shoulder, I climbed on top of him and stretched out on his back, molding our naked bodies together as I continued to nibble toward the crook of his neck.

He tasted and smelled so good. Warm, soft, and strong all at once.

He reached behind him to tunnel his hand into my hair, fingers massaging my scalp and caressing my ear. A shiver raced over my skin, and I bit down at the juncture of his neck and shoulder, mouth wide, tongue savoring him—marking, but also scenting both him and his wolf, drawing them deep into my lungs.

A low rumble vibrated through his body, and the hand in my hair squeezed, holding me close. Then he rolled over so I once again lay on my back, and he fitted himself between my thighs. His weight and warmth pushed me into the mattress, and I welcomed him with a contented sigh, loving that he enveloped me, dominated me.

"How do you feel?" he asked, one big palm wrapped around my nape, the other behind my back.

"Pretty damn good at the moment." I draped a long leg around his thigh and lifted my hips to rub against his rigid flesh. I was already wet and swollen for him. "You could make me feel even better."

He groaned but clamped my hip to hold me still. "You're not too tired?"

"No."

"You're sure?"

I nipped his ear and then pulled his head down to mine. "Shut up and make love to me, Erik. I promise I'll let you do all the work."

My lips met his and kissed away his resistance, my arms locked around his neck, my legs encircled his hips.

He growled and sank into me, pushing up and inside my body at the same time as he licked my mouth. Withdrawing, he stroked in again, establishing an even, controlled rhythm that drove me wild. The languorous pace felt good, spiraling me on a gentle wave toward climax.

But I wanted a tsunami.

I scraped my nails down his back to his ass and dug in. "How about we go fast this time and take it slow after that?"

The breath shuddered from his lungs. "How about we go slow this time, and then tomorrow, we'll see how you feel and take it slow again?"

"Gods, you're such a killjoy." I moaned as he slid his hand down my back to my hip and tilted it upward. His pelvic bone rubbed in the perfect spot, keeping the same rhythm but somehow nudging a little deeper every time, hitting both my pleasure points. "Right there. Oh, don't stop. Erik, you feel so good."

"I don't plan on stopping." The timbre of his wolf marked every word.

Same as mine. There was no way my hussy of a wolf would miss out on this.

I arched my spine, panting now, and when he lowered his head to suck on my breast, I cried out in ecstasy, his tongue feeling like warm, wet velvet. He bit down with just enough pressure that I jerked against him, my knees splaying wide in surrender, my sheath flooding with heat.

His tempo picked up, and he gripped me tightly, kissing across to my other breast. "You're so hot. And the way you tighten around me… Oh, gods. Come for me now, Kristin. I can't hold on much longer."

He didn't need to ask twice, and when he licked up my chest and bit down on the crook of my neck, as much an erogenous zone as anywhere else, I shattered around him, calling his name as I came apart in breathtaking waves.

His rhythm fractured, and he growled as he shuddered into me, pulsing sharply before collapsing over my body.

I smiled, holding him close. So much for going slow. Although, he had held out until the very end.

I sighed as he rolled onto his back, sliding from my body and taking me with him, so I snuggled into his side. My fingers curled into the crisp hairs on his chest, and my eyelids drooped. Then, I slipped back into oblivion.

The next time I woke, it was to the delicious aroma of French toast, sugar, and strawberries. I opened my eyes to the bright midmorning sunlight and saw Erik standing at the window, wearing black boxer briefs that molded an impressive ass. Even doing the simplest tasks, his muscles bulged beneath tanned skin.

Mmm. Maybe I could have *him* for breakfast.

He turned to find me watching him and raised a brow, correctly interpreting my thoughts, which wasn't hard when my gaze dropped to his other impressive package.

"In case you didn't notice, I made you breakfast," he said, indicating the tray on the nightstand. "No more making love until we get the okay from Kat. You were out like a light after last time."

I sighed. "Did I mention you were a killjoy?"

"Yes, right before you came apart in my arms."

I sat up and let the duvet slip from my shoulders. His eyes followed the progression and feasted on my breasts, which had puckered in expectation. To my satisfaction, his body responded, hardening beneath his cotton briefs.

He blew out a frustrated breath, but instead of launching

himself at me like I'd hoped, he yanked open a dresser drawer and pulled out a yellow tank top that said *Follow Your Destiny* across the front. It was one of my favorites.

"I had Gina bring over some clothes from your apartment in Missoula." He tossed me the top. "Put it on, please. I've been waiting to make you French toast and strawberries for a week. I won't be able to enjoy feeding you if you're naked."

A smile tilted my lips as I slipped the material over my head. "I'll still be partially naked."

He tossed me a pair of fuchsia-colored panties. I put them on, too, because he was being so sweet. Otherwise, I might have tormented him a little longer.

His desire to feed me the meal I'd requested after the first time we'd made love gave me hope that he also wanted me for his mate. Sappy tears welled in my eyes. I looked down, rearranging the covers as I blinked them away.

When I glanced up again, he was placing pillows against the headboard. Then he climbed in beside me and reached for the breakfast tray.

"Don't you want any?" I asked, noting the single plate, glass of juice, and cup of coffee.

"I already ate. This is for you." He cut a piece of the warm toast, making sure to add a sugared strawberry on top, and held it up to my mouth.

The sweet and savory flavors burst on my tongue as I indulged. Mmm. He'd outdone himself.

"How is it?"

"Delicious. Thank you."

"You're welcome." He fed me another bite.

Afterward, I had a sip of black coffee, just the way I liked it. "So...does this mean we're dating? I mean, now that the curse is gone. It is gone, isn't it?"

"No sign of it anywhere. And believe me, I've looked." He lifted the fork to my mouth again.

I ate the food but tasted little of it this time as I anxiously waited for him to answer my other question. When he didn't respond right away, doubt weaseled its way into my heart. What if he didn't want to be with me?

Inside, my wolf huffed.

Well, I don't know, do I? It's not like he's declared his intentions. Mate.

Yeah, easy for you to say.

"Is that what you want, Kristin? To date me?"

I swung my gaze to his face, but he was staring at the tray, methodically cutting another piece of toast for me.

"If that's what you want."

He sighed, obviously exasperated, and met my eyes. "I asked what *you* wanted."

"Well, I asked first."

"Yes, I want to...date you. Exclusively. Maybe that's asking a lot in too short a time, but my wolf is possessive. Besides, no males here will dare look at you sideways, knowing you're mi —dating me."

A thrill raced along my skin. "So, is it just your wolf who's possessive?"

He paused. "No."

I bit my lip to stop from smiling. "Okay, then. Let's go steady. See how things develop."

"Steady?"

"Mm-hmm. That's what my mom used to call it."

He fed me another morsel. "Does this mean I have to give you a pin or something?"

"What kind of a pin?"

"I don't know. Isn't that what human males do?"

I laughed, unable to contain my happiness. "You can give me a kiss instead. I may even let you get to second base."

He placed the knife and fork on the plate, moved the tray to the nightstand, and then dug both hands into my hair. Swooping down to claim my mouth, he pressed me back against the pillows. His lips molded mine, taking control, and he stroked his tongue inside.

I linked my fingers at his nape. When his arms slid around my body in that dominant way of his, holding me tight, I hoped things might spiral out of control. His leg lay heavy over mine, and the hard ridge of his erection jutted into my hip.

Then he nibbled along my jaw, down my neck, and bit hard at the juncture of my shoulder and neck. Instinct took over, and I moaned, my body flooding with more heat, my hips tilting into position for him.

He slowly released me, licking where his teeth had marked me. Finally, he lifted his head, eyes the brilliant golden brown of his wolf. He growled every word. "Consider yourself pinned."

I huffed out a breath. "Not fair."

"All's fair in love and war, svassa."

The Norse endearment was one my father had called my mother. My desire changed to a warm, gooey feeling, and I snuggled into the arm he'd curled around my shoulders. "Which one are we? Love or war?"

"Both. You're too strong, and your wolf's too dominant not to fight me on things, which is good. As Alpha female, it's important you take the initiative and express yourself. You might have a different perspective on a situation or see something I miss."

"Is that how it was with your parents? Your mom was Alpha, too, wasn't she?"

"Yes...but..." His tone filled with sorrow...and regret.

"But what?" I stroked my hand across his chest.

"The curse corrupted their Kyssa. The Dverg who sculpted the stone wolf knew my mom well. She considered him a friend."

My eyes widened. "Is he still alive?"

"Yes. He's on the run, but we'll get him. It's just a matter of time."

"Why did he do it? Is he in league with Hati and Skoll?"

"I don't know. He sent the cursed sculpture to my parents as a mating gift. That feels personal to me. But it doesn't matter. As soon as we find him, he's going to pay with his life—the same way my parents did."

The pain in his voice was palpable. I lifted my head to see devastation in Erik's eyes. "Oh, Erik, I'm sorry. Tell me what happened."

He cleared his throat, his fingers tightening on my shoulder. "I told you some of what the pack went through during those years. How twisted everything became. My father, as Alpha, was no exception. Like many of the males, he became obsessive, jealous, and filled with distrust and suspicion. His life was no longer about protecting the pack or fighting Hati and Skoll but about digging in and guarding what was his. He was even jealous of me. He regretted teaching me how to cross to Asgard. Thank the gods he did, though, or we'd have been cut off completely."

"Didn't anyone say anything to him? Try to reason with him?" I asked.

"No, because they were all affected, too, in different ways. It was a terrible time."

"What happened to your parents?"

He took a moment before answering me. "My dad believed my mom was cheating on him with his brother—Dahlia's dad. They were both strong, dominant males, each a little crazed by this time, and they fought." His hand fisted on top of the covers. "My dad killed my uncle. Then he…he killed my mom."

"Oh gods, Erik. No."

He huffed out a breath. "He tore out the throat of the female he'd sworn to love and protect for all time. Before the curse, he meant those words. I remember how devoted he was to us when I was a pup. The entity didn't have as strong a hold then. There was no way he would have hurt my mom."

Tears welled in my eyes, blurring my vision. My heart ached for him and his family. For the entire pack. "What did you do?"

"I ran to help, thinking they were fighting an intruder. Our family bond had degraded over the years, as had my dad's Alpha connection to the pack, but on that day, the attack came through loud and clear. When I arrived, he was covered in her blood and howling with grief. I think that was the first moment of clarity he'd had in years."

"Did you...did you..." I couldn't bring myself to ask if he'd killed his father.

"I didn't have to. He looked at me and told me we were under attack from the inside and that I had to lead the Varda. Then he clawed out his throat. His passing was so sudden and violent that I felt the curse rebound into me. For the first time, I became aware of it, which saved me because I was able to fight back—the same way you did. Except the curse was much stronger by the time you tackled it." He hugged me tight. "Thank the gods you survived."

We clung to each other, Erik holding on for all he was worth as I wept quietly.

"How old were you?" I asked, my voice thick.

"Twenty-three. I fought inside the domr to be Alpha after that. It was a long and bloody battle, and many good wolves died, but I knew I had to win, or the Varda was lost. I was the only one aware of the curse. Afterward, with Odin's help, I siphoned it from the rest of the pack and contained it. The change in the Varda was immediate, like a layer of pollution had lifted from among us."

"You'll meet your parents again someday." My voice was thick with tears, and I tilted my head to gaze at him. "They died fighting that evil. They'll be welcomed home to the woods outside Valhalla."

He shook his head, his mouth twisting. "I've looked. No one's seen them. Maybe now that the curse is defeated, they can pass over Bifrost to Valhalla." He raised my chin. "You've given us such a gift, Kristin. The Varda will survive because of you, and the world will be safer."

Pleasure surged through me—and determination. I'd do more than just defeat the curse. I'd do what I'd planned to do for fifteen years.

Avenge my family.

"It'll be safe when I've killed Hati and Skoll. I have control of my magic now. I can suck away their life force and chop off their heads or shoot out their hearts or something. I may even kill them slowly for what they did to my family. My pack wasn't strong like the Varda. The Valdyr I grew up with didn't stand a chance."

His eyebrows rose, and he opened and closed his mouth several times before speaking. "Kristin, as much as I love the idea of you, or anyone else, chopping off Hati and Skoll's heads, you can't."

Excitement bubbled up. "Yes, I can. I've trapped Hati before, and that was when I didn't know what I was doing. I used the raw magic from my mom's funeral pyre to form a cage. This time, I'll use their own magic against them and drain their life force. They won't know what hit them."

Inside, my wolf growled, and my eagle screeched. They also wanted Hati and Skoll dead. "Odin gave me this power for a reason—to kill Hati and Skoll—and I intend to use it."

Erik pushed a hand through his hair and then rose from the bed. I sat up, watching him with growing unease as he paced to the bathroom and back again.

Finally, he stopped in front of me. "When I said you couldn't kill Hati and Skoll, I didn't mean you weren't able to. I meant you're not allowed to."

"Allowed?" I frowned, not believing my ears. "That's insane." Kneeling on the bed, I clenched my hands at my sides. "This is my destiny. For my family. It's not something I need permission to do."

"And all the families that die in the upcoming apocalypse… don't they count for anything?"

"What are you talking about?"

"The Varda's spent eons studying the ancient texts, gleaning what we could about Ragnarök and Hati and Skoll's role in it. We've had the best minds analyze the nature of their magic and how it relates to cosmic events. Fenrir's sons are tied to the sun and the moon."

"So?"

"The myths say Ragnarök will occur when Hati and Skoll catch and eat them."

I laughed, but it was a harsh, ugly sound. I rose from the bed and stood in front of him, my hands clenched into fists by my side. "Right. What was I thinking? By all means, keep the sons of Fenrir alive." I stepped forward and jabbed him in the chest. "Maybe if the Varda had done what they should have and killed them years ago, my family would still be alive."

Erik stiffened. "That's not fair, and you know it. We don't take the myths literally, but we do search for the truth behind them. How do you think Hati and Skoll destroy the celestial bodies they're bound to?"

I almost rolled my eyes. "Maybe they shoot a rocket into them or something, I don't know. But if I kill them, they can't do that."

"If you kill them, you might do exactly that. We've hypothesized that—"

"Hypothesized! You don't know for sure? Why not ask Odin?"

"The gods don't dole out answers. They speak in riddles and prophecies."

"Odin was pretty clear when he gave me the magic to destroy them. You said I was here for a reason. What better reason could there be than to rid the world of its greatest evil?"

He reached out a conciliatory hand. "Kristin, you don't understand. Greater minds than mine have come up with this theory. And yes, it's only a theory, but so was Galileo's belief that the earth revolved around the sun. If either Hati or Skoll are killed, their magic could rebound and destroy the sun and moon." A hard glint entered his eyes. "No one is allowed to do that."

I stepped back, and he dropped his hand to his side. "There's that word again. 'Allowed.' Well, I hate to break it to you, but you can't tell me what to do."

"Yes, I can. I'm your Alpha, and I lead this pack. Odin knows I want you here, but if you can't abide by this decision, then…"

"Then, what?"

"Then you'll have to leave."

A chasm yawned between us, growing bigger by the second. How could I let Hati and Skoll walk away unpunished for what they'd done? My family had been torn apart—literally.

And why had Odin given me the power to eradicate the sons of Fenrir if he didn't intend for me to use it? Erik was wrong.

"So much for you wanting my opinion on things."

The ringing of his phone cut off his reply. He picked it up from the dresser. "Yes?… I'll be right there."

He ended the call and looked at me. "They've located Bjarg Faegir, the Dverg who cast the curse. We're going in with a full-level assault."

I jumped from the bed. "I'm coming with you."

His gaze pierced me. "I only want Valdyr I can rely on at my back. If Hati and Skoll are there, they must be kept alive. Can I trust you to do that, Kristin?"

I opened my mouth to reply, then slowly closed it. I couldn't answer him—wouldn't answer him—because I just didn't know.

CHAPTER 24

Kristin

Twenty minutes later, I sat squeezed between two huge rekkrs, with three more, including Erik, sitting across from me as we flew over the mountain range. In the distance, snow-covered peaks shone brightly against the clear blue sky.

Closing my eyes, I tried to focus on the rhythmic *whump, whump, whump* of the stealth helicopter blades above my head and the vibrating metal below my feet. I tried to find my center. But it was impossible. The erratic beat of my heart and my whirling thoughts kept me in chaos. I needed to calm down and think about the mission, not the chasm that had opened up so suddenly between Erik and me.

It was a gap I wasn't sure I wanted to close.

Allow the monsters—who'd killed my family, who'd wreaked havoc on the world for centuries—to live? Never. Erik's desire to keep Hati and Skoll alive made no sense. They were the worst kind of evil, and I alone had the power to eradicate them. As much as I wanted to be with Erik and be part of his pack, what he'd asked me to do was impossible. As well as wrong. He'd see that eventually.

Go.

The word reverberated down the Alpha bond from Erik, and his rekkrs leapt from the helicopters—the one that carried me and the ones flying around us. They changed into their wolves in midair, landed on all fours, and raced flat out into the woods. I jumped up to follow, but Erik's hand on my arm stopped me.

My wolf snarled at him. His snarled back—bigger, deadlier.

Stay back and help the injured wolves. Then he, too, sprang out the helicopter door.

I watched him fall, my hurt warring with my anger. Did he want me to stay because I could save lives or because he didn't trust me?

Just before he hit the snow-covered ground, he shifted into his wolf, not missing a beat as he joined the other rekkrs. They fanned out across the mountaintop, but I knew their ultimate target was a small opening in the rocks ahead of them.

The element of surprise would be theirs, but not for long. If Bjarg Faegir was holed up in that cave, he might have an escape route that burrowed deep into the mountain. Or he could fight, using magical weapons he'd most likely forged himself.

As the helicopter circled above the advancing wolves, I recalled what Dahlia had told me about the Dvergar. They were generally of smaller stature than humans, but they were fierce, strong, and well-versed in weaponry and magic. Their eyesight was poor in sunshine, so they kept indoors or underground as much as possible during the day. It would be to the wolves' advantage to draw Faegir out into the open.

A sudden explosion rocked the mountain, and the helicopter wavered in the percussive blast. I crouched at the open door, holding tight to the frame, my eagle eyes sharp as I tried to discern what was happening. Smoke rose to the east, and the rekkrs converged, Erik in the lead.

Something niggled at me. *Erik, the smoke's not right. I can see colors in it. Magic mixed with the explosive.*

It doesn't smell right, either, he replied.

The wolves slowed but continued to circle, covering the mountainside. Movement caught my eye in the opposite direction—a darting figure. My eagle screeched inside.

He's by the tree line!

The wolves raced after him as multiple explosions detonated at once. The smoke obscured my view but not my connection to the pack. I could feel them choking on the smoke, and I created a magical wind to sweep the poisonous mist away.

Then I jumped from the plane, intent on Faegir.

Stay back! Erik roared at me. *We have rekkrs down who need assistance.*

I ground my teeth in frustration as I landed on the ice-packed snow. Faegir could use magic. Who else but me could fight him? It wasn't like the injured wolves were dying. I didn't have to hold their life forces to their bodies. Their bones and tissue would regenerate in time.

Hesitating, I considered going against his orders, but my wolf snapped at me. *Pack!*

I'm doing this for the pack.

No. For you. Not alone now.

What the hell did that mean?

Faegir had crawled down another hole with the wolves hot on his heels. They shifted, then lobbed something into the hole. Another explosion. For the first time, I noticed the helicopters had dropped packs of weapons to the ground for the Valdyr to use.

This was a well-planned assault by deadly warriors. They didn't require my help anymore.

Disgruntled, I made my way over the rocks to the injured wolves. My wolf nipped metaphorically at my heels.

What? I asked, annoyed.

Alpha. They need us.

I repressed a sigh and hurried up.

I reached the first wounded Valdyr and crouched by her side. I had never met the warrior. Young with short dark hair and dusky skin, she tried to be stoic and brave, but I sensed her relief at her Alpha's arrival.

"I'm okay, Fyrsta," the female said, her eyes lowered in submission. She was in obvious pain.

"I know. But I'm going to check you out anyway." I scanned the female's naked form, looking for leaks in her aura. The colors were muddied, and the pattern chaotic, but the life force was tight to the warrior's body—a good sign.

"You're going to be just fine. I'm Kristin, by the way."

The rekkr looked at me askance, widening her green eyes before she lowered them again. "I know who you are."

"Good. That means you'll call me by my name from now on and look here when you speak to me." I pointed to my face. "Otherwise, I'll think I have food in my teeth or a booger up my nose."

The rekkr's lips twitched despite her pain. After a moment, she met my gaze. "A booger? What are we, five?"

Relief flooded through me, and I laughed. Thank the gods, I'd knocked myself off that pedestal.

"Talking about snot with my Alpha does not inspire confidence," the rekkr continued. "Watching you fight Linnea, however... Let's just say you have some moves I'm dying to learn."

My wolf huffed happily, chest puffed out, and chin raised. *Take care of pack.*

Okay, I get it now. You were right. They do need me.

To the young warrior, I added, "We'll spar later after you've got the all-clear from Kat. And nobody's *dying* to do anything here. Not on my watch."

Then my instinct roared, and my wolf lunged forward, teeth bared, fur bristling.

I spun around.

Skoll stood ten feet away, a shining beacon of beauty dressed in a gorgeous Italian suit, the buttons open at his throat to reveal an opalescent pendant lying between well-developed pecs. His long golden hair glistened in the sunlight, and his sky-blue eyes gleamed as he smirked at me.

"Oh, I don't know," he said, fingers flexing. "I intend to kill as many Valdyr as I can before I take you to my brother."

Anticipation rose as I stared at that beautiful, repulsive face. *Finally!*

I barely stopped a triumphant laugh from bursting out of me. This was what I was made to do, what Odin intended for me.

Stepping calmly between the son of Fenrir and my packmate, I dropped my arms by my sides. My wolf crouched, as excited as I was, ready to attack. Behind me, the injured Valdyr growled, and I sent a reassuring caress down the Alpha bond.

"You think you can take me that easily?" I asked. "I seem to recall it didn't work out for you—or Hati, whoever it was—last time."

He shrugged. "That was Hati. And we didn't know you could fly. Now, you're easy pickings, surrounded by soon-to-be-dead wolves. It's a pleasure to deplete the ranks when I can."

He raised his hand and hurled a ball of green fire at an injured wolf who lay on the ground about fifty feet away. I used the wind-like fingers to grab the magic and re-paint the deadly strike into softly falling petals. They floated harmlessly over the vulnerable Valdyr. Skoll's magic was my raw material to sculpt however I liked. I even added a butterfly to please my artist's eye.

But the magic was also his life force, his aura, and once I got ahold of that, I could do anything.

Skoll countered by lobbing multiple strikes simultaneously at several wounded Valdyr. I deflected them all in different ways, changing their intention from deadly to benign—puppies, feathers, chocolate hearts. I was showing off just a little.

He turned to me, his glee now a menacing scowl, and bombarded me directly in a continuous assault. I absorbed it with ease, making me stronger and him weaker.

When he stumbled and tried to cut off the flow of energy to no avail, I smiled. "You are so fucked."

Erik

I leaned over the grizzled, dirty Dverg who'd caused such hardship and heartache for the Varda. I was hard-pressed not to kill the vermin as he lay bound and gagged on the earthen floor in his workshop about a quarter mile underground.

The place looked like a cross between an artist's studio, a witch's hovel, and a mad scientist's laboratory. I would have to send a team down to comb through the objects, many of which appeared ancient and most likely magical. Others seemed new, making me wonder what they were and if someone had hired the Dverg to create them.

Gunn and several other senior rekkrs, including Linnea, stood around the room, battered and bruised. Some remained in their solid, naked form while others chose the misty blur of the helmingr. They all stared with deadly intensity at our captive.

Our intelligence had been flawed. The original cave we'd identified as Faegir's hiding place had been a trap, a diversion to conceal the existence of his workshop deep in the mountain.

The entrance was expertly concealed. We might never have found it if Kristin hadn't spotted Faegir from the air using her eagle's eyes. Luckily for us, she'd been there. Which was a whole other can of worms, one I didn't want to delve into right now.

She was the pack's Alpha, intended by Freyja to be my mate. I was sure of it, yet I didn't know if I could trust her.

Something my mother had said to me, days before she died,

popped into my mind—that love without trust isn't love at all. She was thinking of my father, no doubt.

Grief, raw and fresh over my parents' death, washed through me, and I gritted my teeth to keep from howling. At my feet, Faegir whimpered and writhed on the ground, obviously seeing something in my face that scared him.

Needing answers, I ripped away the Dverg's gag and threw him against a worn rock wall, hands fisted in the creature's dirty clothing. "Why?" I roared. "She was good to you. She considered you a friend."

I didn't need to tell Faegir I referred to my mother. The rat understood, and for a moment, his terror turned mulish. "Good to me like a little puppy. I didn't want her friendship."

"Then you tell her to get lost. To leave you alone. You don't spend hours with her, month after month, talking about art, showing her your work. You don't poison her and everyone she cares about." My canines lengthened, sharpened in my fury. "You were special to her. She even invited you to her mating celebration." My voice was little more than a growl.

"To see your father befoul her?" Faegir's eyes gleamed with possession. "He took what was mine. I loved her."

Shock hit hard, and I reared back. The Dverg twisted and fell to the ground, panting, his already dirty clothes freshly soiled and stinking of shit.

About to go supernova on the worm, I flickered in and out of the helmingr. My wolf was on me hard, wanting free to tear out his throat, but I wanted the pleasure of ripping him limb from limb. I bent forward, my hands clawed. "You murdered all those Valdyr, put the world at risk, because of unrequited love? You corrupted an entire pack because you couldn't stand to see the female you wanted love another?"

I grabbed Faegir's neck and lifted him against the wall again. The Dverg struggled for breath, fingernails scratching my wrist, his legs kicking the rock behind him.

"I'm going to make this last, Faegir, and you're going to wish you'd never set eyes upon my mother."

"Mer-cy…ple-ase."

"Like you gave her mercy? You had almost forty years to reverse the curse. Forty years of it twisting into the minds and hearts of the pack. You don't deserve mercy."

I sliced my claw over the Dverg's ear, and it dropped to the ground. Warm, bright blood spurted out and ran over my fingers. Faegir choked on his screams, which were caught in my crushing grip on his throat.

"There's nothing you can say to stop me. And when I'm done, I'll pass you on to the next wolf and the next. I'm not the only one whose family you destroyed."

"Ha-ti…Sk-Sk-o-ll."

The words penetrated my rage, and for a moment, I almost ignored them, so strong was my need to crush the maggot with my bare hands. My wolf howled with frustration, knowing I would relent—had to relent.

I took a deep breath and loosened my grip. "What about them?"

"Trade." Faegir's throat was so damaged it was hard to make out what he said. "Infor…ma…tion."

It was probably a stalling tactic. I would hurt the maggot even more for lying. Still…

"Gunn, bring me some water."

My second-in-command grimaced, most likely fighting his own battle with his wolf, then moved to a tap in the corner and poured dirty water into a mug. He passed it to me, and I forced Faegir to drink.

"You have ten seconds."

"Promise me mercy first," Faegir croaked. "By your honor, if my information is good, you'll grant me mercy."

I pulled back my lips in a snarl and pushed my face toward the Dverg. Saliva dripped off the razor-sharp edges of my teeth.

"Mercy…if it's good, worm."

Faegir's eyes darted around the room, landing on several arti-facts. "I made something for the sons of Fenrir. It unbinds them for short periods of time from the sun and moon. They can move freely in ways they never could before, and they can come together during the day or night."

I smiled. That information was old. My wolf gave a happy toss of his head as an image of fangs sinking deep into Faegir's throat floated through my head. "I've seen it. In fact, we have one. Skoll was sloppy."

I drew my hand back and punched the Dverg hard in the liver. Faegir crumpled to the floor and curled into the fetal position. Blood seeped from the corner of his mouth.

"Wait… There's…more," he wheezed.

Something in his tone, resignation maybe, sent my instinct ringing. Fuck. I'd wanted to make the vermin squeal.

"You're lying, Faegir." But I knew the intel was good.

"No, I swear it. I made something else for the twins. It will herald Ragnarök."

Silence fell. That telltale muscle twitched in my cheek. "How?"

"All the worlds and everything in them, including the sun and moon, will stop. All but the Jotun. I keyed the amulet to Hati and Skoll's blood. They've amassed an army in Jotunheim and advance on Asgard as we speak."

"What do you mean, stop?" I asked, a tremor passing through me.

"Just that. Everything in the nine realms will come to a stand-still. The gods will be easy slaughter for the Jotuns, and the sons of Fenrir will finally free their father."

Odin's bloody eye. Hati and Skoll would have unlimited time and access to Fenrir's prison. They would break through Odin's defenses eventually.

"What about us? The Valdyr were created from the blood of the twins' Jotun mother. Will we be affected?"

"No. But you and your pack are no threat to them. You may be the Fyrstr of the Varda, Erik Kron, but you are one to their thousands. It is well known you are the last Valdyr able to cross Bifrost to Asgard."

And whose fault was that? Now, I wanted to hurt the worm even more. "How do I stop them?"

"Go to Asgard and wake the gods—if you can."

I towered over the Dverg, who cowered on the ground. "What I don't understand, Faegir, is why you would agree to help them. If Ragnarök comes to pass, you'll die too."

"Some will endure. I'll be among them. I always survive."

He positively gloated. I wanted to forget my promise and kill the Dverg slowly. But the information was good, and I had no time to waste.

"I promised you mercy. You shall have it."

I moved too quickly for the Dverg to comprehend my intention. One second, he lived. The next, I ripped out his throat. Blood ran warm and thick down my naked chest. I spat out the offending flesh and shifted into the helmingr so the carnage dripped away. Faegir stared at me with dead, open eyes. I leaned down and closed them.

"That's your mercy. A quick and painless death. No surviving this time, worm." Then I turned and strode from the room, my rekkrs hot on my heels, every one of them looking grim, their wolves shining in their eyes.

How the hel could I stop this? It was unthinkable—the gods paralyzed; their sanctuary unguarded.

"The sons of Fenrir haven't factored in the dead Valdyr that run in the woods outside Valhalla," Gunn said. "Heroes, every one of them. They'll fight 'til the bitter end."

"They'll fight the army, not Hati and Skoll. The twins will be busy freeing their father unhindered."

"So, you'll cross over and confront them yourself?" Linnea asked. "It's suicide, Fyrstr. Maybe if only one lived, but two?"

"What choice do I have? Sit back and watch the worlds crumble? Maybe I won't have to fight them alone. If I can wake the gods, we might have a chance."

"And if you can't?" Gunn asked.

I stopped and faced him in the doorway of the cavernous workshop. "Then we prepare to die."

On Gunn's bleak nod, I stepped into the worn tunnel that led back to the surface only to be bombarded by a cacophony of wolves shouting down the Alpha bond in confusion, some filled with elation, others with fear and dread.

One filled with calm determination.

My wolf howled with the same confused emotions, but I felt only panic. "Holy Thor, she's killing him."

I shifted and raced up the sloped tunnel and stairs toward the surface, my big padded feet eating up the distance.

The workshop must have been warded against external communication. I'd been so intent on interrogating Faegir that I hadn't realized I was cut off from the rest of the pack.

From Kristin.

Pain at her betrayal pushed me to go harder, faster.

If I couldn't get there in time, it might not be Hati and Skoll who started Ragnarök after all.

Kristin

I hunched above Skoll, who lay slumped on the snow-covered ground. My hands hovered over him, burning from the mass of energy I'd siphoned from his aura. Almost done. He'd been amazingly strong, amazingly arrogant as he'd tried to pull his life force back from me. When it finally sank in that he was about to die, it wasn't fear in his eyes but disbelief. The fucker. I wanted fear. The same fear my family had felt when he'd destroyed them.

I leaned closer, my face the last thing he would see before he took his final breath. "Time's up," I said. "I hope you rot in hell, you mother—"

A brick wall smashed into me from the side and knocked me away from him. My connection to the monster severed as I skidded across the hard-packed snow. Fur and fangs filled my face. "What are you doing?" I screamed.

Erik snapped at me in wolf form. He pinned me to the ground, hot breath wafting up my nose.

I turned my head and saw Skoll reach out a hand. He looked back at me, then vanished. "No!" I cried and used my magic to throw Erik off. He shifted in midair and landed on two feet, a huge, furious male, all bulging muscles and raging eyes.

"You almost killed him!" He advanced on me with quick, long strides, his hands squeezed into tight fists.

"That was the point!" I was just as angry and barely restrained myself from hurling more magic at him.

"After I told you what would happen—that he must be kept alive? You broke my trust."

That stung, and my wolf howled inside. "You told me your theory of what might happen. Well, I have a different theory, and I acted on it. I'm not your lackey, Erik. I don't just do what you tell me to do."

"What I told you to do—asked you to do—was to put the pack first. You've had it rough, Kristin, but so has every wolf here. We work as a team. We don't put personal vendettas ahead of what's good for the pack."

I laughed in disbelief. "Keeping Hati and Skoll alive is good for us?"

"Keeping the pack alive is good for us. And for the rest of the world."

My mouth twisted with derision. "Yeah, well, not everyone wanted me to stop. Why would Odin give me such power if he didn't want me to kill Hati and Skoll?"

"I don't know, and you may never have the opportunity to find out. The Jotun are attacking Asgard as we speak. If they succeed and Fenrir escapes, Ragnarök will come to pass." His eyes hardened. "I suggest you and Gina go find somewhere safe to hunker down."

He turned away and said something through the pack bond to the other wolves. Static interfered, and I couldn't understand him, almost as if the connection had faded.

I grabbed his arm—the muscle solid and the skin warm beneath my hand. "I didn't hear you."

He looked at me, eyes almost black, that muscle twitching in his cheek. "That's Odin's choice, not mine. Goodbye, Kristin."

"I'm coming with you! I'm Alpha female of this pack."

"Are you?"

Panic welled. Is that why I couldn't hear him? Had Odin severed the bond? Had he not wanted me to kill Skoll? "You need me. We're a mated pair, chosen by Freyja herself."

"I need someone I can trust, mate or not." He walked away from me, and the others followed. "Don't come after us."

As one, they shifted and sprinted away toward the helicopters. The wind tugged at my hair as the metal birds took off, leaving me on the mountaintop. Alone.

CHAPTER 25

Kristin

THE SILENCE WAS DEAFENING. EVEN MY WOLF WAS STRANGELY quiet.

The triumph I'd felt while draining Skoll of his life force had faded, leaving behind a sick, empty feeling.

Erik had left me. The pack had left me.

A cold wind blew through my clothing, moaning eerily. I pressed my hands to my stomach, palms still warm from stealing Skoll's aura. The heat seeped through the material of my top to my skin, but still, I shivered. I'd nearly killed one of Fenrir's sons and had been seconds away from it before Erik had stopped me.

I'd almost had justice for my family.

It was doubtful I'd get a second chance.

I searched for the anger that had burned so brightly just minutes before but couldn't find it anywhere. Instead, pressure built around my heart. I took a deep breath to release it, then another, but it didn't help.

For Odin's sake, the world would be a better place without Hati and Skoll.

Wouldn't it?

Erik? I called out through our bond.

No answer. No sense of connection whatsoever. Only a loud, lonely echo that had me blinking furiously to clear the wetness from my eyes.

Erik? I tried again, louder this time.

Gone, my wolf said.

What do you mean, gone?

Pack gone.

I tried to quell my rising panic, to swallow past the lump that had formed in my throat, but it didn't help. He'd told me not to follow them while he and the rest of the Varda went to fight Hati and Skoll, to save the nine worlds.

Without me.

Oh gods, what have I done?

I hadn't been thinking of the pack, the world, or even getting justice when I'd tried to kill Skoll. I'd wanted vengeance. At any cost. I'd been blinded to reason in my need for revenge.

I could have just weakened Skoll, caged him. Maimed but not killed, as Erik had asked.

Now, the best I could do was stand on the sidelines and pray my former pack succeeded. Pray that everyone I cared about stayed safe.

Erik no longer trusted me. He didn't want my help.

The wind died suddenly, and I heard the pounding of my heart in my ears. *Thump, thump. Thump, thump. Thump, thump.*

I needed to leave. Now. I had no place here. Not anymore.

"Screw that!"

My words boomed back to me from across the mountaintop. I turned and charged to the edge of the nearest cliff. The moment I leapt into the abyss, the Alpha bond snapped into place.

Oh, thank Odin. I'd never experienced such sweet turmoil as when that cacophony of noise and images hurtled toward me through the bond—controlled chaos as the Varda mobilized for the coming disaster.

Shifting into my eagle, I flew in the direction the pack had headed, my wings eating up the distance, my eyes sharp, seeking the slightest movement. I spotted two sets of Valdyr wolves, different from Erik's group, headed the same way. I adjusted course and flew over their heads.

Then I heard Erik. *I'm crossing over now. Whatever you do, guard the bridge.*

Erik! I yelled, but I was too late, and his presence winked out of existence.

Bridge? What bridge?

Gunn, tell me where you are!

The pack's second-in-command focused on me down the Alpha bond. I sensed his surprise along with a simmering frustration. *Go away, Kristin. We don't need you.*

Yes, you do. By Odin's will, I am still Alpha female of this pack.

You gave up your right to lead when you put the pack in danger for your own personal vendetta.

Shame wormed its way through my heart. *You're right. I'm sorry. I made a mistake—a big one—but I'm coming whether you want me to or not.* I was determined to make a difference in this fight. *Maybe you don't need my help, but Erik does.*

You're too late. He's already gone.

Gone where?

Where do you think? To Asgard, to wake the gods before it's too late. And he doesn't need you. He needs a miracle. We all do.

The bleakness in his tone sent shivers down my spine. I beat my wings harder, letting instinct guide the way.

I'm coming.

I would be his miracle.

Erik

I stepped barefoot off of Bifrost and knew immediately something was wrong. Nothing moved—not the air, not a buzzing insect, not a cloud in the sky. It looked like even the sun stood still.

Turning slowly in a circle, I listened for sound and scented the stale air, alert to anything that might indicate life still existed in the gods' world.

Halfway around, I spotted Heimdall sitting on his horse, resplendent in white leather, his blond hair shining in the sunlight. Strapped to his back was a sword, and hanging from the saddle was his famous horn, Gjall, which he would use to call the gods to battle during Ragnarök.

Relief shot through me before I realized neither Heimdall nor his horse moved. They were perfectly sculpted—life captured in stone.

Approaching slowly, I said, "Vel finna, Heimdall, Guardian of the Rainbow Bridge." The small hope I'd nurtured died when silence reigned.

Breath tight in my chest, I walked around the living statue. I touched the stallion's flank. It was cold and hard beneath its pelt. Heimdall's leg felt the same under his clothes as if living flesh had petrified.

After a brief hesitation, I tried to push them over, but they stayed upright, solid as a mountain.

My eyes dropped to Gjall. Just looking at the famous horn made my heart pick up. If anything could wake the gods, surely this was it. Fingers trembling, I grasped the instrument, half expecting to be killed on the spot for such audacity. When nothing happened, I lifted it from the saddle, surprised by its lightness.

The simple golden horn was cool in my hands and slightly battered. A worn leather strap was looped around the middle. It seemed strange that such an important artifact wasn't treated with better care.

Placing it to my lips, I blew softly. Nothing happened—no sound, no vibration, no release of air. I tried again, this time asking Heimdall for forgiveness before I blew as hard as I could into the mouthpiece. Still nothing.

"Odin's bloody eye," I cursed.

Respect, my wolf snapped at me.

I winced, acknowledging my mistake. It was one thing to take the gods' names in vain on Earth but another to do so in their own home. What fool wanted to wake Odin's wrath because they couldn't control their need to fucking swear?

A shiver ran down my spine. Holy hel. Maybe that would work.

"Odin!" I yelled as loud as I could. "Heimdall! Freyja, you tart! Thor, you overgrown, meathead motherfucker! Get your lazy asses down here. We're in serious trouble!"

I took a deep breath. "The Jotun are coming, and Fenrir's going to piss all over you before he cuts off your heads unless you *wake the fuck up*! Quit diddling the help, pull your pants up, and save your sorry asses before it's too late!"

I kept hurling insults, getting meaner and more vulgar every time until I was hoarse and blue in the face. Defiling someone's character was hard work.

Finally, I said, "Odin, you all-seeing, old-man-smelling dumb fuck! You couldn't foresee shit if you didn't step in it first!"

I prayed for a stirring in the air, a shrill reprimand, a death blow, whatever, but nothing came. Slumping over in defeat, I placed my hands on my knees.

What else could I do? Other than Heimdall, I had no idea where the gods lived.

I raised my head and looked toward the mountaintop where I'd met Odin the last time I was here. Maybe I should try there? I knew it was a long shot, but I didn't have anywhere else to go...

My gaze dropped to the base of the mountain and the path to Fenrir's prison.

Except there.

Time was a funny thing in Asgard. The sons of Fenrir could have been here for days or weeks already, even though Skoll had been on Earth just hours before. Perhaps they'd made their way to the lake that encircled their father's island—while I'd been yelling insults at the gods like an idiot.

Perhaps Fenrir was already free.

My stomach heaved at the thought. I sent up a quick prayer to the gods, even though no one listened, then leapt forward and shifted into my wolf. My huge padded feet took great strides across Heimdall's paddock before jumping the fence and heading toward the mountain.

It might be the death of me, but no way would I allow the sons of Fenrir to free their father. Not on my watch. And not without a fight.

Kristin

I spread my wings and slowed my descent to a small mountain meadow, about five miles west of Wolf Ridge, that teemed with Valdyr.

The concentration of colors in the area overwhelmed me, and I almost lost myself to the otherworldly beauty. The intensity of the hues was similar to the colored walls of the domr when I'd fought Linnea.

The bridge, the magical one that connected Earth to Asgard, had to be nearby. What had Dahlia called it? Bifrost?

Shifting back to my female form, I landed among hundreds of grim-looking Valdyr. Some sat off to the side, cross-legged and eyes closed as if meditating. Others, armed to the teeth, set up defensive positions.

Feeling vulnerable because of my nudity, I shifted into the blur of the helmingr. I knew the Valdyr wouldn't care, but I'd spent too much time around humans for it not to make me uncomfortable—especially since most everyone else was dressed.

I barely received a glance from the busy rekkrs, let alone a show of submission. Definitely no bowing or scraping here. Which was good. I'd wanted to be knocked off that pedestal. But a little respect would have gone a long way toward making me feel like part of the pack again.

"Hey, Blondie! Catch!"

I spun just in time to see Gunn toss me something. Solidifying, I caught a pair of black leggings and a T-shirt before a pair of runners hurtled toward my head. I scowled at him, but he'd already walked away.

After scrambling into the clothes—which fit, to my surprise—I ran after him. There must be something I could do to help. Odin had named me in a frickin' prophecy, for gods' sakes.

I caught up with him as he supervised the unloading of a rocket launcher from the back of a truck.

"What the hel are you expecting?" I asked.

"Your worst nightmare."

My worst nightmare was Hati and Skoll. I suspected their father would be much worse.

And Erik was going to fight all three of them...alone.

"Is there some way I can get to him? To help. Odin brought us together for a reason."

"You can't." He waved a sharp hand toward the Valdyr who sat grouped together on the ground with their eyes closed. "None of us can. We lost too much time to the curse. Erik's on his own."

I glanced at the meditating Valdyr. "What exactly are they doing?"

"Trying to cross."

"Cross what?"

"The bridge!" His nostrils flared with exasperation before he turned back to the truck. "Look, I don't have time to explain. Fenrir may already be free, and the gods dead. Hel knows it won't be enough, but we have to be prepared for whatever comes across."

My wolf huffed with indignation at Gunn's tone, but I understood. We were both stuck here while Erik went up against the sons of Fenrir—alone. Unless I could find the bridge.

Using my eagle's eyes, I searched the area, so glorious with color, especially around the meditating Valdyr.

"What does it look like?" I asked.

He scowled, his wolf snarling in his throat. "If I knew that, I wouldn't be over here while my best friend and Alpha kills himself on a suicide mission. I'd be at his back, like always."

The Valdyr quieted around us.

I refused to be cowed. "Well, what does Erik see? Surely, he's told you."

"I don't know…a blank canvas."

"Blank?" Dismay crashed through me. My hopes of saving Erik slipped away. "All I see are colors."

Gunn stilled. "What kind of colors?"

"The same ones that surround the domr or a funeral pyre." I reached out and touched one of the swirling energies. It pooled in my hand and heated my fingers. "It's pure creativity. Concentrated life force, I guess. It's about as far away from a blank canvas as you can get." Tears pushed at the back of my eyes, and I crushed the color until it crumbled and drifted to the forest floor. I had no way to get to Erik after all.

"Kristin, what did you just do?" Gunn's voice barely broke a whisper as he stared at the rainbow swirl on the ground.

I looked up at him. "I touched the colors. It's the same thing I do when I save a life. Or take one. I just manipulate the aura."

"Can you do it again?"

"Of course."

Suddenly, he grabbed me by the arms. Excitement replaced the desolation I'd seen moments ago. "They call it the Rainbow Bridge, sometimes the Burning Bridge. If you can find it and touch it like you did that other color—solidify it—then we might be able to cross over. All of us." An exuberant whoop burst from his lungs. "We may have a chance after all."

Hope rose, and I scanned the meadow, squinting this way and that, my own excitement rising. But I couldn't see a bridge, just a mass of gorgeous colors.

"Why a blank canvas?" I asked.

"It's useful for the meditation. You probably don't need it. Erik said to think of sifting worlds like painting a picture in your mind's eye."

"Okay." I reached out and grabbed a color, bringing it into our world. "Maybe I should just start painting." I grabbed another color and another, moving faster as my artist took over, losing myself to my creation. The other Valdyr stopped what they were doing and gathered around.

"Oh, sweet Frigg," Gunn murmured after a moment. "There it is."

Erik

I carefully maneuvered the hidden trail in the sheer, rocky canyon that led to Fenrir's prison. I'd shifted to my Valdyr form when I arrived so I could step exactly where Odin had shown me seven years ago. One wrong move and the trail would crumble beneath my feet, dropping me down deep crevices lined with razor-sharp rocks. If the fall didn't kill me, the scorpions and vipers that lived in the pits would.

And if I did survive? I'd have no way of getting out.

A whisper of sound reached my ears, twine being pulled taut, and I fell into a defensive crouch, my heart racing. An arrow whizzed over my head.

"You missed, Bro. That's a hundred to me—in thousands, not tens, this time. Fresh, crisp bills."

Thor's balls. Hati!

My wolf howled savagely as my gaze darted up the canyon. I pinpointed the Jotun's position on a ledge that jutted from the rock face. His pale blond hair was pulled back in a low ponytail, and his dark eyes shone.

"What took you so long, Fyrstr? We've been here for weeks," he said.

Calculating the trajectory of the arrow that had just missed me, I traced backward to a small crevice on the opposite side of the path. I couldn't see Skoll, but I knew Evil Bastard Number Two had to be there.

Two more arrows whistled toward me, and I jumped high in the air to avoid them. I snagged a tree root growing out of the canyon wall and pulled myself up behind a small outcropping. If only I'd been able to carry a weapon with me.

"In case you haven't figured it out, my brother is royally pissed," Hati said, a delighted grin creasing his perfect face. "Your little bikkja got him good. He's still not right. Although there's something in the air here, isn't there? It's energizing. I can't wait to relocate once dear old dad's been set free."

"If Fenrir gets out, all of Asgard will burn," I said, working out my next move. "The real estate won't be nearly as valuable with smoke blocking the view."

"Yeah, I thought of that, but I'm okay with destruction too. I haven't pillaged in centuries. So much fun."

Three more arrows thunked into the rock beside me. I shrank lower. Damn, those were close. I couldn't stay here much longer. But where could I go? I could shift into the helmingr, but fighting was difficult when I couldn't connect flesh to flesh. Plus, I couldn't move as fast in the helmingr, and to beat Hati and Skoll, I'd need speed and agility—not to mention a miracle.

"Kristin would have killed him if I hadn't intervened. That must count for something."

"Nope." The voice sounded like it had been dragged through broken glass and rubble—and it was far too close. I leapt sideways without thinking, letting instinct take over as the curved blade of a scimitar sliced toward my head, missing me by inches.

How the hel had Skoll gotten behind me?

My sole chance was to make it to the portal in the rock face that led to Fenrir's prison. Only my blood—my essence—could open the gate. Once I was through, it would close behind me, locking me in and the sons of Fenrir out.

I landed on the trail in wolf form, long legs and padded feet racing over the ground. Maybe I could surprise them and gain a few crucial seconds.

The twins cursed, and arrows flew around me. One missile sliced through my ear, and another hit my left flank, grazing the skin. I prayed the tips weren't poisoned.

Behind me, the trail crumbled away. Try as I might, it was impossible at this speed to stay entirely on the path Odin had mapped out for me. My big paws set off avalanches of stone that were as dangerous as Hati and Skoll.

But maybe that meant the twins couldn't follow.

No. They come, my wolf said, focused on the bare rock ahead that was the prison entrance.

Just when I thought I might make it, I stumbled, and my vision began to blur. Ah, hel, there must have been something on the arrowheads after all. The hissing of snakes and gods only knew what else, in the pits below, was loud in my ears as my landings became wobbly.

All I needed was one last leap. I stretched out my lupine body, intent on the nondescript rock face, and shifted back to my Valdyr form. Reaching toward the granite, I anticipated the sharp nip in my palm from the stone portal as it soaked up my blood before opening.

Instead, searing pain and shock crashed through me as Skoll's sword sliced through my wrist. My hand hit the ground before my body did, rolling to within a few inches of the gate. Blood poured from my wound and splattered onto the rock.

The key to Fenrir's prison.

The gate disintegrated before my eyes, leaving the pathway open.

Panic and horror welled. I tried to roll inside so the door would shut behind me, but Skoll's sword pierced my thigh and embedded deep into the dirt. Agony ripped through me. I tried to shift into the helmingr to free myself, but I was too weak and couldn't maintain the energized state. Four more arrows hit me —in my other thigh, my arms, and my chest—pinning me in place like a frog about to be dissected.

Blood and saliva bubbled up my throat, and I coughed, struggling to breathe. White-hot pain seared every nerve. Then the agony slowly faded as cold seeped into my body, into my heart.

I'd failed.

Even worse, I'd led the sons of Fenrir straight to their father's prison. Gods damn it, they'd played me. They'd driven me hard, so I'd run exactly where they wanted me to.

I'd been an easy pawn. A sucker.

Their gloating faces stared down at me. "Always a pleasure doing business with you, Fyrstr." Hati ground the hilt of Skoll's sword further into my leg. "If it's all right with you, we'll collect our weapons on the way out…with Daddy-o."

Skoll leaned in, and for the first time, I noticed that the beautiful Jotun looked haggard, almost hideous, like he'd been to hel and back.

Unexpected pride swelled within me. My mate had done that.

"Too bad you'll be dead by then," Skoll rasped. "Father wanted to kill you himself."

One remaining breath. I drew as much air into my lungs as I could, needing to hurt the monster in whatever way possible. "He's gonna hate you, you ugly piece of shit."

Rage gathered on the Jotun's face before his fist pounded down. But my eyes had closed, and I didn't feel a thing.

The only pain I felt was in saying goodbye to my wolf and failing to protect my pack, the gods, and the worlds. And my unfulfilled bond to Kristin.

Always Kristin.

CHAPTER 26

WHEN THE LAST VALDYR DISAPPEARED INTO THE FLARING kaleidoscope of colors at the far end of the rainbow-colored bridge, I lost all contact with the rekkrs. I'd been mentally cut off from each one as they'd crossed over, and worry about what was happening on the other side churned my guts.

Now it was my turn—finally—and I ran toward Asgard, surrounded by the magical energy of the gods, my heart in my throat.

What if Hati and Skoll had been waiting for Erik, for the pack, when they arrived? They might be dead already. Every one of them. And I'd led them there like lambs to the slaughter.

At the end of the bridge, I slowed and closed my eyes, then stepped through a wall of color that flared like the aurora borealis, almost overwhelming in its intensity. When velvety grass tickled my feet, and sweet-smelling air teased my nose, the bond snapped back into place, bringing with it intense relief. The pack was alive and well, running in wolf form at full speed, Gunn in the lead.

I found myself standing in a pasture in the middle of a beautiful, lush valley with a snow-topped mountain towering in the distance. The sight was similar to valleys on Earth, but everything here seemed sharper, brighter, more majestic.

Amazingly so.

I tried to locate Erik and thought I caught some faint impression of him, but then it slipped away like water through my fingers.

Gunn, is Erik with you? I can't sense him.

No. I don't know where he is, and I can't help you find him. Instinct pulls us this way.

The urgency that compelled the rekkrs to the northwest raced through me as well, but instead, I was drawn to the northeast—to the mountain.

That's where I needed to be.

Chest tight, agitation making my skin crawl, I ran forward then shifted into my eagle, taking off with long swoops of my wings.

As I gained height, I looked beyond the pack, far into the distance, and saw the edge of a shining sea. The shore was lined with ships. Dread whispered up my spine.

Jotun, my wolf said.

Odin's bloody eye, there had to be thousands of them. Too many for the rekkrs to fight—especially after running all that way.

Others will help.

Who?

Those who've sacrificed.

My heart skipped a beat. Of course. I'd been so focused on Erik that I'd forgotten about my parents, my brothers, and every other Valdyr who'd died a hero and now lived in the woods outside Valhalla.

I could see my family again if they survived the upcoming battle. If I survived.

And I wanted that desperately—with Erik by my side.

More determined than ever, I focused on the mountain, beating my wings as fast as I could. I searched for Erik with my eyes and my heart.

What had Gunn said? He went where instinct led.

I shut down my fear, my racing thoughts and riotous emotions, and let the drive that had compelled me this far lead the way. Retreating to a quiet place inside my eagle, I closed my eyes and opened fully to the magic of Asgard.

Swooping to the base of the mountain, I flew above a rocky gorge that ended against a sheer rock face. Something lay at the edge. Something bloody and torn. Something—

Oh, gods. *Erik!*

I landed hard beside him, shifting as I hit the ground but keeping my eagle eyes sharp so I could see his aura—or what was left of it.

"Hold on," I cried, horror ripping through me at the sight of his decimated body. "Please, svassr. Hold on."

The term of endearment slipped from my lips. *Beloved.*

Freyja's breath, I did love him. I couldn't lose him now.

Grabbing the trickle of life force that seeped upward from his mangled chest to pool in the air around him, I gently threaded it back into his body. The filament had a delicate, almost brittle quality. If I wasn't careful, it would break.

Even knowing that, I had to fight the urge to shove it back inside and seal him up.

Tears poured down my face as I worked, but I didn't dare let go of his aura to wipe them away. When they landed on his skin and washed away rivulets of blood, I barely controlled my sobs.

"Please, Erik. Stay with me."

His beautiful face was leached of color where it wasn't spattered with blood, and his nose and lips were smashed. Four wicked-looking arrows and a sword were driven right through his arms, legs, and chest.

Pinned like a bug to the ground.

"I'm here now. You're going to be okay." Gods, I prayed my words were true.

His skin no longer looked so ashen, and hope budded in my heart. Then his chest moved, and he coughed. Blood poured from his mouth and mangled chest, causing his eyes to flutter, then still. I felt a tug at my hands as his aura tried to leave his body again.

"No, damn it! You're not going anywhere."

Maybe I could do what I'd done to Linnea in the domr. I'd used the colorful energy—Asgard's energy—to heal her wounds. I could do that here—the energy was all around me. But that would mean letting go of Erik's aura first.

I tied a careful knot in the energy stream I'd been holding and sealed it to his body as best I could. His aura pooled behind the stopper. It would be like a dam bursting if released. I had to work quickly, or I would lose him for good.

With one part of my mind holding his aura in place, I broke off the ends of the arrows and then heaved him up by his shoulders so the shafts slid free of his arms and chest. After tugging the pointed heads from the ground and tossing them aside, I laid him back down.

His arms bled, but I ignored those wounds and focused instead on his chest. Drawing on the energy of Asgard, I placed my hands over the damage and imagined the cells repairing themselves.

But even after the flesh knit back together and the bleeding stopped, he still didn't open his eyes.

I scanned his leg where the sword had pierced deep into the inner thigh. Standing, I pulled the weapon free. Fresh blood gushed out, and again, his aura tried to break free of the seal.

Pushing my hands directly into the wound, I searched for the ends of the severed artery, which had retracted back onto itself in opposite directions. But there was too much blood, and when I did find the ends, they slipped from my fingers.

I needed something sharp to grasp them, but what? I remembered Linnea forming claws at the ends of her fingertips when we'd fought in the domr. I knew I had to do the same—if I could. I sent the image to my wolf, who didn't understand.

I need your claws!

Shift?

No, just your claws!

My wolf howled in frustration, unable to comprehend my meaning. My desperation grew. I mentally grabbed my wolf's claws and shoved them through my fingertips.

It worked.

Snagging the two parts of the artery, I brought them together and used the magic all around me to sear them back together. It held, but I kept a hold of it until life-giving blood pumped through. Immediately, the pressure behind the seal decreased.

Relief swamped me. I almost collapsed on Erik, but he was still too weak. His chest moved with shallow breaths.

I finished healing his leg and then removed the arrow from the second leg. Thankfully, it had missed the artery and driven straight through muscle and bone. I had to tug hard to free the shaft, and Erik moaned in pain.

"I'm sorry, sweetheart, but you'll thank me later. I promise."

It wasn't until I changed position to heal the final wound in his arm that I realized his right hand was missing, leaving behind a clotted, bloody stump.

Horror almost choked me. "Oh, no." Raising a tear-wet face, I saw his eyes had opened.

"Kristin," he whispered.

I gently laid his arm back down and knelt by his head. My hands cupped his cheeks. "You're going to be okay, Erik. I've healed the worst of it. Everything except your hand. Do you know where it is? If I can find it, I can try to reconnect it. Or maybe you can grow a new one. Has anyone ever done that before?"

He shook his head, then looked toward the rock face. For the first time, I saw a passageway carved into the rock and lit by the minerals within. I'd been so intent on healing him that I hadn't noticed it before.

"Hati. Skoll," he ground out. "They...waited for me. Fenrir's prison. I let them in."

His last sentence was so tortured it broke my heart. "It wasn't your fault, Erik. You couldn't have fought off both of them."

"It was...my fault. I led them here." He closed his eyes. "They played me."

"We'll worry about that later. After you've recovered."

"No time. If Fenrir's...freed, the world will be...destroyed. We have to wake the gods." He pushed himself onto his elbows, his face contorted in a painful grimace. "Try...calling."

"What do you mean? Just call out their names?" Then it occurred to me he might mean the kalla, the howl a male Valdyr sent out to his chosen female. If the female responded and Freyja sanctioned the union, the goddess would bless the couple with a magical bond called the Kyssa.

I turned hot, then cold, then hot again at the thought. "Are you talking about the Kyssa?" The romance of that sacred bond was sighed over by all young females, and I'd grown up hearing tales of famous love matches. "Does it still work if the female calls for the male?"

Erik looked at me, confused, and then his eyes widened. "Freyja's breath, that might do it. If we...invoke the Kyssa, if I call for you, the goddess is magically bound to respond. It's her sacred responsibility to seal us in the kyss or...separate us forever."

Our eyes met. His wolf shone through, turning the irises a blazing, golden brown. "We have to try, Kristin. We can...ask

Freyja to break the bond afterward. I won't tie you to me…forever."

A dull pain imploded in my heart. Not exactly the proposal I'd been waiting all my life to hear.

This so wouldn't end happily.

I dropped my gaze and saw the blood on my hands and arms —reminding me of the blood that would cover the world if we didn't succeed in waking the gods. I had no choice.

"All right," I whispered, unable to meet his eyes. "If you call, I promise I'll answer."

His undamaged hand squeezed mine. "Thank you. And thank you for coming for me, for saving my life."

I looked up. No matter my personal feelings, I was Alpha female to his male, and we had a job to do. I squeezed his hand in return. "I'll always come for you, Erik. We're in this together. And I'm sorry, so very sorry, about earlier. I should never have tried to kill Skoll. The pack, the safety of the world, always comes first."

He nodded, then closed his eyes and tilted back his head.

A low, melodic howl filled the air. My wolf cocked her head and listened. She was excited, and I ignored my reluctance.

Why wouldn't I? This was Erik's wolf calling to me. The purity of the emotion—love, desire, need—was evident in the clarity of his kalla. It was incredible to hear.

My wolf threw back her head and answered his call, the sound vibrating through every cell of my body. The howls blended together in beautiful harmony, creating a rich symphony that brought tears to my eyes.

I had no idea how long we sang to each other, lost as I was in the magic of the moment, but when a hand grasped mine—small, warm, and somehow infinite—I knew I was in the presence of the divine.

Slowly, I drifted back to earth and opened my eyes. Freyja knelt between us, holding our hands so we were joined in a circle. I gasped when I saw Erik, completely healed—his face was as beautiful as ever, his color healthy, his grip strong. Even his severed hand had been replaced.

The goddess was as stunning as Gina, with the same voluptuous curves and long, dark hair. She wore a simple peasant-style dress in a verdant green covered by a cloak of feathers—falcon, by the looks of it.

It reminded me I was naked.

Freyja smiled, and then both Erik and I were clothed in tight black leather from top to bottom, with perfectly fitted boots on our feet.

"It's the least I can do," Freyja said, her smile so beautiful it made me want to weep. "I would have chosen something prettier for your mating, but you'll need to fight soon. The sons of Fenrir are at the lake's edge."

The words made no sense to me, but when I glanced at Erik, he looked grim.

"They won't get any farther," he said and tried to stand. She held him easily in place.

"In a moment. After we've finished." Freyja closed her eyes, and a stirring in the air lifted the hair from my brow.

"Thank you, Goddess," Erik said, "but it's not necessar—"

"Hush, Fyrstr."

"But we just wanted—"

"Hush." This time, the word reverberated through my body, and I felt the physical weight of it in my veins. The goddess had spoken.

Then, it felt like my heart was gently clasped and threaded with warmth. Looking down, I saw what looked like strands of molten gold extending from my chest. Similar strands extended from Erik's, and when they met in the middle, they twined together to form a knot.

Light flowed out from it, traveled back along the strands, and then disappeared. I gasped as the pulse surged through my body, carrying with it the essence of Erik. I could feel him in every cell. Could hear him in my thoughts.

Mates.

Ulf-verr. Ulf-vif.

Husband. Wife.

I realized I was sobbing, tears streaming down my cheeks. When my gaze met his, the same onslaught of emotions was reflected on his face but in that restrained, tight-jawed way of strong males that made a female want to nip them.

Freyja had forged an overwhelming connection between our hearts and minds that hid nothing and never would. I felt his desire and need for me, his gratitude and respect. But I also felt his regret to have tied me to him through the Kyssa.

That hurt. And what was worse, he felt my hurt and was sorry for it.

Gods, I had nowhere to hide. My heart had been turned inside out, and every unrequited feeling was on display for him to dissect at his leisure.

"No, Kristin," he said, aware of my thoughts. "It's not like that."

"Of course it is. How could it not be?"

Freyja *tched* her tongue and pulled us closer, like a mother hen gathering in her chicks. "The strongest wolves often have the hardest time letting go. Trust in my decision for you." Then she kissed us on the foreheads, joined our hands together, and stepped back, dressed now in the same leathers I wore. "I must awake the Allfather before it's too late. War is upon us."

Then she disappeared, leaving behind the loveliest scent imaginable.

I lifted my eyes to Erik's, wanting desperately to retreat and lick my wounds, but I had nowhere to go. He was everywhere. A part of me, just like my wolf. And his concern almost crushed me.

"Don't pity me," I said. I yanked my hands free and stumbled back.

"I don't."

"You do. I felt it."

"For Odin's sake, Kristin. I was…upset for you. That's all."

"I'm fine. There's nothing to be upset about."

He rubbed his hands over his face, and I could almost hear him thinking I was being difficult. I glared at him.

He sighed. "I'm sorry if my caring has made you uncomfortable. Believe me, that's the last thing I want, but I don't know how to stop. I'll speak to Freyja about severing the bond as soon as I can. For now, there are bigger things on our plates. Like the end of the world."

Casting his glance to the ground, he picked up Skoll's weapons and held them up, sword in one hand, arrowheads in the other. "Take your pick. I assume you're coming with me."

His words and actions said one thing, but his emotions screamed his reluctance. He didn't want my help. He wanted to fight the sons of Fenrir alone. Gods, he'd never trust me again.

I grabbed the arrowheads, knowing the sword was too heavy and would only slow me down. "Damn right, I'm coming with you, whether you want me to or not."

Marching past him toward the entrance, head held high, I gasped when he grabbed my arm.

He stepped close so we were nose to nose and growled down at me, "I don't want you to come, Kristin. You're right about that. But it's not because I don't trust you. It's because we won't win this battle. You and I, Ulf-vif, will die."

Then he grabbed my hair at the nape of my neck, pulled back my head, and kissed me.

CHAPTER 27

Erik

I KNEW I SHOULD GET MY SORRY ASS DOWN TO THE LAKE, WHICH was the last defense in Fenrir's prison, but for the life of me, I couldn't let go of Kristin.

Blood rushed through my veins, making me hard and heavy, sensitive to every touch. The feel of her beneath my hands—soft curls, cool leather—set me on fire. My tongue flicked into her mouth, hot and wet, wanting more.

She tasted like the headiest wine.

But that was just the physical, the smallest part of what I felt. If I thought making love to her when our wolves were joined was a mind-blowing experience, then kissing as a kyssed pair was something else altogether. I felt not only my own desire but hers as well, amplified a hundred times over.

Even knowing the end of the world was in the balance, all I wanted to do was strip off her clothes, lay her down, and make love to her. Then do it again. And by the way she strained toward me, I knew she wanted the same thing.

It took every bit of my strength to drag myself away. Our eyes met. We were both breathing like we'd run a marathon.

"Holy Freyja," she said.

And I laughed. I couldn't help it. It'd been a hel of a day. "Now I know why newly kyssed pairs are always getting caught with their pants down. How the hel do you think about anything else?"

"How the hel do you do anything else?"

I shook my head and stepped back. Immediately, her feelings of loss and uncertainty washed over me. Hel, I felt the same.

The tension that had eased for a few moments filled me again, and every muscle tightened. Somehow, I had to filter out our bond. It would be hard enough fighting Hati and Skoll with my own emotions running riot through my body. I couldn't do it with hers there too.

"I'm sorry," she said.

"Don't be." I rubbed her arm. "This is why the newly kyssed go on long honeymoons—they have to learn to live in each other's heads and hearts, not to mention deal with their overwhelming physical desire." I shoved my other hand through my hair and sighed. "I need to block the bond somehow, or we have no chance of beating Hati and Skoll. We may be the shortest pairing in history."

She picked up the arrows she'd dropped, not meeting my gaze. "Okay. Do it, then, so we can go."

I hesitated for a second, regret a tight band around my chest, and then I closed my eyes and went inside myself—into the hjarta. I sensed the pack bond between us right away, but that was surface compared to where I had to go. Freyja's bond was deeper. Much deeper.

For years, I'd walled off the curse. I should be able to use the same technique to block the connection with Kristin.

My wolf growled at me.

We don't have a choice, I said.

Our mate.

She won't be for much longer, not if we don't stop Hati and Skoll. And there's no way I can do that while Kristin's newly inside me. I need your help.

My wolf flattened his ears, tilted up his muzzle, and howled. Then the bond appeared, and I realized with surprise that the source was located within my wolf—within both our wolves.

The animals truly were the heart of the Valdyr.

But if I built a wall around the bond, would I be sealing my wolf inside?

Yes.

Okay, that wouldn't work.

I moved away, following the emotional connection toward Kristin, and then stopped. Maybe if I built a wall on top of it, like a boulder on a water hose, the emotion wouldn't be able to get through. Or perhaps I could twist it. Kink the hose.

If I could get the flow down to just a trickle, that would help.

Will that work? I asked my wolf.

Yes. No.

What does that mean?

No twist.

But the boulder idea will work?

My wolf gave a mental shrug.

Thanks. You're a lot of help.

Turning my attention back to our mating bond, I built a mental wall on top of it. I thickened the base and made it as heavy as possible until the glowing energy disappeared. I had no idea if it had worked.

Opening my eyes, I saw Kristin staring back at me, looking a little panic-stricken.

"I can't sense you anymore—not like I did," she said.

I forced a smile. "That's good." Other than the pack bond, Kristin was gone from my head and heart.

It hurt.

She shoved the arrows into a satchel that had grown out of

the leather suit near her hip. Freyja had provided for all of our needs.

"All right, then. Let's go," she said.

"Not so fast." I squatted down and, using the tip of my sword, scratched out a diagram of the prison in the rock dust. "The tunnel inside the mountain will seem to last forever. It doesn't. Just when you think it'll never end, you're there. At the end is a huge cavern with an underground lake. Fenrir's prison is on an island in the middle of the lake. Whatever you do, don't let the water touch you."

"Got it. No swimming."

"Absolutely no swimming. I don't know what's under the surface, but I know it's not good."

"How do we get across?"

"We don't." The absence of the stone longship hanging from my neck felt heavier than if I were wearing it. I pointed to the lakeshore. "I usually call for the boat here, but I can't this time—which is probably for the best. No matter what happens, Hati and Skoll cannot get to the island."

She nodded. "Anything else?"

"Yeah. Don't shift. It may tempt them to shift too. Their wolves are savage and will kill us on sight. We want to drag the fight out as long as possible to give Freyja more time to wake Odin."

I rose, and when a sheath grew on the back of my leather tunic, I tucked the sword into it. Thank the goddess, our suits adjusted to our fighting needs.

"Okay. Now we can go." Grabbing Kristin's hand, I entered the cave and quickly led her down a path lit by fluorescent minerals.

A tremor ran through Kristin's arm, and I almost stopped. I wanted to race with her back to Freyja and demand she keep my ulf-vif safe. Leading her to almost certain death was the hardest thing I'd ever done.

But I knew Kristin would accept nothing less.

"Will you tell me about your magic?" I asked. The knowledge might come in handy during the fight. "What else can you do besides healing and draining someone's life force?"

"I can create physical things, but they disappear as soon as I stop thinking about them—like the bridge."

"What bridge?"

"The one I built between Earth and Asgard."

I stopped and turned to her, my mouth dry with shock. Why hadn't I thought to ask her that before? "Of course you did. How else would you get across?"

"Not just me, the rest of the rekkrs too. They're fighting the Jotun alongside the Valdyr who've already died and live in Asgard. My family will be there. When my mom died, she told me that they were all together in the woods outside Valhalla."

Her voice cracked at the end, and it nearly crushed me. I pulled her closer—I couldn't help it. "Did you see them?"

"No. I came straight here." Her body cleaved to mine for a second before she pushed away and cleared her throat. "Ragnarök, remember?"

Right. We had nine worlds to save.

A new determination rose to get her through this fight alive so she could see her parents and brothers again. Whatever happened to me, she would survive.

I resumed our trek, quickening our pace.

When the trail dipped down, I squeezed her fingers. "We're transporting." Then, my body disintegrated and reformed as we crossed the portal between Asgard and the prison.

I crouched low and pulled her next to me. Her breath came in heavy gasps.

It's close now, I said down the Alpha bond. *Loki's luck, we'll have the element of surprise.*

We crawled forward silently until the path opened onto an

enormous cavern with a large pitch-black lake in the middle. A mist rose above it that emanated an unnatural gray light.

Hati stood at the water's edge with his hands on his hips. Skoll paced up and down on the beach behind him, throwing rocks into the lake. He still looked furious.

More than anything, that worried me. The haggard-looking Jotun was unpredictable. If he shifted into his wolf, we would be dead in minutes.

There's no scent here. No breeze, she said.

That's good for us. They won't smell us coming. Can you drain them again like you did before? There's no sunbeam or moonbeam for them to jump out on. If you incapacitate them until Odin arrives, that's probably our best chance.

She examined Hati and Skoll before gasping silently. *They have no aura.* She turned back to me and scanned me. *Neither do you.*

Fisting her hand over my heart where my aura should be the strongest, she turned her empty palm upward. *There's nothing to grab onto. Gods, Erik, I'm so sorry.*

I braced my shoulders and let my wolf shine through my eyes. *Don't be. We'll just have to incapacitate them the old-fashioned way. Go for the jugular first and then the femoral artery. And whatever you do, don't hesitate. Go for the kill. Instinct tells me things are different here.*

Just then, Hati lifted his arms, chanting something. Sparks flew from his fingertips, and the lake boiled before settling down to its unnatural stillness. Skoll yelled and stalked back to him. They argued, but the air snuffed out the words.

Watch for fireballs. That's their favorite. I pulled the sword from the sheath on my back. *I'll take Skoll.*

I cupped her cheek. *Stay alive, svassa.*

Kristin

I rushed forward, running hard and fast at Hati. I landed as quietly as I could on the rounded stones beneath my feet. Erik kept pace with me on my left side, gunning for Skoll. The twins yelled at each other as they gestured toward the island, which worked in our favor.

My wolf's claws pushed through the tips of my fingers like when I'd healed Erik, and I flexed them in readiness. I'd spent the last twelve years training for this, and I was damn well going to do it. Even if I didn't kill them, I'd come so close they might as well be dead. Then I'd serve them up on a platter to Odin and let him deal with them. Maybe he'd imprison them like he had their father.

When I was close enough to reach my quarry, I jumped, pushing off the rocks for extra momentum. But Hati spun at the last second, his arms raised defensively as I attacked. Still, my claws ripped deep across his face and chest.

Just not deep enough. I missed his jugular by inches.

Beside me, Erik fought Skoll. Rough thumps and pained grunts filled the air, but I didn't dare lose focus—even for a second—to take a look.

Hati retaliated in a whirlwind of motion, the blood flying from his cheek, his left eyeball torn and bloody. He sliced with his claws across my belly. The leather suit was all that protected me, and I gave silent thanks to Freyja.

But he came at me again and again, claws, feet, fists, and teeth, and I found myself giving ground, moving defensively to stay alive. A blow from his boot landed in my middle, knocking the breath right out of me. I stumbled backward, and my shoes slipped on the rocks.

He dived on me, but I wedged a foot between us and shoved him off with a grunt. Turning over, I scrambled away, only to be caught by the ankle and dragged back.

"How cute," he mocked. "The widdle Valdyr thinks she can defeat the big bad Jotun."

Rolling back, I closed my hand over the arrows in my pouch and glared up at him. "My, what big eyes you have. Too bad I almost cut one from your fricking head."

"It's my teeth you should be worried about, female. All the better to eat you with."

He lunged for my throat, but I struck with the arrows and embedded them in his jugular. I tried to swipe my fist sideways to slice the vein, but he reared back too quickly. I kept coming, my claws out, slashing at his legs.

He hurled a white fireball at me, and I leapt out of its path, but he followed immediately with a second one that hit me directly in the chest, feeling like it crushed bone. My suit protected me from the fire, but the force knocked me into the mist, high over the black water.

Odin's bloody eye. I would lose Freyja's suit if I shifted. The leather pants and tunic were the only things keeping me in the game. Trying to figure out another way to save myself, I played with my magic. I felt a stirring around me, but I couldn't pinpoint it.

What are you doing? Erik yelled. *Shift!*

Letting go with a silent curse, I transformed into my eagle, and the suit plunged silently beneath the surface. I swooped across the lake, wings wide, eyes sharp, ready to evade another fireball from Hati. But nothing came. Instead, he leaned back on his elbows, watching me, and grinned.

Realization hit, and the blood pounded through my veins. I headed for shore as fast as I could, but the mist thickened around me. I could still see the beach, see Hati approaching Erik as Erik pummeled Skoll in the head, but it was getting harder and harder to fly to shore.

Erik, Hati's behind you!

I know. Get your ass back here.

I can't!

You can. You're the Gullari. Figure it out.

His attitude annoyed the crap out of me, but I let it go—I couldn't afford to lose focus.

The mist took shape and tried to strike me down like a fist. I flew in a serpentine pattern, veering sharply whenever the fog attacked. I'd almost made it back when I was hit from above and knocked out of flight. I spiraled down, plunging toward the black water, but I managed to stabilize just in time. Anger surged, and I mentally shoved back at my foe.

A hole appeared where I'd punched. It was quickly filled, but the fog hesitated.

Pressing my advantage, I cleared a path to the beach. The mist fought back, hitting me and blocking my way. Another blow sent me careening downward, and I barely avoided touching the water's surface, which made the mist...happy.

It didn't laugh or shape itself into a smile, but I got a definite feeling that it gloated over my near demise. That didn't make sense if the mist was just a magical device created by Odin to protect the prison. If it was alive, however, that was a different story—one that worked in my favor.

Life equaled energy, which meant it had to have an aura.

Maybe not the colorful aura I was used to, but an energy source nonetheless. Perhaps it was the opposite of what Erik and I had, which was why I couldn't manipulate his aura here when I'd tried.

I put as much force as I could into my next strike, the equivalent of a two-ton wrecking ball, and for a second, I stunned the entity. Taking advantage, I grabbed onto it and siphoned off its gray aura. It tried to pull free, but I held tight and fought for control.

Erik, the mist is alive. I can drain it.

No! That's what's keeping Hati and Skoll away from the prison. Can you communicate with it?

I stopped tapping the entity and tried to just hold on, but it was like riding a bucking bronco. *I don't think so. Even if I could, it's too mad to cooperate.*

I'd almost reached the shore when the fog reared back and struck again. I tumbled down, still too far out over the water. In desperation, I thickened the part of the mist I still controlled, creating a slide beneath me. Skimming down, I landed on the beach, safe from the entity.

But when I shifted back and opened my eyes, I stared into the maw of Skoll's deranged wolf. Foul-smelling breath invaded my nose as razor-sharp fangs, dripping with saliva, snapped at my throat.

"Skoll, stop!" Hati yelled. "We can use her."

The huge wolf hovered at the edge of tearing me to pieces.

I turned my head to see Erik and Hati, both looking battered and torn, squared off a few feet away. Erik's sword was poised to strike the son of Fenrir, while Hati had a fireball hovering in his palm.

"Choose, Fyrstr," he said to Erik. "We can continue this fight, and I'll let Skoll kill your mate, or you can step back, and we'll talk."

Erik never lowered his sword, never took his eyes from Hati, but he did take a half step back. "So, talk."

CHAPTER 28

<u>Erik</u>

MY WOLF HOWLED AT ME AS HE THRASHED BACK AND FORTH JUST under my skin, trying to get out. It was all I could do to keep from shifting.

Stop! They'll kill her as soon as you appear. Trust me. She's my mate too.

My wolf subsided just enough so I could think. If I didn't do what Hati asked, they would torture and kill Kristin, but I also knew I couldn't—*wouldn't*—take them to the island. And she wouldn't want me to.

Kristin, are you hurt?

No. Erik, don't negotiate. I can still fight. If nothing else, I'll force Skoll to kill me.

You won't! That's an order. You said you could control the mist. Does that mean you can create things out of it like you did the bridge?

Yes. I created a slide to get back to the beach, but even that was hard to do. I don't know if I can gain control of it again—or if I do, for how long.

You just have to hold it long enough to—

"Saying your goodbyes?" Hati interrupted us. "If I'd known you cared so little, I wouldn't have offered to save her. Have it your way." He flicked his wrist, and Skoll lunged forward until his jaws clamped down on Kristin's skin.

"Stop!" I lowered my sword and turned to her.

Her eyes were closed, and she looked calm like she'd accepted her fate.

Not gonna happen. "I'll take you across, but she comes, too—alive. You can leave us there when you've rescued your father."

Hati laughed. "You can rot there for all eternity—the way my father was supposed to."

"Erik, you can't help them," she rasped, barely able to project her voice past Skoll's jagged grip.

"Yeah, I can. They're going to get across anyway. It's simply a matter of time. And the island may be the only safe place once Fenrir kills Odin."

Shifting back into his Jotun form, Skoll hauled Kristin up so her back was pinned to his front, his claws at her bruised throat. They were both naked, but it mattered little to either of them. Skoll was intent on pain, not pleasure, and he drew red, dripping streaks across her skin as his claws sank in.

It was the scent of her blood, rich and coppery, even more than the sight of it, that enraged me, and I barely contained my wolf within my bones. My jaw clenched so hard I feared my teeth might shatter.

I'm okay, Kristin soothed. *It's nothing compared to the injuries Gina's inflicted over the years. Trust me, I can handle it. I'll heal.*

Having to fight every instinct to go to her, I turned and marched to the lake's edge, sheathing my sword in the scabbard. The twins were so arrogant they didn't even take my weapon.

Do you know what a Viking longship looks like? I asked her.

I have an idea, but that's way too big. I can't—

You have to. Bring the ship to shore, then carry us over the water as far as possible. The twins can't be able to jump back when the boat disintegrates.

You're asking a lot.

I know.

I peered out over the water, lifted my arms, and muttered the first phrase in Old Norse I could think of. It was nonsense, really, just a rhyme my brother and I had made up as pups—back when we played at being heroes and Hati and Skoll were nothing more than a scary dream.

"Odin's breath, give me knowledge; Freyja's touch, the bond of love; Thor's hammer, lend me power; all to guard the heavens above."

The twins hovered eagerly on either side of me, Kristin still clutched in Skoll's arms.

They appeared to have bought the story hook, line, and sinker. Which, Odin willing, was exactly what they would do—sink. As for what would happen to them afterward, only the Allfather knew.

I need to touch the mist, Kristin said.

I watched from the corner of my eye as she pressed back into Skoll—as if she were afraid of the water. Skoll rasped out a laugh —an ugly, demented sound—and shoved her forward. When she landed on the rocks at the water's edge, she surreptitiously slipped her hand into the gray vapor.

I saw the entity strike like a snake. Hard. Vicious.

Kristin grabbed it and closed her eyes. The mist roiled and churned in front. I could only imagine the battle going on inside Kristin's head.

I played along, lifting and waving my arms like a conductor. I repeated the Old Norse phrase over and over, my movements matching the fog's frenetic dance.

Beads of sweat broke out on Kristin's brow and upper lip, and worry gnawed at me. What if she didn't have the strength to rein in the mist? Odin had created it, and the magic was powerful, but he'd also created Kristin.

She was the Gullari, our savior. And I had faith in her.

Still, I shifted into a better position to attack Hati. This close to the water, I might be able to push the Jotun in. Unfortunately, that would leave Kristin vulnerable to Skoll, which made my stomach roil as violently as the fog in front of me. I began counting down from ten in my head, wanting to give her time to succeed but not wanting to lose our advantage over the twins.

Before I reached three, the mist thickened, and a Viking longship took shape.

Sculpted out of the fog, the boat was long and narrow with a striped square sail rising from the center. At the bow, a terrifying dragon figurehead led the way; the stern of the ship was its tail. In between, ten unmanned sets of oars dipped uniformly into the water and rowed the boat to shore.

I bit down on my tongue to keep from smiling. *How does it feel to know you've saved the worlds?*

The chickens aren't hatched yet, Fyrstr. Let's get Fenrir's spawn dumped in the lake before you start thinking Ragnarök's been averted.

The boat glided to a stop a foot from shore. Hati shoved me. "Do us the honor of going first."

I darted a quick glance at Kristin. *Is it solid?*

For now. By the way, how were you planning to get us off the ship when I can no longer hold it? Which could be any second.

You're going to fly.

And you?

I jumped onto the ghost ship, trying to look like I'd done it a million times before, then walked to the stern and looked out toward the island. *I'm Fyrstr of the Varda, Kristin. I'll do whatever I have to do to make sure Fenrir stays locked up.*

Kristin

Asshat. Erik, the jerk, planned on sacrificing himself. Well, I would do whatever I had to in order to save him too. We hadn't come this far for only one of us to survive.

Hati followed Erik onto the ship and positioned himself beside the mast. He practically vibrated with excitement. I could hardly wait for him to realize his mistake—as he tumbled into the water.

He said something to his brother in another language and then motioned to Skoll, who grabbed me and tossed me onto the deck before following. I had to concentrate to keep the fog in line as I skidded across the planks.

"Let's go," Hati barked.

Erik grasped my hand and pulled me up. It felt good to be close to him again. I could draw from his strength. Turning my head toward his chest, I shut down my other senses—which made it easier to concentrate on controlling the fog—and instructed the phantom longship to head toward Fenrir's prison.

Around me, the mist burned with outrage as the ship dipped its oars into the water and did my bidding. I'd siphoned off just enough of the entity's energy to weaken it but not enough to leave it defenseless if something happened to me.

It was like walking a muzzled pit bull that wanted to rip off my head, and I had no treats in my pocket.

How far? I asked.

As far as you can.

That'll make it harder to get back to shore.

I know, but the twins are bound to renege on their agreement. As soon as they feel safe, they'll toss us. We need to know it's over for them when we bail.

Just then, the fog retaliated, striking hard, causing the ship to shudder. Erik squeezed his arm around me as I scrabbled for control. Tightening my mental grip, I siphoned off more energy until the entity settled down again.

"What's going on?" Skoll asked, his hand tight on the rail.

"Maybe it doesn't like you," Erik said. "You really didn't think this through before you climbed aboard Odin's ship, did you?"

"Odin sleeps. My father will kill him before he even opens his eyes."

"Are you sure about that?"

"Yes. You're out of your league, Fyrstr. All of Jotunheim is behind this strike. The magic we used to incapacitate the gods is beyond your comprehension."

Erik shrugged. He leaned against the dragon's tail as if relaxed, but his arms tensed around me in readiness. "I may not understand magic, but I know a goddess when I see one. Of course, maybe Freyja was just sleepwalking when she joined me and Kristin in the Kyssa."

The twins fell silent, and I turned my head to look at them. Fenrir's sons stood still, staring at each other over the rudder at the back. Did they speak to each other telepathically the way I did with Erik? Were they regretting their decision to get on board?

Well, if they weren't now, they soon would. I'd make sure of it.

I closed my eyes again, my cheek pillowed on the rock-hard planes of my ulf-verr's chest, the leather cool against my skin.

His hand brushed up and down my bare arm. *Kristin?*

Yes.

Being kyssed to you, even for such a short time, is the best thing that's ever happened to me. I am blessed by the gods to have found you. Fly for me, svassa.

Then he grasped my waist with one hand, my leg with the other, and threw me high into the air—just as Hati and Skoll attacked. I shrieked with shock and outrage as I soared through the gray mist before shifting into my eagle, desperate to hold on to the fog.

Below me, I saw my enemies shift into their wolves, claws out and teeth bared, and land on Erik, who had no time to do anything but wrap his arms over his head. Thankfully, the suit protected him.

For now.

I swooped back, furious at Erik for tossing me and at Hati and Skoll for trying to kill my mate. Diving down, I extended my talons like curved razors and tore at one of the wolves. It leapt around and snapped at me, just missing my tail feathers.

Jump, I screamed to Erik. *I'll catch you.*

No, I'm too heavy. Disintegrate the boat.

Damn it, Erik, get off right now, or I'll sail it straight to Fenrir.

I came around for another pass at the wolf—Skoll, I guessed, from the deranged look in his eyes. I flew just close enough to distract him from Erik but miscalculated how fast he could move, and he crunched down on my wing. I struck with my talons, gouging deep into his eyes. Painful howls filled the air, and he let go.

Barely able to fly, I made a rough, lopsided circle. The fog took advantage and bombarded me with heavy blows, tugging and twisting as it tried to free itself from my grasp. Below me, the boat shuddered, throwing Hati off Erik.

He jumped up, his suit untorn and only a scratch on his cheek. Unsheathing his sword, he darted forward, but the planks under his feet wavered, and he stumbled against the dragon's head. Holes appeared in the deck between him and Hati, and the lake swirled, deep and endless, below.

Shit. I was losing control.

I solidified the boat once more and then flew hard at Skoll, who thrashed about blindly on the deck. When he was near the edge, I headbutted him in the flank. He teetered unsteadily and then slipped in his own blood and tumbled overboard. The only sound when he hit the water was a soft plunk as he disappeared beneath the surface.

Exhilaration coursed through me, and I circled a few times, making sure he didn't come up for air. *He's gone, Erik! I knocked Skoll overboard!*

A burst of pride shot down the Alpha bond. *Of course, you did! I told you that you were amazing.*

I think the actual word was extraordinary.

That too.

I could hear the smile in his voice, which made me smile. But we weren't out of danger yet—far from it.

I landed on top of the mast, barely able to balance with my wing hanging at an awkward angle.

On the ship below, Erik battled the giant wolf, sword in hand, and I noticed his suit had grown a hood. He looked surprisingly unhurt for having been almost eaten.

By the way, my wing is broken. I won't be flying back—with you or without you. You damn well better win.

He sliced crosswise and caught the tip of Hati's tufted ear. *This is what it's going to be like the rest of our lives, isn't it? Me telling you one thing, and you doing another.*

My breath caught, and if possible, my heart beat faster. Did this mean he thought we had a future together? He didn't sound upset or even resigned that I'd somehow trapped him in our Kyssa.

If you think I'm difficult, wait until you meet my brothers. They'll eat you alive.

Yeah? I'm not very tasty.

Hati bounced off the stern and lunged at him, but Erik swung the sword up and clipped his muzzle.

And my dad. He'll have you by the throat the minute you step out of line.

I would hope so.

The huge wolf rolled, and his long back claws raked across Erik's torso. Thank Freyja, the suit protected him, making it an even fight. Grabbing Hati's paw, he twisted, and the last of Fenrir's sons crashed onto the deck.

But the worst is my mom. You should see what she can do with her magic. It makes the male side of the family look like kittens.

I like cats.

He drove his sword point through the wolf's Achilles tendon and into the planks below. Hati howled and yanked his leg free by ripping through the tendon, then limped backward until he hit the mast—directly below me.

After yanking his sword loose, Erik quickly hurled it like a dagger. I thought he aimed high until I saw the blur of movement below me. Hati had shifted so rapidly that I hadn't even seen him scaling the mast to get to me. Erik's sword plunged through his spine, and he faltered—only a few feet away from me.

Looking into his eyes, I saw his hatred and disbelief as he fell backward, almost in slow motion, and plunged beneath the still, black water.

Shock and relief tumbled through me, and I scanned the lake, searching for any ripples—any sign that the sons of Fenrir had survived. Nothing.

Bubbles of happiness began to burst in my body. Had we done it?

And what about Gina? Is she going to tear up my infirmary again?

I turned my eagle head and met Erik's gaze. He leaned with one hand on the railing, the other on his thigh, catching his breath. A wolfy grin tilted his lips.

Barely containing my elation, I said, *Nah. Gina's not so bad. She'll just wreak havoc on your security systems. And Gunn.*

He limped slowly toward the mast, looking up at me. I shifted back to myself, holding my right arm, and quickly checked on the mist. It was surprisingly subdued.

Erik climbed the sturdy wooden pole, never taking his eyes from mine.

At the top, he lifted me into his arms. "That wasn't so bad, huh?"

More happy bubbles exploded—fizzing like champagne under my skin—and I laughed up at him. "Not bad at all. Let's call the twins back and do it again."

"Nope. I've got other plans." He leaned in and captured my mouth, savoring me. "Asgard's not a bad place to honeymoon— although we'll have to bring our own food." He pulled back just far enough to look into my eyes. "What do you think?"

A lump formed in my throat. "If you undid whatever you did to block our bond, you'd know what I think, Ulf-verr."

The tension that had invaded his muscles melted away. He grazed his fingers down my temple and under my hair. "You didn't have a choice in our Kyssa, Kristin. It was either take me as your mate or watch the worlds burn. I want you to have a choice."

Lifting my good arm, I palmed his cheek, loving that his eyes had turned all wolfy. "Thank you. I'll take it into consideration. Okay, I've considered it. I choose you."

For a second, he stopped breathing. Then he drew in a sharp breath. "As in forever?"

"As in, just try and get rid of me."

He let out a whoop of laughter and hugged me so tight my arm hurt. But I didn't care. The pain made the happiness cascading through me that much sweeter.

He kissed my forehead, eyelids, nose, cheeks, and chin before finally taking my mouth. I welcomed him in, my lips parting eagerly beneath his, my tongue rubbing against his tongue.

A blast of love seared through me, and then he was there—all of him—his presence at the very core of my being. His thoughts, his emotions, his desire ratcheted up my own a thousand percent.

Sighing in unison at the reconnection, our kiss gentled, and we took a moment to soak up the essence of each other. It was like sinking into a hot bath after trudging miles through a blizzard.

His bliss and wonder astounded me. "Really?" I asked. "That's how you feel?"

"That's exactly how I feel." His hands cupped the back of my head, fingers massaging through my hair. "I can feel your emotions, Kristin, but I need to hear them out loud. Say the words. Please."

Tears welled and trickled down my cheeks until I tasted the salt on my tongue. "I love you, Erik. So much so, I can't breathe at times."

He pulled me back into his embrace. "Me too. I never thought it was possible to love someone this much. You're everything to me, Kristin." He brought my hand to his mouth and kissed my palm. "I don't know what I would have done if you'd said no."

"I don't know what I would have done if you'd let me go."

He huffed out a laugh. "I do. You would have fought for us. We've already established that you'll do whatever you think is right no matter what I say."

"Yeah, and look where that got us."

"On top of an angry fake boat with you naked in my arms. That's not so bad."

We laughed and almost kissed again, but my wolf yipped at me.

Pay attention!

I realized that the mist had been quietly seeping from my grasp as I'd been kissing Erik. I caught the entity by the tail. It whipped around and snapped at me. The boat shuddered.

"It's okay, svassa," he said. "You can let it go. I don't know about you, but I could do with a nicer ride."

I crinkled my brow. "Well, I'm sorry to say, but this is the best I can do."

He pulled a stone pendant of a Viking longship from around his neck. "I can do better."

"What's that? You weren't wearing it earlier. Is it part of Freyja's suit?"

"No. It's from Odin. And you'll see soon enough. Let the mist go."

"What?" I peered into his eyes, looking for signs of a concussion. "Did you take one too many blows to the head?"

"Nope." He tossed the pendant high in the air. It peaked and began to fall. "Let go."

I watched the pendant drop. "Ah, hel." Then I turned my head into his chest, closed my eyes, and released the entity. We lost our perch and plummeted down, but I knew we'd be safe. Erik was far too pleased with himself to drop us to our death.

He landed feet first on a surface that sounded solid, holding me close. Opening my eyes, I saw he stood on the deck of a large Viking longship much larger than the one I'd created from the fog. And it was built from actual wood. That floated. And steered itself.

"Are you telling me you had the ability to do this the whole time?" I asked.

"No. I didn't bring the pendant with me. I didn't have time. I felt it around my neck once I stepped on board your boat."

"Why didn't you tell me?"

"I didn't want you to get your hopes up. Chances were, even with the ability to call the longship, I wasn't coming back."

I hugged him tight, realizing how close we'd come—and the enormity of what we'd done. We'd stopped Hati and Skoll from freeing their father, but had we killed the twins in the process?

"What happens now? Are Hati and Skoll dead? You said that would be disastrous."

"I know." He put me down and walked with me to the railing, holding my hand. I could see the island in the distance. Around us, the mist had returned to normal.

He looked down at the lake. "My instinct tells me we haven't seen the last of the twins. We won the battle but not the war."

"Truth," came a booming voice from behind us.

CHAPTER 29

Erik

I TIGHTENED MY ARM AROUND KRISTIN'S WAIST TO KEEP HER upright. She was dressed once more in the leathers Freyja had given her, but I didn't think she'd even noticed. Her thoughts and emotions whirled chaotically through our bond. I could hear and feel them.

Odin stood no more than four feet away, tall and strong, wearing a horned helmet and holding his spear, Gungnir, dangerously by his side. Around him, his great plum-colored robe billowed despite the lack of a breeze, and his red hair and beard glowed even though the sun didn't shine. The ever-present eye patch covered his missing eye.

He looked different from how he usually appeared to me. Today, he'd taken on the mantle of what he was—king of the gods —and I suspected the spear wasn't just for decoration.

Odin spun it in his hand and grinned. "I use it to impress the ladies."

Kristin's jaw dropped, and I was hard-pressed not to laugh. Instead, I nuzzled a kiss on the top of her head. "Svassa, this is

Odin. Odin, meet my ulf-vif, Kristin."

"How d-do you do?" she whispered.

The god came forward and shook her trembling hand. "I'm fantastic, Kristin Gullari, Fyrsta of the Varda. I had a lovely, long sleep. I would have slept longer, but Freyja insisted I awaken. I told her the two of you had it under control. Congratulations, by the way."

"For saving the nine worlds or kyssing my mate?" I asked.

"Both. I'd like to give you a gift for your nuptials. Are you registered anywhere?"

She looked at me, eyes round, as if to confirm what she was hearing. It reminded me of my first meeting with Odin. I'd been bloody and battered after a series of brutal fights in the domr to become Alpha. I had wanted to bow and scrape before him, while Odin had just wanted to talk about the fights—beer in hand.

"No, not yet," she said. "We'll…um…let you know."

"Please do." He leaned on the rail beside us and looked out toward the island. "So, Fenrir is contained and Ragnarök averted for another day. His sons were quite ingenious in their plan. I can hardly wait to see what they come up with next."

"They're not dead, then?" My relief was palpable, yet at the same time, I felt weary, knowing Hati and Skoll would soon be up to their old tricks.

"No. The lake is infinite darkness. If you had tumbled in, you would have fallen forever. But the twins carried sunlight and moonlight with them, captured in a pendant like the one you found after Skoll attacked your compound. The light ripped a hole in the darkness."

"Where are they now?"

He shrugged, then moved toward the bow of the ship, also carved in the shape of a dragon. "Recovering, I'm sure. Their minds will have been ravaged by the darkness." He nodded to Kristin. "A fitting punishment for what they did to your family."

Her breath caught on a small sob, and I squeezed her waist in support. She'd been waiting a long time for her revenge before giving it up to support the Varda. She'd sacrificed it for me. For us.

It was nice to know she'd get justice for her family after all.

On the island, Fenrir appeared over the top of a sand dune. He was so ugly it almost hurt to look at him. Around his neck and trailing behind him glinted the pretty ribbon called Gleipnir, forged by the Dvergar eons ago. A fetter so tight even he, with all his strength, couldn't break it.

"Fenris-Wolf," Odin said in solemn greeting.

The Jotun watched him, then turned his gaze to Kristin and me, and I tightened my arm around my ulf-vif. I hadn't forgotten the monster's threats of rape and murder.

"One down, eight to go. It will not go easy for the rest. These two barely made it," Fenrir said. Even the rasp of his voice was ugly.

"I disagree. Their bond is like that ribbon around your neck. Struggle only makes it stronger."

"We'll see."

"You have no understanding of love, Fenris-wolf, let alone sacrifice. The quota will be met."

Fenrir smiled—a horrific baring of his teeth. "I only need one, Odin One-Eye. And then your day will come." He turned and disappeared over the dune.

The ship dipped its oars into the water and reversed away from the island. I stepped up beside the god, who, to my surprise, looked troubled.

"Is there anything you want to tell me?" I asked. It was the second time Fenrir had spoken in riddles, and for once, I wanted to have all the information. But I knew that wasn't how the gods worked.

Odin smiled, his problems seemingly forgotten, and clapped a hand on my shoulder. "There is. Don't keep your in-laws waiting."

Kristin

I found myself standing in the midst of a battlefield teeming with the detritus of war. Dead and injured warriors—both wolves and Valdyr—littered the ground, and weapons of war were scattered everywhere. A smattering of gods wove in and out of the chaos. No one had to tell me which ones were gods...I just knew.

In the distance, the great Jotun ships retreated in defeat.

I looked longingly at the Valdyr and wondered if my family was among them. "I should help with the injured."

Erik laid his hand upon my shoulder. "I'll help you. And then we'll find your family together."

Before I could take a step, Odin materialized in front of us, this time as an old man with a long, white beard and grizzled hair. A gnarled wooden walking staff was clenched in his hand, replacing the spear he'd held earlier.

"Asgard will heal their injuries," he said. "Your mother searches for you."

He stepped aside, and I saw a Valdyr female with her back to me. She had long brown hair streaked with a touch of gray. Everything within me stilled, and then emotion rushed up, choking me.

Erik squeezed my fingers, his concern beating at me through our bond. "What's wrong?"

Unable to speak, I just shook my head. My wolf yipped happily and ran in an excited circle. Still, doubt plagued me. It had been twelve years.

Lifting my hand toward the female, I tried to speak, but a lump had formed in my throat. Tears welled, and the image of the woman wavered.

Finally, I squeaked, "Mom?"

With a gasp, the older Valdyr spun around, and I let out a happy sob as Gale's beloved face broke into an elated smile.

"Kitta!"

We ran together, crying, and I melted into my mom's warm, strong arms—so familiar and safe I thought my heart might break. I inhaled deeply, and her healthy scent filled me with joy.

"You're here! Thank Odin, you're here!" my mom cried. "My sweet ulf-ungr."

I felt twelve years old again and reveled in it. Maybe I would pretend the last fifteen years had never happened.

Standing right here, Erik said.

My laughter bubbled down the bond to him. *Sorry!*

With a teary smile, I pulled back from my mom and reached for him. "Mom, I want you to meet—"

A solid ball of energy smashed into me and held on tight. I stumbled backward into Gale. Erik reacted instinctively, grabbing the young, dark-haired male and yanking him off of me.

"No, Erik. It's Finn!"

He hesitated, and Finn took full advantage, ducking out of his grip and then kicking his legs together. Erik toppled over, but he was too well trained, and he pulled Finn down with him and sat on his chest.

"Holy Thor," my brother said. "He's good!"

"Of course he is," I said, my heart filled with pride, and I felt Erik's ruffled feathers smooth.

Then, huge arms enfolded me from behind. A big barrel chest shuddered against my back, and a scratchy beard pressed against my cheek. "Oh, gods, Kitta. *Kaerr dottir*. You're finally here. I've been so worried. I couldn't stand the thought of you being down there all alone."

"Dad," I cried and twisted in his embrace to bury myself against him. Now I really felt twelve years old, and my body shook with happy sobs. Other arms encircled me, and I knew the rest of my brothers, Adam, Joran, and Garet, surrounded me. I turned and hugged each one of them, marveling that they looked exactly as I remembered—dark like my mom and as big as my dad. Their cheeks were wet with tears.

A little help here.

I poked my head up from the mass of male bodies to see Finn, forever eighteen, circling Erik in an attempt to take him down again. Erik was doing his best to stay upright while not hurting my brother. Finally, in exasperation, after Finn head-butted him in the chest, Erik flipped him onto the ground and knelt on his back, holding him in place.

Then he looked up and stilled.

Oh, crap. All three of my brothers, my dad, and my mom glared down at Erik. I tried to fight my way to him, but no one would let me through. Then, my mom stepped to the front of the pack.

Finn groaned dramatically when he saw her, and my stomach sank. The little bugger.

My mom's voice was soft and smooth but so deadly it sent shivers up my arms. "I don't know exactly who you are, but I can guess, which means I'll give you a warning first. Let my son go, or I will rip off your balls. Slowly."

Erik rose steadily, hands in the air, never taking his eyes from my mother. He took one step back, then another, then he met my gaze. "Meow."

I burst out laughing, used my own magic to push my overprotective clan out of the way, and ran into Erik's arms. "Welcome to the family!"

EPILOGUE

<u>*Odin*</u>

ODIN LAID ONE ARM ON THE RAILING THAT OVERLOOKED THE crowded rotunda at Wolf Ridge and raised his tankard to his lips.

A shapely hand appeared next to his as Freyja solidified beside him, looking resplendent as usual in a sheer white dress, her luscious dark hair falling to her waist.

Her demeanor was pensive, at odds with the merrymakers below, and he passed her his drink. She took it without hesitation, drank deeply, and then handed it back. "Thanks."

He knew, of course, what bothered her, but he didn't mention it. He never did. Not unless she brought it up, which she never did. Instead, she skirted around the issue.

"This is quite the celebration—a Kyssa and Fenrir's defeat," she said.

Odin's gaze found Erik and Kristin in the crowd, their arms wrapped around each other and their lips pressed together. "Yes."

"You chose well with those two," Freyja said, "but you may have put us all at risk with your second choice."

His eyes darted to the far side of the room where Gina and Gunn nattered at one another. "They have chemistry," he said.

She huffed derisively. "She's way too good for him."

Then Gunn leaned forward and stole a kiss from Gina, who melted in his arms and dragged him into a dark, private corner.

Odin barely stopped himself from laughing. "Maybe she's planning on slumming it."

Freyja frowned and crossed her arms over her chest. The goddess of love couldn't be objective on this one. "He's not ulf-verr material. You've put all of our lives at risk with those two."

"You more than anyone should know that love can blossom in the most unlikely places. The Valdyr and the witch are a good match."

Freyja narrowed her eyes at him, then disappeared. She reappeared on the crowded rotunda floor and made a beeline for the dark corner Gina and Gunn had found. But halfway there, she came to a halt. Her gaze lifted to Odin's, and he saw pain and uncertainty there. Regret. Then she vanished.

His heart hurt for his friend.

Freyja had done what she had to twenty-two years ago. She'd done it for him.

He sighed, and the air around him wavered. The mantle he wore crushed him tonight—more so than usual.

Gulping down his ale, he changed his appearance so he would blend into the crowd and went to find his own source of amusement, reminding himself they were celebrating a victory tonight.

One of nine.

Tomorrow, they'd have to fight again.

THE GODS HAVE GAMBLED.
NINE TIMES SHALL THE WAGER BE ANSWERED.
NINE TIMES MUST LOVE PREVAIL...
OR THE END COMES.

In Missoula, Montana, Odin's wølves fight to save the world from *Ragnarök*.
One Kyss at a time...

Thank you for reading **Wolf's Reign**!

Want more of Erik and Kristin? Sign up for my Newsletter at MadelynLayne.com and receive a bonus epilogue, featuring Erik and Kristin on their honeymoon…in Asgard!

Looking forward to Gunn and Gina's book?

Wolf's Witch will be up for pre-order in 2024! I'll announce the details in my upcoming Newsletters.

Also, please leave a review! I greatly appreciate you taking the time to tell others why you loved Wolf's Reign. It allows me to keep writing this wonderful series. 🤍

FREE BOOKS!

Sign up for Madelyn Layne's Newsletter and get access to free books, bonus material, and exclusive content.

Madelyn's Newsletter:
www.madelynlayne.com

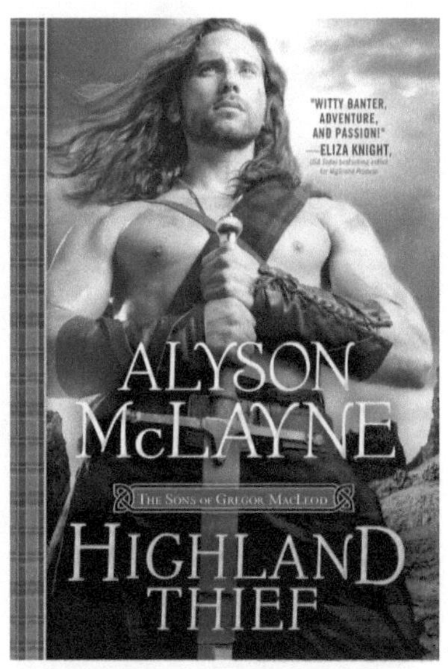

Interested in more of Madelyn Layne's writing?

Madelyn also writes adventure-filled historical romance set in the wilds of Scotland under the pen name Alyson McLayne. Check out her critically acclaimed series The Sons Of Gregor MacLeod and meet one of Erik's ancestors in Highland Thief!

I also have a free series sampler called First Dates With Alyson McLayne that features all five books. Happy Reading!

GLOSSARY OF TERMS IN WØLVES OF ODIN:

WORDS:

- **Allfather:** Odin.
- **Bikkja:** A Valdyr slur from Old Norse, meaning a female dog.
- **Domr:** A sanctified circle the Valdyr use for high rituals, in which Odin and the pack's Alpha male or female bring judgment upon a Valdyr or other creature.
- **Domari:** The Valdyr who sanctifies the sacred circle.
- **Fyrsta:** Alpha female of the pack.
- **Fyrstr:** Alpha male of the pack.
- **Handsal:** A ceremony that bonds a wolf to his or her pack.
- **Helmingr:** A magical merging of the Valdyr with their wolf. The helmingr happens the first time the wolf rises and the last time upon death. A strong Valdyr can enter the helmingr at will.
- **Hjarta:** A Valdyr resides on two planes: the physical plane of Earth and a spiritual plane called Hjarta—or

heart. Kristin's wolf uses the image of a rock—a spherical geode—with thousands of crystals inside to describe the supernatural realm of Hjarta. Each crystal can be interpreted as an individual cell, or dimension, within the spiritual plane. Bonded wolves, whether they are kyssed pairs, family, or packmates, share these special cells. A wolf can exist in one or all of them, all at once.

- **Hringr:** A sanctified circle used for celebrations or rituals.
- **Hundr:** A Valdyr slur from Old Norse, meaning a hound dog.
- **Hyrr:** A Valdyr funeral in which the dead are cremated in a magical fire and their essence is sent back to Odin.
- **Kalla:** The howl a male Valdyr sends to his chosen female during the Kyssa. If the female responds and Freyja sanctions the union, the goddess will join them in the Kyssa.
- **Kaer dottir:** Dear daughter.
- **Kyssa (kyssed, kyss, unkyssed):** The magical bond, sanctioned by Freyja, that joins fated mates. Equivalent to human marriage.
- **Rekkr:** Warrior wolf.
- **Svassa:** A term of endearment for females, meaning beloved.
- **Svassr:** A term of endearment for males, meaning beloved.
- **Ulf:** Wolf.
- **Ulf-einn:** Lone wolf.
- **Ulf-mynd:** When the souls of the wolf and the Valdyr merge.
- **Ulf-risa:** The rising of a female Valdyr's wolf. A rite of passage.

- **Ulf-rist:** The rising of a male Valdyr's wolf. A rite of passage.
- **Ulf-ungr:** Young wolf.
- **Ulf-verr:** Husband.
- **Ulf-vif:** Wife.
- **Valdyr:** Shape-shifting wolves created by Odin to guard Fenrir and prevent Ragnarök.
- **Varda:** The strongest Valdyr pack—descended from the original pack created by Odin.
- **Vel Finna:** A formal greeting. Also used to say goodbye.
- **Yla:** The howl a wolf sends out during the Handsal, asking to join the pack.

RACES/CHARACTERS:

- **Bjarg Faegir:** The Dverg who carved the stone wolf.
- **Dvergar (plural) Dverg (singular):** A race of magical alchemists and mountain-dwellers who live in Nidavellir. They are generally shorter than humans.
- **Fenrir (Fenris-Wolf):** A monstrous wolf. Son of Loki and a witch Jotuness.
- **Freyja:** Norse goddess of love, sex, marriage, fertility, and war. Also the goddess of seiðr.
- **Hati:** A wolf-shifting Jotun whose magic is tied to the moon. Son of Fenrir and twin brother of Skoll.
- **Heimdall:** Norse god in charge of Bifrost. He will call the gods to battle during Ragnarök.
- **Jotun:** Race of Giants. Enemies of the Norse gods.
- **Loki:** Trickster god. Blood brother of Odin and father of Fenrir. Murderer of Baldur.
- **Mimir:** The wisest of the Norse gods.

- **The Norns—Urd (past), Verdani (present), Skold (future):** The Norse Fates who weave the great tapestry of life and care for Yggdrasil at the Well of Urd.
- **Odin:** All-father of the Norse gods and ruler of Asgard.
- **Skoll:** A wolf-shifting Jotun whose magic is tied to the sun. Son of Fenrir and twin brother of Hati.

PLACES/EVENTS:

- **Asgard:** Home of the Norse gods.
- **Bifrost:** Also called the Rainbow Bridge. Bifrost connects Earth to Asgard.
- **Hel:** Citadel of Niflheim.
- **Nidavellir:** World of the Dvergar. Interchangeable with Svartalfheim.
- **Niflheim:** World of the dead.
- **Ragnarök:** A prophesied apocalypse that is brought on when Fenrir escapes his prison and devours Odin.
- **Valhalla:** A paradise for warriors killed in battle and deemed worthy by Odin.
- **Well of Urd:** A well in Asgard that waters Yggdrasil.
- **Yggdrasil:** The World Tree at the centre of the nine worlds.

SPECIAL OBJECTS/ANIMALS:

- **Gjall:** Heimdall's horn with which he'll summon the gods to battle during Ragnarök.
- **Gleipnir:** A leash of ribbon that binds Fenrir until Ragnarök. Made by the Dvergar, it's the only fetter strong enough to hold Fenrir.
- **Gungnir:** Odin's spear. Gungnir is said to never miss its target.
- **Sleipnir:** Odin's eight-legged steed. Birthed by Loki.

ACKNOWLEDGMENTS

I finished the first draft of Wolf's Reign way back in 2013. My kids were barely a year old at the time, and the manuscript ended up sitting on my hard drive, twiddling its non-existent thumbs. I tried shopping it around to a few publishers/agents, but I couldn't get a bite.

And then in 2016, I entered it into the Golden Heart contest (under a different title and pen name)—which, at the time, was Romance Writers of America's premiere contest for aspiring writers. It made the finals! That opened up a lot of doors for me and led me on a wonderful journey of finding my writing tribe, becoming a published author (different sub-genre), and expanding my knowledge of the business side of things, which eventually brought me all the way back to Wolf's Reign...and self publishing.

Along the way, I've had numerous critique partners, beta readers, teachers, and friends who gave me feedback on Wolf's Reign and provided me with lots of writing and publishing advice. In particular, Christyne Butler, Tina Beckett, and Jenny Greene—for critiquing every chapter; Angela Campbell, Eileen Cook, Diana Muñoz Stewart, and Iona Jones for beta reading; Carol Opalinski, Layla Reyne, Jaycee Jarvis, Melonie Johnson, and Brenna Aubrey for fun, support, and answers to my endless questions; and to Sarra Cannon for teaching me how to take that leap from author to publisher.

Also a big shout out to my friend, critique partner, copy editor, and proof reader extraordinaire Kari Cole.

Lastly, to my husband, Ken, who gave me the time and space to write. I love you so much. Words alone cannot express how much I appreciate all you've done for our family (especially the 6 am hockey practices!).

Thank you to everyone!

ABOUT THE AUTHOR

After earning her degree in theatre at the University of Alberta, Madelyn Layne moved to the west coast of Canada and worked in film for several years before buckling down and finishing her first published book.

She lives in Vancouver with her prop master husband, twin eleven-year-olds, a sweet, sucky chocolate lab, and two cats who are always up to something.

Madelyn loves coffee, listening to podcasts, and watching Harry Potter with her kids. In case of emergencies, she keeps a stash of chocolate in the cupboard, which she savours late at night when she's writing…and everyone else is asleep.

Visit Madelyn's website:
www.madelynlayne.com

ALSO BY MADELYN LAYNE

Wolf's Kiss

Wolf's Reign

www.ingramcontent.com/pod-product-compliance
Lightning Source LLC
Chambersburg PA
CBHW051432190726
48289CB00001B/149